*About the author*

Brian Grehan is a retired ⌣ ⌐
County Dublin. He professes an abiding passion for the west of Ireland, the game of cricket, and writing. His first book, of short stories, was called "The Well Travelled Road".

# The Leenane Inspector

**Brian Grehan**

Published by New Generation Publishing in 2016

Copyright © Brian Grehan 2016

First Edition

The author asserts the moral right under the Copyright, Designs and Patents Act 1988 to be identified as the author of this work.

All Rights reserved. No part of this publication may be reproduced, stored in a retrieval system or transmitted, in any form or by any means without the prior consent of the author, nor be otherwise circulated in any form of binding or cover other than that which it is published and without a similar condition being imposed on the subsequent purchaser.

**www.newgeneration-publishing.com**

 New Generation Publishing

To *Deirdre*, who walked the road.

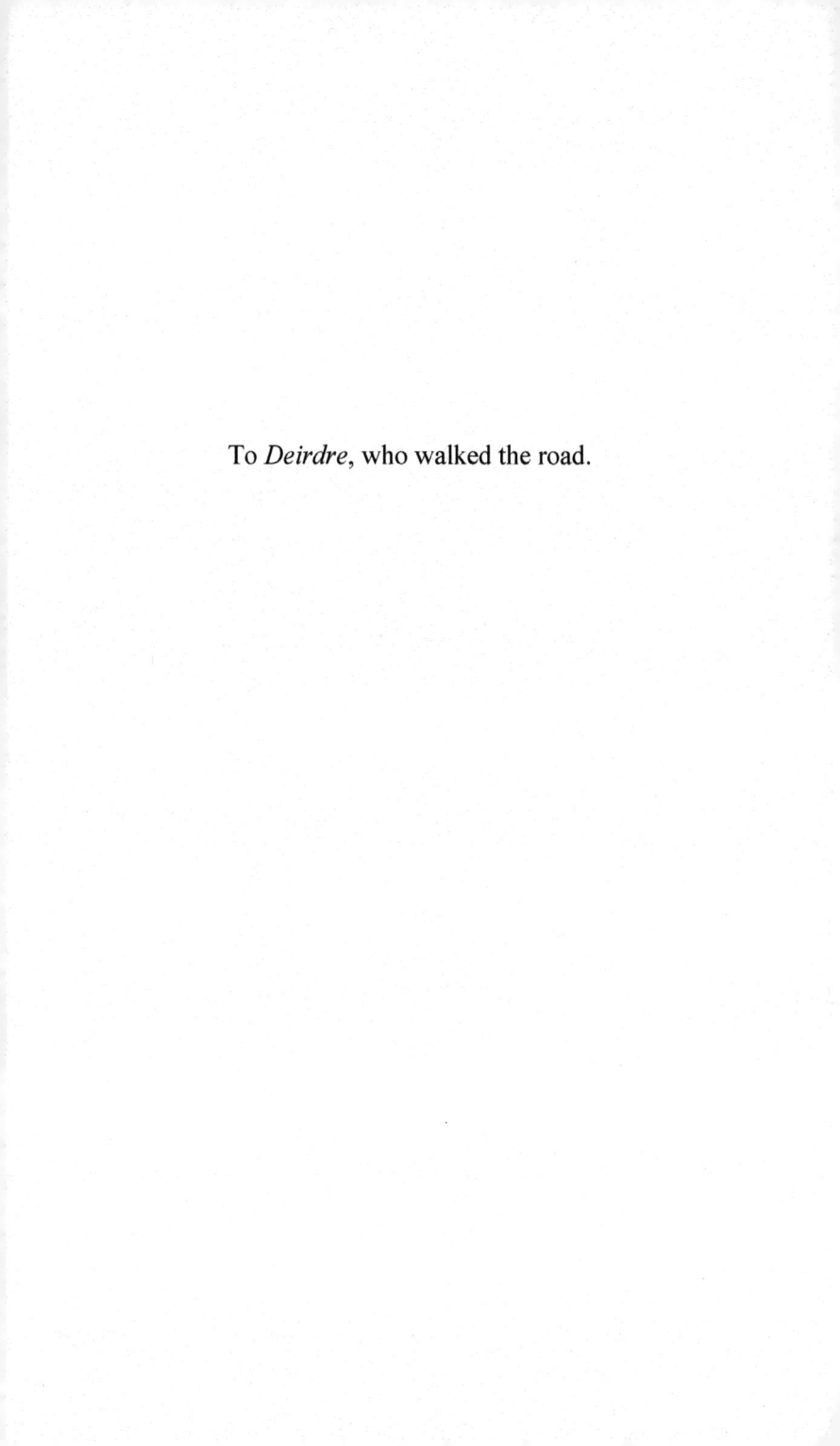

*"How can men feel themselves honoured by the humiliation of their fellow beings?"*

　　　　　　　　　　　　　　*Mahatma Gandhi*

*Inscription on memorial in Delphi valley, County Mayo.*

# Chapter 1

## *West down the Road*

The taxi pulled up and a man emerged, suitcase in hand. Tall and thin, oval faced, brown eyed, wearing a black suit. He tipped the taxi driver well, elated after hearing the second half of Ireland's World Cup draw with England in Cagliari on the radio. The air was still, with the first faint stars out, and one was brighter than the rest, below a crescent moon hanging over a mountain on the far side of the fjord. After pausing to admire the Victorian façade of the hotel, he entered the foyer, and strode to the check-in desk. The receptionist was busy on the telephone, but smiled and waved to him. He yawned and stretched. It had been a long day.

"You have a reservation for me? Wyatt is the name."

"We have indeed Mr. Wyatt. For four weeks. Department of Marine and Fisheries. We've kept room 236 for you on the second floor. It's secure, with space to set up an office for your work, which Mr.Halpin told us is important. He said you'll be needin' some couriers from time to time. Here's your key. Would you fill this in please?" She beamed as she handed him a Registration card.

He signed the card, dating it June eleventh, nineteen ninety, and slid it back across the counter, asking her to ring Clontarf Nursing Home in Dublin, and to put the call through to the phone on the desk in the corner of the foyer. She nodded.

When through to the Nursing Home, he was told his mother was asleep and could not be disturbed. Frustrated, he put the phone down, consoling himself that he had at least tried.

"Please let me know if we can help you in any way, Mr. Wyatt. My name is Brigid. You're welcome to Leenane, and I hope you enjoy your stay. Can I get someone to help you with your suitcase?"

"Thank you…..er Brigid, but no thanks, I'll take it up myself." He felt tetchy after the journey, and wondered how much she knew about the reason for his visit. A low key arrival would have been better. And for Halpin to think it would be all over in four weeks. Bullshit, there was no way.

After lugging the suitcase up the curving, wrought iron staircase, he entered the room, and looked around. It was, as the girl had said, at the rear of the hotel, and secure. His case unpacked, he put his computer and files on the desk beside the window.

With everything set up, he showered, relaxed in a chair, and gazed out the window. The craggy landscape was now draped in twilight, but his mind was a morass.

He wondered if he was doing the right thing. Who knows or cares, but he must stop thinking this way. Be positive. Halpin had said he needed a challenge, and a change of scenery. Wyatt had to admit he had slipped into a rut, treading water for years in his Government job. But after the trauma in his private life, did he really need this? It was too late to change horses now, he muttered.

His boss was one cute hoor. Brussels was onto the Department to sort out water pollution problems in the west, and to get himself off the hook, he'd picked Wyatt to do his dirty work, and investigate the allegations. Yes, he'd picked him, with no experience of rural living, being born in Dublin, educated in England, graduated from Trinity, and rarely straying beyond the Pale.

He stood up, stretched, and strolled to the mini-bar, where he poured a double whiskey. Back by the window, he gulped the liquid, and felt it flame the back of his throat. Pensive, he continued staring out the window.

Yes, he felt like a pawn in their game, and he didn't trust Halpin. And he had abandoned his mother in Dublin. He'd left her alone, just when she needed him, and that bothered him. Her mind had deteriorated rapidly of late, and now she would often forget his name, but she was his mother, he missed her, and had qualms about leaving her. Halpin had dangled the lure of promotion, pension, and extra money in front of him, and he'd swallowed it, just like a fish. Hook, line, and sinker.

Drink knocked back, he pulled the curtains over and flicked the lights on, before scrutinising his plan for the week ahead. Tomorrow morning he would meet skipper Tommy Joe O'Malley, a local fisherman, and spend the day checking out the waters in Killary fjord and Clew Bay. That perked him up, and the activity would take his mind away from the memories of his past, the demons bedevilling his sleep. Later in bed, he reached for his tablets, on the table beside his bed, before switching the light off. He realised how much he had become dependent on them.

After breakfast, he stood in the foyer, viewing a framed1870's newspaper page that hung on the wall. It was about the visit of Queen Victoria and her husband Albert to Leenane, and their welcome by the Irish peasantry, before they drove around Connemara in style in a charabanc. Another framed page, from 1915, concerned English battleships sheltering in Killary fjord during WW1. No fear of Killary fjord being used as a sanctuary nowadays, not with all those salmon cages cluttering its waters, he muttered.

By the brightness of a window in the lounge, he read the newspaper. In it was an article on Nelson Mandela, released some months earlier, after twenty seven years on Robben Island. There's a man who examined his life, he thought, but I suppose he had plenty of time to do it. He scanned the rest of the pages, reading about another fatal bombing in the North of Ireland. He wondered when the carnage there would end, and grimacing, folded the paper, and left the room.

He went over to Brigid, and asked if there was any mail for him.

"Nothing for you, Mr Wyatt, I'm afraid. You'll be out all day then? Shall I take your key?"

"Yes, I'm away for the day. I'm on my way now, but I'll hold onto the key, thanks. Where's the harbour, by the way?"

"Out the door, a few hundred yards left up the road." Spoken with a smile that would light up the day.

He left the foyer pulling the rucksack onto his back, and crossed the road to the garden at the fjord's edge, where he gazed at the landscape. Purple rhododendrons were still in bloom, and wildflowers abounded in all shapes and colours. Mountains, dotted with rocks, crowded in around him. The calm sea inversely framed the sky, mountains, and clouds above. Spellbound, he felt his heart uplifted, and sighed in wonder, before trudging up the road to the harbour in his wellingtons, taking a few photos for his files on the way.

At the harbour, lobster pots were piled in pyramids on the pier. Tar black currachs lay upside down beside them like giant stranded beetles. The air stank of seaweed and fish.

A stocky, middle sized man bounded off a fishing boat onto the steps of the harbour, securing his vessel with a rope. His peaked cap, pulled over a weatherworn face, didn't hide the scar below his right eye. He wore a green Aran sweater and matching wellingtons, and held out his hand.

"You're welcome to the wild west, Mr. Wyatt, Tommy Joe O'Malley at your service". A smile creased his face, as his calloused handshake crushed Wyatt's fingers.

"Thanks Tommy Joe, it's a beautiful place you live in. So peaceful too, I envy you. But I'm sure the weather isn't always as good as it is today? By the way, can you tell me what those ridges running up the mountainside over there are?" Wyatt flexed his fingers as he spoke.

"They'd be the lazy beds for growin' potatoes back in the Famine times. Our history's a heavy burden on us down here, God help us."

"Oh. And that mountain behind the hotel, The Devil's Mother I believe it's called, is it easy to climb?"

"Ah, you mean *Magirli an Deamhain*, The Devil's Bollocks. That'd be its *real* name. The people up in Dublin, they went to change it, afraid they were it might cause scandal to the visitors comin' here.Yes, for sure you can climb it from behind the hotel. Would you be thinkin'of climbin' it then?" He took off his cap, and scratched his head.

"I might, but I wonder why it's called that?"

"You may find out some day when you climb it." Tommy Joe replied, grinning.

"Ok, let's get to business. I'd like to travel around Killary fjord, see some fish farms, then do the same for Clew Bay, and make the most of the weather."

"Famous. But the weather, it may change. And we must pick up my brother on the way. There's work to be done on the fish cages while we're at them."

"Oh, so you're a fish farmer?"

"I am for sure, me and some others in Westport. You know now Mr Wyatt, lots of families down here are dependin' on the fish farms for their livin'. You know too, when we joined the Common Market way back, the Irish fisherman, he was sold up the Swanee by the Government, so the Irish farmers could get their grants and subsidies. Sold out completely like gobshites we were. An' now the seas are overfished, an' fish stocks are at their lowest ever. It's like another famine, a fish famine." His voice was bitter.

"I'm sure there's truth in what you say. Anyway let's get moving, while the weather holds out." Wyatt thought it better to humour Tommy Joe for the moment, as he negotiated the steps into the swaying vessel. They sped across the fiord to a pier on the other side, where a man waited beside a pile of plastic containers.

"This is Bun Dorca harbour, where the Queen Victoria once landed. And this is my brother, who works with me. Michael, this is Mr Wyatt from up in Dublin."

"Pleased to meet you." As they shook hands, Michael mumbled something inaudible to Wyatt.

"Don't you be worryin' about what he said Mr.Wyatt. Michael, he doesn't be sayin' much these days. No, not much at all" Tommy Joe's voice had a bitter edge, as he helped lift the containers on board. Then he throttled the engine, steering the boat out to the centre of the fjord, and west towards the open sea, finally stopping near a fish cage.

"Salmon." Tommy Joe said as he started emptying one of the containers into the cage. Inside the cage, Wyatt recoiled as he saw thousands of fish threshing about like lost souls in a fishy Hell.

"What are you doing, Tommy Joe?"

"We're havin' a problem with lice below the cages. We have to treat the fish with the disinfectant to stop them dyin'. We fed 'em a while ago." Tommy Joe said, putting the empty container back in the boat. The smell of chemicals stung the air.

"Hold on a minute, while I take a sample." Wyatt took a plastic bottle out of his rucksack, and leaned over the side of the boat to fill it with water from near the cage. As he put the sample back in the rucksack, before labelling it, he turned and saw Tommy Joe glowering at him, his face contorted.

"So that's your game is it? Comin' down here to spy on us. Inspectin' everything we do, checkin' if we're doin' it right. Takin' them samples, then writin' them down in a book. And then some effin gobshite in Dublin, him checkin' your work, then writin' about it to Brussels. "He paused to spit over the side of the boat, before continuing.

"Then some effin gobshite over there inspectin' it, then writin' to someone else, and so on, until someone who hasn't any effin idea at all about fish farmin', who's never been anywhere next, nigh, nor near a fish farm in his life, and hasn't a clue about it, will decide to end our way of making a livin'. Is that your game now is it, Mr Wyatt? "

"No. It's not my game, as you put it. Let me explain

Tommy Joe, I'm here to do a job as best I can. I've hired you to help me do part of that job. I've nothing against you, and I'm sure you've nothing personal against me. But I have many other things to do besides look at fish farms. Everyone has to make a living you know." Wyatt was irate, and Tommy Joe fell silent, before speaking again.

"You're right for sure. We've a lot more places to be seein' today. Bad cess to it, no good ever came out of a row." Wyatt sighed with relief, glad both his and Tommy Joe's anger had abated.

The morning was spent zig sagging across Killary fjord, stopping at the fish cages, treating the salmon inside, while Wyatt took water samples, and photos. When the boat moved seawards, with InishTurk in its wake, and Clare Island looming ahead on the port side, he noticed the waves lashing the boat were growing larger, jagged like teeth, with the wind whipping in hard from the west and lifting spray off the waves.

"We must make more speed, the weather, she's set to turn." Tommy Joe roared, revving the engine to full throttle.

The boat took off, bucketing in the waves, soon lifting into the air at the top of the rollers, before smacking down on the other side. Wyatt shuddered every time the boat landed in the water, and regretted having eaten the breakfast.

"Tommy Joe, could we abandon Clew Bay for today, and make a dash for home? I've had a hundred crash landings so far, and the weather looks like it may get worse."

Wyatt then took off his rucksack, and put on his oilskins.

"You're right there. We might be best shelterin' in Westport, but we'll give it a lash for Killary. There's a gale rising, force 6 to 8, I'd say. I'll turn her now."

He swung the boat in an arc into the teeth of the raging storm. Michael was baling out water with one of the plastic buckets he'd used earlier to delouse the fish cages.

"Are you ok there Mr Wyatt?" Tommy Joe shouted over the roar of the waves, as the rain started to pelt down.

"Yes. I'm alright." Wyatt replied, feeling anything but. The nausea of seasickness hit him as the boat rocked around then took off again over the waves, before whacking into the seething mass on the far side. Soon he'd vomited everything over the side. Even then, his stomach retched for the next two hours until they reached Leenane harbour.

Wyatt peeled off his oilskins, as he stepped weak-kneed up the pier steps. It was then he realised his rucksack was missing. In panic they searched everywhere in the boat, but in vain. It was gone, vanished. Wyatt was torn between shock and disbelief.

"Must have fallen overboard Mr Wyatt. 'Twas a mighty swell, as bad as I've ever seen on the west coast, eh Michael?" Michael nodded his head.

Or conveniently fallen overboard while I was puking my guts up. At least I still have my camera, Wyatt thought. A mighty swell indeed. Wyatt grimaced.

"Thanks Tommy Joe, I don't feel great now. I'll be in touch about next week."Wyatt had his doubts about Tommy Joe and his brother.

"The sea, she's your best friend an' your worst enemy. A few hot whiskies, an' a nice seaweed bath, an' a good woman to wash your back, then you'll be right as rain. I have to go now an' empty the lobster pots before droppin' Michael home. I'll say goodbye to you now Mr. Wyatt. Next week's fine for me. Stay between the ditches." Tommy Joe stepped back into the boat, and soon vanished like a wraith into the mist that had fallen, as the rain spat bullets into the sullen waters of the fjord.

As Wyatt trudged through the foyer his stomach heaved, he reeked of puke, and water dripped onto the parquet floor. He squelched through the empty reception area, up the stairs to his door, finally retrieving the key from his sodden shirt, glad no-one had seen him in the state he was in.

Inside his room, he emptied the water from his wellingtons, and left them to dry in the bathroom, before falling exhausted onto the bed. He stank, but didn't have the energy to take a bath. What had started with promise that morning, had ended in frustration. A day's work wasted. It might be the way of the world down here, he thought. All his work now rested at the bottom of the sea, or did it? Had Tommy Joe duped him? Who knows? But without the man's sailing and navigational skill they would not have got safely home. Had he been set up? He was too tired to think any more. Drowsiness dragged him down. His eyes closed, and he sank into a deep sleep.

# Chapter 2

## *A Vigil Keep*

Where am I? Wyatt thought, jolting awake, his mind jumbled. Someone was knocking on the door. His head was splitting. He jumped out of bed, and stumbled across the room.

"Who's there?"

"I've come to clean your room, sir."

"It's ok, come back later."

"All right, sir."

He got up, and put the Do Not Disturb sign outside on the door handle. Back in the bathroom, he swallowed some aspirins, his hands shaking. He grimaced into the mirror, thinking he looked a wreck. His stubbled face had a sickly yellow pallor, and he looked, and felt, a lot older than his thirty five years. At least his body was lean, from playing sports over the years.

His watch showed two o'clock in the afternoon, and he realised he had slept right through. No wonder the maid was beating down the door. They must have thought he was unconscious. Then it hit him he had slept without taking any sleeping pills, and he felt better. No point in trying to do any work, at this stage of the day, he reckoned. The need for a drink was more urgent.

After a lingering bath, he shaved, dressed in jeans and lumber shirt, and went downstairs to the foyer. Brigid was on duty. He was glad she hadn't seen him the day before in the state he was in, when he'd squelched through the hotel.

"Well, Mr Wyatt, there you are. Are you feeling all right? We were getting a bit worried about you. I'll get the maid to attend to your room right away." She picked up the phone.

"I'm ok Brigid thanks, it was just a seasickness hangover. I'm right as rain now. Can you tell me what's on down here on a Saturday night? I'd like to get out and about for a few hours."

"You're in luck, tonight there should be a good time down in the village in Traynor's pub. Once a month there's a sing song there, and tonight's the night. People come from far and near to join in. I might even be going there myself later on."

"Good, that sounds perfect. What time does it start?" Inside he felt glad she was going. At least he would know someone.

"About half past nine, give or take an hour. You know how it is down here." She smiled in a shy way.

"I don't really, not yet, but I'm starting to get the idea. Thanks for the information. Could you ring Tommy Joe O'Malley, and say I'd like to book him and his boat all day Monday from ten o'clock. I'll meet him at the harbour."

"I will indeed." She lifted the phone to make the call.

After a snack he left the hotel, and strolled towards the village. A purple haze had settled on the landscape, and all was quiet. Then a curlew's cry rasped from the water's edge, slicing the stillness. As he walked down the road, he trod with a lighter step, not worried that he was behind in his work schedule. Halpin won't be happy, he thought, but so what? Halpin will have to be patient. Funny, before I would have worried, but down here things don't seem to have quite the same urgency.

Inside the pub, he paused to look around. The acrid cigarette smoke hit his nostrils. A hush came in the room, as people stopped in mid-conversation to glance in his direction. They acted as if nothing had happened, but he knew he'd been checked out.

The packed bar was low and long, with a piano tucked away in a corner. The roof had black beams criss-crossing the white-washed ceiling and walls, casting shadows across the room. In the corner near a turf fire, he spotted an empty table. He ambled to the bar, eyes peeled, ordered a drink, and carried it to the table, where he could observe the whole room.

At the bar, a group of girls giggled over their drinks. One of them stood with her back to him. Her raven hair was tied in a green ribbon, and she wore a green dress short enough to show off her legs. He kept glancing in that direction. After a while the girl turned towards him. It was Bridget. She nodded towards him, before turning back to her friends. Some minutes later she gathered her drink and cigarettes, and sauntered over to sit beside him at the fire, flicking her hair back as she sat down. The flames from the fire lit in her eyes, and shone on her hair.

"You picked the cosiest corner in the room Mr Wyatt."

"Yes,...I....I did. Out of the limelight here too, that's the way I like it. You can call me Jim, by the way, you're off duty now Brigid." God, why am I so nervous? He thought. You'd swear I'd never chatted to a young woman before.

"I am indeed. My friends call me Bridie."

"I like that name, can I call you that too?" He said, trying to sound nonchalant.

"Yes, sure you can." She smiled, and he relaxed.

"Great, I hope that makes me one of your friends too. I was hoping you would be here tonight." She blushed, and looked down at the floor.

"I often come here with my friends. There's not many places to go around here, if you're looking for a bit of fun, and don't have a car."

"I'm a stranger here, a blow in."

"I'll be your interpreter, if you like." She smiled, lifting a ginger ale to her lips.

"The place is jammed, I wonder when the show starts?"

"Show is right. It's more like a lot of eejits making a bloody show of themselves. Mind if I light up?"

"No, go right ahead. Hold on, speak of the devil, I think something's happening."

A squat, white haired man had walked to the piano, took the mic in his hand, tapped it and held it to his mouth.

"You're all very welcome here tonight. We'll get the ball rollin' with a song from Father Flynn, from Leenane church up on the Westport road, who's travelled down to be here tonight. Let's give him a big *bualadh bas*."

When the clapping abated, Father Flynn sang a song of deep emotion that kept the audience enraptured. Wyatt recognised it as *Boolavogue*, a rebel song about the rising in 1798.

A local county councillor named Ned Halpin followed, singing *The Fields of Athenry*. The MC mentioned everyone's job before they sang.

"Bridie, I know that one, it's sung at all the football matches in England."

"It is. But most don't know it's about transportin' Irish prisoners to Van Dieman's land, Tasmania to you. It's got a local connection too. I'll explain it someday."

Next up was Sergeant Barry McSweeney from Westport, with a song about the banks of his own darling Lee. This got a mild reception from the crowd.

A square, rugged, grey haired man then took the mic. Eamon Carney, the owner of a company mining for gold in the Delphi valley rendered *My Darling Clementine*. There was muted appreciation from the inebriated audience.

Next up was a big man with red hair and beard, who sang *Kevin Barry*, without the mic. No mention was made of his job. The MC seemed embarrassed by him, moving quickly to the next song.

"Bridie, who is he? I don't think I'd like to tangle with him."

"True for you, that's Aengus McFadden, and I'd keep out of his way if I were you. He's from Ballytoher in the Gaeltacht, and has republican sympathies. I'll say no more."

Distracted by her words, Wyatt didn't hear the name of the next singer, who got such a reception, he did an encore. After a similar response to the next song, another encore was promptly given.

"Good heavens Bridie, who is that man, I didn't catch his name? Most of the other singers had better voices than him, but he got two encores."

"Well, he's Sean Glynn, the Bank Manager from Westport."

"Does that make a difference down here?"

"Yes. We all look up to him, I suppose. Everyone around here is probably indebted to him, in one way or the other. In fact, you could say that in this area, *He's Got the Whole World in His Hands*." She laughed as she spoke.

"I get you. Good heavens, I think Tommy Joe's going to give us a bar now."

Tommy Joe had walked unannounced to the piano, then turned and spoke to the crowd.

"I want to dedicate this song to someone who's just arrived here in Leenane, who's a stranger in these parts. Yes, it's Mr. Wyatt I'm talkin' about, that's him over there in the corner, him who's come down all the way from Dublin to inspect our ways of doin' things, and tell us how we should be doin' things. This song's for you Mr. Wyatt. Mr. Inspector." A sneer curled his lips, and the room went silent.

*"When all beside a vigil keep, the West's asleep, the West's asleep,*
*Alas and well may Erin weep, that Connacht lies in slumber deep……"*

The tension rose, as the song moved to its climax.

*But hark a voice like thunder spake, the West's awake, the West's awake,*
*Sing oh, hurrah let England quake, we'll watch them die, for Erin's sake."*

The applause raised the rafters. It was the biggest of the night. When the din died down, Tommy Joe stood staring across the room, in Wyatt's direction. Straight into his eyes.

"And now I'd like to call on the Inspector to give us a tune." Tommy Joe smirked as he placed the mic on the piano. The audience roared its approval, some banging their glasses on the table.

"Jesus, Bridie, what'll I do?" Panic gripped his body.

"You'll have to sing of course, you *amadawn*."

"I can't sing a note, I never could."

"Look, you've got to get up an' do something. For God's sake, just get up and sing *Molly Malone*, and they'll all join in." Slowly he rose.

As he walked to the piano, his knees knocked, but when he spoke into the mic his voice wasn't quivering as much as he was inside. After explaining his lack of a singing voice, he asked the crowd for their help in the chorus, then broke into the song, which he'd learned years earlier at drinking sessions in Trinity College. It was the first song of the night that involved the audience, and they joined in the singing, ending with a rousing cheer for him. Waving back to them, he left the mic on the piano, and returned, relieved, to the sanctuary of his corner by the fire.

"Thanks Bridie, for helping me out of that jam. I don't know what I would have done without you. I think I may have got away with it." He took a long slug from his glass.

"I think you might have too, they liked you for having a go."

Tommy Joe strode to their table, placing a pint on the table in front of Wyatt.

"There y'are, this one's on me. Everyone loves a trier Mr Wyatt. Cockles and Mussels my arse. I'll tell you one thing you've the neck of a jockey's bollocks, but take my advice and stick with the day job." Tommy Joe winked, and returned to his cronies at the bar.

"Thanks Tommy Joe, I'll drink to that. See you on Monday." He called after him.

Soon Father Flynn came to their table, and held out his hand.

"Welcome to our little community Mr Wyatt."

"Thanks Father, it's a beautiful place." They shook hands.

"Yes it is. There's an old Irish proverb..... Let he who is without faith walk the road to Leenane."

"I can appreciate that saying, Father. With the rhododendrons out everywhere you could be in the Garden of Eden."

"Indeed you could. I don't know if you're of our persuasion, but you're very welcome to our Sunday mass tomorrow morning. My church is not the one here in the village it's just a few miles farther down the Westport road."

"Thanks Father, you never know." Father Flynn bade him good night, and left the hubbub in the pub.

Soon Ned Halpin came over to Wyatt's table, and presented him with a pint, before shaking his hand.

"There you are James, you've earned that. We're all hoarse from singing along with you. You changed the format of the evening. No harm in that. It was getting to be a bit predictable. Best bit of craic we've had for ages. Ned Halpin, independent Councillor for this area. Put it there."

"Thanks Mr. Halpin. Excuse me, but how did you know my first name?"

"Sure isn't my brother Seamus your boss up in Dublin? It's my job to know what's goin' on in this area."

"It's a small world. I might need your help sometime on this project." Looks like Seamus Halpin's pulled another one on me. Looks like maybe he has a pair of local eyes and ears keeping tabs on me, Wyatt thought.

"You can rely on me for anything you want. I'm at your service at all times." Halpin handed him his business card, then turned to talk to someone in the crowd.

The pub was heaving, with no sign of the night ending. It was after one o'clock, well past his usual retirement time. Wyatt felt tired but happy.

"Bridie, I have to go now. It was a great night. How are you getting home?"

"I'm staying with my friend Mary Coyne, she lives up the road. I better go over and rescue her,I can see she's got tangled up with a few local lads, the worse for drink. I'll see you at the hotel on Monday, Jim."

"Sure Bridie. Thanks, I really enjoyed tonight."

"Me too, *Slan abhaile*." Bridie moved back to the bar, and as Wyatt headed for the door a tall, blond man, in a blue shirt, blocked his way.

"Sergeant McSweeney's the name, just came over to say hello, Mr Wyatt. If you ever need any help anytime, let me know."

"Thanks Sergeant, I enjoyed your song. Hopefully I won't need to trouble you, but you never know."

"You're right, you never know, bhoy. Anyway, I hope you have better luck than the last fellah that was here before you, if you know what I mean. Good night to you now."Saluting, Sergeant McSweeney headed back to the throng at the bar.

"Good night to you too." Wyatt replied, shaking hands, before stepping out into the gloom of the night. Outside he hesitated, feeling alone and exposed. The Sergeant's last words resonated in his ears, and he felt like he'd just been punched in the stomach.

# Chapter 3

## *The Water is Wide*

The bells clanged their Sunday call to midday Mass, as Wyatt leaned his rented bike against the stone wall of the church car park, and gazed about him. Built of granite, the small church had a high spire. It stood beside a table- top mountain, where rain streams had gouged runnels, tumbling to a river below. A veil of cloud hung above the mountain, and a breeze blew in soft from the west. Chance of a shower later, he thought.

Inside, a crowd had gathered, as it was the only mass of the day. Men were grouped in the porch at the back, yet many seats were empty at the top of the church. He walked up the aisle, and sat near the altar. Single men and women sat on opposite sides of the aisle, perfumed and pretty in their finery, the smell of damp clothing permeating the air. Early on in the Mass Father Flynn changed his vestments, and sauntered to the pulpit. His sermon droned on, ranging from the Gospel of the day, to man's insatiable greed. The priest spoke of the damage gold mining in the Delphi valley could do to the local environment, as an example of the latter. Finally he said a short prayer of remembrance for Frank Duffy, whose anniversary happened that month, and prayed the mystery of his disappearance would soon be resolved. It hung over the parish like a curse, he said. After speaking the priest paused to gaze about the congregation, as if he knew one of them knew the answer.

Wyatt checked his watch as he left, shoes scrunching the gravel path. The Mass had been a long one. Father Flynn stood near the church gate, talking to some people, and he walked over to him. The priest turned to shake his hand.

"Ah, it's good to see you came to our Mass after all Mr.

Wyatt, I'm so glad you did. I hope you enjoyed our little ceremony. Maybe you'll come again."

"Yes, I did enjoy it Father, though I wouldn't describe it as a little ceremony. I agree with your views on protecting the environment. I'd like to talk to you more about this matter, some other time maybe."

"You're welcome anytime, anywhere. The devil has many disguises." A frown furrowed the priest's face.

"I suppose he has. There's one thing on my mind, though, that maybe you might clear up."

"I'll do my best. Yes, what is it?" The priest asked, worried, his eyebrows arched, as he looked up into the taller man's face.

"That man, I….I think he was called Duffy, the one that you prayed for today. Tell me who…who is, or was, he?"

"You mean you don't know?" A look of surprise creased the priest's face.

"No."

Father Flynn leaned over, lowering his voice.

"I can't say too much here Mr.Wyatt.There's too many people around here with prying ears. I can't believe they never told you."

"Told me what?" The priest hesitated, looking about him, before replying.

"Frank Duffy, he… he was…well all I can say is he came down here from Dublin about four years ago. He vanished over two years ago. He's presumed……well he's still missing. Excuse me, there's someone over there I must speak to. We'll talk about it some other time."

"Ok Father, let… let's do that."

On his way back to his bike, Wyatt felt a hollow feeling in his stomach. Duffy vanished? Maybe murdered? Unbelievable. His mind reeled, as he pushed the bike towards the road, and a dry feeling came in his mouth, the one he usually got before a panic attack. Bridie came into view just then, walking across the far side of the car park, wheeling her bike. He remembered then that she was one of the reasons he had come to Mass that morning, maybe the main one. He wheeled his bike towards her.

"Good mornin' Jim. I'm heading back to the village now. Goin' my way?" She smiled as she spoke.

"Yes, are you alone?"

"I am."

"Good. Yes, I'd love to go with you. That's a grand bike you've got there."

"It's an old jalopy I got from my mother. It's a Raleigh, an upstairs model. They don't make them like this anymore, or so my mother says. It does the job anyway. It's reliable, and it gets me around. Shall we go?"

"Yes...yes, let's go." The panic in his body began to recede, as he pushed the pedals, and spun down the road after her.

A ray of sunshine split the clouds, lighting the landscape in a magic light, as they pedalled along the meandering road back to the village, and his spirits picked up more on the way. She declined his offer to join him that evening for dinner, saying she had an arrangement later with her friend Sharon. But she did agree to a coffee in the local pub. They parked their bikes outside, went in and found a table by the turf fire in the corner. They each ordered coffee and a sandwich.

"Do you live near here Bridie?" As he spoke, she took the scarf from her head, letting her hair tumble around her shoulders. Her blue eyes pierced his, and he caught his breath.

"Not far, as the crow flies. Over beyond, on the far side of the bay near Bun Dorca in the Delphi valley. It's near a half hour on the bike, give or take. I live there with my mother, and my younger sister Nora."

"And what about your father, is he not there too?"

"No, he died nearly ten years ago, God rest him. And I have an older brother Matthew. He's working on the buildings over in London."

"I'm sorry to hear about your father. It must have been hard on your mother."

"It was, she worked herself to the bone to get us reared.

She said learning was the best gift you could give your children. But now she's crippled with arthritis, though she doesn't go on about it, but sometimes it does get her down. She…she…. used be a grand dancer in her day, but now she barely gets around the house, even with a stick. We've had some bad times, but thanks be to God and our neighbours, the worst is past." She lifted the mug to her lips.

"I think Tommy Joe O'Malley lives over in your neck of the woods. Is he one of your neighbours?"

"Yes he is, and one of the best, too. He's a great help to my mother. He's a cousin too. His father and mine were brothers."

"Really?" The O'Malley clan seems to be big around here."

"It is for sure, more than you might know."

"And what are you hoping to do yourself, Bridie?"

"Well…I…I'm working now to help my mother put my sister through University. My brother in London is not much help to her, or anyone for that matter."

"And what then?"

"Oh,…I… I'll think about doing something when the time comes. I'd love to be a dancer. Or…or maybe…. maybe…. I'd like to to become a Genealogist."

"That's really interesting. I like the last one especially."

"You do?Tracing a person's or a family's history. Yes, that's what I'd like to do best of all. It's fascinating. I like delving into other people's lives. Everyone has a story to tell. I've just started a course on the subject. And tell me, what about you, and your family?" She sipped her coffee.

"There's nothing much to tell, I'm afraid. My father left when I was six years old. My mother's in a Nursing Home in Dublin. I have no other family to speak of."

"Oh….. thats sad. How long has she been in the Nursing Home?" Her face wrinkled in a frown.

"For a while before I came here."

"I suppose you won't get to visit her much from down here?"

"I hope to, whenever I get a chance."

"I suppose you'll write a lot to her anyway, then?" He began to feel edgy.

"I owe her a letter, a long one. I intend to rectify that matter tonight". He stood up, lowering the dregs of the coffee in a gulp.

"Well Bridie, what are your plans for the afternoon, since you're booked for tonight?"

"I was going to watch the currach races in the bay. They start in a few minutes. It's a big thing here every year, and good fun too. Would you like to come along?"

"Yes, why not?"

They left their bikes at the pub, and ambled down to the harbour, past an old whitewashed, horseshoe shaped entrance where the forge had once been. A sign advertising hire of scuba diving gear hung on a wall. He wrote down the telephone number, thinking it a good way to check out the wide, deep waters of the fiord. Luckily he still had his PADI qualification. The sharpening wind from the south west was whipping up white horse waves in the bay, and a salty tang hung on the breeze. The clouds lifted and broke into crazy shapes on the mountain peaks, as the sun burst on and off through the blue patches. Even still, the air stayed warm and humid.

A crowd had gathered at the sea wall, looking across the expanse of ruffled waters in the bay. Tarblack currachs gathered at buoys marking the start of the race. Each currach had a crew of six, wearing diverse Aran sweaters. The crowd cheered as the parishes represented were announced on the loudspeakers.

A shot exploded, and a roar rent the air as the currachs took off, cleaving the wind and waves. Many of the crews had now discarded their shirts and jerseys, exposing lean, white torsos, bending back and forward over their oars. Wyatt sensed the awe of some primal force in what he was watching.

Another roar erupted when the winning currach crossed the line. It was then Wyatt realised the crowd were speaking in Irish.

"I wonder who won the race, Bridie?"

"The team from Ballytoher Gaeltacht won it. There's McFadden, he's the big redhead who sang last night in the pub, over there with the team. He's from there."

"Should we go over and congratulate him?

"No, it's best not to. I'll tell you why some other time. I think we should go now."

"Yes, you're right. I've stuff to do at the hotel, not to mention writing to my mother."

"And I'm off to meet Sharon, my dancing partner. We've a mountain of practice to put in before the Ceili in the town hall, two weeks down the road."

"Oh....I didn't know.... maybe I could come and cheer you on?"

"Why not? We'll need all the help we can get, *Slan Abhaile*." With a wave she pushed off on her bike, and in a slow spinning movement, hair streeling in the wind, swept past the whitewashed, thatched cottage at the corner, in the direction of the village. She looks good on a bike, Wyatt thought. He waved after her, watching her all the way until she vanished around a bend in the road. He sighed, mounted his bike, and cycled back to the hotel.

That night he wrote the letter to his mother. It was a long letter. It took a long time, longer than he expected. In it he mentioned meeting Bridie, and the currach races, and the rhododendrons and the wildflowers, and other things he thought she'd like to hear about. I hope she'll understand most of it, he reflected. I hope it's not too long. I'll send it to the Matron of the Nursing Home, with a covering note, and ask if someone would read it to Mam. Later he got stuck into his work schedule for the coming week, but after a while gave up the task. The priest's words about Frank Duffy drifted back into his mind, confusing his thoughts. He tried to remember the Sergeant's last words to him as he left the pub. Something about having better luck than the last guy. Seamus Halpin is going to have some explaining to do tomorrow, he fumed, fear gnawing his gut. A fitful night's sleep followed, before he reached for the sleeping tablets in the drawer beside his bed.

He rang Halpin early in the morning, hoping to get his spoke in first, but Halpin was engaged at a meeting. Wyatt left a message to ring back, and returned to his room, annoyed that he had forgotten about the weekly management meeting on Monday mornings. It would finish at half past ten on the dot, he remembered. He sat at his desk, reviewing his plans for the week ahead, drumming his fingers on the desktop while he waited. The phone rang at ten thirty five.

"James, good to hear your voice. I intended ringing you, but you got there first. People up here have been asking about your progress. I kicked to touch of course, told them to be patient, but I *was* hoping to have something on my desk by now. So how goes it?"

"Progress is being made, Mr. Halpin, but I....I... was caught in a storm at sea last week, which has delayed matters. All...all my work was lost overboard. "

"Hmm...ok, well.... that's a pity, but there's pressure building on me. You know how it is up here. They don't understand how it is where you are. By the way you can call me Seamus, we're all on the same side you know."

"Yes, I know. You can tell them I nearly drowned, if you like."

"Ok James, I can understand how frustrated you must feel down there on your own."

"I'll be sending you my first report next weekend, when I have my samples back from the lab."

"That's good. Anything else I can do for you, James?"

"Yes, I have a couple of questions. One, you never told me your brother lived here."

"So you've met already. I can see you're putting yourself about. Well it never occurred to me to mention it at the time. But he should help matters, if needed." Wyatt suspected Halpin's brother could be a spy in the camp for Seamus Halpin back in Dublin.

"Number two, what about Frank Duffy? Why wasn't I told about him? My predecessor vanished without trace, but no one told me in advance? This assignment is a lot more complicated and dangerous than I thought. Why did you not tell me?" There was a pause before Halpin replied.

"Ok James, you're right, it *is* a complex project. The Frank Duffy case was before my time as head of Department. Also, he was sent there at the instigation of other Departments, including the Garda. It was a completely different operation. As far as I'm aware he was a plant, put there to gather information on Republican activities in the area. The job was a cover, and as he was successful in his surveillance duties, they left him there longer than intended. Yes he vanished, but there's no evidence to prove he was murdered. He just disappeared."

"I believe you should have told me anyway."

"Maybe, but why bring up issues which are not relevant now? The bottom line is there's a pressing European aspect to your assignment. You're there where you are now. I believe you're the right man for the job. Don't you?"

"Yes, of course I do." Cunning bastard, trying to pass the buck as usual. Should be on the stage, Wyatt raged to himself

"Well ok then, let's get back to the case in hand. I need your first report on my desk by next Friday. Agreed? Without fail."

"Yes Seamus, sure."

"That's fine then James, I'm looking forward to getting it then. Good luck." The phone line clicked dead. Case dismissed.

\*\*\*

Wyatt's skin tingled in anticipation as he walked up the road in the morning sun, rucksack on back, towards the harbour where his hired wooden currach lay moored. The thrill of scuba diving again made his blood pump. Gannets shrieked in the air, before plunging into the waters below. The stench of fish and seaweed hung in the air. The morning mist on the fiord had almost burnt away. The water was flat as a pancake. Perfect for diving, he thought. Excitement coursed his veins. The van with the scuba gear was parked on the pier. Tommy Joe helped him load the gear onboard, then left, saying he would collect the boat at six o'clock that evening at the same place. Wyatt put his wet suit on, and stepped into the swaying vessel.

He started the outboard engine and guided the boat to the centre of the fjord. The sea mist had now vanished. As he watched the sun arc higher in the sky, he felt encouraged, thinking it would help visibility in the deep waters. When he came close to a salmon fish cage, he cut the engine, dropped anchor, and lifted the oxygen cylinder onto his back. After checking the diving equipment, he tied a bag with empty sample bottles around his waist, pulled the oxygen mask down over his face, before toppling backwards into the water.

The sea seemed bottomless, as he sank down. His torch sent a shaft of light through the phosphorescence, and he dropped deep into the depths. He circled around, taking samples at differing levels, before moving in close to a fish cage. After diving into the shadow below the cage, he took more samples, then swam around the sides of the cage, stopping to stare at the teeming mass of fish flesh inside, trapped in their watery prison. A life sentence for them, he thought. There were up to 50,000 fish in the two acres inside the cage, each living in an area the size of a bath. The crushing of fish, off each other and the cage walls, caused fin damage, infections, and fish deaths, and the chemicals used to treat this problem led to water contamination. Lice were the big killers of wild fish outside in the fjord, attaching themselves to the skin of the salmon, and making them die a cruel, lingering death. He grimaced at the thought.

As he swam along the outside of the cage, past the hatch where the fish were accessed, he had an idea. He decided to take a grilse out and check it for contamination and lice. It could be damning evidence. It was tempting. Not ethical, but neither was what was going on inside the cage. After moving closer, he slid back the grill panel, put his hand in, grabbed a young salmon, and stuffed it into his bag. As he went to shut the grill, a clumping noise erupted nearby. A huge wave hit him, smashing him against the side of the fish cage, before everything went black.

When he awoke, he was staring into the fish cage, and hundreds of startled fishy eyes were gaping back at him. Fear, then panic, numbed his body. He felt dazed, in an unreal world, and his left arm hurt like hell. Fish were escaping through the open grill panel. Hundreds of them were squeezing through the gap, out into the wide, open waters of the fjord, following the thousands that had already escaped. They were swimming the gauntlet of fish cages strung out along the fjord, in a race to freedom. He clutched the side of the cage, and waited, resting until he felt stronger.

The brightness dazzled his eyes, when he resurfaced. He pulled back his mask with his good hand, and then used the same hand to steady himself against the cage top. While he rested, he scanned the water, bewildered. His boat was gone. Looking about in panic, he saw bits of wooden debris floating in the water. The boat had been blown to smithereens, and he realised that fish were still escaping in thousands from the cage below the surface.

He hung onto the cage for some time, cold, dazed, and exhausted. It seemed an age before he saw Tommy Joe's trawler heading in his direction. Soon he was hauled out of the water, and ferried back to the harbour in silence. Wyatt felt numb and wondered if he was suffering from shock. His left arm ached like mad, and everything seemed far away, unreal.

Back at the harbour, he stood on the pier, groggy, arm throbbing, staring dumbly at his oxygen tank and sample bag on the ground in front of him, before he spoke.

"T...thanks Tommy Joe. I'm not sure what happened. Look...looks like there was an explosion somewhere near the boat. I was just swimming around, taking samples. Then bang. Your boat's blown to bits, I'm afraid. That will be sorted though."

"No worries, Inspector. It's only wood, and it can be replaced. Looks like you're going to be famous all over Mayo. Maybe not in the way you'd want to be. But famous you'll be, for sure. You'll first need to go get yourself checked out at the hospital. I'll report everythin' to the guards. If you like, I'll not mention you opened the hatch in the salmon cage."

"How do you know I opened the hatch?"

"Would you look at the bloody fish still wriggling about in the bag there? It didn't fly in there, did it? Your head's not workin' right, Inspector. I'll get the priest and finish the job for you. I'll give it the last rites." Tommy Joe picked a stick from the ground, took the fish from the bag, whacked the salmon on the head, and popped the dead fish back into the bag.

"I'd prefer if you didn't mention it at this stage to the guards."

"Great, whatever you say Inspector. You have my word. It might help with the claim too. Tongues 'll wag though. You'll sort out the loss of the boat, an' the fish too? The cost could be mighty."

"Of course, you'll be compensated for both." Wyatt knew Halpin wouldn't be a happy camper, when he got the news. But right then he didn't give a damn how Halpin felt.

Tommy Joe brought him back to the hotel. He limped up to his room, and changed into clean clothes with difficulty, his bad arm aching. Within the hour he was visited by two detectives from Galway, there to check out the explosion in the fiord. One wrote while the other asked the questions. They were experts in explosives and armoury, and wanted full forensic details. He explained what had happened, saying everything was a bit hazy, omitting he had opened the hatch on the fish cage. They told him he was lucky, a local Garda would be in touch with him, and he should get himself seen to, straight away. They thanked him and left.

Evening shadows slanted across the landscape, when he returned from Castlebar hospital. The doctor had confirmed his arm wasn't broken. The damaged ligaments would need several weeks rest, but his arm must be kept in a sling. The doctor's last words rang in his ears.

"From what you've told me, you're a very lucky person, Mr. Wyatt. You could have been seriously injured, or worse. You're also suffering from post- trauma shock. You must have complete rest for the next two weeks. Please call back in a week."

"I'll do my best Doctor." Complete rest? He thought to himself. If only. The pain killers are a help, though.

# Chapter 4

## *Down in the Valley*

Wyatt spent the next two days in bed. The painkillers had numbed the pain in his arm, but he slept fitfully, fatigued, visions of fish escaping into the fjord, and the chaos following the explosion spinning endlessly through his head. A phone call came from the local Garda, who wanted to interview him about the incident. Damn, he swore, after agreeing to meet them next morning at the hotel. As he put down the phone he recalled Tommy Joe's remark about being famous all over Mayo. He was impatient to get back to work outdoors, in spite of the doctor's advice. First he had to get his report to Halpin in Dublin. But he wondered how, with all the interruptions.

After breakfast he entered the lounge, and sat by the window, newspaper in hand. He scanned the pages, relieved there was no mention of the explosion. He put the paper down, glancing out the window. A Garda squad car with lights flashing pulled in and parked outside the hotel. He hurried into the foyer, and saw Sergeant McSweeney talking to another guard. The Sergeant turned and approached him.

"Sorry for your trouble, Mr. Wyatt. You remember me, Sergeant McSweeney. But please call me Barry. No serious injuries incurred from the incident yesterday, I trust?"

"No Barry. I was lucky."

"That's good. Look, I'd like to speak to you in private about the explosion, but only if you feel up to it. Just a few questions like. My colleague here Guard Kenny will take notes. If you want, I can wait or come back tomorrow. You must still be a bit shocked. It was a hell of an explosion."

"Now is ok, let's do it. I'll order a few coffees, and we

can go to the lounge." Wyatt said, drained, but anxious to get it finished. Better to face the music now, he thought, they must be following up the visit of the two detectives. They sat in a secluded corner, near the window. The Sergeant offered him a cigarette, but he declined. It was five years since he last smoked, after that bleak night, but he had never felt more like having one. The arrival of the coffees eased the craving.

Wyatt related what he could remember, but omitted that he had been diving near the damaged salmon cage.

"Tell me, why did you use scuba gear if you just wanted to take water samples?"

"I wanted to take samples from varying depths. Water quality can vary at different levels, you know."

"I do know, bhoy, just checking. And did you get samples from below the fish cage in question?"

"No….no..not really. I was going to, but the explosion changed everything. I was only approaching it. What do *you* think happened to the boat?"

"We don't know yet, we're still doing the forensics. Our findings so far show that the explosion wasn't due to an engine fault. Most likely it was caused by dynamite, detonated by a time fuse or by remote control. Either way you're a lucky man, you could've been aboard, or close by when it happened. Your injuries *are* consistent with you being in the region of the fish cage."

Wyatt saw Guard Kenny scribbling away on his pad. He drained his coffee cup, and refilled it.

"As I said I was moving in that direction, but I hadn't got there, when all hell broke loose. Are you saying someone tried to murder me?" Wyatt felt a knot tightening in his stomach.

"Maybe, but we're not saying anything definite at this time. We're trying to piece the jigsaw together, you know like. Do you have any enemies? Enemies who might attempt to murder you?" McSweeney's eyes narrowed into slits as he spoke.

"No…no.. not that I know of. You tell me."

"We don't know either. I wish we did. All we do know is dynamite was stolen from the gold mining company up in the Delphi valley. We'll be doing forensic tests to see if it matches that used here today. I suggest you give no information to the media, if they approach you. I'm sure you're not in a fit state to comment anyway?"

"Yes…yes.. good idea, I agree with that sentiment. I…I just want to take it easy."

"Thanks for your time Mr. Wyatt. We'll let you know of any developments." The Sergeant stood up, and turned towards the door.

Wyatt followed him, tugged his arm, and asked if he could speak to him alone. McSweeney agreed, and nodded to the guard who left the room.

"Ok we're alone, so what's worrying you?"

"It's the Frank Duffy case. It's been on my mind a lot. I want to get it sorted in my mind. Can you tell me what happened to him? I swear I won't divulge anything you tell me. My lips are sealed. It might be relevant to the explosion on the boat." There was a pause.

"Well, you're the quare one, and no mistake. Personally I don't think there's any connection, but we never rule anything out in the force. The Frank Duffy case file is still open. It's a mystery I want to solve too. No body was recovered you know. I hope to find out what happened, some sweet day, by God I do." The Sergeant punched the palm of his hand as he spoke.

"Look Barry, I might be able to help. Could you let me have a copy of the case notes?"

"In strictest confidence of course." Wyatt added, eyeballing McSweeney. The Sergeant said nothing, stood up, and paced the room, flexing and unflexing his hands, before finally replying.

"By God, you're putting me on the spot, and no mistake. What you're asking is highly irregular. It's not kosher, like. But…..but... ok, look, I trust you. And by God I'd do anything to unravel that case. It's cost me many a sleepless night. I'll let you have a copy, in absolute secrecy. *And* this conversation, it never happened. Ok? And now I must be off to check how our sub aqua team are doing at the crime scene."

"Ok Sergeant, you have my word."

They shook hands, and McSweeney left the lounge, joining his colleague in the foyer. They spoke briefly, then left the hotel and drove towards the harbour.

Wyatt returned to his room, exhausted, slumped on his bed, and fell into a deep stupor. He woke in a panic, wondering if it was all a bad dream. The scuba gear on the floor confirmed it wasn't. So did the twinge in his shoulder. He went to the bathroom, and swallowed some painkillers. He tried to sleep once more, but still the image of thousands of fleeing fish flitted through his head, and the clump of the explosion kept thudding in his ears.

Eventually he got up, frustrated, and busied himself tidying up his room. His injured hand hampered him as he hung his wet suit in the bathroom. He left the mess on the carpet for the cleaning staff. After checking and re-labelling the samples, he put them in a row beside his computer. He remembered that the first test results would be back from the lab the next day. A rancid stench came in the room, and he realised the salmon in the bag was going off. He hastily placed it in the sink in the bathroom, and scraped flesh from the outer skin, taking samples from the organs, before putting each in a separate bottle. He then duplicated the procedure, labelled each bottle with his good hand, while steadying the bottles with the injured one.

Afterwards, he started to input the data onto his computer, and update his first report to Halpin. But when he lifted the computer lid he gasped. Someone had broken into his computer. The hair he had sellotaped to the lid and the body of the computer was broken. It was located near the back, in an area where it would not be seen. He logged in and checked the data on his hard drive. It was still intact. Somebody was spying on him. It hit him like a bolt, but he reasoned no vital information had been lost, as the lab results would not arrive until the next day. Then he remembered the cd's he had hidden in the back of the wardrobe, and rushed to check if they were still there. When he found them intact, he calmed down a little.

No need to get excited, he told himself. A slug of whiskey from the bottle hidden in his bedside locker soothed his nerves. It wasn't a complete surprise, he reasoned. After all, he *had* put in his own computer security check, in case something like this happened. You can't trust anyone, he muttered. Yes, somebody was spying on him. But that person, or persons, didn't know that he *knew*. He decided it was better to keep it that way. He could then feed them whatever story he wanted, and they would be none the wiser. If he stayed cool, maybe he could turn this development in his favour. The idea of keeping two computer files now seemed a good one. So did the idea of another gulp of whiskey.

In bed later, he tried to concentrate on the words of the Famine book he had bought. He soon gave up, frustrated, his mind again embroiled in events leading to the explosion in the fjord. Someone was out to injure, or maybe murder him. He had been lucky, and survived with only a minor injury, but the what-might-have-been preyed on his mind. Got to stay positive and move on, he thought. But what would he say to Halpin? And what would he do in the coming weeks to cope with the boredom if he was confined to the hotel? *And* it was coming to his bad time of the year. I need some pills, he muttered, panicking. But before he had reached into the drawer for them, his eyes closed, and his head slumped on the pillow. He dreamt that night, and Tommy Joe's words about being famous all over Mayo kept going through his head.

Next morning he woke, and gazed around the room. It again looked dishevelled. This won't do, he fumed, and spent the next hour tidying it up. He labelled and packed all his water sample bottles. If he got them out today he knew they would be back from the laboratory on

Thursday. He called reception and booked a courier.

The courier arrived within the hour. During the waiting period, he entered all the information onto his computer, before saving the data onto a disk, which he hid in a recess in his wardrobe. When he handed over the packages for delivery, he breathed a sigh of relief, and felt at last things were moving.

Back in his room, he glanced at the latest edition of the local newspaper. A headline about pollution in local drinking water caught his attention. There had been an outbreak of *Cryptosporidium* in the water in the area recently. It seemed to be caused by inadequate monitoring of local drinking water by the council. The council had denied this, saying that their sampling methods were compliant with normal environmental standards. The problem was the council's monitoring, which was carried out once a month, and then was only done at the tap. This was inadequate in high risk areas, as it did not cover the sampling of raw water, nor did it cover treated water at each treatment works. Something is rotten somewhere, he seethed, as he read on in disbelief.

It seemed the reason that proper monitoring of the water was not being done by the council, was to save money. He was stunned. Apart from the effect on local people's health, it would be disastrous for the country's tourism reputation if this became known abroad. It would cause global reputational damage. He wondered how this could happen in a country whose biggest asset was its clean image, and unpolluted environment. Not to mention the millions being spent abroad each year promoting the country. It just didn't make any sense. Realising this matter was part of his brief from Halpin he cut out the article and filed it. He later decided to spend the next day investigating the onshore water in the locality.

That night he checked the weather forecast. There would be a spell of settled weather over Ireland in the coming week. High pressure was drifting in from the Atlantic. Just what he needed to catch up on his workload, he thought. Before retiring to bed he sat in front of his computer, opened a file which he labelled "Head Office Reports", and another which he called "The Real Story". The moon was full and high over the mountains, and a silvery glow had spread throughout the room, when he'd finished updating each file. Finally, he saved the data onto two separate discs, and hid them away.

Next morning he hired a car, and filled the boot with specimen bottles, a packed lunch, and some books. Outside, the sun was climbing in an indigo sky, the mountains a tawny canvas on the fjord. Inside he felt the negativity of the previous day fade. Today he felt glad to be alive.

His first stop was the car park near Aasleagh Falls, over the Mayo border, at the entrance to the Delphi valley. The cataract there descended from a valley surrounded by sheer mountains, and a rainbow arced over the waterfall. After climbing up and around the falls, he walked further up into the valley past empty wooden fishing beats, along the banks of the winding, swirling river, and took water samples as he went.

Later he returned to the car park at Aasleagh Bridge, and drove on into the Delphi valley. He passed Bun Dorcha harbour, and stopped in the valley to take samples in the rivers and streams. After parking near an arched bridge beyond the Adventure Centre, he took his packed lunch, crossed the road, and climbed over a wooden stile, leading down to the river bank.

At the edge of the river, he spread out a cloth on the grass, and sat down, eating his lunch in the heat of the sun. As he chewed a sandwich, he looked around. There were rippling circles breaking on the surface of the river, as trout rose to take the flies skimming over the eddying waters. Swallows zig zagged up and down the banks, patrolling the scene.In the river was the blue sky above, and the mountain pinnacles around him. Further upriver he spotted the source of the river. It flowed from the lee of a mountain, into a dark lake with fishing boats in it.

Shadowed by the mountain, it moved along in a curving sweep. It swirled past clumps of reeds by banks where water hens and ducks swam in and out. Then onwards, under the arched bridge past where he lay, and down towards the sea.

Lunch eaten, he scanned the countryside with his binoculars. On a nearby mountain, a sheepdog herded a flock to lower pastures, and he heard the strange cries of the farmer to the dog, echoing through the stillness. In the lower fields, cattle grazed. He decided to check the streams in that area, in case there was contamination from fertilizers used in the surrounding fields. But first he cleaned up after his lunch.

In the distance, Ben Gorm towered. Contours of green lazy beds were etched on the mountains, beside deserted ruins, which harked back to Famine times. Wyatt was fascinated by the lazy beds since he'd come to the area. His mind recalled what he'd just read about those godforsaken days. In that era, the poorer Irish people were forced by uncaring landlords to eke out a living in this area, on the poorest land on God's earth.

The best of the land then was nothing more than peat bog and bare rock. Women carried seaweed and sand up from the shore in baskets on their backs. Men cleared rocks and stones from the hillside, and mixed what was in the baskets with whatever soil and manure they could dredge up. Desperation drove them to grow their potato drills in the desolate terrain, but disease hit them in the end. All that time, despair and hunger stalked the land.

The people who tried to make a living in these conditions were anything but lazy. The name came from the practice of re-sowing the drills with seed potatoes from the crop being dug. Nine months later a new crop would be harvested, and the process repeated. Then the fatal results in the Famine times came. What appeared to be fine potatoes were re-sown, only to turn out blighted, when dug up nine months later. The poor, living like this, were always one step away from hunger, starvation, and death.

The lazy beds, like graves, were stark testimony to the fate of most of these poor souls. Of those who survived the starvation and disease, most ended up emigrating on coffin ships, following the words of the Irish proverb. *Seek the fair land, beyond the brow of the hill.*

Many small villages around Killary fjord were devastated. After the Famine, the government had brought in sheep farmers from Scotland, and turned the area around the fjord into one large sheep farm. Gone were those who toiled the lazy beds. Gone to God knows where. Their epitaph was the corduroy contours, now overgrown with grass, terracing the hillsides. He sighed, and moved on.

After checking some streams for pollution, he drove along rhododendron bordered roads, until he reached Doo Lough (Black Lake), and stopped to take more samples. There was an eerie feel to the place, and no fishing was going on. Later he took soil samples from the adjoining fields. In the afternoon he drove west until he came to a Famine monument overlooking the large dark lake. When he read the inscription on the stone, he felt a tingle through his body. *Doolough Tragedy 1849. Erected to the memory of those who died in the Famine of 1845-1849.* The words cut deep into his being. He shuddered.

Around a bend in the road, he followed a sign pointing right for Lioscarney. The road twisted for miles through forests of high pine trees, before a cone shaped mountain loomed ahead like a dead volcano. It had a small white building on top, and he recognised it as Croagh Patrick, the Holy Mountain. Later he came to a picnic place in the valley behind the mountain, and parked there. He continued walking with a rucksack on his back. The afternoon sun was now hot on the back of his neck. A stream flowed through the valley. After taking some samples from it, Wyatt scanned the valley, now in the lengthening shadows of the evening sun on the mountains, and saw a man far away, bent double over the stream. As he got closer he saw that the man was large, very large, with a blue lumberjack shirt, and a cowboy hat, and a griddle in his hands, which he was shaking hard.

"Howdy dude. Pete's the name" The big man spoke first, straightening his back, and extended his hand, as he spat into the clean, flowing water. He *was* large, Wyatt thought.

"Pleased to meet you. Jim's my name. You look like you're panning for gold." Wyatt's hand felt like it was being crushed in a vice.

"Sure as hell am, sir. I didn't get my nickname of Panhandle Pete for nuttin'. Come all the way from Texas to be in this here place."

"Really? How interesting. And are you having any luck so far?"

"Sure as heck I am. This place's loaded, an' I really mean loaded. High grade stuff too. Say, you're not from the government are you?" He lifted his stetson hat and scratched his blond head. He had clear blue eyes.

"No. Not really. You can relax about that. I'm just out for the day. I won't disturb you any more then. Nice to meet you."

"You too, sir." The big blond man saluted, and bent down again to his task. As he did so, Wyatt saw a green bag lying on the grass. On the outside there were a number of white x marks, and below these the words in large letters, DANGEROUS, HIGH EXPLOSIVES.

Further up the stream Wyatt took more samples. He wondered what effect gold mining might have on the water quality in the area. And the blasting of river beds and rocks? It could be disastrous for the landscape, he reckoned. He needed to check it out further. After walking back to the car, he placed his samples in the car boot, and saw then that he had used up all his bottles. As he drove home, the mountains changed to a golden colour in the evening sun. *So* there's gold in them thar hills, he thought, smiling to himself.

Wyatt made a note to contact Ned Halpin, the local

councillor, to arrange for testing of the local water and sewage plants, later in the week. Back at the hotel, he spent the evening labelling and sorting out all the water samples of that day. Then he updated his files on the computer, and hid another CD copy away, after deleting "The Real Story" file from his hard disc.

After a hot bath he retired to bed to read his book on local history, and the Famine. He thumbed through it until he reached the chapter about the Doo Lough Tragedy.

*When the Famine was at its worst, nearly six hundred starving people came to Louisburgh, seeking food or admission to the workhouse. Spurned there, they were told to go see the two paid Poor Law guardians whom they said were holding a board meeting at Delphi Lodge the following day. The next morning about four hundred of these starving wretches, some in rags, some half naked, all barefoot, took off on the bitterest of cold spring days, hope in their hearts, treading through over ten miles of the wildest, bleakest countryside in Ireland. When they came to Glenkeen, they had to ford a swollen river due to heavy recent rainfalls. Between there and Doo Lough (Black Lake), they took a high goat track, fording more streams, until they reached Delphi Lodge. When they got there, the two guardians, Colonel Hograve and Mr Lecky were at lunch (or playing cards, legend has it). They could not be disturbed. The starving, miserable people huddled wet and freezing in the pine trees outside. When the two gentlemen finally came out, they refused to give them any relief, and told them to return to Louisburgh. At this time, there were no roads through the dangerous pass between the Sheefry Hills and Mweelrea Mountain, only high, narrow goat tracks up above the Black Lough. Darkness was falling, when a raging gale brought a hail storm in from the north-west. When the refugees passed over a cliff called Stoppabue, severe gusts of wind drove many off the cliff to their deaths in the dark lough below. The survivors continued northwards through worsening weather. Those who did not perish on the way, did so at the second crossing of the swollen Glenkeen River. None of the four hundred survived.* Later, the book slid from his fingers to the floor, as his head fell asleep on the pillow. The tears had dried on his face.

# Chapter 5

## *Atlantic Waves*

The Great Escape. The headlines caught his eye next morning, when he read the local newspaper in the hotel lounge. There was front page coverage of the incident in Killary fjord, reporting that 50,000 fish had fled to freedom from a salmon cage, and escaped both up and down the fjord, after an explosion on a nearby boat. *And* there was an unnamed person scuba diving nearby when the incident happened. The Garda enquiries were ongoing. Of course, he thought, and why wouldn't they be? No connection had been made yet between the theft of dynamite from a company mining for gold in the Delphi valley nearby, and the explosion on the boat. But people had their suspicions. The Garda had described the occurrence as "bizarre and mysterious". He froze. The article had a sinister tone to it, and the fact that *he* was the mystery scuba diver in the water, sent a shiver down his spine. Famous all over Mayo he was indeed, just as Tommy Joe had predicted. In panic he rummaged through all the major national papers. There was no mention in any paper of the incident. He relaxed then, but wondered how long that situation would last. His head still felt dizzy, and he now had a dry taste in his mouth. Perhaps the media would soon be on his trail? He'd better lie low for the present. But how could he, for God's sake, in a place like this? When he got back to his room, he rang Halpin.

"James, good to hear from you. Everything ok?" He surmised from Halpin's words, that he hadn't heard anything yet about the incident.

Wyatt apprised Halpin of the explosion in the fjord, excluding the fact that he had opened the grille on the salmon cage. When he finished, there was a pause before Halpin spoke.

"Hmmm….this is serious James. Our budget has been literally blown out of the water, no pun intended. I'll have to meet straight away with Finance and try to square things up. Mmmm…….. yes, this is very serious indeed. Finance will just have to realise that this is a matter of grave national interest. Look, I really don't know how this will end up. They may want to pull the whole project. At least you were just an innocent victim in what happened. It's vital I have your first report in my hands by Monday morning. You understand?" Halpin's voice now had a strident tone.

"Mr Halpin, surely you realise it's *not* all about money. Someone may have tried to murder me for doing my job. Surely *that's* the most important thing. I didn't sign up for an assignment as dangerous as this. I don't even know if I want to continue putting my life on the line." Wyatt paused for a while before continuing.

"We must be on the right track though, if someone wants to stop me that badly. If something is right to do, the cost doesn't matter. Surely *you* can see that?"

"Yes James, I suppose you're right, look I'm sorry. I…..I was a bit shocked by the news. By the way, please call me Seamus, we're all on the same side you know. *Of course* your safety is of prime importance. We've already lost Frank Duffy. It would be damn careless, to lose a second person…. ha,ha,ha."

"It's no laughing matter Seamus. *And* I thought you said Frank Duffy was *before* your time, and not relevant."

"No…no you're right there, it's not a laughing matter. As I said before it's a serious situation. But I'm under pressure here, after the furore in Brussels. And now the damn Finance mandarins here in Dublin will be on my back too. I really need that report without fail, James." Smart bucko, passing the ball back, Wyatt thought.

"I've already told you that you *will* have it. I've given you my word. What more can I do? Deliver it by hand?" His nerve ends jangled, and he craved a drink. Just one drink.

"Well, now that you mention it James, why don't you come up for a few days next week. We can discuss your report's initial findings, and develop our strategy from there, in the light of these dangerous developments. Your nerves must be frayed with all that ballyhoo yesterday. Why don't you have a little break, and visit your mother, who I believe is in a nursing home up here." So, he has a heart after all, Wyatt thought.

"Ok Seamus, *that's* a good idea, as soon as I feel a bit better. I need to lie low from the media down here too."

"Right then, that's agreed. See you next week, James." The receiver went dead.

He still felt groggy, and decided to rest awhile, but first went downstairs to check his mail. A tall, thin young man stood in the foyer.

"Mr Wyatt? I'm Noel Kenny from the Mayo Times. May I speak to you for a minute?" The man produced an ID card from his pocket.

"About what?" Wyatt felt edgy. He needed to rest, and he needed a drink. He knew he should tell the man that he wasn't feeling well, but he hadn't the will.

"Can we find somewhere more private?

"Let's go into the lounge." Better to face the music, and get over it, Wyatt thought. They went to the far end of the room and sat down.

"Mr. Wyatt, I have reason to believe *you* were the mystery scuba diver in the bay yesterday, when the boat was blown up." The tall man eyeballed him, and took a notebook from his pocket.

"Firstly, who said I was that person, and second who said the boat was blown up?"

"Sorry Mr Wyatt, we have to protect our sources. But I *can* tell you that the Garda have confirmed the boat was dynamited, using the same kind of explosive as had been stolen from a nearby mining company the previous week." So it *was* deliberate. Wyatt was shocked.

"Ok, so I *was* scuba diving in the fjord at the time it happened."

"May I enquire what you were doing?"

"I was doing my job, and minding my own business."

"Which is?"

"It's confidential. I work for the Government. Department of Marine and Fisheries."

"I see. Do you have any reason to suspect anyone would want to harm you?"

"No."

"Had you reached the fish cage before the explosion happened?"

"No. I was swimming *near* the cage."

"You were crushed against the cage by the force of the explosion, and injured your arm?"

"Yes."

"So you *were* quite close to the cage? Did you at any stage open the grille through which the fish escaped?"

"No. Why would I want to do that? I told you I had not reached the cage when the boat blew up."

"So you *were* heading for the cage?"

"I didn't say that. I was swimming around near the cage. That's what I said."

"Of course you did. Thank you for your comments Mr Wyatt. Goodbye." The tall man stood up, shook Wyatt's hand, and went outside into the sunshine.

Wyatt's head ached from the non-stop events of the morning. I must be in shock, he thought. I never knew how easy it was to lie. I need a walk to clear my head. I should be relaxing but it's impossible. He left the hotel. Cirrus clouds straddled the mountain peaks, as he strolled up the road towards the harbour. Heat was rising with the sun, and the azure sea lay placid before him. Shrieking gannets scythed into the waters in the middle of the bay. Must be fish out there, he thought. I wonder if it's any of the escapees?

When he reached the harbour, he saw Sergeant McSweeney's squad car parked by the road. Tommy Joe's boat was anchored out in the fjord, with some scuba divers swimming nearby. The Sergeant spotted him and came over.

"Feeling better I trust, Mr. Wyatt?"

"Yes, a little muzzy still, thank you Sergeant. How's the investigation going?"

"As well as we could expect. Luckily, due to the good weather, we could be out of here in the hour."

"That's good. Have you had any developments?"

"Yes. We've connected the theft of the dynamite from the gold mining company in the Delphi valley to the explosion. Preliminary conclusions, but fairly reliable, and we *will* do more forensic tests. All I can say is that we're following a definite line of enquiry. I may need to speak to you again, before we've finished. "

"Ok Sergeant. I see you've hired Tommy Joe's boat."

"We always try to use people with local knowledge, bhoy. He knows every ripple in the bay out there."

"Yes, indeed. I need to speak to him. I'll wait here. By the way I'll be in Dublin most of next week."

"You're not leaving us, are you?" the Sergeant's eyebrows arched in surprise.

"No, not at all. In fact, quite the opposite. This project may go on longer than expected."

"That's good then. We'll get to the bottom of this little escapade, so we will." McSweeney had a half smile on his face.

Later when the Garda had left, Wyatt talked to Tommy Joe. He told him of his pending trip to Dublin, and that he needed to know the name of the company who owned the fish cages in that part of the fiord. Tommy Joe scratched his head beneath his cap.

"And *why* would you be needin' to know that, Inspector?"

"Look, Tommy Joe, you're going to have to give me a bloody invoice anyway from that company for the lost fish and the boat. Aren't you?" Wyatt felt his pulse pounding.

"Yeh, ok, just hold onto your hat Inspector, I suppose you're right there. It's called Atlantic Waves. I'll have the invoices for both things for you before you go to Dublin."

"Thanks Tommy Joe. See you then."

His head cleared a little after the stroll back to the hotel. Bridie was on the telephone behind the reception desk when he entered the foyer. When she saw him coming she put down the phone, and handed him two large envelopes. His pulse throbbed faster. The first reports were back from the test centres.

"There you are Jim. Are you ok? Is your arm alright?" Her face seemed worried.

"Yes, Bridie, it's fine, it's only a strain. Nothing some rest won't cure. The head's a bit woozy though. Anyway it's a chance to catch up on my paperwork. You've just reminded me of something. I need to book a courier for Dublin. I'll bring down the bags shortly. How are your dance rehearsals going, by the way?"

"Fine, they're goin' just fine. Sharon and I are practising every moment God spares. I see you're making a big splash in the papers, yourself." She had a grin on her face.

"I suppose you could say that. Look, if anyone from the media calls looking for me, just say I'm not available. I'll be away in Dublin from Monday next for a few days, anyway. I have to visit my mother, and there are a few other matters to deal with. Hopefully things will have cooled down when I get back."

"You mean you want me to tell little white lies for you Jim Wyatt? Well……ok…I ..I will this time. But don't you go makin' a habit of it. There will be a payback, you know." She said, eyes twinkling.

"Am I not going to cheer for you at the Ceili? Will that not be enough?"

"Maybe it will. Must go now, there's a call comin' in."

Back in his room, his hands trembled as he slit open the envelopes. The first one was from the test centre in Galway. He skimmed through the pages of technical data. Then he read the summary conclusions on the final page. In general, the test samples were clear, and the overall outcome positive.

He sat down and perused the data from the duplicate samples. He had sent these at the last minute to a private laboratory in Castlebar. When he'd finished, he scratched his head, and slowly re- read the report. Once more there was a tightness in his gut. The results were negative. The outcome was the opposite of the Galway tests. Both tests were taken from the same specimens, but with opposite results. He was incredulous and wondered what was going on. There *was* severe water contamination in the fjord where the bulk of the salmon cages were located. This would adversely affect wild salmon, as they swam up through the fjord to the rivers to spawn where they were born. He rose, went to the window, and looked over at the shadow-crossed mountains. Thank God he had decided to do a double check of his own accord, he thought. It was a gut instinct, but it looked like he'd uncovered a hornet's nest. Though inconclusive, it seemed the Galway samples had been tampered with, *or* a mistake had been made in the testing. The next tests would confirm or deny his hunch. Wyatt walked across the room to the whisky bottle on the cabinet beside his bed, lifted it to his lips, and took a long slug from the bottle. He then wiped his mouth with the back of his shirt sleeve, and placed the half empty bottle on the desk near his computer.

The rest of the night passed in updating his report for Halpin. Yes, by God, he would give Halpin a report and a half. Something to get his teeth into.He thought he would make it as long and technical as he could. He'd put in only the Galway test results. And all about the drinking water pollution. And the gold mining pollution. And the river pollution. And the soil pollution. And the Fish Escape story. What Halpin wants to hear and more, I'm sure. No problems. No conclusions. He'd keep the Castlebar results up his sleeve for the moment. It was late in the night when he finished the twenty fifth and last page, and decided he would check it in the morning. His back ached, when he stood up. He stretched, and took a last swig from the whisky bottle, now only a quarter full, before falling into bed, exhausted.

Next day he pored over every page of the report. And then read it again.He then printed a copy, and sent it off by courier to Halpin. Afterwards he saved the data onto two cds. He hid one cd in the wardrobe as before. The other was stashed in a drawer in the bathroom. Somebody was after the information. He worried that he needed a more secure hiding place.

The weekend passed swiftly, updating his Real Story file. As he did this, the gravity of the situation sank in. It was a potential political bombshell. And a potential nightmare for Seamus Halpin. There were lots of breaches of EC legislation. The laws were on the statute books alright, but there was no enforcement. It was hands-off management of the situation all the way. He realised lots of things needed to be done urgently. *And* he had only started his investigations. There was the tampering with the Galway tests. Could Ned Halpin be behind it? Possibly. When he finished typing the report, he walked around the room, until he sounded out a creaking floorboard by the window. After prising it up, he placed a plastic bag containing the cd of his Real Story report underneath, and replaced the floorboard. He realised security would be a problem in the coming days he would be away, and decided then to bring all the test documents with him to Dublin.

\*\*\*

The converted red bricked nursing home had once been a large Victorian residence, and had a curving, gravelled entrance, bordered by giant eucalyptus trees, that swayed in the sun and the breeze. Inside the main lounge, people sat in rows on chairs and sofas, some in wheelchairs. Some slept. Others moved around on frames, while some walked about unaided. Like the living dead. Although heads stared in his direction when he entered the room, many had a distant, vacant look in their eyes. In the centre of the room was a large TV, and some residents were staring blankly at the screen. His mother lay asleep in a chair at the back of the room, beside a bay window, that overlooked a flower filled garden. He remembered years ago, when she tended her beloved flowers and pottered around the garden. He felt a lump come in his throat. The heating was on, the air in the room warm and clammy. No wonder they were nearly all half asleep, he thought.

"Mam, it's me." He shook her gently on the shoulder.

"Oh….it… it's you again Charles." Her eyes blinked awake, a frightened bird- like look in them. She had called him by his father's name.

"No, it's me, James. Don't you remember me?"

"I must pack my bags now."

"Why, mam?"

"I'm going home."

"But why do you want to go home?"

"Christmas is coming. I have to get my shopping done. I must shop early for the presents, before everything is gone. I don't belong here. I have to be going." She tried to rise but fell back into the chair, her eyes closing.

Afterwards he rose and left her, promising to call back later to collect her, and bring her home. She said she would be waiting at the door with her bags packed. Outside on the driveway, he bent to pick up a eucalyptus cone from the gravel. He inhaled its menthol smell, and looked over the roses in the garden to the window where his mother had been. He spotted her silvery mane of hair framed in a windowpane. She seemed to be slumped again in sleep. He pictured her again, many years earlier, bent over in her own garden, tending her plants and flowers. That was the time she was happiest. Maybe it was the only time. He sighed as he crunched the pebbles on the driveway, out onto the roadway, towards the bus stop. He sighed, feeling sad and helpless.

Next day he arrived at Halpin's office at nine o'clock sharp, and was ushered into the old, familiar, musty smelling office.

"Sit down James, make yourself comfortable. The usual?" Halpin asked, smiling, seemingly at his affable best.

"Yes please."

He placed a steaming mug in front of Wyatt, beside the pile of papers littering the desk, and then sat back in his worn leather chair. After placing his glasses on the bridge of his nose, he leaned back in his chair and read through some notes, before finally speaking.

"Well James, I must congratulate you. You may have been slow in coming up with the first report, but it was worth the wait." The usual back- handed compliment, Wyatt thought.

"Good. You're happy with the findings?"

"Yes. Just what the doctor ordered."

"It's only a preliminary report you know. There's a lot more research to be done."

"Of course, of course, tip of the iceberg. By the way, the name's Seamus, we're all fighting for the same cause." Halpin twiddled with the end of his moustache as he spoke.

"Of course sir, sorry, Seamus."

"And how are you, after that carry on in the water?" Halpin leaned forward in a concerned manner, elbows spread on the desk.

"A bit shook, to be honest. I wasn't expecting that kind of reception. But I'm sure I'll be fine."

"Good. Valour in the line of fire, old boy. I'll make sure it goes on your file."

"Here are the two invoices for the damage." Wyatt slid the envelope across the desk.

Halpin sliced it open, and studied the contents. After a few minutes, his mouth tightened in a grimace.

"Good heavens. One hundred thousand. Twenty for the boat, and eighty for the fish and cage, and cleanup. They must be mad. That's twice as much as I forecast to Finance." Then maybe you got the forecast wrong, Wyatt thought.

"I'll leave that to you to sort out."

"Mmmm…it's not going to be easy. Those boyos in Finance are tighter than a duck's arse, you know. Money is scarce everywhere. But I think I have them on our side. They were impressed with your first report, the length and scope of it. Agreed it was a good start. Nothing too contentious in it, either. It should help keep Brussels at bay too. "

"I'll also need a cash advance, Seamus. Expenses are running much higher than expected."

"Certainly, no problem. Just fill in this requisition docket, and I'll sign it."

Wyatt slid the docket back across the desk. Halpin's eyebrows lifted as he signed the form.

"Two thousand? That should do you for the duration."

"I have some outstanding bills to pay."

"By the way, have you seen today's paper James?" Halpin pushed the Irish Times over the desk to him. On the front page, halfway down was the headline…… Mystery Explosion in Killary Fjord.The same details as before, except he *was* named as the scuba diver, employed by Marine and Fisheries, in the water near the fish cage, when the boat was demolished. The story also mentioned that some of the fish seemed to have escaped into the upper reaches of the Delphi valley, rather than heading out to sea.

"I'm not too surprised, Seamus. It's hard to keep a secret in this little country of ours."

"Too right you are. You're as well known as a beggin' ass now, as they say in the country, James. More coffee?"

"Yes please."

After refilling the mugs, Halpin took his empty pipe from his jacket pocket, tapped it in his hand, placed it in his mouth, and started sucking it. As he studied his notes and the report on his desk, he took out a pouch of tobacco, and filled the pipe, before lighting it with a match. Soon the air was filled with a vanilla flavoured aroma. He tapped the desk with his pipe.

"Right James, to business. Where do we go from here? It's a good start, if rather an expensive one. And a dangerous one too. We need more information, and more reports. A lot more.Continue doing what you're doing. But be careful how you go, mind who you talk to. The explosion may not have been meant to injure you. It could have been just to frighten you, a warning. Or maybe it was a complete accident? You keep doing what you're doing, and I'll keep buying time from Brussels. Agreed?"

"Agreed Seamus. Here are the documents concerning the first tests, backing up my report."

Later, after the test data had been copied, and he'd received his cash advance, Wyatt left the drab Government building, promising Halpin another report in two weeks. He was satisfied with the outcome of the meeting, but wondered what Halpins attitude would've been, if he had given him the Real Story details.

After a quick lunch in McDonald's in O'Connell Street, Wyatt lodged the money in his bank account, and walked up to Parnell Square. He passed the Parnell monument, before resting awhile at the Garden of Rememberance. Later, he crossed the road, and entered the Companies Registration Office. Clutching his queuing number, he sat on the bench seats and waited. When he was called to the counter, he requested a company search on Atlantic Waves Ltd., giving the registration number he had taken down from the invoice. After paying the search fee, he sat down again to await the outcome. A short time elapsed before he was called back to the counter, and handed the document. A quick scan showed six directors/shareholders. He spotted Tommy Joe's name first. There were other names he did not recognise. He started, as the name Eamon Halpin caught his eye. Ned Halpin, the local councillor, mmmm. SeamusHalpin's brother. He held his breath. How interesting. The last name was Minerva Nominees, a limited company. He needed to know who was behind this company. After paying another search fee, Wyatt sat down again to await the second report.

It turned out to be a shelf company, one that didn't trade. There were two directors. One was a solicitor called Sean O'Neill. The other was a Seamus Halpin. Wyatt felt like he had been punched in the gut. He looked around to see if anyone was watching him, before rushing from the building.

# Chapter 6

## *By the Waters and the Wild*

When he got back from Dublin Wyatt hurried to his hotel room, to check if the two hidden cds were intact. He first searched the wardrobe. The cd was gone. He panicked, then rushed to the window, pulled back the carpet, and lifted the floorboard. The cd was still there, the Real Story one, the vital one. A wave of relief washed over him, but he felt he was swimming alone against the tide. The fact that the two Halpins had a financial involvement in Atlantic Waves Ltd., the company operating many salmon cages in the fjord, was a bombshell. *And* the results of the second set of tests were due back the next day. What story would they show? He had a hard copy of the stolen cd, so no real damage was done this time. He replaced the cd under the floorboard, pulled the carpet back, then walked to his desk, and picked up the whiskey bottle. It was empty.

That night after dinner, Wyatt bought another bottle of whiskey at the bar, and brought it, with his book, into the lounge, sitting in front of the turf fire at the end of the room. He glanced around. He was alone. Reading a book gives one an air of respectability, even when one is getting drunk, he mused. He tried to focus on the story of the Famine in the book, but his mind kept drifting back to the events of the past week. As if he didn't have enough to cope with, especially at this time of year. The whiskey helped though. Its fiery taste on the back of his throat soothed the hurt, and kept the melancholy at bay. Here's to oblivion, he muttered, and raised the trembling tumbler to his lips.

Time passed in an alcoholic haze, and he was dozing off before the fire's dying embers, when he sensed a presence beside him. He woke with a start, and turned around. It was Bridie. Before he could speak she had taken some turf sods from the wicker basket, and thrown them onto the fire.

"There. There's one thing I can't abide, and it's a dyin' fire. It's so cheerless and sad. A good blaze'll warm the cockles of your heart. And how are you Jim Wyatt? Gettin' better, I hope?" She said, smiling, and flicked her hair back.

"Yes, thanks. My physical wounds are healing, but I've got to go back to the hospital again tomorrow. I'm afraid it's my mental state that's the problem. Care to join me in a drink?" He tried to appear nonchalant, but inside still felt the hurt. But he was glad to see her.

"Thanks, but not tonight. I'm meetin' Sharon later. We've some serious dancin' practice to get done, the Ceili's coming up on Saturday week. We need to polish up our act. I'll just have a mineral." Her eyes flashed for an instant on the half empty whiskey bottle.

"Is there somethin' on your mind, Jim? You don't look good at all. You're not your usual self. Is it this hullabaloo with the explosion, and the media hoohah that has you like this?"

"No....no..not really. It's not that. I can handle all that stuff. Really I can." He replied, trying to sound convincing.

"Then please tell what is it that's on your mind, if you don't mind me askin'?"

"Well,…well..it…it's sort of personal, it's not something I've ever discussed with anyone before. I…I find it hard to talk about."

"Oh well…I… in that case I'm sorry for askin'. Maybe I should be goin'then." She stood up.

"No…no Bridie, please don't go. Its better that I speak to someone, instead of keeping everything wrapped up between me and a whiskey bottle. Please…please sit down, while I fetch your drink." She sat down again beside the fire, and waited.

"I don't want to pry into your private life, if you don't

want." She said later as she sipped her lemonade.

"I *do* want you to. I suppose I just couldn't level with you up to now. It's hard to talk about it, you understand?"

"I *do* understand. But please tell me what's on your mind."

"Well,.....it... I suppose it all started when I fell in love in my last year in Trinity. She was studying medicine. Her name was Emma, a redhead, and a beauty, from York in England. We...we got married six months later. It was just a small ceremony in a registry office in Dublin. Emma was a few months pregnant at the time, but our parents didn't know. Seven months later a bonny blond boy arrived, Sean, the apple of our eyes." Wyatt paused to lift a whiskey to his mouth, and his eyes glazed over.

"And then?"

"Times were tough. It was hard to make a decent living even with our degrees. But we survived. Until that night,...that...that awful, awful night."

"But what happened Jim?"

"Well....well... like most dreadful things it started with something simple. Emma had gone out to meet some friends. I....I took the car down to the supermarket to get some food for the morning. Sean was six at the time. I brought him along for the ride, as I often did, and I'd buy him a little treat just to see him smile and his eyes light up. This time he...he didn't make it. No,... he didn't make it." Tears dribbled down his cheeks, and he took another mouthful from his glass.

"Do you want to go on, Jim? I can see this is not easy for you to talk about."

"Yes...yes.. I do...I do...I have to go on now. I was coming onto the main road turning left, when something Sean was doing in the back seat caught my eye.....it...it sort of distracted me. I think he was trying to open the window or something. I took my gaze off the road for a moment. Then BANG, the van smashed into the back of my car at speed. When I recovered from the impact, I looked back to see Sean asleep like an angel on the back seat. There wasn't a mark on him. He *seemed* to be asleep. But...but he *wasn't* asleep. He ...he was dead. His...his neck was broken. I had forgotten to fasten the seatbelt on him. And it….and it was all my fault." His voice quavered as he took another drink.

"Hush now, don't you blame yourself. It was a terrible accident."

"Well, that was only the beginning of the nightmare. I'll spare you the details of the inquest, and the funeral. And Emma's reaction. She...she never forgave me for my stupidity. Our marriage went downhill rapidly after that. I suppose there were other factors too. We were divorced within two years. She went back to live in England. And now all I have are my memories. Black memories. My punishment is to live the rest of my life with the nightmare of that night. Time hasn't made it any easier. Every year at this time, I just get into this black bout of depression and start drinking for days on end, or even longer. And after that time of the year passes, I somehow get back to normal, until the next year, and the same sad merry- go-round starts all over again. Sometimes I wonder if I will pull out of it, or do something worse, and worse than anything I keep wondering why it wasn't me that got killed...me who caused the accident. If you could only swop lives." He gazed into the fire, a faraway look in his eyes.

"You poor, poor man. Don't be so hard on yourself, Jim. It could have happened to anyone." She grasped his trembling hands.

"I know, but unfortunately it happened to *me*. I can't change things now, I know that. I just don't know how to get out of this hell hole in my mind. Still I feel better to have spoken to someone about it. To someone who doesn't mind listening to a self- pitying drunk." He squeezed her hands.

"Jim Wyatt, you're going to have to stop blamin' yourself over that terrible accident, and then drinkin' yourself silly to forget it. Yes, it's a really dreadful thing to have happened to you, but you're goin' to have to get your head right and move on. Is your arm recovered enough to go cyclin' a bit? I've got a few days off. We could go off tomorrow for a spin down to Renvyle, while the weather's still holdin' good. It'll get you out of yourself. Are you on?"

"Hmm….well, my arm does feel a lot better. I'm sure it will be fine, but I have to go back to the hospital for a check up with the physio in the morning. I've got stuff coming back from the test centre too."

"I asked you if you were on." Her blue eyes bored into him.

"Yes….yes..you're right, I'm supposed to be on sick leave anyway. Let's go for it. Yes, let's do that."

"What about your arm then?"

"It'll be fine. I'll cancel the physio."

"Good, we'll leave at eleven then. Good night Jim. You must try to get a decent night's sleep. I have to go now, Sharon will be wondering where I've got to." She dashed out the door, and blew him a kiss as she went.

"I will." He called after her. A few minutes later, he picked up the near empty whiskey bottle, and trudged up the staircase to his bedroom.

They met next morning outside the hotel, both clad in shorts. She has the legs of a dancer alright, he thought. The sun was rising in a cobalt sky, the fjord flat in the windless air, a hush everywhere, bar some bleating sheep, and shrieking gulls. Walkers strolled by, in shorts and boots, sticks in hands, heads covered from the sun.

"They'll be mostly heading for the Green Road walk, up by the Killary, where the old Famine trail is." Bridie said, as she pushed off on her bike, rucksack stuck in the basket at the front.

"Maybe we could do that walk together, sometime." Wyatt said, following in her wake, after he'd secured his rucksack on the back of his bicycle.

"Why not, maybe when your arm is better?"

"Yes, I agree. Let's go. You're the navigator today."

They climbed the hill out from the fjord breathing hard, and he admired the shape of her legs and body from behind her, as she rose from her saddle and pumped down on the pedals. At the top of the hill they rested, and looked across Maam valley where pine forests blanketed brown boglands, and over to the twelve Bens of Connemara, then onto Renvyle peninsula jutting west to the sea. They did not speak. The only blots on the landscape were the fish cages clogging up the Killary fjord.

They came upon a church further on, which overlooked the Maamturk Mountains. Bridie stopped, and said she wanted to go inside to say a short prayer. At first he declined to join her, but then changed his mind, and went in a few minutes later to say a prayer for Sean. When he returned to his bike ten minutes later, he was surprised how much better he felt.

They cycled on south, by Kylemore House, a castle of gothic granite, lake fronted, and mountain behind, with a large white cross near the top.

"It's a boarding school for girls, run by the Benedictine nuns. They came here from Ypres in Belgium, after being bombed out of there, in World War One." Bridie said.

"Would you like to have gone there?"

"No, not really, it's only for the well off, the gentry. Anyway I don't believe in boarding schools. They're no substitute for the home, my mother always said, and I agree with her. I wouldn't want any of my children to go to one."

"You're probably right." Wyatt said, not mentioning he had attended one himself.

Soon they got to Letterfrack, and veered west at Veldon's pub, opposite the old industrial school. A flock of starlings flew across the road and settled on the telephone lines. Wyatt held his breath, when the birds took off again, criss crossing the sky like giant locusts. When they got to the village of Tullycross, Bridie suggested heading down to Lettergesh beach, for a lunch break. He agreed, saddlesore setting in, his arm starting to ache.

They freewheeled down a meandering, rhododendron road, towards a coral sanded beach, and parked their bikes near the road. Bridie said not to bother locking them, as no one ever did in that neck of the woods. Rucksacks on backs, they trod the rough track worn into the cliff face, dropping, until at last they reached the sands. A river cut through the beach, but stepping stones straddled it, and they hopped across on these, laughing as they went, afraid of dropping the rucksacks. After ambling along the strand, they sheltered in a large sand dune, with marram grass streeling above them, and facing the westering sun. It was all quiet there, save the squawling seabirds, and cows lowing on the other side of the inlet.

Bridie laid out a picnic on the ground, on a red chequered cloth.

"It's one of the advantages of workin' in a hotel, if you're friendly with the chef." She smiled, as she laid out an array of foods on the cloth.

"And it's one of the advantages of staying in a hotel, if you know your way to the bar." Wyatt said, placing a small bottle of red and white wine on the cloth.

Later, food eaten, wine drunk, drowsy and languid, he lay back on the towel that was stretched across the sand dune, and dozed off in the sun. When he opened his eyes, Bridie was lying beside him, eyes closed. She had changed into a black bikini, and he became aware of the sensuality of her body. And he felt attracted to her, in an overpowering way. And he leant over, and kissed her on the lips, desire mounting. She woke with a start.

"Jim Wyatt, what do you think you're doin'?"

"Kissing you, what do you think I'm doing? I couldn't resist the temptation. What's wrong with that?"

"There might be somebody watchin', that's what." She jumped up, tossing her hair back.

"So what, it's not a crime to be attracted to a beautiful woman."

"I'm gettin' in for a swim. Care to join me? That'll cool your ardour."

"Why not, let's go."

Soon they were splashing about in clear Atlantic waters. He looked down, and gasped at the clarity of the water, webbed by sunbeams. Small fish darted about on the bottom. It was unpolluted and pristine. He wondered if Killary fjord was once like this. The water felt warm too, thanks to the Gulf Stream.

Afterwards, after drying out in the sun, they changed, and continued their journey westward. Along the road they came upon a cloud of white seedlings hovering ghostly in the air. Bridie took a seed in the palm of her hand and blew it to him. A kiss, she said. Later, as they freewheeled down an incline, hedges of fuchsia trees bled by the roadside. Beside them, rainbow wildflowers waved in the breeze, and he felt uplifted. Further on, as he gazed at the rocks jutting out of brown boggy soil, and the purple heather clumps everywhere, nature's constant survival struggle hit him. Maybe he could learn from that struggle, he thought. Maybe he could fight harder to overcome his difficulties.

They reached Renvyle House, tired but happy. The ancient, granite building lay behind a shelter of high trees. A sign for horse riding on the beach hung at the entrance gate. He asked Bridie if she would like to have a go. Her eyes lit up. She said she loved horse riding, but hadn't done it for years. Neither had he, he replied, so let's go for it, let's have a go, and make fools of ourselves. She agreed.

A while later, astride their horses, they followed their guide, a young teenager, clip clopping along the road until they reached the turn for the beach. From the roadway, Wyatt saw the curving line of waves wasting white on the shoreline, stretching away into the distance.

The horses cantered to the water's edge. Across the bay, Mweelrea Mountain was majestic, ochre in the evening sun. He held his breath. They tightened the straps on their riding helmets, as the horses turned, and lenghtened their stride along the edge of the shoreline. Their hooves spewed water and sand into the air, as the beach stretched out ahead of them, infinitely unending, and deserted. On the way back they let the horses have full rein, and they stretched into a gallop along the edge of the tide. The wind whipped into his face, along with spray from the waves. Wyatt felt exhilarated, and heard Bridie whooping with excitement behind him. Later they returned to the hotel, exhausted, but exuberant. The young girl led the horses, steam rising, back to the stables.

They entered the hotel, and ordered coffees in the lounge. Wyatt walked around the foyer, perusing old photos lining the walls. He liked the sense of history in the place. He felt exhilerated after the ride, and resolved to do something out of character. Bridie came over and thanked him for suggesting the horse ride, and said she had never enjoyed anything as much.

"Me too, say Bridie, how about us staying here for the night? We could have dinner here, the restaurant looks really good. Of course I'll have to check if they can fit us in. Well, how about it?" He held his breath.

"But this place is posh, Jim. I've never stayed here before. I couldn't afford to, in any case. And I've nothin' to wear. All I have is a blue dress, the one I wore last night."

"And all I have is a spare shirt and trousers. You'll be grand. Say you will." He pleaded.

"Well ok, twist my arm, I will." She said, after a short hesitation.

They crossed the lobby to the reception desk. Wyatt asked for a double room for the night. A grey haired, bespectacled lady peered at him. He saw her gaze at his hand. He still wore his wedding ring, as it was too tight to take off, and he hadn't got around to having it cut off. The lady seemed reassured by this. She checked her computer before replying

"Yes, we do have rooms. Would you like a double or a

two single bed room?"

"We'll take the double bed, for just one night." He replied.

"Good, it's room 35. Are you staying in Connemara for long? "She handed him the keys.

"No. We head on to Galway tomorrow."

He thanked her, took the keys and they went to the room. It was spacious with a view of the sea. A sea view is relaxing, just the job, he thought. Wild red roses in vases decorated the room. He glanced at Bridie, but she did not seem happy.

"Are you alright Bridie? Why do you look so sad? Do you not like the room?"

"No.The room is lovely."

"Then what's wrong?"

"Nothin', it's just nothin' at all."

"Come on Bridie, tell me what's bugging you." He put his arm around her shoulders.

"Well, you had a nerve bookin' a double bed without speakin'to me. You could have taken two single beds."

"Why didn't you speak out to the lady?"

"She would have known I was from the area. You signed us in as a married couple, didn't you?"

"Yes, it just seemed the easiest way to do it, that's all. It doesn't mean anything. I hope you understand."

"Ok I do, but don't you go readin' too much into it."

"I won't."

That evening Bridie emerged from the bathroom. She wore her blue dress, and was smiling. Her cheeks had a red tint from the sun and wind, and her black hair hung long and shiny.

"You're pretty as a wild mountain rose." He said and kissed her softly on the lips.

The restaurant was dimly lit with long dark beams across the ceiling. On the tables were wild red roses and candles. They found a shadowy corner, intimate, with a view onto the main dining area. He ordered an Italian wine, hoping it would impress her. And after each had supped their glasses, the night passed fast in a cocoon of romance, with a frisson in the air. He found Bridie not only young and beautiful, but also fun to be with. And when she smiled, she seemed to light up the room with her smile, and that made him smile too. He felt smitten by her, and wondered if she felt the same about him.

The night went, and as they rose to leave the restaurant, Wyatt looked across to a large table in the middle of the room, where a group of people were making a lot of noise. Many wine bottles lay on the table, mostly empty. He started, as he recognised some of the faces seated there.

"Bridie, some of those people I'm sure I've seen before. Do you know them?"

"Yes, I see Eamon Carney, the owner of the minin' company, and Sean Glynn the bank manager, and Ned Halpin, the councillor."

"Hmmm... interesting, I think we should leave discreetly now." They did.

Back in the bedroom Wyatt breathed a sigh of relief.

"Phew, I'm glad I saw them, but I'm happier they didn't see me."

"Why's that Jim?"

"I'll explain it some other time."

"Thanks for a lovely night." She kissed him softly on the lips.

"Thank you for today, and everything." He pulled her closer, and her dress slipped a little down her shoulder. They kissed long and hard.

"Don't you be gettin' carried away now, Jim Wyatt. Don't forget you have to stay on your side of the bed." She said, and pulled herself away.

"Whatever you say." He said, and moved to the other side of the bed.

A while later as he lay in the bed, lights out, Bridie came from the bathroom, framed white in moonbeams shafting through the windows. She got into the bed on her side.

"I forgot to give you a goodnight kiss." She said, and

snuggled over to him. Her body felt soft and warm, her legs long and entangling.

"Hey, you're on my side of the bed. You're trespassing, but I won't hold that against you, no, not at all." He said, and their mouths came together.

"And I see you're arm is miraculously cured." She said, and put her arms around his neck.

And then she spoke soft and gentle to him, kissing him in a way he had long forgotten, and embraced him in a way he had long forgotten. And he did the same back to her. And she never went back to her side of the bed.

When he awoke in the morning there was no one in the bed beside him. Bridie had already showered, dressed, and was seated in an armchair by the window, reading a magazine. She told him she had ordered breakfast in bed.

"Better to be up early and make a quick getaway. We don't want to meet any of that crowd that were at the big table last night." She said.

"How right you are. Good thinking." Wyatt rolled out of the bed, and headed for the bathroom. There was a ring on the door. Breakfast had arrived.

Soon they were cycling back to Leenane in a morning mist, and he wondered if he had ever before had such a wonderful day and night. He felt the answer was never, but he didn't talk about it. On the way, he asked Bridie about the giant redhead at the currach races. She said he was a well known republican, dangerous, and suspected of subversive activities over the border. He was someone not to be trusted.

They parted company at his hotel. She said she was going on to her mother's house.

"Maybe you'd like to visit my mother Jim, during the week, when you're out and about on your work. She'd love to meet you. She doesn't get too many visitors."

"Yes, I'd like that, Bridie. What about Wednesday? I've stuff to get done here before then."

"Good, that would be fine. She'll like that. And thanks for a lovely day yesterday. Maybe it got you out of yourself. Anytime I'm feeling down in the dumps, I'll think of that horse ride on the beach."

"And will you think about the afterwards?"

"And I'll think of the lovely night afterwards of course. Now don't you go worryin' again. Goodbye." She smiled, and kissed him softly on the side of the face, before pushing down the road towards the village.

# Chapter 7

## *Woman of the House*

The weather had changed for the worse. After breakfast, Wyatt peered out the window, realising it had to happen. Pellets of rain peppered the panes. Mist clouds piled high on the mountains, and a westerly gale whipped up the waves in the fjord. The rain then started to slant down even harder. Better to work indoors on the second set of lab results he'd just got back, he thought. After the weekend with Bridie, he felt elated, and had slept the following nights, without drink or pill. He was smitten, and wondered if she felt the same about him. He hoped she did, but he would like to know for sure. Maybe she would give him a sign.

Back in his room, he plugged in the kettle, and sorted the reports from the two test centres. These covered the samples taken on the day of the explosion, and included the samples of the salmon taken from the cage. He put two spoons of coffee into a mug and poured in the boiling water. No milk or sugar. He needed it strong and long. It would be that kind of day. He had a mountain of work to plough through.

The data from the official centre in Galway again gave a clean bill of health to all the samples, including the salmon. How predictable, he thought, and tensed, as he sliced open the second envelope, containing the results from the centre in Castlebar. As he scanned the pages, he inhaled sharply. The results were again the opposite of the official ones. *And* the samples from the salmon were included. The Castlebar results confirmed the salmon *was* contaminated. He gulped again, and tried to focus his mind on what he was seeing. His suspicions were now confirmed. There *was* something sinister going on. Someone *was* tampering with the samples, *or* altering the results from the Galway centre. *And* someone had broken into his computer in the hotel, and stolen one of the cds from his wardrobe. He took another swig of coffee, strolled to the window, and stared out at the teeming rain. Then he began once more to mull over everything.

It was plain he was just a pawn in a game. A deadly game it seemed, in the aftermath of the explosion on the boat. The stakes were high. The Halpin brothers had a financial interest in the salmon cages. That might work to his advantage later, if he played his cards right. But there might be more to it. He needed to delve deeper. *And* he needed more time. If he kept his head straight he might be able to buy that time. It was clear he was completely on his own. There was no one he could trust, except maybe Bridie. But she was on the hotel staff, and someone had taken information from his hotel room. No, he banished the thought, she surely could be trusted. But better not to involve her at this stage.

He rang Seamus Halpin to tell him that he would have the second report to him in Dublin within two days.

"Good stuff James, that's a relief. I had a torrid time last week with Finance, concerning the bills for the boat and the lost salmon. It wasn't going so well until someone came up with an ingenious way of charging the whole bloody lot back to Brussels. So I think the payment will be ok. I should know for sure at the end of the month. So no more surprises, ok?" The fact that you and your brother have a financial interest must be a big incentive to ensure Brussels picked up the tab, Wyatt thought, imagining Halpin sitting back at his desk, puffing smoke circles up to the ceiling, and smiling smugly.

"Yes Seamus, please don't worry. I don't intend to get blown up again."

"We have a meeting next week in Brussels. I'd like to have that second report before then."

"You shall Seamus, don't worry you shall."

"What's in your plans for the coming week, then?"

"I'm going to arrange a visit with your brother to check out a few local water treatment plants."

"Oh, really, is there a drinking water problem down there?"

"Not that I'm aware of. But you never know. Anyway that's what I'm here to find out, isn't it?"

"Of course, yes of course James. You keep the work going old chap. I'm looking forward to that report." The line went dead. Wyatt replaced the receiver, and gritted his teeth, thinking Halpin sure had a way of getting under his skin.

Wyatt began to tidy up his room. The clutter had been bothering him. When he finished, he sat in front of his computer to start the report. The telephone rang. Damn, he muttered, and picked it up. Reception said a Mr Halpin, the county councillor, was on for him, but the line had been lost, and did he wish to talk to the man? He said he did, and waited for the call to come through. As he waited, he wondered if Halpin had spotted him in Renvyle with Bridie on the last weekend.

"Ned Halpin here Mr Wyatt, do you remember me? I'm the County councillor."

"Yes of course I do, you're my boss's brother, if I remember correctly."

"Spot on there. Let's cut the formalities then. I'll just call you Jim, and you call me Ned. Ok? It's just a routine call. I've been meaning to call you to see if there's anything I can do for you."

"Well, there is actually, Ned. I need a list of all the waste water treatment plants in your area, as well as details of your systems and procedures for testing. And ditto for all the drinking water facilities."

"Why? Is there a problem?" Wyatt wondered if Halpin had been tipped off by his brother.

"Not that I'm aware of. These are just routine checks. Are there any problems you know about, Ned?"

"No, there aren't any. Anything else I can do for you?"

"Yes, there's one thing. I'd like a report on all water,

waste or drinking problems, if any, experienced over the past five years in the area, and how they were resolved." He thought he detected a hesitation at the other end of the line.

"Ok Jim. You'll have what you ask for. It will be next week before that happens. Will you collect, or will I get the stuff delivered to the hotel?"

"The hotel would be perfect."

"The hotel it will be then. Anything *else* I can do for you?"

"Yes Ned, there is another item. This matter is highly confidential, and must stay that way. I need a letter signed by you, authorising me to visit any of the water treatment plants, or all if necessary, to carry out whatever checks are appropriate. These will be done on a random basis without warning, for maximum effect. You understand the need for secrecy. If the plants know in advance, it could undermine everything."

"Of course Jim, we wouldn't want that, would we now?" He's definitely not pleased, Wyatt thought, and felt he must be doing the right thing.

"No, we wouldn't. And thanks for your help Ned, it's much appreciated."

"You're welcome anytime Jim. Always like to be of service. Keep in touch. Goodbye."

Wyatt put down the phone and rubbed his hands together. Ned Halpin hadn't spotted him in the Renvyle hotel with Bridie, and now was anxious about the upcoming audit checks on the water treatment plants. No doubt his brother had been on to him earlier in the morning. But at least for the moment, Wyatt felt a little bit in control.

After reflecting on the conversation for a few minutes, he decided to do some delving in advance of receiving Halpin's information, and put a call through to the Mayo Times newspaper. Eventually spoke to the reporter who had interviewed him earlier.

"Are there any developments in the case?" Wyatt made

the running.

"Not really. The Gardai are still investigating."

"They're ongoing, no doubt. You want some news?"

"It depends. What is it?"

"Well, apart from the uninteresting fact that I'm alive and well, and recovering, I can tell you that the company who suffered the damage from the explosion have been compensated. A substantial amount, too. Approved for payment, but not yet paid."

"How much was the compensation?"

"I can't say. Why don't you speak to one of the owners of the company?"

"Ok, can you give me their names?"

"Yes, on two conditions."

"Which are?"

"First, I need information on all water contamination stories in your paper over the past five years, and details of how they were resolved. Second, my name is not to be mentioned to anyone, or printed in your paper, regarding any information I give you."

"Its a deal, we never divulge our sources to anyone. You should know that. Now please tell me what *your* information is, Mr Wyatt."

"The company is called Atlantic Waves Limited."

"And who are the owners?"

"Well, I can tell is that Tommy Joe O'Malley is one of them. He should confirm what I've told you."

"Ok, Mr Wyatt, I'll follow it up. You'll have your information in about a week. Thanks for the call."

"You're welcome."

Wyatt put the phone down, satisfied.

He paced the room a number of times, sat at his computer, and began his second report to Halpin. This is going to be a long one, Wyatt thought, as it included the boat explosion. He changed the story relating to the salmon sample, and wrote that he found the fish floating dead in the water after the explosion. This would back up his story that he had never reached the fish cage. He noticed the reports on the tests from the official test centre, were couched in legal terms and caveats that let them off the hook, if the results turned out to be incorrect. Many hours, and thirty pages later, he stood up, yawned, and stretched. He felt he had written enough to keep Halpin and his cohorts happy. There was technical stuff to beat the band, and nothing too controversial. It seems to be what they want, even if it's not the truth, he reckoned. They seemed to lap it up.

Wyatt had dinner, read the newspapers, and booked a courier taxi for Dublin the next morning. When he turned his mind to chapter two of the Real Story, he felt a tingle inside as he stared at the computer screen. Then he inserted the cd, and re-read chapter one, mulling over the details. There was no doubt now, that the details in this report would cause shock waves in the Department. A web of environmental problems existed, which even at this early stage, would embarrass the government, at home and abroad, if they got into the public domain. But how was he to handle the situation? The question bedevilled his mind. When he had finished writing, he'd decided the best thing to do now was nothing at all. Just keep doing what he was doing, feed them what they want to hear, and keep the shocks in the Real Story until the end. There must be more of the same out there, or maybe worse? But where was it all leading to? And how would it all end? Better not to dwell on that now. And he must be more careful *where* he stored the documents about the Real Story. The room was unsafe, he needed somewhere safer. He resolved to continue with the duplication of the lab tests in Galway and Castlebar.

The need to find a secure haven for the information badgered his mind. But where is safe, for God's sake? Wyatt fumed, running his hands through his hair. He stood up, and stretched again. God, he was tired. After putting away all the information again under the floorboard, he yawned, feeling ready for bed.

Visions of Bridie came to mind, as he relaxed in bed, and read his book. Wyatt wondered what she was doing. Probably rehearsing her dancing steps for next Saturday's competition. He knew he owed her a lot. He hadn't touched a drop of whiskey since the Renvyle weekend. That was unheard of for him at this time of year, since the night of the accident. Yes, for sure he owed her a lot. She was off work until the middle of the week, and staying with her mother. He must get her mother's phone number. Since that weekend he had an urge to see and speak to Bridie every day. The visit to her mother's house couldn't come soon enough. Soon his eyelids drooped, and darkness came.

In the morning, the gales had abated to sunshine and showers. Wyatt studied the map Bridie had given him, and packed his rain gear and sample bottles into his rucksack. He secured the rucksack on the carrier at the back of his bike, and moved off. His bike spun along the road west into the Delphi valley, and he did a few detours on the way. Between the showers, he took water and soil samples from fields and streams close to where he saw sheep and cattle grazing. There were few trees in the valley, with most twisted into grotesque shapes by the wind. No hiding place here, he thought. Mist clouds raced across the sky, obscuring the sun on and off, and threw dappled shadows onto the mountains. He felt happy as he labelled the samples and placed them in the rucksack, thinking that was what he was there to do.

On arrival he saw an ancient Irish cottage, whitewashed walls, thatched roof, and an extension with a slate roof. The smell of turf smoke hung sweet in the air. Outside, a black and white sheepdog rose from its slumber, stretched, and barked as Wyatt approached. A few scrawny hens clucked in the yard. Bridie looked out above the half door, and waved to him, saying not to mind Scotty the dog, that he didn't bite.

"Come on in Jim, I'll introduce to the *Bean an Ti*."

"I beg your pardon?"

"In your language, it's the woman of the house."

Inside, her mother sat beside the fire in a rocking chair, beneath the ticking clock on the mantelpiece, bent over, as she poked the turf with her walking stick. She wore a black cardigan, and had thick and silvery hair, over a narrow face, wrinkled with age. A beauty in her prime, he thought.

"Ma, this is Mr. Wyatt from the hotel. He's come to visit you." Her mother rose, leaned on her stick and shuffled across to him, back slightly bent over, her arm outstretched.

"You're a thousand times welcome Mr Wyatt. You'll have a cup of tea?"

"Of course, thank you Mrs O'Malley. Please call me Jim." She ushered him to a rocking chair beside the fire, saying it was her late husband Dessie's chair, and only special people were invited to sit there. They sat sipping their tea, as Bridie entered the room and said her cousin Michael had just called with the water and the fish.

"Oh, do you not have your own water supply here?" Wyatt asked Bridie.

"We do. But for the past two years, we can't drink the water here. We're afraid to use it. Tommy Joe lives beyond, over the hill, and has his own well. He gets pure spring water from it, and usually gets Michael to bring us a bucketful every day. And some fish into the bargain, if we're lucky." She smiled as she spoke.

"And have you complained to the Council about the problem?"

"Ah, we have for sure, many times."

"And what happened?"

"They're working on it, that's what they'd always say."

"Well, you're lucky to have such good neighbours. But still you shouldn't have to wait that long."

"Probably not, but they're doing their best. It's not easy for them. But Mam's not too fussed. She likes the daily visits with the water."

"I see. Do you mind if I check out the water and the soil on your farm, Mrs O'Malley?"

"No, not at all, you go right ahead, you go and do whatever you want."

Later, as Wyatt got to know Bridie's mother better, he asked her if she found it lonely living in such a remote area.

"Ah musha, I don't be at all lonely Jim. Haven't I Bridie and her sister Nora, and my son Matthew sometimes coming to visit me from London and shure isn't Tommy Joe and Michael livin' just over the hill? And the priest comes callin' here sometimes. I can't get to mass anymore, with the arthritis, and I miss that a lot. And shure haven't I the radio to listen to? And a good book to read? I can't be fussed now with the television, unless there's dancin' on it, or a good old weepie picture, or the news. And can't I see the sun rising behind Ben Gorm in the morning, and goin' down behind Mweelrea in the wesht in the evening? And I can hear the larks singin' in the meadow, and sometimes there's the cuckoo, and best of all is when the blackbird is in full flow. And haven't I the farm and the animals to look after as well?"

"Yes, I suppose there are some good things about living down here."

"And if I ever start to feel lonely, haven't I got all my memories, from this very spot on God's earth, memories of times with Dessie, and the good times we had, even when the life was hard, and the children were young. And the dancin' and the music we'd make here in the kitchen of a weekend, and Dessie sittin' there playin' the tin whistle, sittin' in the chair just where you are now, and me maybe doin' a jig or a reel on the flagstones. And with everyone joinin' in for a Kerry set. And if I'm still feeling lonely now, don't I talk to Dessie, as if he was sittin' there in that chair instead of you. And to tell you the truth Jim, with all the great things we have these days, I'd rather be back sometimes in them days when we had nothin', but we had each other, and we *needed* each other."

"I think I understand."

"Shure I'd *die* if they ever took me away from here. This is where I was born an' rear'd, and this is the place where I've always lived, and it's here that I want to be laid to rest. But before then, there's nothing I'd rather have than a little grandchild on my knee in front of the fire there." Her eyes were moist now, and had a faraway look, as she twisted the rosary beads in her hands.

"You're right, there's something about a place like this. It gets into your bones. I believe you were a great dancer in times past. By the way, are you coming to the Ceili on Saturday night to watch Bridie?"

"Yes, I am for sure, Tommy Joe said he'd bring me in his van. I'm so excited. I've been looking forward to it for months. And will you be there?" The sparkle was back in her eyes.

"I will. I wouldn't miss it for the world."

Later Bridie took him on a walk around the farm. It spanned fifty acres, grazed by sheep and a few cows. While they walked, her mother pottered around the cottage, cleaning and putting away the crockery. Afterwards, he asked Bridie to excuse him while he took some samples. As he did this, a thought clicked in his mind. The cottage, with its remote location would be the perfect hiding place for his files. He put the samples into the rucksack on his bike, and walked back to the cottage. The day was nearly gone. The dying sun had put a gold shroud on the mountains, and swallows dived and ducked high up, anticipating better weather. A perfect hideaway place it would be indeed, he decided.

Bridie's mother was delighted when he asked her if he could leave some old files that cluttered his hotel room, in her cottage. No problem at all it was. She said it might mean he would come visitin' more often to her house. Probably, he replied. He bade her goodbye, as he walked out into the yard, back to his bike. Bridie followed him.

She walked down the boreen with him, and he wheeled

his bike. He said he missed her not being at the hotel during the week. She blushed, and looked down, then said she missed not seeing *him*. She kissed him lightly on the cheek, saying she had to rush as she was late for her dance rehearsals, and turned back towards the cottage. She soon disappeared round a bend in the road. He gazed after her, sighed, and mounted his bike.

Darkness was falling as he cycled down the hill towards the village. His conversation with Bridie's mother had reminded him he must write to *his* own mother. This time it would be a short letter, maybe with a few photographs. He must do that when he got back to the hotel. He felt disappointed Bridie hadn't been more intimate after their weekend together. Yes, she was friendly as always, but he had been expecting a bit more. Still, she was probably nervous with the coming dancing competition at the Ceili House. She would probably be fine when that was over. He hoped so.

# Chapter 8

## *Ceili House*

Next morning, Wyatt packed all the files in his bedroom into his rucksack, put the rucksack on the back of his bike, and headed for Bridie's mother's house. On the way he stopped in the village to post the letter to his mother. In it, he'd said that he'd met a girl called Bridie, and had fallen for her. He wondered if she'd understand any of what he'd written. He put the letter into the green post box with Queen Victoria's name, embedded in a wall by the roadside.

Bridie's mother was surprised to see him back so soon, and said Bridie had gone shopping in Westport. He was disappointed that Bridie wasn't there. Her mother showed him to the spare bedroom. He thanked her, and entered the room, closing the door after him. He found a loose floorboard, hid the files under it, and replaced it. That'll do for the moment. Back in the kitchen, Bridie's mother handed him a cup of tea and buttered scones.

"You're very welcome to stay here anytime Jim, you know that."

"Thanks Mrs O'Malley, for the offer. You're very kind. You never know."

After the tea and scones, he rose to leave, saying he would see her at the Ceili.

"You will for shure. It should be a great night." She smiled, and waved at him over the shut half door, as he ambled back to where he had left his bike leaning against the wall.

\*\*\*

The minibus parked outside the Parochial Hall, and the

crowd poured out onto the gravel path. Wyatt observed the Hall was in the grounds of the church where he had attended mass. The packed car park hinted at the huge interest in the Ceili. Overhead a crescent moon balanced in the night sky, spangled with winking stars. A tingle touched his bones at the thought of seeing Bridie again. He *had* missed her.

Wyatt traipsed behind the raggle-taggle crowd into the white, corrugated building, and paid at the door. Inside, a maple dance floor stretched the length and breadth of the hall, lit by neon strips that hung by wires from the ceiling. No chance of any intimacy here, he thought. At the top end of the white, barn- like hall, the Ceili band belted out music from the podium. People sat in rows at the back, and lined the busy dance floor. Most seemed immersed in serious conversations. He noticed that many were drinking tea or minerals, and realised then it was an alcohol-free evening. A sobering thought, he reflected.

Wyatt spotted Bridie, as she sat with her mother, and a young, black haired girl. He went over and sat with them, meeting Bridie's younger sister Nora. Bridie told him normal dancing would go on until eleven o'clock, when the competition would begin. She was dressed in a plain green dress, but said she would change for the competition. She seemed nervous, biting her lip. Her mother suggested that they should take the floor for a dance, as it might help Bridie relax a bit.

"Why not, but I warn you, I have two left feet when it comes to dancing." He muttered.

"Not bad for a beginner." Bridie smiled as she steered him around the floor, and explained some of the different steps and dances. After a while she gave up with a sigh.

Soon he started to perspire, and his legs ached. He excused himself, citing his injured arm, and they returned to their seats. Bridie continued dancing with her sister, while he chatted with her mother, as they sipped lemonade. She explained to him some of the intricacies of the steps and dances. *The Kerry Set, The Walls of Limerick, Jigs, Reels, and Hornpipes*, and some more. The dance that really caught his fancy was *Shoe the Donkey*. He scanned the dancers and spectators in the hall, and felt the buzz of anticipation, and he sensed that everyone was having fun, despite the lack of alcohol.

Bridie rejoined them, saying she would have to leave soon to get ready for the contest. It was fifteen minutes to countdown. She sat down beside him, and as she listened to the music, he noticed her moving the fingers of her right hand over the flat palm of her left hand, in time to the music. When he asked her about this, she said.

"I trace the steps that I have to do for each dance with two fingers of one hand on the palm of the other to make sure I can remember all the steps in tempo. You do it when you're watching the others performing. It's a trick of the trade. I'm off now." She smiled, as she rose and headed for the changing rooms. Wyatt blew her a kiss and wished her good luck. He felt a nervous twinge in his stomach.

While Wyatt was talking to Bridie, Father Flynn had arrived, and chatted to Bridie's mother, saying how great it was to see her, and she looking so well, and that Bridie hadn't picked up her dancing skills off the ground. Then he turned to Wyatt, and extended his hand.

"Mr Wyatt. It's good to see you again. You have good taste, I see. She's a grand girleen, and a great dancer too."He spoke as they shook hands.

"She is, Father. You're right on both counts."

The priest glanced around him, then leant close to Wyatt, and muttered that a protest meeting would be held in the near future, he wasn't sure where, about the gold mining in the Delphi valley, and would Wyatt attend? In a neutral capacity of course, but his presence would be a great support to the local community. It was the biggest natural disaster facing the area since the Famine. Wyatt thought quickly. Yes, it *was* an environmental issue, and within his brief, but something inside him made him hesitate. There could be political problems, and he could be exposing himself to danger again. On the other hand, he liked the priest, and felt he was doing the right thing.

"Ok. I'd be delighted to attend Father. Just as an observer, you understand, I'll stay in the background."

"Thank you, Mr Wyatt. I'll speak to you soon." The priest shook both his hands, and moved on.

On the stage the compere picked up the mike, and read out the rules of the competitions. There would be set dancing with teams of four, then a doubles competition, followed by the grand finale of the evening, the singles area finals. A hush came in the hall, as the dancers filed onto the stage. Bridie wore a green and black dress with celtic motifs, black tights, her black hair tied back with a green ribbon. Wyatt thought she looked stunning. It seemed as if there was no one else on the stage.

After his efforts on the dance floor, Wyatt had some idea of the skill and effort shown in the competitions. And then Bridie was onstage, dancing her two dances at the end. He marvelled how high she kicked her legs, and how easy she made it look, smiling all the while. He jumped to his feet to cheer when she finished. This was followed by waiting, and nail-biting suspense. Bridie and Sharon were announced as winners of the doubles prize. A further wait ensued, as he peppered for the winner of the singles to be announced. When finally the judge pronounced that Bridie was placed third, with her friend Sharon coming second, his heart fell. Her mother said Bridie had made a few mistakes that were not typical, but by finishing third she would qualify for the county finals in Westport a month later. She'd have a chance to redeem herself then. He nodded, but felt deflated. It wasn't the outcome he had expected, but then he wasn't an expert.

He waited until Bridie eventually appeared, clad again in her green dress. Her eyes seemed a little red, and her eyeliner had run down her face.

"Well done Bridie, you did great." He hugged her close.

"Thanks Jim, but I should've done better. Anyway I'll

have time to improve for the finals next month. Mam and Nora are off home now with a friend. Some of the crowd are headin' to Traynor's pub to wind down after the excitement of the dancin'. Would you like to come? I need a drink and someone's shoulder to cry on."

"Of course, I'd love to." He put his arm around her, and they left the hall together.

Although well past midnight, the smoke filled pub still heaved, a blazing turf fire at one end, a group playing Irish music at the other end, and a wild feeling in the air. Bridie teamed up with the other dancers at the bar, while Wyatt had a drink with Tommy Joe.

"I see you're getting' to know the locals, Inspector." He said, winking and nodding in Bridie's direction.

"Yes, you could say that. Is there any woman in your life Tommy Joe?"

"Nare a one, Inspector, but I *do* have a healthy interest in women, in case you're thinkin' otherwise." They both laughed.

"Thank God for that, that's good to know. Tommy Joe, can you tell me why there is such a problem with the drinking water in Bridie's house?"

"It's a long story, a bit too long for tonight."

"Ok, maybe another time. Will you be going to the meeting about the gold mining in the Delphi valley?"

"I will for shure."

"See you then." He moved on, sensing Tommy Joe wasn't for discussing serious matters.

He and Bridie met later near the fire, drinks in hand. She seemed in better form, and more relaxed.

"God, I needed that drink. I really did. I'm only beginning to feel normal again."

"You were great, you really were. And you looked great too."

"You say all the right things Jim. You're kind. It does help to have someone to lean on, to get over things. *Jesus*, there it goes again." The musicians had launched into a new tune at breakneck speed.

"There goes what, Bridie?"

"That tune. That feckin' reel."

"What about it?"

"Oh.... nothin'. Nothin' at all." She seemed hesitant.

"Come on, out with it, tell me, what's bothering you."

"That reel they're playin'. It's the one I danced to in the final."

"So what, and why does it matter so much? What's it called anyway?"

"It's called "*My Love is in America*".

"So?"

"It's the one I made a bags of tonight. Jim, let's go outside. There are too many people in here. Earwiggin', I'm sure some of them are. I need to talk to you alone." Her face had crinkled in a frown.

They walked out the door, drinks in hand, and crossed the road to the wall facing the placid, moonlit waters of the fjord. They put their drinks on the wall, and gazed seaward. She lit a cigarette, and paced up and down, distracted, before sitting at a wooden picnic table. He sat beside her, and took her hand in his.

"Come on Bridie, out with it. What's on your mind? You can tell me. Is it the dance result or what?"

"I think I need a drink Jim. God, I left my drink on the wall. Jesus, I'm not thinkin' straight atall." She inhaled her cigarette.

"I need one too. Don't worry, I'll get them. I'll be back in a minute." She seemed stressed again.

"There you are." He placed the pint glass on the table, and she took a long mouthful before speaking.

"Jim, I just don't know how to start to tell you."

"How about making a start?"

"Well.... ok then,......it...it was nearly a week ago, just after our weekend together in Renvyle, that I got a letter from my boyfriend Francis Kenny in New York, to say that he was coming home for a month. He'd been away for nearly two years. I wasn't expectin' that, I can tell you."

"Your...your boyfriend?" Wyatt struggled to get the

words out.

"Well, he's more than a boyfriend really. We're engaged to be married."

"Engaged to be married?" Wyatt felt a hollow feeling in his stomach.

"Yes. We...we're engaged, but...but we never bothered with rings. We've known each other since our schooldays. We both felt buyin' a ring was a waste of money. Better to save the money instead. Money was tight, and he had no choice but to go to the States, lookin' for work. He's a carpenter. He...he's got a work permit now, but he's been so busy making money over there, that this is his first time home in two years. We used write all the time, in the beginnin'. But now that he's comin' home, I don't know what to feel. My head's still spinnin' with the news. I....I hope you understand."

"Well....of course I understand, you must be really excited. Congratulations. That....thats great news. I'm delighted for you." Inside though, he was churning. He realised that must be the reason for her below par dancing, but it all seemed unimportant now. Wyatt had a sour taste in his mouth. He gazed into the night sky, and saw the moon obscured by a large cloud. How appropriate. He lifted his whiskey glass to his lips, and in one swallow emptied it. She grabbed his arm.

"Jim, I'm sorry, I really am. But I had to tell you now, not later. I know I should have said something before. But I didn't mean to deceive you in any way. Maybe if I had told you, things would have been different. But I don't regret anything we did together though, and I hope you don't either. It was special, but I didn't know where we were headin'. Maybe it's just as well Francie is coming back now. It puts my life back to normal again."

What about my life? What does that count for? He felt like screaming the words at her, but didn't.

"Jim, we can still be friends, can't we? Real close friends. Say yes. Please say yes." She gripped his hands in hers. Her eyes were moist.

"Of course, you have no need to worry on that." He kissed her cheek.

They returned in silence to the pub. The place was still packed, music flying, people dancing, turf fire blazing away, life going on. Some people had started singing, and others were huddled in talking serious drink talk. It all felt unreal to Wyatt now. As they sipped their drinks, he wondered if he had imagined the conversation outside, but knew it was wishful thinking. Then Bridie informed him that she was staying with Sharon that night in the village. He said goodnight then, and left saying he had a headache. As he stumbled out the door, he felt his back pierced by a multitude of eyes. He trudged in wan moonlight up the road, and back to the hotel. Alone.

In his room, he found the half- full whiskey bottle he had stashed in the wardrobe, and filled his tumbler to the brim. Feelings of rejection and inadequacy ripped through him, as he thought back over what had happened. She was a young girl with her own life to live. He just wasn't part of it though, was he? That was the nub of it. Damn, why was life so complicated? He drank a mouthful of whiskey. And it happened just when he seemed to be getting his life together. She had played a part in that happening, for sure. Life wasn't fair, was it? He drank another mouthful. Well, nobody died this time, that's something, I suppose? He lifted the glass to his lips, and emptied it, then refilled the glass. Better get over it. They could still be friends. Of course they could, here's a toast to friendship, he muttered, lifting the glass. He was glad of what had happened between them, even if it was only a short affair. Now it was over. He was older and wiser.With baggage. He lowered the whiskey in one swallow, and clunked the empty glass on the table.

He lay in bed but sleep wouldn't come, despite all he'd drunk. His mind raced. He'd been dogged with bad luck all his life. And now when he thought things were on the up, this had to happen. She had deceived him and led him on, then left, leaving him with a bitter taste. Maybe she was not that innocent after all? Maybe she knew something about what had been stolen from his room? The thoughts swirled around in his head, until the last, dark hour, just before dawn.

# Chapter 9

## *Where the gathering is to be*

The sun was bright in the room when Wyatt awoke. His head throbbed. He glanced at his watch. It was past midday. He jumped out of bed, swearing. The empty whisky bottle on the table beside his bed, reminded him of events the night before. Bridie's revelations now seemed like a bad dream. He craved another drink, and cursed the empty bottle as he tossed it in the bin. A while later, as he left the bathroom, he felt better, his head helped by the tablets, and his body cleansed by a bath.

Downstairs, Wyatt picked up his post, and newspapers, putting them on a tray with a pot of coffee and toast. He sauntered to the lounge, and sat by the bay window. Bridie's engagement still tortured his thoughts, and he felt betrayed and bitter. He was glad she was off duty that day. He couldn't begin to think of how to deal with their relationship, and wondered how he would ever talk to her again.

Wyatt scanned the papers, as he sipped his coffee, and noted Brian Lenihan's slide in the Presidential polls. Then he glanced at his post, and started. There were two large envelopes, and one small one. He scanned the room, seeing there was nobody about. First he opened the large envelope. It was from the Mayo Times reporter. The hand written note with the documents said that he might be a bit shocked by the contents. He deferred reading the report, and put the note back in the envelope.

The second large envelope was from Ned Halpin. Inside it was the signed Letter of Authorisation to visit the water plants, with details of the waste water treatment plants, and the drinking water facilities. It also contained a report of the problems experienced over the past five years, which Wyatt scanned before replacing in the envelope. The other, smaller letter he knew was from his mother, recognising her spidery handwriting. He put it in his pocket, gathered up the documents, and returned to his room. He sat in front of the computer, and spread the contents of the two large envelopes in front of him. It was going to be another long day of forensic analysis. He sighed, but at least it would take his mind off last night's happenings with Bridie.

Just like the marine test samples, there were conflicting pictures between the drinking water problems reported by the Mayo Times, and those given by Ned Halpin. Maybe a lot of the defects had been rectified, or maybe not? Getting to the truth would be the problem. It was worrying. He wondered how a country with such large rainfall could have a problem with drinking water, something didn't add up. And then there were the waste water treatment plants. The newspaper said some villages still had no waste water infrastructure, and mainly used septic tanks. In many cases in villages where water facilities existed, they were ineffective due to overloading or inefficient operation. H'mmm.... Waste water treatment at plants below EU standards? Polluted water being discharged into coastal waters and rivers? What next? He grimaced as he read on in dismay. It was a horror story. How could this be allowed to happen? Who was accountable, and to whom? It didn't make sense. A lot of questions needed answering.

There was a report too, on the gold mining venture in the Delphi valley, which he studied. He reckoned it might be of use at the pending gathering. Then he gazed at an article which made him feel nauseous. It didn't feature in Ned Halpin's report. Surprise, surprise, he thought. The place in question, he decided, though a long way off, would be his first port of call.

Midnight had gone when he finally got around to reading his mother's letter. She was glad he had found a girlfriend. She sounded nice, she said. If she only knew how it was now, he thought. She liked the photos he'd sent her, saying how lucky he was to be in such a lovely place, and how she envied him, it sounded so much better than the hell she was enduring in the nursing home. Guilt sliced through him. She was looking forward to his next letter, and had packed her bags to go home at Christmas. He sighed, folded the letter and put it back in the envelope, and left it on his desk. At least she got my name right this time, he muttered.

\*\*\*

The bay curved in a half moon shape, and was covered in a mass of green seaweed. There was slime everywhere. On the water, on the beaches, on the rocks, on every slithering, slimy place. The whole place was covered by stinking green seaweed. There were tidal flats in the bay into which two rivers drained. He took some photos, and walked around the emerald sea of pollution. It was called sea lettuce. Not the kind I'd fancy for my salad, he thought. He'd read in the Mayo Times report, that there had been a commercial proposal a few years ago, to build a multi- million drying and processing facility to convert the green algae into fish food, but nothing had happened. A Government Task Force was looking into the matter. Typical, nothing happened, he fumed. He'd travelled a long way by taxi to view this green sea of slime, and was glad he'd come, even if it sent a shiver through his body. Seeing is the truth, he muttered, however disgusting. Wyatt tiptoed to the edge of the green mass, and took samples.

Wyatt gazed about.There were many fine houses in the area. Some new ones were dotted along the shoreline. He wondered how frustrated they must be at this fiasco. A solution at hand too, and not taken up, but why? He needed to find out. He guessed the building of the new houses by the sea, and inadequate sewage treatment were the reasons for the green mass. It was a lovely place to live if only the blooming green tide would vanish. Something was rotten somewhere, and it was not a pretty sight for the tourists. He sighed, and shook his head.

Next morning Wyatt rang Ned Halpin, to inform him of the two waste treatment plants he planned to visit that day. Afterwards, he decided to visit different ones, but not tell Halpin. The managers had looked surprised when he arrived, and showed them his Authorisation Letter. From their reactions, he knew they weren't expecting him, and he was glad. Catch them off guard, when they're not expecting it, he thought. The best audit check. The nearest beaches to both plants had recently lost their Blue Flag status. What a coincidence. It's another disaster for the tourist business.

That night he assembled the data he'd gleaned that day at the treatment plants on his desk, and analysed the details. Then he compared his findings with the information from the Mayo Times. It was late when he finished. He felt disappointed, and ashamed, but not surprised, to find most of the reported problems and allegations in the newspaper were vindicated by his findings. And most of them were still not sorted out.

Next morning, he decided to do an initial report about the waste water problems, while they were fresh in his mind. Bridie was at the reception desk. She told him that there was a message from Father Flynn, saying there would be meeting on Friday at eight in the Parochial Hall. He thanked her, and took the note. It was their first conversation since the night of the Ceili. She seemed standoffish, he thought, and avoided eye contact. The reality of their short affair ending, hit him again. He tried to think of something to say, but couldn't find the words. Back in his room, he immersed himself again in perusing the data he'd gathered the previous day.

The problem emerging was a lack of proper management at the water plants. Why? Were they being compromised? Most of the problems seemed to arise from insufficient or inaccurate sampling of the waste water. He couldn't fathom it. The cost of waste water sampling was low. And the pollution of beaches near the plants was due to poor waste management. Some pollution problems were due to the Council discharging toxic waste through the plants into the sea. The buck stops at the top. He grimaced. Ned Halpin will have some explaining to do.

Later that afternoon he cycled to Bridie's mother's house to store the new information. He now wondered if it was now a safe storage haven, since his break- up with Bridie.

"You'll have a cup of tea?" Bridie's mother seemed hesitant,

"Sure Missus O'Malley, a quick cuppa would be grand. I have things to sort out back at the hotel."

"Bridie told me Francis Kenny will be home tomorrow. He's a grand lad. You'll both get on famous. It's such a long time since he went away. His family are delighted he's home. A fine family, they are for shure. I wonder has he changed at all." She smiled, and placed a tray on the table near the fire.

"I'm sure we'll get on."But he didn't really think so.

"You know you're welcome in this house anytime Jim. You'll still keep comin' to visit?"

"Of course, why wouldn't I?"

"Shure that's grand then. I was worried, that's all. And your mother, she's well?"

"Yes, I've just had a letter from her. I'll be writing back to her tonight. I'll send her your wishes. I'm off now." He lifted the latch on the half door and sauntered down the gravel pathway to his bike, and wheeled it to the roadway. Twilight had put a purple tint on the mountains, as he leaned on the pedals. The breeze brushed his skin, and the bike skimmed along the road. He grinned as he gazed up at the streaks of gold in the sky, and wondered why people went crazy to dig gold out of the earth at huge cost, when they could look up, and check it out for free in the evening sky.

Late that night he finished the letter to his mother, and felt satisfied. Visiting Bridie's mother made him want to keep more in touch with his own mother. He still felt bitter that Bridie had misled him, and despaired of how to handle it. But maybe things will get better in time, he hoped. He reached for the whisky bottle beside the bed. My whisky and my book are my best friends now. At least they're not fickle.

\*\*\*

The oblong trestle table was covered by a green baize cloth, with pitchers and glasses of water on it. It stood on the platform where the band had played on the night of the Ceili. The hall was still lit by strips of neon suspended by wire from the ceiling. All the important people sat behind the table, facing the packed crowd. He recognised most of them from the night in the Renvyle Hotel with Bridie. Father Flynn sat sandwiched in the centre.

Below, on the dance floor, people sat on wooden chairs. Wyatt stayed near the back of the hall. Before the meeting began, Tommy Joe arrived and sat beside him, tipping his cap and nodding. Wyatt saw Bridie on the far side of the hall, beside a dark-haired young man. He wondered if it was her fiancé Francis. Then he started, as he spotted Mc Fadden, the giant redhead, in the distance, and wondered what the hell he was doing there.

After a short prayer by Father Flynn, Ned Halpin, the County Councillor, kicked off the proceedings about the Delphi gold mining project. Results were positive so far and justified more investment to develop the mining near Lioscarney, at the back of Croagh Patrick, he said. It will be great for the county of Mayo and the country. The Government were backing the project. Jobs would be created, long term jobs. Everbody in the area would be better off. They'd be mad *not* to vote for it. It was the chance of a lifetime. It was now or never. They owed it to their children and grand children to back it. And so on.....

Muted clapping followed when Halpin sat down, twenty minutes later. It seemed everyone wasn't as sure as he was, about the mining, Wyatt thought. Then Sean Glynn, the bank manager from Westport spoke, endorsing what Halpin said, and said his bank would of be happy to supply whatever finance was required. And why wouldn't he? Wyatt muttered. The priest then asked for questions from the audience.

"And what the fuckin' hell about the dynamitin', and the killin' of our fish stock, and the pollutin' of our rivers and water, and then with the rivers going into the sea itself, even pollutin' that too. Sure what good is all that to the people livin' here atall? We might as well be in fuckin' Timbuktu." Tommy Joe had stood up as he spoke, twisting his cap in his hands, and jabbing his finger at Halpin. Halpin jumped up.

"I'm glad you said that, Tommy Joe." Halpin snarled, lips narrowed to a slit. "A lot of people mistakenly think like you do. But they're wrong too, just like you. We have the most stringent environmental regulations for operations like this. Glencorrig Mining has the highest health and safety standards in the country. You can rest assured on that matter." He sat down, frowning, and fuming.

"Words are cheap Mr Halpin. You can talk what you like, but where we live, some people don't even have proper drinkin' water. And there's raw sewage pourin' into the sea in places that you know about too Mr Halpin, and nothin's being done about it either, an' nobody's losin' their job or anythin'. An' you know it too, Mr Halpin. So why should we believe any of the words that come spoutin' out of *your* gob?" Tommy Joe's face was red as he shook his fist in the air.

Halpin jumped back to his feet, eyes bulging, face contorted, and banged his fist on the table.

"I reject these allegations. As you say Tommy Joe, words are cheap. The people I represent on the local Council are doing a fine job, in difficult circumstances. I think you're reacting emotionally, maybe because of difficulties in your personal life, but I believe you owe me and my colleagues an apology."Halpin sat down, glaring at Tommy Joe.

Father Flynn tapped his glass with a spoon, and stood up, a frown on his face.

"Gentlemen, order please, we're here for a frank exchange of views in a rational and peaceful manner. It's an emotional matter I know, but let's keep our heads, for God's sake. Anyway, we're lucky to have someone who's here in a neutral capacity, who can say something on the subject. I now call on Mr Wyatt to say a few words." The priest sat down.

"Fair ball to yeh Inspector." Tommy Joe muttered beside him, grinning. Thanks a lot Father for putting me on the spot, Wyatt thought. Thanks a bloody lot. He stood up. He hadn't intended to speak but felt moved by the truth in Tommy Joe's words, and the hypocrisy in Halpin's.

"Reverend Father, gentlemen and ladies, I'm here merely as an observer. My responsibilities lie elsewhere. But they do cover the environment, and that affects everyone. The environment is a giant jigsaw of interrelated parts. When somebody does something here, it affects someone else there, and so on. So I'd like someone here tonight to clarify the type of mining proposed in extracting the ore. I understand it's to be open cast mining, because it's the cheapest. Sodium cyanide might be used to strip the rock. This could mean poisonous dust generated would be wind- blown up through the Delphi valley, polluting the rivers and lakes, and eventually even polluting the sea itself. If that's the case, we have a problem, a major problem. It would be an environmental disaster for this area, jobs or no jobs. We're all responsible for protecting what God and nature has given us. We're custodians of the land here, for our lifetime. The land will be here long after we've gone, wherever we're going. We must protect our heritage. No sell out, I say. Wyatt sat down.

The crowd applauded, and Wyatt heard Father Flynn's "hear, hear" ring louder than the rest. He knew he might have overstepped the mark, especially in his closing words, as he'd got carried away.

"I can assure you, your fears are without foundation." Eamon Carney, the squat, stocky manager of Glencorrig Mining Company had bounded to his feet. He was rocking from the ball of one foot to the other, and his eyes flashed in Wyatt's direction as he started to speak.

"We're a reputable company, and we have permission from the Irish Government to pursue our lawful business interests in the Delphi valley. We've got all the required permits from the Council and the Garda have ensured compliance with the laws of the land. We want to give something lasting back to the people of this area, apart from jobs. I am therefore committing substantial company funds to the building of a new school here, and the restoration of the church and the Parochial Hall where we're gathered tonight. I was going to make this announcement later, privately, to Father Flynn, but now seems a more appropriate time." He sat down to loud yahooing, staring in Wyatt's direction all the time. Round one to the miners it looks like, Wyatt thought. He now felt like another voice in the wilderness. An adjournment was called for refreshments.

He took his tea and scone to a quiet corner and sat down. Ned Halpin came over, sitting beside him.

"Jim, I trust you'll disregard those outrageous remarks of Tommy Joe. They're a pack of lies. There's no truth whatsoever in them. We've had our differences over the years. He was taking advantage of the situation to have a go at me, you appreciate."

"Ned, I don't believe my fears about open cast mining were answered by Mr Carney. And he seems to be dangling money in people's faces to get their support. I'm not convinced. There are many pollution problems already in the area, without adding to them."

"Are you referring to your visits to the two water plants, which incidentally were not the ones you told me you would be checking." Halpin's eyebrows arched as he spoke.

"Oh yes Ned.... of course...of course... I meant to tell you, I had a last minute change in plans. It shouldn't have made any difference as I'm sure all the plants were well prepared for a possible visit."

"They were all prepared of course Jim, there's nothing to hide."

"Indeed Ned, you're right, I wasn't referring to problems at the plants."

"Then what *were* you referring to, may I ask?"

"You may ask Ned, but at this stage I'm not at liberty to say. My enquiries are not yet complete, and are highly confidential. You understand?"A vision of the green sea lettuce tide flashed through Wyatt's mind.

"Of course Jim, I'm glad you found everything in order at the two plants." If you only knew, Wyatt thought.

Father Flynn called the meeting back to order. Many local landowners were swayed by Carney's offer, stood up, and spoke of supporting the mining plan. Obviously they have visions of the Gold Rush and striking it rich in their minds, Wyatt thought. Father Flynn spoke then, saying he appreciated Carney's offer of financial help to the parish, but that it wouldn't affect the right decision being made. We need to think long and hard, he said. Not a decision to rush into. We should all pray for God's guidance in this difficult matter. We only had one bite at the cherry. He finished, saying they should dwell on the issues, pray, and meet again in a month's time.

Carney had the final word, offering to sponsor a hurling match between two local clubs, and put up a cup and money for the event. *And* there would be free drinks later that night for all in Traynor's pub. The crowd dispersed then. Carney's offer seemed to have won their hearts, if not their minds, Wyatt mused.

The pub was packed, a smoke pall halo hanging in the air, and a log fire blazing in the corner.Trays of free drinks lined the bar, everyone helping themselves. The air hummed with excited chatter. The musicians in the corner were drowned out by the hubbub. They soon gave up playing, and joined in the banter and free celebrations.

Father Flynn shook Wyatt's hand, and thanked him for coming and speaking.

"You got me out of a spot of bother there tonight Jim, thank God. We're not going to let those cowboys ride roughshod over us, are we? You'll come to the next meeting?"

"No problem Father. I'll be there." Wyatt excused himself and moved over to the bar, where he saw Bridie with her boyfriend. A sparkle from her finger caught his eye. When he came over to her, his eyes were on her hand.

"Like it Jim?" She held her hand up, so he could clearly admire the large, sparkling diamond.

"Beautiful. Congratulations Bridie. Well done. And this must be Francis." He held out his hand.

"Pleas'd to meet yah Jim, I've heard a lot about yah. Have another drink? They're on the house yah know like." Francis had a shy smile on his face, and a full pint in his hand.

"Why not, never look at a gift horse." He gave Francis his empty glass, and took the full one.

"I'm sure you're glad to be home, after your years in the Big Apple."

"Shure I am. It's all work over there, and not much time for play."

"Anyway, you've got something to show for it." Wyatt said, nodding towards the ring, which Bridie was showing off to a crowd of her girl friends at the bar.

"I have for shure. Blood, sweat, and tears went into gettin' that ring."

"I'm sure. Well done again." Wyatt drifted away, a hollow feeling inside.

Later he bumped into Tommy Joe at the bar.

"Good on yeh, Inspector, ye gave the gobshites somethin' to think about." Tommy Joe winked, as he took a slug from his pint.

"No love lost between you and Halpin either. Surprising,

as you're both involved in a business venture."

"What's that you're talkin' about Inspector?"

"Atlantic Waves is the company I'm talking about. Have you bought a new boat yet with the compensation money?"

"Yeh, we're in business together for a few years alright. That doesn't mean I agree with him on everythin'. And I don't. He's a big man down here alright, but he's not right in everythin' he does or says. We've ordered a new boat alright. Delivery's comin' in a few weeks."

Tommy Joe nodded towards the giant redhead at the far end of the bar, talking to some locals. "I'm going to kill that bastard McFadden some day."

"Why?"

"Why? Because I hate him with a vengeance, that's why."Tommy Joe's lips curled in a snarl.

"But why do you hate him that much?"

"Some day Inspector, you may find out. But for the here and now, there are some things you're better off not knowin'." He winked, and turned to some friends near him.

Wyatt decided to leave then. As he turned to go, he noticed Bridie and Francis on the far side of the pub, seemingly embroiled in an argument. Francis looked drunk, his head and body seesawing. He started to go over to bid them goodnight, but changed his mind. No point sticking your nose in when you're not asked, his mother had always told him. He took satisfaction at their disagreement, but did not feel proud of the feeling.

# Chapter 10

## *Jenny Picking Cockles*

The following week Wyatt's sleeping problems recurred. Despite downing late night whiskies he still woke on and off. Visions of Bridie came constantly into his mind. Sometimes she seemed to be fighting with her fiance Francis, or sometimes just dancing on the stage, and sometimes he dreamed of holding her close in his arms. Sleep came hard after that. The nights dragged, and in the daytime he felt fatigued. He worried about becoming an insomniac. It was getting to him, and he decided to do something about it. Later that week, he walked to Leenane village, bought a book on hill walking, resolving to get out and explore the area, and hoped that might do the trick.

Next Saturday morning, the weather was set fair, so he put his plan to work. As he strode through the foyer, rucksack on back, Bridie looked up from her desk. He strolled over, and exchanged banter about the weather. She then lowered her head and continued poring over her work. He sighed, wondering if she ever thought of the day they cycled to Renvyle. She looked tired and pale. Maybe she too was having trouble sleeping at night? Then his thoughts switched to Cleggan, a fishing port on the way to Clifden, where he was going, and he wondered how long it would take to get there. He brought his water sample bottles, so he could combine work and play. Before setting off on his bike, he re-checked his route.

It was midmorning, and the white washed village of Moyard came into view. Wyatt paused there at a roadside grotto near the harbour, and said a prayer. He moved on, and was freewheeling down an incline, when thoughts of the gold mining meeting drifted through his head. Ned Halpin seemed to have a finger in every pie down here. Was he getting something out of it from the mining company? Was there a conflict of interests? Possibly, but locally he was Mister Big, and would probably get away with it. It might be seen by the locals as a smart move, creating jobs, even at the environment's expense, and making something out of it as well. And why was Tommy Joe so vehement against McFadden, the giant redhead? There must be a story there, and it must go deep. He would love to find out what the story was.

The sharp, winding climb ahead interrupted his thoughts. After pushing hard in low gear to the halfway point, Wyatt alighted and wheeled his bike to the top, sucking in the air. There was a picnic table at the side of the road. Perfect. He placed his rucksack on the table, and took out his sandwiches and coffee flask. As he started to eat, he surveyed the terrain. Afar were brown bogs, stuck between pine forests and lakes, the sea silvery to the west. Behind, the Twelve Bens, defiant, quartz tops glittering, mist clouds atop their peaks. How he wished for their strength and durability. He resolved to do some hill walking in the area before he left the west. After eating he rested awhile, then remounted, and continued his journey. The road stretching before him was flat and narrow, twisting and turning. Loose stone chips flew up beneath his wheels, and the whiff of tar tainted the air.

Fishing boats bobbed in the harbour at Cleggan. Their diesel fumes, mixed with the reek of fish, polluted the air. The fishing village nestled at the neck of a narrow inlet. A notice stated boats sailed daily to and from Inisboffin Island, about forty minutes away. He took some water samples near the port, and followed a rambling road south along the jagged coastline.

Omey Island lay before him. Wyatt was tired, and decided this would be his final destination. His luck was in, as the tide was out. It was a tidal island, and could be reached only at low tide, about every seven hours. He cycled over the causeway, parked his bike by a sand dune, and strolled around, taking samples as he went. Soon he stood beside a sandswept graveyard, where he read the epitaph of those drowned near Cleggan in a major disaster, in 1927. Forty four souls lost. So many families in the area affected, with many souls buried beneath the sands of Omey Island. He read the litany of names, and walked across the island, heart heavy. The island, stark and beautiful, had famine ruins scattered around, and many holiday homes. As he strode through the deserted dunes and ruins, his mind wandered, as he wondered how people survived there, generations ago. A lot didn't, and perished in the Famine, or emigrated. Life was simpler then. Starve or emigrate. Not much of a choice, was it? On his way back, he glanced sideways, and saw in panic that the tide was sneaking in fast from the side of the island. He rushed to reach his bike, and just made it over the causeway, before the island became cut off again by the sea.

On his journey back to Leenane, Wyatt stopped to take samples near a lobster and shellfish farm at Arhus. Further up the road he saw a sign for Rossadillisk beach, and followed it. Near a gate at the end of the narrow road, a Mini car, with UK Registration, was parked. He left his bike beside the car, humped his rucksack onto his back, and climbed over the stile into the field. He gasped. The field before him, stretching down to the beach, was a multi-coloured mosaic of wild flowers. A few cows grazed here and there, and in the middle of the field stood a lone woman. She wore a short brown coat, and bent to pick some flowers. When she stood straight again, she turned and gazed out to sea. Wyatt passed close to her as he walked towards the beach. He lifted his hand in greeting.

"It's quite something isn't it?" Wyatt said, waving at the sea of flowers.

"Oh yes...yes it is. It...it's a very special place. It's super. I hope you don't mind me picking these flowers."

"No, not at all, they're nature's gift, and there's more than enough left for everyone." He smiled and moved on.

Later, as Wyatt paddled on the coral shoreline, the sun was hot on his neck. He had used his last sample bottle in the sea. He let the waves lap over his feet, and looked seaward. Far out, fishing boats were silhouetted, inching along the rim of the horizon, with the sea a shimmering mass. When he turned inland, the mountains far away dipped in and out of mist clouds. He sucked in air, thinking there was no other place he'd rather be.

The woman he had seen earlier came into view. She approached him barefoot, walking along the tideline, dress hitched, and occasionally bending low to pick shells off the beach. This time he looked straight into her face when they met. She was tallish, with brown eyes and hair, and had a serene smile. Beneath the short brown coat, she wore a black dress and carried her shoes in her hands.

"You've caught me breaking the rules again, I'm afraid, I plead guilty." She laughed, showing him the coral shells she had gathered in a white plastic bag. On the hand holding the bag was a gold wedding ring.

"You're forgiven again. But don't let me catch you again, take this as your last warning." He grinned.

"Thank you…thank you. I'm sorry. I promise I will behave."Her voice was soft and friendly, with an English accent.

"If you don't mind me asking, what brings you to such a place? It's rather remote, are you on a holiday, or visiting relatives?"

"No…no…..I don't mind you asking….not at all. It…it's…my husband John…well.. he…he died five months ago." The smile slipped from her face.

"Oh…. I'm very sorry to hear that."

"Thank you. It…it… well it was all so sudden. He had a heart attack in his car when he was stopped in a traffic jam coming home from work. It came out of the blue. Bang. It was a complete shock." She paused for a minute." We…..we had known each since we were children, and were married for eight of the happiest years of my life." She choked, and wiped her eyes with a handkerchief.

"I'm so sorry, but…but still what…what brought you to this place?"

"I….I really can't say. I just couldn't get over the

whole thing. I've never gone out at all since it happened. I couldn't bring myself to, instead I went into myself. Yesterday, I was at home in Hull as normal, just enduring another day, nothing special, feeling the usual dark clouds hemming in around me."She paused to dry her face again.

"Really, and what happened then?"

"Well…I….I just got the urge to go to Ireland. I don't know why. We'd never been to Ireland before, but we'd talked many times of coming. I just felt I had to go. I can't explain it. I packed a few things, and drove to Holyhead, and arrived in Dun Laoghaire this morning."

"You mean you drove all that way today?" Wyatt was astounded.

"Yes, and I did it without stopping. I kept going. And somehow I arrived here about an hour or so ago."

"So, you…you mean you arrived here by chance?"

"Yes……yes, that's it. I just can't explain it, as I said. Maybe it was John's will, from up above. But when I saw that field full of wildflowers, and the sea beyond it, and when I walked through the field, I knew I had arrived at where I wanted to be, or where *he* wanted me to be. I felt at peace for the first time since John died. It was like a spiritual feeling, as if he had guided me here somehow. I…I just can't fathom or explain it. No rhyme or reason. But I…I do feel happier now."

"Well, I must admit there is something about this place today that goes right into you, right into your soul. Still, it's an unusual story, I…I don't know what to say either."

"Then best say nothing. You…you must think I'm a crazy woman, picking cockles on the beach, and coming up to a complete stranger, and unburdening my soul to him. You probably can't wait to get away from me. And I don't blame you."

"No …no…not at all, actually I do believe what you say, it's not a story you'd make up. And I'm glad to be the one to hear it."

"That's so kind of you to say. I'm normally shy to strangers, you know. Rather prim and proper really. But there was something I felt inside when I met you. I felt I could say all those things to you, even without knowing you. I don't know why. And now I must say I feel the better of it."

"Good. Now that we're no longer strangers, my name is Jim Wyatt." He held out his hand.

"I'm Jenny Marsh." She took his hand, smiling.

They walked back through the wildflower meadow, and he explained the purpose of his visit to the area that day, while she paused occasionally to pick flowers for her collection, before they reached the gate where the car and bike were parked.

When they got there, Wyatt's back tyre was flat. Damn, a puncture, he muttered. Damn again, he fumed, realising he had forgotten to bring a repair kit. He was furious that he, normally so precise and so careful, had cocked up. How stupid can you be, he raged, and in front of a woman he barely knew. He pumped the tyre until red in the face. Nothing happened. Then he saw a gash on the side of the tyre. He felt better then, knowing a repair kit would have made no difference.

"Can I give you a lift somewhere Jim? I'm not in any hurry. You can put your bike on the roof rack."

"Well…yes… thanks Jenny. That would be handy."

When they had packed away the bike and his rucksack, she asked where he was going.

"I'm heading back to Leenane, on the Westport road. By the way, I saw a nice seafood restaurant earlier in Cleggan, overlooking the harbour. Maybe we could stop there for a bite."

She agreed, and soon they sat at a table in the bay window of the restaurant. The view was onto the harbour, where fishing boats swayed beside the pier. Jenny went to the bathroom while he studied the menu. She returned in a short time, spruced up, lipstick and makeup on. Wyatt found her attractive, her manner easygoing. They both had the house speciality, pan fried fresh scallops, straight from the fishing boats outside, washed down with a fine

Bourgogne, all served by Eamonn, the pleasant local restaurant owner. Over the food and wine, they relaxed more. They laughed about the whole coincidence of how they met, and what might have happened if he had to make it home walking. She told him she was an only child, and didn't have any family of her own. Though not for the want of trying, she added. She worked as a freelance journalist for a woman's magazine in Lancashire. Apart from his work, Wyatt spoke little about himself, preferring to listen, and he wasn't bored. When the bill arrived she insisted on paying half of it, in spite of his protests.

On the way back to the hotel, he asked when she would return to England.

"I'll think about that tomorrow Jim. Tonight I just want someplace to rest my weary head. All this travelling and fresh air, not to mention the food and wine, is catching up on me I'm afraid."

It was dark when the mini pulled up outside the hotel. He took the bike down off the roof rack, while she gazed at the hotel's faded Victorian façade.

"It's well for some people, staying in a posh place like this. I'd better look down the road for a cheap bed and breakfast, though it may be hard to get a place at this hour." She smiled as she spoke.

"The hotel has self catering apartments. They're very reasonable. I'll go in and check, if you like."

"Oh, yes please Jim, thank you, that...that would be super."

A while later, after she'd signed in and parked her car, he escorted her to the door of her apartment, carrying her hold all bag. She opened the door and turned around.

"Thank you Jim, very kind of you." She took the bag from him.

"Thanks for the lift, Jenny, you saved my bacon today. Say how about joining me for dinner in the hotel tomorrow night. That is, if you're still here." She hesitated a few moments before speaking.

"I have some writing to catch up on. This looks the

very spot to do it. Yes, I'd like that very much Jim, super." She moved closer to him, putting her free hand behind his neck, and kissed him softly on the lips. He felt her body close, and the odour of her perfume. She pulled back, bidding him goodnight, and vanished into the brightness inside.

Later he lay in bed, his book in his hands, but he wasn't reading it. This time his problem was *going* to sleep. The day's events washed through his head like waves onto a beach. Their chance meeting was hard to believe. Then the puncture happened, farfetched but true. Yes it *had* happened, and he felt drawn to this woman he had met in such a strange manner. Something about her reminded him of his former wife Emma, who came from York. Not in her looks, but in a way in a way he couldn't fathom. She seemed near his age, mid thirties, maybe a few years younger, and he felt attracted to her. He wondered if she felt the same, but guessed probably not. He was disappointed she hadn't asked him into her apartment, but deep down reckoned it was for the best. He shouldn't be letting his imagination take over. She probably just found him an amusing, local sounding board, and would be out of his life and back in England in a few days, but then again, maybe not. For God's sake, she was still in mourning, forget it. He tossed and turned the rest of the night.

Next morning there was a hand delivered letter for him at reception, and he opened it. It was from Jenny. She apologised and said she had contacted her boss, and had to go on to Sligo to research a project she was working on. She had to leave early as there were a number of places to visit, and hoped he would forgive her hasty departure, and the postponement of their dinner date. But she would return on Wednesday, and stay a few nights in the same apartment, and would love to have dinner with him on any of those nights.

Wyatt took the letter and a coffee into the lounge, sat by

the window, and read it again. A polite fare thee well, he surmised. He was stupid to have read anything into a casual, if unusual, meeting of two lonely people. He sipped the black liquid, then squeezed the letter into a ball, and threw it into the litter bin in the corner of the room. He could now write the affair out of his mind. At least he might sleep better. Before going back to his room, he decided to book dinner for two on Wednesday night, just in case.

To his surprise another letter arrived on Wednesday, and he recognised her handwriting. She had returned that day and was working in her apartment, and looked forward to the dinner that night. She would meet him in the bar at eight. He realised she must have checked if he'd made a booking in the restaurant.

His body tingled as he waited for her in the bar, and he wasn't disappointed. Her dress was black, knee length, conservative, but revealing in the right places. A string of pearls hung around her neck, and a red ribbon bound her auburn hair. He complimented her on her dress. She thanked him, and said she had bought it in Sligo, as she'd brought nothing to wear to dinner with her. He noticed she was wearing her wedding ring on her other hand. They both had *Kir Royales* before heading into the restaurant.

The waiter took them across the maple floored restaurant to a table by the bay window. On the table were flowers and a candle. He felt happy inside. It was an intimate location, looking onto the waters of Killary fjord, ochre after the sunset.

"Oh Jim, this is a super place, I really love it so." She giggled with excitement.

"Glad you like it Jenny. So did Queen Victoria."

"Really?"

Wyatt told her of the hotel's most famous visitor, while the waiter lit the cinnamon scented candle and took their orders. He had Connemara lamb, while she ordered Sole on the bone. He suggested his favourite wine Chateau Neuf du Pape, and she agreed. Sated, they lingered, looking out the window at the changing landscape. When the sun went down, the candle threw flickering shadows over her face, and she looked alluring in a mysterious, seductive manner.

"I'm dying to know what took you so suddenly up to Sligo town, I thought you were just trying to get away from me."

"No. You're wrong there. It was genuine. You can blame your most famous poet, Mr. Yeats."

"Oh, you mean W.B.Yeats?"

"Yes, he's the very one. I have to admit I've always been mad into his poetry, and I've studied his work and life for many years. Almost a lifelong obsession, you might say." She lifted the wineglass to her lips, before continuing.

"I talked my editor into letting me write a story for the magazine about Yeats. I'd broached it many times before, in vain, but this time, probably because I was here, she relented. I visited Lissadell House, Dooney Rock, Lough Gill, where the Isle of Innisfree is, Drumcliffe where's he's buried, and Knocknarea. All the places in Sligo associated with him. It was a smashing experience. A fleeting visit, but I feel a lot closer to him now, and his work."

"What's so special about him?"

"Well, he had a way with words. Words alone are certain good, you know? And there's his lyricism, and romanticism. And he understood how women feel. Do you?" She touched his hand.

"I'm not sure. So far I haven't been too successful." He sipped his wine.

"Oh and how's that Jim?"

He told her briefly of his marriage break up. She seemed moved by it. A silence fell.

"It's all in the past now Jim." She took both his hands in hers.

"Yes Jenny, let's talk of something more cheerful. Tell me some of Mr.Yeats's famous words?" She paused, sipped her wine, before looking into her half-full glass.

"Wine comes in at the mouth, and love comes in at the eye." Her brown eyes were now boring into his.

The words were a spark that lit a candle inside him. Wyatt looked back into her eyes, and felt his blood throb in his veins. But inside, something warned him to hold back. Don't make a fool of yourself again, he thought. Not so fast. She's in mourning for her husband. She doesn't feel the way you do. He wanted to suggest something to her, but hesitated, the fear of rejection gripping him. They each had a brandy to finish the meal. She seemed to have read his mind, and when he paid the bill before they rose to leave, she moved close to him, touching him on the leg with her hand under the table. She called him her shy one of the heart, and said she would go with him that night to an isle in the water.

Without further talk, they left the restaurant, and he sensed what was implied. He held her hand in the foyer and went to turn up the staircase towards his room, but she pulled him back, saying

"Best you come to my place tonight, Jim. It may not be as salubrious as yours, but it's more discreet. Maybe we'll come here another night." She kissed him full on the lips.

When they entered the bedroom in her apartment, he saw that the twin beds had been moved together.

"Expecting company?"

"You never know your luck."

"Hey, I forgot my pajamas."

"They won't be necessary." She put her arms around his neck, pulling him down, whispering in his ear, and said she'd spread her dreams beneath his feet, and he must tread softly, because he might be treading on her dreams.

"I will, I will, I will."

Later sleep descended deep on him, and when he woke, dawn's light palely lit the room. He quietly dressed and departed, leaving Jenny asleep, and before returning to the hotel, he left a note on the table. In it he asked her to dinner again that night.

That afternoon, he called to reception to collect his mail, and saw a hand delivered envelope addressed to him. He recognised her handwriting, and his heart raced as he opened it. Jenny apologised, she couldn't make it to dinner that evening as she had to finish her article and it was way behind schedule, all his fault of course. She said many things could tempt her from her craft of verse. The following night would be fine, but she must return to England the day after.

Disappointed, he immersed himself in catching up on his own work backlog. All his samples from the trip to Cleggan had to be sorted, labelled, logged onto his computer and sent for testing. After booking the restaurant, he sent a note to Jenny confirming their last night together. His mind wandered a lot while he worked. Usually it was her face he saw. He wondered if it was the same for her.

When he passed through the foyer the next night, on his way into the lounge to wait for Jenny, Wyatt noticed Bridie working in reception. They did not speak as she was busy on the telephone. Jenny arrived again right on time, through the door.

"You look lovely." He kissed her lightly on the lips.

"I'm wearing the same outfit as the other night. You'll have to forgive me, I'm travelling light."

"I'm sure you're wearing something that I can't see, that you didn't have on, the other night."

"Jim Wyatt, you're a cad." She said, smiling, waving her handbag at him.

The night flew by in a cocoon, and when at last they left the restaurant, he had his hand around her waist. They stopped at the foot of the staircase. He turned to ascend it, and this time she didn't refuse to follow him, and kissed him long and hard inside the room. Afterwards, as they lay together in bed, passion's play ended, he said, heart thumping, that he thought he was falling in love again, and wondered if she felt the same. She said she'd never give all the heart and that love would not seem worth thinking of, to passionate women if it seemed certain, and they couldn't dream. And he told her to dream on, as he kissed her.

Then they embraced again, and later a deep slumber descended, until he woke late in the morning, and found this time it was she who had left. There was a note on the table. In it she said she had to leave early before the hotel staff arrived, but she had left him something as a souvenir. She hated emotional farewells, and was full of conflicting emotions, but was sure things would settle down when she got back to England. She would write to him, and yes she felt she might be falling in love too, in spite of not wanting to give all her heart. He read the note a second time, folded it, and put it in the drawer beside the bed.

# Chapter 11

## *At the Great Hurlin' Match*

Wyatt sat in the hotel lounge, read the newspaper, and mulled over the draft of his latest report to Seamus Halpin. It concerned the water treatment plants and the green lettuce sea. He worried about getting the balance right, with Halpin's brother so deeply involved. His mind drifted back to Jenny's note, and he wondered if she would write as promised, or if he should dismiss the affair as a romantic fling, and her in such a vulnerable state of mind? Probably the latter, he decided. Women, just as he was trying to get one woman out of his mind, he'd replaced her with another. Still, his spirits had perked up. And he was sleeping better. Yes, there was something about her, more than something. She made you smile, and relax, and other things too. His mind kept wandering.

"Take these souvenirs with you Jim Wyatt. Your room rate doesn't allow for overnight visitors." Bridie spat the words at him in a shrill voice, and threw a brown paper bag in his direction. It landed in his lap. The heads of an elderly couple sipping tea in the corner of the room turned sharply in his direction.

"I…I can explain everything, Bridie." He mumbled, staring numbly at the red frilly underwear in the bag.

"I'm sure you can. I'll adjust your account in the meantime." She glared at him as she spoke.

Before Wyatt could reply, she had swivelled around, and stormed out of the room. He looked over at the elderly couple. They smiled knowingly at him, nodding their heads, and continued sipping their tea. He left in a hurry for his room.

Wyatt focused again at the report. The words seemed jumbled and meaningless. He needed to clear his head, and his hands trembled. After he'd left the report and Jenny's brown paper bag back in his bedroom, he rushed from the hotel without looking left or right, and cycled to the village, hoping the exercise would clear his mind. As he pedalled along the road, it hit him. Jenny had said in her note that she'd left him a souvenir. So that was it, but the joke had backfired on him, big time. But why was Bridie so venomous? After all it was *she* had given *him* the push. Women. He gritted his teeth.

As he turned onto the Westport road, Wyatt gazed across the fjord, and saw the water crinkle in a gust of wind. The scene was interruptied by a commotion in a nearby sports field. He pulled in beside the road and watched a group of men hitting a hurling ball around near some goalposts. They all wore working clothes, sleeves pulled up, and were raucous, swearing and laughing a lot. He spotted Tommy Joe's stocky torso, and Sergeant McSweeney, tall and elegant, cuffs rolled up on his blue shirt.

"Over the bar, said Lory Meagher." Tommy Joe shouted, and pucked one over from far out.

"There was only one Ringie, bhoy, and he came from Cork, and he knew where the goal was." McSweeney shouted, and let fly a low shot for the goal. It went wide.

"You big yahoo, you should go and get your eyes tested. Now Nicky Rackard, the Wexford giant, he would've had that shot bulgin' in the back of the net. " Tommy Joe bellowed at the Sergeant, who grinned back.

During a lull in play, Tommy Joe approached Wyatt, a hurley stick in each hand.

"So there you are Inspector, let's see what you're like in a man's game." Tommy Joe stuck a hurley in Wyatt's hand.

"I'll do my best, but it's not my cup of tea you know. I've never played in a real hurling game in my life."

"Look Inspector, we're in a fix, we're short a goalkeeper for the big game with Ballytoher next Sunday in Louisburgh. This is our final practice. Just get you over there between the sticks and we'll see what you're made of."

Wyatt peeled to his shirtsleeves, and walked towards the goal, musing. So the hurling match sponsored by Glencorrig mining company was happening on Sunday? He'd forgotten about it, but obviously the locals hadn't. And he also hadn't told Tommy Joe of the hours he'd spent in Trinity College in the summer evenings, pucking a sliothar about on the rugby pitch with some students from the country. He'd enjoyed the experience. It helped sharpen his reflexes for cricket, his first sporting love.

After a while he began to get the feel of the hurley in his hands, and the eye contact in connecting with the ball. He stopped a few, missed a few, but felt he'd done ok.

"We'll make a hurler of you yet." Said Tommy Joe, showing him the proper grip for holding the hurley.

When the practice was over, Tommy Joe came over and shook his hand.

"You're in Inspector. It's my call, I'm the captain. Be here for the bus at twelve on Sunday. Keep the stick and ball and get a bit more practice against the wall in the handball alley beyond the hotel."

"Ok Tommy Joe, thanks, I'll do that. It should be a bit of fun."

"Divil the bit of fun it'll be. It'll be war with that bloody Ballytoher shower. Out and out bloody war it'll be. In the ould days if we played in their place, and won, we'd be stoned on the way home. The same would happen to them if they beat us here. Old memories die hard around here. Anyway it's not often we get the chance to win a bit of silver in this place." Tommy Joe eyeballed him as he spoke.

"Ok, I get the picture." Wyatt spoke, and realised the match was like an All Ireland final to the locals. He tied the hurley to the crossbar, mounted his bike, and pushed down the road. His head felt clear again. But he felt a nervous pang inside, as Tommy Joe's words sank in.

Back in his room, he stared again at his draft report for

Halpin, and it finally hit him, what exactly he should write. He spent the rest of the day revising the data, and decided to put in a no- holds- barred account of the pollution problems.The plain, unadulterated truth it must be, he thought. After all that was what he was here to do. Or was it? Maybe he was just a pawn in a game, an expendable pawn. It was time for Seamus Halpin to realise something had to be done. No more cover ups, he vowed, of the polluted drinking water, the inefficient water treatment facilities, and the mass of rotting seaweed drifting on the shoreline. Something had to be done and quickly. Still, he *was* sticking his neck out. He felt as isolated as a curlew crying on the shoreline.

Wyatt sent off the report to Halpin the next morning, and rang Noel Kenny in the Mayo Times. He asked Kenny for more details of the meetings between the commercial company wanting to harvest the green lettuce tide into fish food for export, and the local Council. Kenny informed him that after two years the company had lost patience with the Council and sourced their needs abroad.

"Yes Mr Wyatt, I think I can get copies of the minutes of the meetings. Have you any news to supply in exchange?"

"Apart from me playing in goal in the big hurling game on Sunday, I've nothing much at the moment. I'll owe you one."

"Ok. I'm sure we're covering the game. Good luck. Wear your helmet." The phone went dead.

He then put in an hour of hurling practice in the nearby handball alley with a soft ball. He was exhausted after it, but felt his touch and reflexes improving.

After showering he felt revived, and headed for Bridie's mother's house to store a copy of the report. On the way to the Delphi Valley, he paused at Aasleagh Falls, and stared at the frothy torrent cascading into the brown waters of the river. In his mind's eye, he imagined large spotted salmon leaping high to climb the falls, striving to get back to the place where they were born, where they would spawn and repeat the never ending cycle of nature. He felt good as he thought these thoughts. They were his dream.

With the documents stashed away, he joined Bridie's mother for a cup of tea in the kitchen. The kettle sang as it boiled away on the hob. The oak table, covered with a flowery oilcloth, was set with her best willow pattern china. She told him she only took them out for visits by the parish priest or the doctor.

"I'm flattered to be in such company." He raised the cup to his lips.

"But Jim, did ye hear the terrible news?"

"No, what news is that?" He put the cup down with a start.

"Its bad news altogether it is. They killed Tommy Joe's dog Shep, they shot him dead they did. Such a lovely black and white sheepdog, he was. The best dog Tommy Joe ever had. Five years he had him. I've never seen Tommy Joe so upset, he was mad with the rage. He said he would kill whoever did it, and he was in such a terrible dark mood, I wouldn't put it past him." She brushed a tear from her eye as she spoke.

"What.... but who shot the dog? And when did it happen?"

"God knows who did the deed, and bad cess to them anyway, whoever they are. It was only last week it happened."

"Why would anyone do such an awful thing?"

"God alone knows." She shrugged forlornly.

"Did Tommy Joe report it to the Garda?"

"I don't know. He said he'd deal with it in his own way, whatever that means, I don't know." She sniffled into her handkerchief.

"Thanks for letting me know anyway. I appreciate that."

"Sure, why wouldn't I? Aren't you like one of the family?"

"Thank you. By the way, how is Bridie? I haven't spoken

to her in ages."

"No more than I have. She spends every blessed moment with Francie. And she's practising for a dance they're having in the hall after the hurling match on Sunday. Would you be goin' to the game to support the parish?"

"Believe it or not I'm playing in the match, in goal. They're hard up for a keeper."

"Musha, that's grand news. I'll tell everyone. You'll get a great cheer from me."

"You mean you're going all the way to Louisburgh for the match?"

"I wouldn't miss it for all the tea in China. For sure I'm going, wild horses won't stop me."

"Ok, but I hope you're not disappointed. Please give my regards to Bridie. I'm off now." He ducked out the door, waving as he went.

Next day a letter arrived with an English stamp. Wyatt's pulse raced as he thumbed it open. It was from Jenny. To her her coy, shy one of her heart. She apologised for not writing sooner. Her mother had taken ill. She missed him a lot. Her editor liked her piece on Yeats, and she hoped to enveigle her into allowing another trip to Ireland to flesh out the story. She would let him know when, and hoped he would write soon. He resolved to do that, and remembered he owed his own mother a letter. He decided to write to both after the match. No need to get carried away, he thought. Once bitten, twice shy, shy one.

Sunday came grey and overcast, rain and high winds forecast. A nervous knot niggled in his stomach, as he walked to the village, where the bus was parked. His hurley stick was gripped tight in his fingers. Can't let the side down, he thought, all eyes would be on him. The Inspector, the outsider. A wet ball could make his life hell. A mistake could cost the match. No hiding place in goal either. Inside the packed bus with the other players, his nerves subsided, as he sensed they too were edgy. Tommy Joe moved about the bus, cajoling the younger players.

Wyatt was impressed, and thought Tommy Joe a natural leader, and held in high respect. He envied him his composure.

The rain started just as the bus took off into the Delphi valley, fumes belching from its rear. As it passed the Famine monument at Doolough, a torrent peppered the panes, and Wyatt tried to look out. The mountains lurked above, mist covered on top, streams tumbling down their sheer sides into the dark lake below.Doolough. The bus made slow progress, between the pelting rain, and the shivering sheep huddling for shelter along the roadside.

Before they took the field, Wyatt saw a pile of yellow plastic helmets on the floor of the dressing room. He sifted through them, trying them on, until he found one that fitted him. He glanced around, and saw that many of the team, including Tommy Joe, were not wearing helmets.

"Say Tommy Joe, why isn't everyone wearing one of these?"

"Musha, why would we want to Inspector? Haven't we our hurleys to protect us? It's a man's game we're playin' you know. We don't want the enemy to think we're scared of them, do we? Still, it's your call, if you want to wear one."

Wyatt was impressed with the numbers watching the game, in spite of the deluge. The crowd was spread around, trying to shelter from the rain and the rising gale force wind. The Leenane supporters waved red flags and banners, and sat in the only stand. The Ballytoher crowd, in green colours, faced them, bedraggled and exposed, on the opposite side of the pitch. The flags on the flagpoles flapped fiercely in the wind.

In the dressing room Tommy Joe jumped up and down, and used every swear word Wyatt had ever heard, and many more, as he tried to lift the team before they took the field, and swished his hurley stick back and forth for effect. Wyatt donned his yellow goal keeper's jersey, nerves knotting in his stomach. The rest of the team put their red jerseys on, and ran onto the pitch, like gladiators into the arena. The crowd cheered.

Pools of water had gathered on the muddy pitch. Wyatt felt his studs sinking into the squelchy surface, as he sprinted to the goal at the Louisburgh end, and donned his gloves. He looked up into the stand, and saw Bridie's mother waving a flag in his direction. Bridie was beside her, engrossed in serious talk with Francie. Neither looked his way.

Wyatt was surprised to see that Father Flynn was the referee. The priest called Tommy Joe, and the Ballytoher captain, the big redhead McFadden, to the centre of the pitch, and told them he would tolerate no shenanigans, to play the ball not the man, and behave in a sporting manner. They both nodded their heads, saying nothing. Eamon Carney, the owner of Glencorrig mining, stood in the centre of the pitch, holding an umbrella blown inside out in one hand, and threw the ball in to start the game with the other, before he scampered off.

*Early on, a high ball drops in the centre of the pitch, between a group of players, who pull together on the ball in mid-air, to a resounding crack. Ash clashes with ash, and bits of broken hurleys splinter the air. The crowd roars. Wyatt sees players digging each other in the ribs with their hurleys, even though the ball is elsewhere. It seems normal to them. Players played without helmets too, fearless going for the ball, and miraculously escaping injury most of the time.*

*As he watches the play, Wyatt flaps his hands to keep warm. The pitch churns into a sea of mud, the rain and wind unrelenting. Physical contact grows. Father Flynn separates the players time and again, warning some of eternal damnation, if their behaviour and language doesn't improve. Nip and tuck. Score for score, all points, no goals. Wyatt has no shots to save. Tommy Joe keeps their dangerman, the huge redhead, marked out of the game. Halftime comes, the game all square. In the second half Leenane are playing against the gale. Tommy Joe is in the dressingroom, giving everyone a bollocking, turning the air blue. He wants more effort, a helluva lot more. A helluva fuckin' lot.*

*The second half is barely started, when Wyatt makes his first save. A low shot comes in from a distance. He stops, lifts, and clears the sliothar, as the forwards rush in. He's looking in satisfaction at the sliothar sailing upfield, when a thump in the back leaves him flattened, and winded in the mud. He looks up, gasping for air, and sees the giant redhead, McFadden, towering above him, then spitting on the ground, and saying:*

*"Get up, ye fuckin' yellow- livered bastard. There's nothing wrong with you a tall. You're as yellow as the jersey you're wearin'." Then he spits again on the ground.*

*Wyatt opens his mouth, but no sound comes out. A few minutes later he's back on his feet. Tommy Joe comes over and whispers not to worry he'll sort the bollocks out. Wyatt nods, stumbles back to his goal, as Tommy Joe takes the free out.*

*Soon a high ball drops into Wyatt's goalmouth. An almighty schemozzle follows, hurleys flailing all around, the sliothar sticking in the mud. The ball finally comes to rest in front of Wyatt, as McFadden flies in pursuit, then trips, and his unhelmeted head lands beside the ball on the ground, right in front of Wyatt, poised with hurley raised high above his head to hit. Wyatt sees his moment for revenge, but he hesitates. Then Tommy Joe whacks his hurley into McFadden's head from the other side, shouting" fuckin' bastard". McFadden is stretchered off, pumping blood from his head. The referee is apparently unsighted, and Tommy Joe escapes unpunished.*

*The momentum swings in Leenane's favour. Only three minutes left, and they lead by three points, mainly due to Sergeant McSweeney's sharpshooting. Then Tommy Joe makes his only mistake, slipping, and lets his marker through. The forward goes for the equalising goal, shooting low and hard for the corner of the net. Wyatt guesses rightly, and gets his stick to the sliothar, deflecting it around the post for a sixty. The sixty is pointed, but the final whistle goes, Leenane winning by two points. Its over. Wyatt is relieved. He's kept his goal intact.*

As the teams trudge off, Wyatt is elated, his mind spinning. Apart from his team winning he'd kept a clean sheet with no disastrous mistakes. He saw Bridie's mother waving in the stand, and waved back. Bridie was not beside her. The rain still poured down.

Back in the dressing room, Tommy Joe shook Wyatt's hand, saying:

"You saved my arse there, and no mistake, Inspector, at the end, and me slippin', lettin' that fecker through like that."

"I suppose I just guessed right, Tommy Joe."

"You did for sure, Inspector. You'll never guess what that bastard McFadden said at the end, that fuckin' big bollocks, when I went to shake his hand, and him with the big bandage on his crown, and the big red splotch on it like the risin' sun."

"No, what did he say?"

"Shake hands", he says, "I'd rather shake hands with a hape of dung." And then he spat on the ground in front of me." Tommy Joe chortled as he spoke." Mind you, he thinks 'twas you split him open, so watch out in future. He's a bad bastard, and no mistake."Tommy Joe's eyes twinkled as he spoke.

"I will keep my eyes peeled, thanks."

Finally, back at the Parochial Hall, the formalities of speeches, and presention of the cup by Eamon Carney were completed. Carney congratulated Father Flynn on his refereeing, before announcing his company would be making a large donation to the Parish building fund. Carney said he hoped the match would become an annual event, with next year's game being held in Ballytoher. Eamon Halpin, the Councillor, thanked Glencorrig Mining for their generosity, praising their work, and spelt out the jobs potential. Father Flynn said nothing.

Then all eyes turned to the Irish dancers up on the

stage, heads high, legs kicking in the air. Wyatt couldn't keep his eyes off Bridie. She looked stunning in green and black, and danced with elegance. Did she glance in his direction? He wondered. Maybe, he couldn't be sure. When the dancing finished, Tommy Joe announced, to raucous cheering, that courtesy of Eamon Carney they could now adjourn to Traynor's pub to fill the cup. Drinks would be on the company, of course.

The packed pub buzzed, under a smoke haze, as young musicians belted out Irish music in the corner, mostly drowned out by the babble of voices. Drinks at the bar flowed as fast as the music. The world and his wife were there. The air was wild, cut with excitement and celebration. Wyatt downed his drink, as Tommy Joe thrust the brimming cup into his hands.

"There you are Inspector. Get that down yeh. This is going to be a night to remember. I can feel it in me waters."

Wyatt swigged a mouthful of the lethal concoction. He noticed Father Flynn approaching, and offered him the cup.

"No thanks, not my chalice you know. Never touch the devil's brew." Father Flynn then turned to Tommy Joe.

"On reflection you got off lightly that time you split Mc Fadden open, Tommy Joe. It should have been a free- in, and a sending- off. But I reckon he had it coming. My father always said it was a dangerous thing to put a hurley in the hands of an Irishman. Now I know why." Father Flynn winked.

"He had it coming for sure, Father. You did the right thing. God will reward you." Tommy Joe chuckled, and winked back.

"Perhaps God will, Tommy Joe, but it's still on my conscience. I want you to say ten decades of the Rosary as your penance for the incident. Promise me you'll do it." He eyeballed Tommy Joe, whose mouth dropped.

"Of course Father, I swear on a hape of bibles." Tommy Joe spluttered.

"A nice cash windfall to the parish too, thanks to Glencorrig Mining." Wyatt continued.

"I'm not happy about that. There's bound to be a price to pay. Nobody asked them for their money. I've a bad feeling about that, it's like selling your soul to the devil. I'll take my leave now I've a funeral in the morning." The priest said, and discreetly left by the back door.

Sergeant McSweeney then approached Wyatt with a pint in each hand.

"There you are bhoy, take that. Fair play to you, your save at the end was important. How's the back?"

"I just guessed right Sergeant. It was a team effort. Your points made the difference at the end. The back's a bit stiff though, but the drink is easing the pain, I guess." He laughed as he quaffed the beer.

The Sergeant leaned over, after first checking that nobody was earwigging.

"I've been revisiting the Frank Duffy file, to see if any new clues might hit me, but divil the bit. I might be able to get you some details, though, if you could supply some information, in exchange, you know like. Exchange is no robbery." The Sergeant winked as he spoke.

"Well now, that's an offer I can't refuse. Let me check it out, I'll let you know."

"You do that bhoy." The sergeant nodded, and drifted into the crowd.

Wyatt gazed at Bridie. She stood near the turf fire, wearing a green dress, accompanied by a group of girls. He guessed they were all part of the dancing troupe. When saw her heading towards the bar, he squeezed in behind her, and tapped her shoulder.

"Say Bridie, I want to tell you how much I enjoyed the dancing tonight. It was great, and so were you, I …I mean you looked great."

"Flattery will get you nowhere. But thanks anyway, Jim. You're the dark horse, and no mistake, with you comin' down here from the city to show us the art of hurlin'. Are there any more strings to your bow?"

Before he could reply, Francie interrupted, and pulled her away to a group of his cronies. He seemed the worse for drink. Wyatt thought she was annoyed by Francie's interruption, as she rolled her eyes to the heavens. But maybe the drink was blurring his judgment? Then he noticed a big man with a cowboy hat and red chequered shirt sitting alone at a table in a corner, and ambled over to him.

"Mind if I join you? Pete isn't it? I met you out panning for gold back of Croagh Patrick if I remember right."

"You sure do dude, sit yourself right down there. Reckon I remember you too from out in the valley. I get to meet a lot of people in my game you know. I'm from the Lone Star state, where you can meet pretty sen-yo-ritas by the score from down south of the border." His handshake crushed Wyatt's fingers.

"Just call me Jim. We've got something in common. Neither of us are locals."

"You're right there dude. Let's drink to that." They downed their drinks, and refills magically appeared on the table.

"How'd you get into mining?"

"Started off bustin' horses in Dallas, then wrestlin' steers at Rodeos, then workin' the oil rigs, then dang it I saw this ad for a mining company, and never looked back since. Love it I do."

Wyatt was deep in conversation with the Texan, when a hand grabbed his shoulder, and pulled him around. When he spun about, McFadden stood before him, his head covered in bandages, and a crimson splotch spreading in the middle.

"So you're the one who did it. You fuckin' yellow-bellied bastard. Hit a man when he's down would you? We've fuckin' waited seven hundred years to get your likes out of this country, an' send you back across the water where you came from." McFadden seesawed on his feet as he spoke.

"Look I'm as Irish as you are, and I didn't hit you on

the ground either, though I can't say I'm too sorry for your troubles." Drink now fanned Wyatt's bravado.

McFadden lunged forward, grabbing Wyatt by the shirt, and pushed him hard across the table, scattering drink and glasses on the floor. Wyatt hit his head on the wooden floor, and lay there dazed and immobile, his back aching. His hands bled from the broken glass. The man was powerful. Wyatt looked up, eyes blurred, as the red giant leered down at him.

"Get up and fight like a man. Let's see yer yellah belly." McFadden reached down and tore Wyatt's shirt. The music and talk had stopped, and silence sliced the air. The crowd moved away.

The big Texan rose, went over to the band, took the Bodhran drum in his hands, and ambled back to McFadden.

"Ever play one of these dude?" He held the Bodhran in front of McFadden's face with his left hand.

"Can't say I have yank, so fuckin' what?"McFadden sneered.

"Well, you're dang well goin' to now, don't you mess with big Pete's friends." The big Texan said and smashed his hand through the leather casing, onto McFadden's nose, causing an instant eruption of blood, mucus, and gristle. McFadden fell to the floor clutching his face, and swore. A melee broke out in the bar, but Sergeant McSweeney quickly calmed things down. Soon some of McFadden's cronies came, and helped him off the floor, swearing revenge, as they left the pub. People drifted back to the bar, and continued drinking, but the atmosphere was now subdued. Wyatt bade the big Texan goodnight, saying his right hand would be the envy of Mike Tyson, and quietly made his way home to the hotel, sore all over but satisfied. Tommy Joe was right, he thought. It had been a night to remember.

# Chapter 12

## *Out on the Ocean*

The day began badly with Seamus Halpin phoning early. Although Wyatt was expecting the call, his confidence had ebbed.

"James, I've got your report in front of me. Look, I'm as shocked as you must be. It's like a bolt from the blue. I can't believe it after all the other good reports, are you sure there hasn't been a mistake?"

"No Seamus, those are the facts."

"Hmmm, this is not good, not good at all. We need to have an urgent meeting, and Finance Department are on my case again. They want to know when the project will be wound up. Well, what say you?" Wyatt pictured Halpin, chewing his pipe, drumming his fingers on the table, as he replied.

"Look, all I need is a few more weeks. I need to do more checks on land and sea. After that we can meet."

"Ok James, two weeks it is, and then we must have our wrap-up meeting. Agreed?"

"Yes, agreed."

Wyatt put down the phone, fuming. Halpin had been curt. Wrap up meeting? I don't think so, he thought. Halpin doesn't like bad news, but who does? Of course his brother is involved too. But what did he expect for God's sake? If he only knew half of what *hadn't* been sent to him. It's the real world down here, for God's sake. But Wyatt worried he'd stuck his neck out too far, and feared it might end up being chopped off. The hell it would, he vowed. Seamus Halpin wouldn't be pulling any plug until he said so. But Wyatt wondered if he was saying the words to reassure himself, as inside he felt more isolated than at any time since he'd arrived in Leenane.

In his mail he found a notice saying the next meeting

with Glencorrig Mining would be held on Friday evening in the Parish Hall. He noted this in his diary, and rang Sergeant McSweeney.

"Hello Barry, I trust you've recovered from Sunday's match?"

"The fracas afterwards in the bar was far worse. I had to restrain a few IRA latchicos from joining in the melee. They were friends of McFadden, and my knuckles are still raw."

"Thanks for the help. Do you remember our conversation in the bar about Frank Duffy, my predecessor down here?"

"Yes, I remember, have you got something?"

"Well...yes I might have. It may or may not be related."

"Shoot."

"First, do I get a copy of your file on the late Mr. Duffy?"

"Well ok, I can offer a précis of the file. What've you got?"

"Tommy Joe's dog was shot last week."

"That's bad news, but it was never reported. I hope Tommy Joe is not going to take the law into his own hands. Anyway, what's that to do with the Duffy case?"

"I don't know, but it might have. People don't usually go around shooting dogs."

"No bhoy, I'll grant you that."

"Have there been any similar incidents in the past few years?"

"No, not that I can recall, I'll check further though. Ok, you'll have your information by the end of the week, but I want more stuff later. Let's say what you've given me was a down payment."

"Ok, thanks Barry." Wyatt put the phone down, relieved.

With the weather set fair, he rang Tommy Joe, booking a trip later that week to check out mussel farming in the fjord and Clew Bay. Tommy Joe said he was flat out but would fit him in. After he'd put the phone down, Wyatt's mind drifted back to his words with Seamus Halpin. Time *was* running out. He knew he should be glad to get back to Dublin in one piece, but somehow he wasn't.

In his mail he found an envelope from The Mayo Times. Inside were copies of the minutes of meetings about the rancid sea of green lettuce. Wyatt scanned through the pages, which covered a two year period, then re-read everything. It appeared Ned Halpin was involved big time in opposing the offer to buy the rotting seaweed for fishmeal exporting. Halpin had been arguing for a better price from the company. The matter had dragged on, until the company finally lost patience, and sourced its requirements abroad. Meanwhile the problem of the green foetid seaweed tide remained unresolved. All talk, and no action. Dear God what next? He fumed, frustrated at what he was reading.

That night Wyatt wrote a letter to his mother, hoping to see her soon, and recounted details of the hurling match. Not that she'd appreciate any of that, he thought. His mother had been more into equine sports than the rough- and- tumble of hurling. She'd been a good show jumper in her youth. When he'd finished, he sent his promised letter to Jenny. In it he said he hoped she'd return soon, and that he'd missed her too, and wanted to learn more about Yeats. He hoped her mother was in better health. At the end, he mentioned his project could finish in a month, and he hoped she'd be back before then, signing off with lots of hugs. That night in bed, he thought a lot about Jenny.

Fleeting clouds flashed crazy shadows across the mountains by the fjord, as Wyatt set out in Tommy Joe's boat. They set the lobster pots, and the boat was steered west into the open sea. Michael, silent as usual, was busy in the stern. They stopped to let Wyatt get samples near some mussel beds in the fjord, his research indicating water pollution was more likely there. Soon Clare Island loomed ahead like a giant whale, and memories of his first sea journey with Tommy Joe hit Wyatt, bad memories, nauseous memories.

"Better weather this time than the last, Inspector." Tommy Joe said, smiling.

"You could say that, I suppose." Wyatt replied, wondering if Tommy Joe had read his mind.

"The mackerel are about." Tommy Joe nodded at the nets bulging behind the boat, below the squawling gulls. He cut the engine while he and Michael emptied the nets, then they put the nets back in the water, and set off again.

"We have company." Tommy Joe shouted, and nodded towards the wash of the vessel. Wyatt saw fins jutting out of the swell.

"Dolphins, they know where the fish are. We always get them in the mackerel season. They're a scourge, they'd eat you out of house and home." Tommy Joe said.

"That's ok, I like Dolphins, but I thought at first they were sharks."

"Smarter'n shithouse rats they are, they'd take your catch in the blink of an eye. We do get the sharks betimes. Not the big ones though, only porbeagle or blue. The Uncle Jack now, he used to fish for the big ones, the basking sharks, over yonder in Achill, way back in the sixties. They caught them in currachs of canvas. Man that was exciting, they were monsters. Wet yourself, you would, and worse. It sorted the men from the boys that kind of fishin' did. I got to go once with him as a lad, an' I'll never forget it, never." As Tommy Joe spoke, he had a faraway gleam in his eyes.

The boat moved smooth around Old Head, into the jaws of Clew Bay, dotted with drumlin islands.

"There are an awful lot of islands out there." Wyatt observed.

"One for every day of the year, they say. At least you don't have to pay to enter the bay, like when Grace O'Malley, the Pirate Queen, she ruled the roost from over yonder on Clare Island. A warrior woman she was." Tommy Joe replied, his jaw jutting proud.

When Tommy Joe stopped again to empty the mackerel haul, Wyatt gazed out to sea. White sails bent in the breeze at the mouth of the bay, and far out, framed on the rim of the ocean, fishing boats hunted fishy shoals in furrowed waves.

Croagh Patrick drifted by, on the port side, cone proudly pointing to the heavens. They came then to the mussel beds, took water samples, and berthed at Westport for lunch.

When they got back to Leenane late in the evening, the half-light of twilight was all around, and the sun was playing rainbow tricks on the placid waters of the fjord. Wyatt took his rucksack off the boat, paid Tommy Joe, and turned to leave, pleased that the weather had been benign this time.

"You see Inspector this is the kind of life it is here. There's ships out there, sailing far out on the ocean, big ships with big nets, that's takin' our livin' away from us. They get the riches, but we have to work like slaves to make ends meet. Sold out we were again big time, but still I wouldn't change my life, even if I could. There's nothin' else I'd rather be doin'."

"You're right Tommy Joe, money isn't everything." Wyatt waved goodbye, and turned down the road to the hotel.

\*\*\*

The Glencorrig meeting was a fractious affair. The hall was thronged, and Wyatt reckoned the hurling match had galvanised the people, with everyone hell bent on a gold rush with jobs and money to beat the band. Ned Halpin, the local Councillor kicked off proceedings, grovelling to Carney for sponsoring the hurling match, and helping with the Church Building Fund. A new day was dawning etc...etc... Pathetic drivel, Wyatt thought, but he could see the crowd's eyes out on sticks, drooling at the prospect of money for nothing.

Wyatt spoke next, aware it might get him into hot water with his bosses in Dublin. He spoke of the negative environmental impact of open cast mining, including its long term implications for the area, and future generations. Eight thousand tons of gold-bearing ore would be taken from the valley, using cyanide, which would poison the soil and the waters. It would be an utter disaster for the countryside, he said. He saw blank stares come on the faces in the crowd, and knew he was losing. They weren't hearing his words, they weren't even listening, and they didn't want to know. Glencorrig Mining was in the driving seat. He sat down to lukewarm applause. A hollow feeling came in his stomach, as he realised his voice was like that of one lost in the wilderness.

Carney, the Glencorrig boss took the floor next, a smug smile framing his face. He believed there was a rosy future ahead for the people of Mayo. In the pipeline you might say, he joked. Recent assay tests were favourable, and it was a commercial find without doubt, and jobs would be created. But for how long, Wyatt wondered. And what will be left when they've gone, a crater in the ground? The company were waiting on planning permission from the Mayo Council, Carney continued, which Mr.Halpin had assured him would be forthcoming by the end of the month. He ended with an offer of free drinks back at the village bar, and the audience whooped with delight. Carney sat down, and his smug smile spread even wider. Wyatt felt deflated and disappointed.

Father Flynn spoke last, and proved the fly in the ointment. He said he would be returning the donation to Glencorrig Mining the next day, in case it was seen as a bribe. The audience gasped, stunned by his words. You mustn't sell your birthright for a mess of pottage the priest said, after all we were only keepers of the land for future generations. We would pass on, but the land would remain, and the valley behind Croagh Patrick was holy ground where St Patrick had fasted and prayed. We should venerate the ground and St. Patrick's memory, not desecrate it. It was a symbol of the people's religious history and hopes, on the upward journey towards God and Heaven. Short term was short sighted the country was being ruined by everyone thinking short term. Greed and self interest was everywhere, and we must respect the land that God has given us. The devil dances in many dresses, and we should remember what happened to the scandal-giver? The priest stated he would start a petition that week in the parish against the mining project, and hoped it would spread countywide, then countrywide. He sat down to polite applause, but Carney's face was dark, and full of fury.

***

Wyatt elbowed his way to the bar to order a pint. He felt someone tap his shoulder, and turned to see McSweeney beside him.

"Can I get you a drink Sergeant?"

"Ok, you do that. I'll wait over in the corner, where we can talk a bit."

"There you are it's great to get a table away from the din, and with a bit of privacy." Wyatt handed him a pint, glanced around, and sat down.

"Here's a copy of a write up on the hurling game, hot off the press. You got a favourable mention in it Inspector."

Wyatt started. It was the first time the Sergeant had called him by his nickname.

"Yes, and that's what they called you in the paper too, bhoy. It has a certain ring to it, and I certainly wouldn't mind being called that in my job." McSweeney grinned as he spoke.

"I get it, and did you get an honourable mention too?"

"Indeed I did, they said I had a Christy Ring- like sharpshooting ability. Now if you're from the banks of the Lee, that's praise indeed, Ringy he was my hero. You can call me Barry, by the way." The Sergeant said, smiling.

"The mining meeting was tough going tonight, Barry. How do you think it will end?"

"God knows Inspector, money talks, but Father Flynn has God on his side. The planning decision is at the end of the month, that'll tell a tale."

"I suppose, how do you think that will go?"

"Who knows? I haven't a clue, but I do have something here for you, wrapped in this newspaper. I couldn't trust anyone else to deliver it, even the walls here have ears." McSweeney said, glancing about as he spoke.

"What is it?"

"Hush while you talk, will you. Even with the noise in here, you never know who might be earwiggin'. It's the bloody report on Duffy you clown, what did you think it was?"

"Ok sorry, I should have figured that."

"Yes, and I suggest you leave here straight away and deposit this report in a safe place, I'm taking a big risk even bringing it here."

"Thanks Barry, I'll take that advice." Wyatt exited the pub hastily, the report tucked under his arm, and rushed back to the hotel.

In his bedroom, Wyatt's hands trembled as he took the folder from the newspapers. Before reading its contents, he poured a large whiskey, aware he was breaking his resolution. After knocking it back, he started reading, and refilled the glass. Duffy had been in the area for three years, working on environmental issues. He was well known and liked, and was into hunting and fishing, and was a good wingshot. Duffy had become friendly with some republicans, through his girl friend, but she was not named. Dammit, why not? He read on. Duffy went fishing regularly in Tommy Joe's boat. The report concluded his disappearance was highly suspicious, but people were reluctant to step forward and give information. I wonder why? Wyatt scratched his head, poured another drink, and re-read the report.

He paced the floor, pensive, and wondered if he'd be better off out of Leenane. Get out before it's too late, better a live chicken than a dead duck. But he wanted to find out more, and he now knew Tommy Joe knew something about the Duffy case. At least he could trust Tommy Joe, but he needed to move fast. He felt as a fly must feel trapped in a spider's web.

# Chapter 13

## *Mist Covered Mountain*

Wyatt smiled, at last the day he'd waited for had arrived. He'd worried would it come before Halpin pulled the plug on the project, and now felt relieved and exuberant. The reality of being into his third month in Mayo sank in, as he watched the rising sun glinting on the mountain, filling his heart with hope for the day ahead.

He knew his time was running out, but he'd studied the weather charts, and waited, and waited, hoping for such a day. It had come mid week too, with less people about. Perfect. Though it was more pleasure than business, he'd brought water sample containers to salve his conscience. He filled his rucksack with drink cartons, and sandwiches. It would be a long day, and a good supply of liquids was vital.

After packing the wet gear in his rucksack, Wyatt checked that his compass, map, and binoculars, were in his pockets. Then he mounted his bike, and sped towards the mountains near the Delphi Adventure Centre, the air brightening all the time. As he glided along, his mind drifted back to Jenny's letter. Excitement tingled in his veins, as he thought of her coming visit, and he wondered how it might go. He felt positive, and everything seemed good in his world, as he skimmed along the deserted road.

Mweelrea, bald grey hill, High King of the Connacht Mountains, reigned majestic over Killary fjord, and backed onto a vast valley surrounded by Ben Lugmore and Ben Bury. He reckoned it would be a horseshoe climb, straddling all three peaks. It was not a climb for the faint hearted, or one to do when the weather was bad. Even on a good day, mist could drift in without warning, and shroud the mountain in a flash. But he had done his homework, and felt today was just the right kind of day to climb it.

Blood pumped through his veins, as he pedalled along the potholed road, the breeze brushing his face. Mweelrea towered ahead, proud, enticing, and gigantic. The mountain attracted him onwards, in some magnetic way. It looked cloud free, but for a thin white veil near the top. His luck seemed to be in, and he pedalled even harder.

Wyatt left his bike locked at the Adventure Centre, and followed a flinty path, flanked by dead rhododendron bushes, until he reached a stone arched bridge, starting his trek from there. After climbing an iron gate into an evergreen forest, he passed some of the Adventure Centre's climbing exercise equipment.

Further on, he crossed a footbridge over a stream, and stopped to observe a hawk, hunting over the bank of the stream. It hovered over its prey, and minutes passed, before it fell like a stone to the ground, and glared around, yellow eyed, defiant, before flying away, a small dead bird in its talons. Wyatt realised then that danger was never far away, even in such a beautiful place. He wished he had the hawk's defiance and survival instincts.

He trod a grassy path by the banks of a river, and passed near to a pine forest. Small waterfalls cascaded in the river, and holly trees sprouted on the banks, near a wildflower wilderness where Mombretia grew in orange clumps between Foxgloves and Cowparsley parasols. Soon he'd entered the shadows of the forest, hoping to find a trail straight through it, but instead the undergrowth thickened, and became squelchy underfoot.

His walking clothes were drenched when he tripped over a wire fence embedded in the marshy grass. Damn, I should have worn my wet gear, he muttered. Soon he left the forest, and crossed the river into open countryside, moving over wet, tussocky bogland, the going getting heavier. He paused for a drink, and sat on a boulder in the centre of the glen, and let the sun dry his clothes, before donning his wet gear. He gazed ahead, and saw Mweelrea looming at the end of the glen, silhouetted against a blue sky, a veil of cloud still on its top. As he strode forward, he felt hypnotised by the mountain, and took a pathway left of the centre of the glen.

Wyatt moved up over more boggy tussocks, past enormous ice age boulders, and stopped to check his map. After walking parallel to a stream, he continued towards a gap in the skyline to the left of the mountain. When he'd reached the end of the glen, he passed some scree under the cliff, and climbed until he reached the gap. He glanced at his watch, and couldn't believe that nearly three hours had passed since he'd begun his journey. At that moment his nerves jangled, when he heard muffled sounds echoing from the far side of the glen, like a series of dull thuds. Like gunshots.

Wyatt paused by a rock, removed his rucksack, and placed it on a flat stone behind him, took out his binoculars, and lay on his stomach at the edge of the sheer cliff face, scanning the terrain. He spied a small group, partly hidden behind a rock outcrop, on the other side of the valley, beneath Ben Lugmore. He stood up then to get a better view, focussing the binoculars. He recoiled, as he made out six people, faces covered in balaclavas, all armed with rifles, firing at targets lined up against the mountainside.

Wyatt could see the recoil of the rifles on their shoulders, but no sound came until the bullets struck the targets. Silencers, he surmised. Just then, one of the group, large in stature, turned, and began scanning the valley with his binoculars. He must be the lookout, Wyatt thought, and wondered why the man looked familiar. The big man froze, then focussed again, zoning in on where Wyatt stood. For sheer seconds the man seemed to be looking straight into Wyatt's eyes. In a flash, he'd dropped the glasses, and raised a rifle to his shoulder. Wyatt dived to the ground. There was no sound, but he heard the hum of bullets as they zinged overhead, and whacked into the rockface behind him, ricocheting all around.

When he peered again over the edge of the cliff, the big

man was bounding with giant steps in his direction. Then it hit him who he was, as he recognised McFadden's shape and gait from the hurling match. And it hit Wyatt too that the giveaway must have been the rising sun in the East reflecting on *his* binoculars. A complete giveaway, what a fool he was, he fumed, gritting his teeth.

Wyatt bent fast to pick a spent bullet from the ground, shoved it into his pocket, grabbed the rucksack and started to run. Panic had his heart in a vice, as he reckoned he had no more than an eight minute start on McFadden.

He sprinted up the sharp rise from the gap. It was so steep in places he had to grab tufts of grass in panic. Sweat poured from him, his breath rasping, as the extra layer of wet gear slowed him down. He looked backwards, saw the glen falling away below him, and guessed Mc Fadden was gaining ground on him, though he could not see him. Above, the summit was invisible in a mist cloud. He climbed onwards and upwards, breathing hard, and sucked in air that was alternately hot and cold, before passing the cairn at the top of Mweelrea.

As he moved quickly towards Ben Bury, visibility dropped all the time. When he looked back again, he thought he could see a large shadow in the mist not far away, barely discernible, but directly behind him.

Alarmed, he ran on up a stony, grassy slope, gasping for air, low rock outcrops jutting on either side. It was like walking on a knife edge, with sheer drops both sides, the mist thickening, and visibility reducing even more. A raven flew out of the mist, swishing close past his head, and honked harshly. He was startled and swore, as the bird of ill omen vanished into the mist. Don't panic, be defiant, he muttered the words, but inside panic welled, and he took a quick bearing on his compass, before moving on to where he reckoned Ben Lugmore should be.

When Wyatt climbed to a gap in the mountain, he looked below him into the huge hollow of Lugmore, Doo Lough lying invisible in the distance. He passed a cairn on the gap and his legs ached. Then as he travelled along a mist- enshrouded ridge, narrow and rocky, jagged and sharp in places, he stumbled over a heap of bones. At first he thought they were human remains, but later realised it was a sheep's carcass. What the hell was it doing at this height? He wondered, as he gasped in air.

A sheer drop into the hollow of Lugmore lay before him, and he realized he was spent. There was no choice but to make a stand there, for better or worse, even if he was the prey, and his hunter had a gun.

Wyatt gathered the dead sheep's bones into a pile at the edge of the cliff, took his yellow wet gear off, and covered the bones with it, in a human shape. Then he hid behind a nearby boulder, petrified, waiting, sucking in the dank air, a rock clutched tight in his fist. Minutes passed, before McFadden's hulking figure bounded from the mist, swearing as he approached.

The figure stopped when he saw the body shape in the yellow gear at the cliff edge, then raised his rifle and pumped a round into the inert figure, the clothes lifting with the impact of the bullets. The man left his gun on the ground, went over and knelt beside the body, and seemed to freeze in shock when he uncovered it.

Wyatt sensed his chance, gripped the rock hard, and quickly covered the space between them, smashing the rock hard onto the base of the giant man's neck. He fell, swearing, but seemed merely dazed, but groggy enough for Wyatt to grab his legs, and hoist him over the edge, into the mist- covered abyss.The body tumbled down, screams rending the air, before finally fading into silence. Wyatt stood and stared into the mist, gasping.

Moments later, Wyatt took the rifle from the ground, released an unspent bullet from it, and put it in his pocket. He flung the rifle as far as he could down the mountainside after McFadden's body, and stooped to retrieve his bullet-riddled wet gear from the ground. When he lifted the bullet-holed jacket, he started as he stared at the skeletal sheep's head in front of him, with its large teeth grinning at him, and the front two teeth shot out. No wonder McFadden was surprised, he thought. Better make tracks before his cronies arrive.

He grimaced before running through a jumble of scree and boulders, over a small gap, and climbed a slope to reach the summit of Lugmore. It was broad and grassy there, with a little cairn. After ascending above the mist into sunshine, he stopped for a drink, and checked his map and compass, and wondered how long it would be before McFadden's gang found the remains of the sheep skeleton, if at all. Would they keep chasing him? Maybe they would, maybe not.

He knew he had to rest as he was exhausted physically and mentally, but couldn't take a chance, and had to keep moving, though his heart felt frozen with fear. What had just happened was beginning to sink in, as he took another drink, and moved on. This must be what a hunted animal feels like, Wyatt thought.

The mist later lifted, and he looked back towards Mweelrea with his binoculars, but there was no sign of anyone. Good, he sighed, but he was still anxious to get off the mountain as quickly as possible. One never knew where they could be, they might have gone back through the centre of the glen to cut him off. After donning his bullet-punctured raingear, he dropped down a boulder-strewn slope, and left Ben Lugmore behind. Then he descended by a series of ridges past low rock outcrops, before stopping to study his map again.

Over six hours had gone since Wyatt had set out. He was jaded and decided to take a short cut, and avoid a way that dropped to a saddle before it climbed another hill until the road came in sight. Instead, he took a route which would take him out by the glen, and he would not have to climb again, but it was a mistake. The short cut proved a disaster, and soon became boggy and squelchy. Every few hundred yards he met gullies and ditches that brimmed with water from the run-off of forestry plantations. His porous wet gear didn't help either, as he tried to skirt around these drains. In the end he had to leap over them, or splash through the boggy, dirty water.

At last he came to a stream, and forded it, using boulders as stepping stones, and as he squelched through yet another boggy area, he came upon the dead rhododendron bushes he'd seen early that morning. The arched bridge next came into view, and soon he was back to where he had left his bike. He sighed with relief to see it safely there. When he mounted the bike, peaty water drained down the inside of his legs, making him feel even more wet and miserable. It had been a long day, and instead of feeling elated, he was wrung out and deflated.

Back in the hotel, Wyatt took a hot bath, and downed some hot whiskeys, before falling exhausted into bed. A fitful night of tossing and turning followed, with the nightmare chase across the mountains being relived over and over in his brain. He wondered if McFadden was dead or alive, if *he* had killed someone, and if Mcfadden's gang were after him. But in the end, he felt too tired to care. He was just glad to have survived the ordeal, and be alive.

Next morning he rang Sergeant McSweeney, and said he needed to speak to meet him urgently.

"What's it about, Inspector?"

"I can't talk on the phone, Barry. But believe me it's important."

"I believe you, give me half an hour."

Over coffee in the hotel lounge Wyatt recounted the previous day's events. The Sergeant took notes, muttering under his breath, before speaking at the end.

"Well Inspector, you sure stumbled on a hornet's nest this time. Are you sure it was McFadden you hit with the rock?"

"I'm as sure as I'm looking at you."

"And you hit him in self defence when he attacked you?"

"Yes, he was armed. He'd fired at me several times."

"Do you have any evidence?" Wyatt handed him the spent bullet.

"Here, is that evidence enough for you?" Wyatt still felt nervous and edgy.

"That's fine Inspector, I'm on your side, I know this fellah, and he's a nasty piece of goods all right. We'll need to find the rifle, though. Pity you threw it away, our forensic boys would have loved to get their hands on it. Right, now let's have your description of everything again, from scratch. You can make a written statement later." Wyatt recounted the details.

"Barry, I'd like to know why those people were firing guns in the valley."

"Practice, they move around so we can never catch them, and they use silencers. We know they're up to no good. Sometimes they use old army ranges for their exercises, and we do know they're at these manouevres, but people are afraid to report their activities to us. They're afraid of a backlash on them or their families if they did, until now, that is. You're the first one I've spoken to, who's had a face-to-face encounter with them. Believe me Inspector, you're a marked man from hereon, if McFadden survives, and if he recognised you. Do you think he did?"

"Yes, I'm sure he knew me, we seemed to eyeball each other for a split second. But I don't think he's alive, he couldn't be. Nobody could have survived that drop." Or could he? Wyatt wondered.

"We'll find out soon enough. I'll have a Search and Rescue team check the mountain around Lugmore straight away. In the meantime, take it easy, stay low, and be careful who you speak to. If you don't have a gun, I suggest you get one, somehow, and quickly."

"Thanks Barry, I'll think about that. One more thing, do you think there might be a connection with the disappearance of Frank Duffy?"

"Anything's possible, nothing's ruled out or in. Take care." McSweeney donned his hat, rose, and strode to the hotel door. He paused there, and turned to face Wyatt.

"By the way Inspector, there was a fire two days ago at

Tommy Joe's house. Nothing serious, nobody hurt. Tommy Joe and his brother were away fishing at the time. Bridie's mother spotted it and called the fire brigade in Westport, otherwise the damage could have been serious. Still, Tommy Joe seems to have had his fair share of bad luck lately, what with his dog being shot only a few weeks ago."McSweeney tipped his hat, and closed the door behind him.

Wyatt sat stunned in the chair, and his mind spun again from the events that had just occurred. He worried too about the workload to be done before his visit to Halpin in Dublin. McSweeney's words about him having to carry a gun, and thoughts of whether McFadden had copped it on the mountain, revolved in his head.

He was still trembling from the mountain ordeal, and everything just seemed unreal. He felt like murdering a drink, but decided first to contact Tommy Joe, as after all they were companions in bad luck. He guessed he would find Tommy Joe at his house, and cycled straight there.

"Bad luck Tommy Joe, any idea how it started?" Wyatt spoke, surveying the blackened roof of the cottage.

"No Inspector, I've no idea, but I'm damned if it was an accident."

"Why's that?"

"Let's just say I have my suspicions, but I'll keep them under my hat for now. It wouldn't have happened either if poor Shep were alive." Tommy Joe spat on the ground.

"Ok, I'm sure, are you still sleeping here?"

"And sure why wouldn't we? What harm would a bit of smoke do to anyone?"

Wyatt felt they had a common bond of tough luck, and told Tommy Joe of his adventures on the mountain. Tommy Joe listened intently, eyelids slitted, until Wyatt had finished.

"For sure you had a day of it, Inspector, bad cess to that bastard McFadden. Please God he got his due desserts, the cunt. Tell me, you said you gave a bullet to the Sergeant.

Do you have another one?"

Wyatt remembered the unmarked bullet he had taken from the rifle, and fished it out of his pocket.

"There." He tossed it to Tommy Joe, who caught it, held it up, and eyed it intently.

"Yes, it's in good nick, I'd like to keep it for a while."

"You're welcome."

"I'd like to mark your cards too about somethin'."

"Yes, what's that?"

"If it ever gets to court, you must say the bastard attacked you, and not that you ambushed him from behind."

"Why's that?"

"Because that's how the law is, Inspector. It's a fuckin' ass it is, but a little white lie sometimes does the trick. Otherwise his family'll come after you in the court."

"Ok, thanks for the advice Tommy Joe."

"You're welcome, and one last thing Inspector."

"What's that?"

"Be careful, an' watch your back. You'll need eyes in the back of your head from now on."

"Don't worry, I'll be on guard." Wyatt shouted back as he mounted his bike, and sped down the road.

Sergeant McSweeney phoned him next day, to say no trace had been found of McFadden's body, or his rifle, on Lugmore Mountain, or in the hollow. Wyatt decided it best to take the Sergeant's advice about getting a gun, and ring Seamus Halpin straight away. McSweeney had also offered, off the record, to recommend where Wyatt might get a pistol, and said he'd get back with the details, and about where Wyatt could get gun lessons.

"Thanks Barry."

"No problem bhoy. But keep all this under your hat, you hear, it's not official. We'll keep looking on the mountain. We haven't given up yet."

"That's good, you never know." But Wyatt felt deep down that no trace of McFadden would ever be found on the mist covered mountain.

# Chapter 14

## *Pay the Reckoning*

A week later, Jenny arrived at the hotel, resplendent in a green flowery dress. As she beamed at Wyatt, he thought her slimmer than before, and more alluring than he remembered. She kissed him on the mouth.

"Oh Jim, I'm so sorry about the lipstick, your shirt's a mess. Have I smudged my lips? I got carried away."She giggled.

"No problem. Nobody's going to be checking, are they? It's good to see you again, Jenny. Your mother's well I hope."

"She's as well as can be expected. The good news is this time I got a higher allowance from my bitchy boss, so I have my own room in the hotel."

"Great, let me carry your bags."

When they went over to the check- in Bridie was on duty. Wyatt remembered they hadn't spoken since the night of the hurling match. She looked up when they came in.

"Mrs Marsh so pleased you're staying here for two nights. We have got one of our best rooms reserved for you, please sign here. I see you don't need any help with your luggage."Bridie smiled, barely acknowledging Wyatt's presence.

"No dear, aren't I lucky? That's super about the room. Thank you so much."

After dinner that evening, they went straight to Jenny's room. While Jenny retired to the bathroom, Wyatt downed a double whiskey, and lounged on the couch, memories of the misty mountain nightmare receding. He wondered if Bridie knew Jenny was the same person who'd stayed in his room previously. Yes, he guessed she must know, yet she'd seemed friendly to Jenny, while staying distant with him. The ways of a woman's mind....hmmm. He took another swig.

Jenny returned, wearing a short white bath robe, and poured herself a Gin and Tonic. She came to the sofa, and sat on his knee, pecking a kiss on his cheek. Her skin was baby fresh, with a pink hue, after the bath, and the smell of her musk perfume was heavy in the air.

"What a lovely, friendly girl that was at reception." Jenny said.

"Yes, her name is Bridie, we're good friends."

"Not too friendly, I trust." Her eyebrows arched.

"No not at all. She's engaged to a local lad."

"I'm so glad to hear that Jim and you here all alone at night, I could be jealous." She moved in closer, the movement loosenening her bathrobe at the front, and revealing goosebumps on her skin. Wyatt smelt the perfume, and the Gin and Tonic in her mouth as they kissed, and her body pressed in on his in the shadows on the couch.

Later he awoke, and found himself lying on the floor of the bedroom, with Jenny propped on a pillow in the large bed, reading a book.

"Ah, awake at last my sleeping beauty. Care to join me? As we're both paying residents, I'm sure you can stay the night here."

"Yes, sounds a good idea, what are you reading?"

"It's a book on Yeats. I have to go to Sligo in a few days to do research for my book. I wangled it with my Boss.... the Bitch. Maybe you'd like to come as well Jim? It would really be fun if you came."

"I'd like nothing better, but I'll have to check my diary first."

"You do that then. Super." She giggled.

Wyatt decided then not to burden her with *all* the details of his adventure on Mweelrea. Instead he just said he'd climbed Connacht's highest mountain.

"Why did you want to climb it, Jim?"

"I don't really know. Maybe it was a challenge. Or

maybe it was for the fresh air, or just for the view. Let's say I was attracted to it…like I am to you." She laughed, as he touched her arm.

"Repentance keeps my heart impure." She said, as she put her arms around his neck, and pulled him nearer to her lips, closer to her body.

Next morning, Wyatt left the lounge, having read the newspapers. The headlines concerned another atrocity in the North. When will it ever end? He sighed. Then he spotted Jenny and Bridie, deep in conversation in the foyer. Inside he felt excited at the prospect of the days and nights ahead in Sligo, with Jenny.

"There's a phone call for you." Bridie called over to Wyatt.

"Who is it?"

"A Seamus Halpin, from Dublin, and he says it's urgent."

"Ok, I'll take it in my room" Damn, what's on his mind this time? He bounded up the stairs to his room, and picked up the receiver.

"James old boy, I've been thinking."

"Yes, about what Seamus?"

"Firstly, I've been trying but I can't get you a gun. It's against the rules as well, you know."

"I didn't know, actually."

"Look James, I'm on your side, you know that, but rules are rules."

"I'm sure."

"Look, I can't help you directly in this matter, but if you were to solve the problem locally, I believe I could get a cash subvention from Finance for a safety matter, such as a burglar alarm. A gun by any other name, get my drift?" Halpin's voice now had a confidential tone.

"Ok, I'll see what I can do down here."

"Ok James, glad that's sorted, but I need you in Dublin tomorrow for an urgent meeting. It's first thing in the morning, is that ok with you?"

"It is a bit sudden, I've got planned visits and

inspections down here. I'd have to cancel them, could we not put it off until next week?"

"No, I'm afraid not, there are things going on up here too. I'll fill you in tomorrow, and I'm sure you'd like to see your mother too." Wyatt paused before replying.

"Ok then, so be it, I'll be there." Wyatt banged the phone down, furious. There's the rub, he thought, the irony in Halpin's remark about his mother cutting him to the quick. Damn.

His plans with Jenny for Sligo were out the window too. He walked across the room, and sat on the bed, head in hands, trying to think ahead. He suspected Halpin was going to make his long- threatened termination of the project in the west. Gradually it hit him there was no doubt about it, the reckoning was nigh. At least there was time to prepare. He would travel to Dublin that evening, *and* he would visit his mother *after* the meeting with Halpin.

Later, after re-arranging his schedule, he went downstairs and noticed Jenny and Bridie still chatting and laughing at the reception desk.

"Sorry to intrude ladies, can I have a word Jenny, in the lounge?"

She followed him in, put her arms around his neck, and smiled as she hugged him hard. He withdrew, telling her he was sorry but he couldn't go to Sligo, and explained about Halpin's orders to leave immediately for Dublin. Her face furrowed in a frown.

"Why did you not put him off 'til next week luv?"

"I tried but he wasn't having any of it." The look on her face suggested he hadn't tried hard enough.

"I have to travel up tonight, I'm afraid." Her face looked even more downcast.

"I suppose it can't be helped, Jim." Tears welled in the corners of her eyes.

"Look, as I said I'm sorry Jenny. It wasn't planned."

"I know darling. But it....it's just so disappointing. The lies I had to tell to wangle this trip from that bitch." She snuffled into a handkerchief.

"Look, maybe you can make up a story to justify another trip?"

"Maybe, but perhaps you won't be here then?"

"I will, I promise. No matter what happens, I'll make it my business to be here."

"Promise?"

"Yes, promise, cross my heart." He kissed her slightly on the lips. As he lifted his head he noticed Bridie entering the room, and taking out some crockery.

That evening he cycled to Bridie's mother's house to collect the hard copies of the reports he'd stored there. It crossed his mind that a fire such as the one at Tommy Joe's house could destroy all his records there. All his work gone up in smoke. He needed to keep duplicate copies in a new location. Bridie's mother invited him for a cup of tea, saying Bridie had arrived, and asked would he mind if she joined them.

"Of course not, there's nothing I'd like better."

"That's good then, we'll be ready in a few minutes."

When he went into the kitchen, a plate of home- made scones and raspberry jam sat beside the tea pot on the table. Bridie was already sitting there, thumbing through a magazine.

"Yummy, my favourite scones. Good to see you again Bridie, when you're not working." She smiled back at him.

"And you too Jim, it's more relaxing here. Are you going back to Dublin?" She seemed concerned.

"Just for an urgent meeting, that's all. I need to see my mother too. I won't be staying here forever you know. Anyway, would you miss me anyway if I was gone?"

"Hmmm….actually…..probably yes. You've part of the furniture here now." She smiled then.

"Which part? On second thoughts, don't answer that."

"It's a good thing that you can visit your mother, I'll say a rosary for her." Bridie's mother said, as she poured the tea.They both waved him off later, hoping to see him soon. You will, he muttered, and waved back, as his bike wobbled down the road.

Before leaving for Westport station, he knocked on Jenny's door. She opened it, and let him in. She wore a grey track suit, with her hair tied back. Her computer lay open on a desk by the window at the back of the room. Her face was in a red rash, as if she'd been crying.

"Sorry for the mess, Jim. And for the way I'm dressed, it's the way I like to dress when I'm working. I find it better for writing, but the view from the window here can be distracting."

"You look fine, it's me should be sorry for messing things up."

"It's not your fault luv. The Bitch just rang. She's playing silly buggers again, she is. She wants me back straight away in Hull, so I couldn't have gone with you to Sligo anyway. I don't feel so bad about it now, but I *was* disappointed at first."

"I don't feel that bad now either, we'll make up for it some other time." He moved close to her and kissed her on the lips, embracing her.

"Now Jim, don't be getting carried away, you've a train to catch."

"Yes, I'm afraid I have." He could feel his control slipping, and felt in a few minutes it would be to hell with the train. But that wouldn't get the job done. He dragged himself away from her.

"Jim, I don't like dramatic farewells. You'll write to me, won't you, when all this has settled down? Please."

"Of course I will Jenny. You have my word." He picked up his suitcase.

"Super. I'll count the days." She blew him a kiss from the doorway as he rushed down the maple steps of the staircase.

Wyatt checked out of the Gresham Hotel in the morning, and walked down O'Connell Street in a drizzle, towards St. Stephen's Green. The scene was dismal, as rubbish blew about the street, in front of garish shop fronts. He glanced at the water- filled statue of Anna Livia in the centre of the street. James Joyce would be proud, he thought, the Floosie in the Jacuzzi. They'd got it right it fitted the image of the city centre like a glove, with the waste papers and packages floating in its waters.

Beggars hung out on corners, and people slept rough in doorways, while junkies shot each other up on the boardwalk of the river Liffey. Many had tattoos, and a lot had multiple piercings on their faces. It was depressing, Wyatt thought. God knows what the rest of their bodies must look like. He grimaced, and moved on. A blind lady was tapping her white stick on the kerb at the corner of Abbey Street, waiting to cross, and he helped her over.

Halpin had a new office, brighter and bigger.It was located the top of the building, with large windows, and a view over the rooftops of Dublin. He was ensconced behind a massive oaken desk, and a coffee machine gave a pleasant aroma around the room. It seemed Halpin had gone up in the world. Wyatt was impressed. Halpin had a person sitting on either side of him, like guardian angels. Hell, I wasn't expecting a tribunal, Wyatt muttered.

"James, grab a pew. Let me introduce my colleagues, John Doyle from Finance, and Roger White from Personnel." Halpin waved him towards an empty chair. Wyatt nodded in their direction, sat down, and placed his briefcase on the floor. He felt uneasy.

"The usual James? Coffee as black as the ace of spades? Wonderful gadgets these, I must say." Halpin said, pressing a button on the new machine.

"Hey presto." He placed the mug carefully on the mat in front of Wyatt. No fear of a stain on his new desk.

"Now let's get to business James. First Mr Doyle has agreed a supplementary budget for your personal safety. Is that correct, Mr Doyle?" Wyatt thought he detected a wink in Halpin's eyes.

"Yes indeed, staff safety is paramount." Doyle wore a black suit, herring bone, red tie, and a grim smile. His body language indicated he thought the safety funds budget a waste of money. You'd swear it was out of his own bloody pocket, Wyatt thought, immediately disliking the man.

"Now let's move on to other matters." Halpin rummaged through the pile of papers that littered his desk.

"There's good news and bad news I'm afraid to relate James. Shall we start with the good news first?"

"Yes please."

"Good, well your early escapade with the blown up boat and damaged fish cage has had a positive outcome."

"Really, tell me more." Wyatt wondered if Halpin was about to unveil the reason behind his elevated office status.

"Well James, it appears that when the young salmon, grilse I believe they're called, escaped from the damaged fish cage, some went out to sea, but some of the little beggars went upstream, much to the delight of the fishermen in the valleys above the fjord. They never had it so good for years, apparently, and catches shot up. We got favourable feedback that the fish- starved fishing tourists were delighted to catch anything, after paying so much money to fish here.

When we later told our colleagues in Brussels about the incident, they were impressed. In fact our French friends informed us that this was a *very* good idea. Apparently every year in the Pyrenees, in a place called....let me see...yes...*Cauterets,* I believe it's called, the locals restock all the rivers and lakes in the area. All highly organised of course, they even use helicopters. They recommended we should follow their example, and do the same each year in the west. We now have proposals prepared to implement this. Hopefully they'll be in operation in many places next year. My superiors are pleased with these developments, very pleased indeed." Hence the new office, and no doubt promotion, Wyatt thought. *And* a bigger pension for sure.

Halpin's face had a smug smile as he sipped his coffee.

"So that's the good news James. Now we must move to the not-so-good news. A lot of changes have taken place since you took up your assignment." As Halpin paused to light his pipe, Wyatt sensed what was coming, and stood up.

"Sorry to interrupt Seamus, but I have information of a serious and confidential nature that I need to discuss with you privately."

Halpin seemed taken aback, and sullenly put his unlit pipe on the desk.

"Gentlemen, if you could excuse us for a while." He nodded towards the door. When they had trooped out, Halpin turned to Wyatt, with a scowl on his face.

"I trust this is as important as you're making out. " He's not happy, that has to be good, Wyatt mused.

"I think you will find that *is* the case." Wyatt spoke as he took a sheaf of documents from his brief case, and placed them on the desk in front of Halpin.

"Firstly Seamus, I must congratulate you on your new office. It's obviously a promotion of sorts, and not easily achieved in days of cutbacks. Something must be going right. Maybe due partly to how things have been going in the west?"

"Maybe, but please get to the point James."Irritated, Halpin picked up his pipe, patted down the tobacco in the bowl, struck a match and lit it. A sweet vanilla smell permeated the room, as a smoke pall rose to the ceiling.

"Ok, let's start with the company Atlantic Waves Limited, which owned the boat that was blown up in the fjord."

"Oh, and what about that?" Halpin snapped.

"You are a director and shareholder of this company."

"What? Who said so?"

"These say so." Wyatt threw the documents he had got in the Companies Registration Office onto the desk. Halpin grabbed them and glanced through the pages, sucking on his pipe.

"There's no law against investing in a company."

"Absolutely not Seamus, but begrudgers might infer there was a conflict of interests, particularly as *you* authorised the compensation for the damage caused by the explosion."

"Are you threatening me?" Halpin's eyes bulged, and his mouth sagged.

"Indeed no, why would I, nothing could be further from my mind, Seamus. But if this information got into the wrong hands, such as a newspaper, things might be misconstrued. You can't be too careful, can you?"

"I suppose, but that's most unlikely isn't it?" He glared into Wyatt's eyes.

"And there's the problem of the tampered tests and reports."

"I beg your pardon, what do you mean?" Halpin's voice was strident.

"I did duplicate tests of all my samples in Castlebar laboratory, and the results were the exact opposite of the Galway tests. I sent you only the Galway ones, all of which were favourable."

"But why…why didn't you tell me before now, I mean about….about these negative test results."

"I needed to do further forensic checks to be sure. Look, here are the correct Castlebar sample results. " Wyatt threw a pile of documents onto the desk, and sat back while Halpin pored through them, taking a sneaking pleasure at Halpin's discomfort, and enjoying the feeling. Eventually Halpin looked up.

"This is dynamite James."

"I agree. If this got into wrong hands, reputational damage could be caused."

"I'm sure." Halpin seemed stunned.

"And there was more skulduggery, somebody tried to access information on my computer in the hotel." Wyatt related the details to the bemused Halpin, before switching to family matters.

"Your brother Ned has political ambitions I believe."

"Yes, he hopes to run in the next General Election as an Independent. He has high hopes."

"I'm sure he has, seeing he's involved in almost everything going on down there. He's a hard worker too, I believe. But these reports on the water treatment plants are pretty damning. Also there's the issue of the green lettuce tide of pollution. *And* he's involved big time in the goldmining venture, which could cause massive environmental damage in the area. Here are the relevant reports." Wyatt threw another sheaf of papers onto the desk, and sat back again while Halpin scrutinised them. After some timeHalpin looked up, and removed his glasses.

"Are there any more bombshells James?" He seemed shaken.

"Well, while we're at it, there's the question of my predecessor Frank Duffy's disappearance."

"What about it, have you solved the mystery?"

"No, I wasn't sent down there as a detective, but I have my suspicions."

"And what are they?" Halpin's jaw jutted, as he leaned forward.

"I can't divulge anything now Seamus, as I said, they're just suspicions. I need more proof, and time."

Halpin paced round the room, stopping at the windows several times, and gazing at the, dismal Dublin skyline. He refilled the coffee mugs before speaking.

"This isn't the kind of meeting I was expecting to have."

"I suppose not."

"There's a lot of information here to sift through, and it's highly sensitive."

"Indeed."

"I'll need more time to do an in-depth analysis, and maybe devise a new strategy."

"True."

"You're sure these new reports are the correct ones?"

"Positive."

"Are they originals?"

"No, they're copies."

"So you have the originals in the hotel?"

"No, I told you about the hotel. They're stored in a safe place."

"Of course, of course, it's important they don't fall into the wrong hands."

"Absolutely, we wouldn't want that, would we?"

"No, that could be disastrous, and we wouldn't want to be blackmailed either."

"I couldn't agree more, Seamus. So, do you now want to continue with the meeting?"

"Let me go and discuss things with my colleagues. I'll be back soon."Halpin muttered, trudging out the large mahogany door. He returned shortly, and sat with a squeak on his leather swivel chair. As he spoke, his fingers drummed the desk.

"James, I've spoken to my colleagues, and we're all agreed you're doing a fine job in Mayo, in difficult and dangerous circumstances. My HR colleague Roger White has agreed a wage increase as a gesture, while Mr Doyle in Finance says you should be given whatever additional time you need to finish the project. How long do you think that will be?"

"That is the question. I wish I knew, you'll just have to trust me. I'll let you know when I get back there. I'm sure you'd like to solve the Duffy mystery too, Seamus? After all, he's a former member of staff."

"Of course, of course, this is a dangerous business. That's why I'm immediately giving you money for your improved security. You're now a marked man, and you must watch your step." Wyatt wondered if this was a veiled threat or a genuine warning.

"You're right Seamus, and there's one more thing I need to protect myself."

"What's that?"

"I need a bullet proof vest."

"Ok, it will be delivered to the hotel later this week."

"That's good Seamus. Anything else to discuss, I must leave now to visit my mother."

"Of course you must see her. No, there's nothing else for now, just be careful."

"I will, but I'll feel better when I get that vest." Wyatt

closed his briefcase, and rushed from the room. As he descended in the lift Wyatt wondered if Halpin had really consulted his colleagues. He doubted it, wily old fox. He looked at his watch. It was well past lunchtime. In all the time he had known him, it was the first time he could remember Halpin foregoing his lunch.

Wyatt strode up the curving, pebbled driveway, flanked by swaying eucalyptus trees, and inhaled the menthol smell. He was happy after his encounter with Halpin, but afraid he had become more isolated. He was treading on a lot of toes, and many might now prefer if he wasn't around anymore.

His mind jolted back to the present when he entered the living area of the nursing home. The TV was switched off, as a priest said the Rosary to a packed room. Wyatt scanned the room for his mother's face, but she wasn't there. He enquired from the Nigerian nurse of her whereabouts. The nurse took him down a long corridor. There was a sour smell in the air.

Finally he entered a room where his mother lay asleep beneath the sheets, like a baby. He shook her, but she stayed asleep.

When he tracked down the Irish matron, he asked if there was a problem with his mother.

"Well to tell the truth, Mrs Wyatt prefers to stay alone. She doesn't like to socialise much with the other people, she likes her own company."

"Is she being sedated?"

"Yes, she is on medication prescribed for her by the doctor, but sometimes she can be an unsettling influence on the others."

"Do the nurses interact with her on a one- to- one basis?"

"They try, but her dementia has worsened since she came here. It's not easy."

"Hmm, does she watch TV, dine with, or have any contact with others in the home?"

"She does, sometimes." Wyatt suspected it was not at

all.

"She always loved flowers and gardening. Could you not get someone to bring her out each day to the gardens, even in a wheelchair?"

"Certainly Mr Wyatt, we could do that. That's a good idea, and it might help her perk up." Wyatt felt better then.

"And maybe try to reduce the sedation too, gradually of course."

"We'll have to speak to the doctor."

"Please do."

He returned to the bedroom, and saw his mother still asleep. "Goodbye Ma." He kissed her on the forehead, and riffled his fingers through her mane of hair, grey as a badger. His heart was heavy, his step slow, as he went back into the lounge. The Rosary was over, the priest gone, and the large TV screen flickered in the corner.

Two patients argued over who should have the remote control, and beside them a row ensued because somebody had sat in another person's seat. It hit him, as he waited for a taxi to take him to the station, how vulnerable people in the nursing home were. And then it hit him, just how vulnerable he himself now was.

# Chapter 15

## *An Isle In The Water*

"You'll get by, Inspector, but you're no Dead Eye Dick." Sergeant McSweeney grinned as he handed the Beretta pistol back to Wyatt. McSweeney had helped Wyatt buy the gun from a retired U.S. army veteran in Westport, and it was the end of their second practice session. Wyatt enquired when the next one would be.

"Stall the ball, from here on you're on your own, I can't do any more for you. You'll need a lot more practice, and I mean that."

"Ok Barry, I've got the message, thanks for your help." Wyatt knew he had to improve a strike rate of one out of three wasn't good enough.

"You're welcome bhoy, take it handy and stay between the ditches." McSweeney said, waving as he ducked into the squad car that had pulled up beside him.

Back in the hotel, Bridie called out as he passed her desk.

"Jim, there's a delivery here for you that I signed for from the courier. I hope that's ok with you, he was in a hurry and I didn't know where you were. It's very heavy."

"That's fine Bridie, I think I know what it is, and you did the right thing, thanks." As he leant over to take the parcel, he smelt the fragrance of her perfume. Her eyes sparkled, and her hair hung loose on her shoulders. Even with no makeup on, her face seemed fresh as a spring morning. He'd forgotten how lovely she looked, and the good times they'd had before, rather he'd blocked those thoughts out of his mind. He sucked in his breath, as he realised he'd been staring overlong at her.

"A penny for your thoughts Jim Wyatt, don't you know it's ungentlemanly to stare too long at a lady? "

"Just because you're on a diet doesn't mean you can't

check out the menu."

"Who's on a diet? You don't look starved."

"Figuratively speaking, you're out of range, you're spoken for." As he said the words, he glanced at her hand, and was surprised to see no engagement ring on her finger. She saw his glance, and replied before he could speak.

"As you can see I'm no longer spoken for."She seemed sad, her eyes downcast.

"I'm sorry to hear that Bridie, I really am. Maybe.... would you like to go for a drink and a chat later?"He hesitated as he spoke.

"Thanks Jim, but I don't think so I haven't got my head straight yet. Anyway, I'd be too self-conscious in a pub, I'd be thinking they were all looking at me, or talking about me behind my back."

"Well ok, I understand, it's not easy. Maybe we could go somewhere else, somewhere more private?" He felt drawn to her again, and every twitch of her face attracted his attention, as if the desire had always been there, but somehow been pushed to the back of his mind. There was Jenny too of course, but he didn't want to think about her just then. After a while she replied.

"I'm working late until Friday night Jim. We could go somewhere on Saturday though, to a place you haven't been before. What about a trip to Inisboffin Island? I like it there, it's beautiful, and I know the weather forecast is good."She seemed tentative, unsure of his response.

"That sounds fine to me, let's do it."

\*\*\*

The ferry left Cleggan, the sea mist dank and dense, a swell on the waves. Wyatt felt queasy, and leant over the side of the boat, peering into the fog for sight of landfall, but nothing appeared. Invisible sea birds squawled and shrieked.

"So much for the weather forecast."Wyatt murmured.

"It's normal for here, it'll burn away later".

Then the engine went quiet and the ferry stopped, bobbing about in the swell. All was quiet as the grave.

"What's up? Don't tell me the boat's broken down." His stomach rocked with the boat, as ghostly currachs appeared out of the mist, and the other passengers climbed aboard. They were helped down into them by the ferry's crew, who told them not to worry, that the tide was out, and the ferry was unable to dock in the harbour, and this was normal in Inisboffin.

"Nobody told me about that in Cleggan." He grumbled, as he stepped into the shilly shallying boat.

They climbed the hill behind the harbour, weighed down by their rucksacks. Wyatt started to feel better, glad to be on terra firma. At the brow of the hill, he turned and looked down towards where the harbour was, and saw it unfold like an apparition out of the mist. The sun split the mist clouds above, and lit the landscape. Within minutes the mist had vanished, and the sun was a blazing orb in an indigo sky.

They continued along the boreen in silence. He scanned the scene of sea and sand ahead, and took out his booklet on the island, poring through the pages. *Isle of the White Cow, where St. Colman came to from Britain, and set up a monastery in old God's time. Cromwell kept a castle there too, where prisoners were sent before being transported to Barbados, and were treated cruelly.* They stopped for tea and biscuits, and afterwards continued their trek along a meandering road. It wound beside a long beach with storm beach stones piled at the back, and ended where a heap of boulders lay strewn across the sand.

After climbing the boulders, they found a cove of silver sand on the other side, littered with large rocks giving shelter from the elements. Behind the dunes were the ruins of an old church, beside a deserted graveyard. They agreed it was the perfect place to rest. They were tired and sweaty, and a dip seemed appealing.

"Last in's a chicken." He shouted, racing to the water's

edge.

"Jim, don't go yet. I can't find my togs." She said, rummaging in her rucksack.

"Looks like you'll have to skinny dip then, I won't look, I promise." He smiled as she blushed.

"Don't be ridiculous Jim Wyatt, anyone could come over those rocks and see me."

"And they might like what they see, I know I would. On the other hand they could look away. Look, I'll join you, if it makes it any better for you."

"No way, and we in front of holy ground." She said, nodding towards the graveyard.

"I suppose, well what are you going to do?"

"I'll just have to wear my bra and knickers." She retorted.

Soon she was with him on the beach, in a black and white outfit, a black bra on top, white underwear below. She looks sexier than in any swimsuit, he thought, and curved in all the right places too, and with the legs of a dancer.

"Race you." He yelled.

They took off for the surf, sand spewing behind them. She won the race easily, but he didn't mind, he had a good view from behind and liked what he saw. She swam far out with strong clean strokes through the webbed water. He trailed her out, and they floated back to the shoreline on their backs, the sun dazzling their eyes. They frolicked about, and held hands, splashing each other. Sometimes their bodies touched in the sea, and once he pulled her close and kissed her lips, and felt her soft against him, and the salty taste, and the feel of her dancer's legs against his below in the water.

"Jim, that's enough of that, we should get back." She said, pulling away. He traipsed after her onto the beach, and they raced up and down the coral sands to dry off.

Later they moved into the graveyard behind the sand dunes. Bridie left her wet underclothes flat on the gravestones to dry. Draped in a red towel, she set out the red chequered picnic cloth on the grass. In the hot air, bees buzzed about the honeysuckle. Sated, they each sat on a flat tombstone, wine glass in hand.

"Feel like talking about it now, Bridie?"

"Well yes…yes… I do. But it's not easy you know."

"I *do* know." He touched her hand, and it was a while before she spoke.

"Francie….God how I loved him…but…well he'd changed a lot since he'd gone away. He drank too much, that was the problem, and he got aggressive when he drank. Well….he wanted me to go back with him to New York I suppose that was the nub of it. And leave my mother behind, but I didn't want to go, and I told him so. We argued too much, far too much. He begged me to go, and swore he'd give up the drink. He even stayed an extra two weeks for me to make up my mind. When I finally gave him back the ring, he flew into a blind fit, and stormed off swearing, and went on a bender for two days. Maybe I should have kept the ring, I don't know.Christ, but I loved him Jim, we were together since we were kids. We had plans, but it's all over, finished, gone forever." She sobbed, and laid her head on his shoulder. He put his arms around her and hugged her. There, there, he muttered.

"What did your mother say?"

"She wanted me to go to the States, to see what it was like. We had a row too, but she's getting over it now."

"And are you?"

"Yes, I think so." She snuffled as she spoke.

"Have you had any word from Francie since he went back to the states?"

"No, he's not the writin' kind, but I'm damned if I'm going to write first, he'd think I was mad after him again."

"And are you?"

"No, it's over. But you can't change the past, only the future, we were together a long time."

"You could still be friends."

"Yes, but I don't really think so. Not the way he left. Anyway I feel the better of talking to you about it. And I suppose life goes on too."

"It does and talking of that, how did you do afterwards in the dancing competition?"

"I didn't, I hadn't the mind to compete with all this hassle going on with Francie."

"Pity, maybe you'll try again when your head is right."

"Maybe, you never know. Or maybe I'll try something else."

"Like what?"

"Well......Genealogy. Remember I told you before I always wanted to do that. Even thinking about the people buried here in this sandy old cemetery makes me curious. All those poor souls buried here from the Famine times too. I'd love to find out the stories of their lives, no matter how desperate they were. I'm going to check out all the gravestones before we leave. I like doing that, and I'll use the details for my research files."

She reclined on a flat gravestone, as the afternoon sun slanted down. All was quiet save the larks singing in the sand dunes, and the waves wasting along the shoreline. They were alone on their island, and she beckoned to him, pointing to a spot on the grass, nodding her head. He moved closer when she lay down, and spread his towel beside hers, asking if her clothes had dried yet. She said who cares about clothes, and pulled him close, her towel falling away, as she pressed against his body. They kissed, and he tasted the tang of salt inside her mouth, and nothing else mattered but that moment. She asked if he loved her, and he said he did, and she said she did too. She lay back on a flat headstone, and pulled him to her gently, in a slow, lingering movement, and the music of larksong soared in his ears.

He had dozed off, and woke to see shadows across the cemetry, and Bridie sitting on a gravestone. She was writing in a notebook balanced on her knees, barefooted, dress pulled up past her knees, hair tied back, cheeks glowing. He quickly dressed.

"I see your clothes have dried out."

"You see right Jim." She grinned.

"Bridie, did I just dream what happened?"

"Would you prefer a dream or reality?"

"Reality I guess."

"Then you're right."

"I'm glad, are you?"

"Guess." She left the notebook down on the headstone, came over to him, reached up on tip- toes, her arms encircling his neck, and kissed him on the lips.

"I suppose that means yes."

"You suppose right, here let's finish off the wine." She drained the last of the bottle into their glasses, sat back on the headstone, and picked up her notebook.

"Hey Jim, I just came across a strange thing."

"What's that? Here's to you anyway." He lifted his glass in her direction.

"Here's to us, and days like this." They toasted, clinking their glasses.

"Aren't you going to tell me about this so called strange thing? Or were you having me on?"

"Oh yes, I almost forgot. While you were asleep, I did an inspection of the graveyard. I must be a bit of an inspector in my own way."

"Ha ha, and?"

"Well, one of the gravestones had the name Wyatt on it."

"Really, is that unusual down here?"

"Yes it is. It was old, weather-beaten, and hard to make out, but I got the Wyatt name definitely. The rest was unclear, and I took a close- up photograph, so I can do some research on it later."

"Thanks, that's interesting."

"No problem, it's what I like doing. There are so many interesting names and stories here, some going way back to the Famine era, the forgotten people of Ireland. I can feel their spirit around me everywhere in this place, it gives me goose bumps."

"And did you feel their spirit when you lay on that

headstone earlier? You were certainly high spirited to say the least."

"And did *you* object Mr Wyatt?"

"No way, but I do feel a bit weird now, knowing there's someone called Wyatt buried here."

"Yes, that's a coincidence. Jim, what's that gun doing there on the ground?" She looked startled.

Wyatt picked up the Beretta from the ground, and put it into his shoulder holster.

"It's my best friend, and my guardian angel. It must have fallen out, I have to bring it everywhere with me now, even to bed." He told her then about the incident on Mweelrea Mountain, which led to him getting the gun, and about the meeting in Dublin with Halpin. He said he'd baulked at wearing the bullet proof vest to the island.

"You should have worn it Jim."

"It would have been silly on a day like today."

"No it wouldn't. *You're* the one being silly, these people are dangerous, you've got to be more careful. I don't want you ending up dead, do I?" Her face wrinkled in a frown.

"Neither do I, believe me. Ok, I *will* wear the vest in the future, and take more precautions."

"Good, you do that. Jenny Marsh is very nice by the way, I really like her, she's so different she's like a breath of fresh air down here. It was terrible that her husband died like that, will she be coming back again?"

"Yes, she's nice. She's a good friend, and should be back again. She's writing a book about Yeats and the west of Ireland, you know."

"Yes, she did mention that. You should bring her to Renvyle House, Yeats used to visit there."

"Yeah, that's a good idea. I might mention it next time she's over." But inside he didn't think so.

"Jim, I want you to know that today is one of the happiest days of my life. The worry that was on me, has lifted and gone. I feel so free and happy, I can't thank you enough." She fiddled with the stem of the empty wine glass as she spoke.

"I'm glad for that, Bridie, but don't forget you did the same for me that time we went to Renvyle, when I was in a bad way. I owed you one."

"Yes Jim, I do remember, now we're quits. But I didn't tell you then about Francie, I hope you've forgiven me."

"Of course I have, it's all in the past now." He put his arm around her, and kissed her cheek.

"And Jim, there is one more thing I want to say to you."

"What's that?"

"When you said earlier that you loved me, did you really mean it?"

"Yes I did, and I do, I'm glad you didn't go to America." He kissed her gently, hugging her close.

"That's great, so am I, I'm just so happy." Her eyes shone.

"I am too."

They packed everything into their rucksacks, the ferry being due within the hour, and set off at speed, following a worn track back to the harbour. On the way they heard a rasping cry from a clump of high grass near a small lake, and Bridie whooped with joy, telling him it was the cry of the corncrake.

When they reached the harbour the tide was full in, with the ferry docked, and everyone embarking from the pier onto the boat. The Connemara mountains, tawny and gold in the evening sun, lay ahead, as the boat chugged it's way back to Cleggan. He looked over the side at the churning waters, reflecting, and felt as happy as he could be, but still had a sneaking feeling he'd not been fair to Jenny. He wondered why, all being fair in love and war. Still, the thought that he hadn't played fair nagged him. Bridie and he had sure got carried away, but today was like some kind of heaven.

Wyatt looked around to see her standing at the side of the deck, gazing at the mountains ahead, hair streeling in the wind, happiness etched on her face. Did she really forget her togs? Mind you, he wasn't complaining. He felt the weight of the pistol chafing his shoulder. Damn nuisance, but he would have to get used to it, one never knew when it might come in handy.

# Chapter 16

## *Ship in Full Sail*

Next morning a call came from Seamus Halpin. He wanted a full and final report on the marine pollution project, and wanted it on his desk within a month. The tone was curt, and unfriendly. He may have relented a bit at the meeting in Dublin, Wyatt thought, but he's cracking the whip now. He gritted his teeth, as he agreed to the request, saying he was working on it. But in his mind he was determined the report would take as long as *he* felt he needed. *And* he would keep a copy stashed away, as his insurance, and Halpin better realise which side his bread was buttered on.

It crossed his mind then how his boss might gain by him vanishing off the scene, just like his predecessor Frank Duffy. Another missing person, another unsolved case. He banished the thought from his mind. He yearned for a drink to steady his nerves, and resolved not to let the bastards grind him down.

He scanned a newspaper in the foyer, the headlines about the Irish Presidential election campaign. Brian Lenihan's "mature" recollection of phoning a previous President had caused him to slide in the polls. Bridie was not at the reception desk when he looked, though he knew it *was* one of her work days. On enquiring, he found out her mother had fallen at home, injured her back, and been taken by ambulance to Castlebar hospital. Bridie was now on a week's compassionate leave. Wyatt rang the hospital, and soon got through to Bridie.

"Sorry about the bad news Bridie, how is your mother?"

"We don't know yet, they have to do more tests. I'm waiting here with my sister Nora. My mother's got spirit, but she's a good age now, even though she doesn't seem to realise it." She sighed.

"Is there anything I can do?"

"Not really Jim, I'll stay here with my sister. Thanks for the call anyway, I do appreciate it."

"It's nothing, keep me posted, bye." He put down the phone.

Before working on his final report, Wyatt decided on a day's fishing with Tommy Joe. Though only an occasional fisherman, he'd always enjoyed the experience. Also a final sample of fish and water, taken inshore and deep at sea, would help confirm his earlier reports to Halpin. He reckoned Halpin might not agree with him going fishing, but today he felt to hell with Halpin.

After booking Tommy Joe's boat for the next morning, Wyatt took a taxi to Westport. He spent the rest of the day there, fitting himself out with fishing gear and tackle in Hewetson's shop in Bridge Street. He enjoyed browsing around, and pretended to be knowledgeable about fishing, as he checked out the gear with the friendly owner. Everything he bought was top of the range, only the best from now on, feck Halpin's penny pinching ways, he muttered. The shop owner's face beamed when he wrote out the cheque. It's great to make people happy, Wyatt murmured, as he staggered back to the taxi, laden with his purchases.

There was a message at reception for him from Bridie next day. She said her mother had had a good night, a better one than she herself had, but there was still no definite news. After reading the note, Wyatt continued out the hotel door, clad in his new waders and water proof garments. He held a fishing rod in one hand, a fishing basket in the other, and felt like an Irish fisherman's version of Don Quixote.

Wyatt plodded up to the harbour near the hotel, and saw that the tide was full in, with Tommy Joe's boat berthed there. Empty lobster pots were piled in pyramids on the pier, and the stench of rotten kelp fouled the air. Tommy Joe's new boat was a thirty footer with cabin, and shaped like a Galway Hooker, its large sail unfurled. It had been bought with the proceeds of Halpin's compensation payment, and had the name *Connemara Queen* on its bow.

He lowered himself into the boat, and sat on a bench near the reeking fish nets, holding his breath. Tommy Joe's brother Michael stood silent in the stern. The sky was a grey blanket, threatening rain, the wind brisk, with a sea mist low over the water. The vessel slipped out into the bay, tacked into the wind, sails billowing, as it moved west towards the top of the Killary. Tommy Joe's face was grim. He seemed tense, and said little, bar a few shouted instructions to Michael.

"Nice boat you have now." Wyatt tried to open the conversation.

"She'll do. Nice price too, Inspector, as you know only too well. Ever been fishin' before?" His half smile indicated that he already knew the answer.

"Not much really. I'm just a beginner."

"Well, you're well togged out for a beginner, good wages or good expenses, is it?" He seems to be coming out of his shell, Wyatt thought.

"None of your business, Tommy Joe, you just make sure I catch some big ones. Ones I can brag about, not tiddlers that got away."

"I will surely, you'll have somethin' to crow about today all right."

"I hope you're right."

"Musha, there's a good spot I know out in the bay. We'll head there now with speed."

Tommy Joe steered the ship shorewards into the lee of a small island, dropped anchor, and furled the sails. As he boat swayed in a rolling motion, Wyatt heard a muffled sound from below the deck.

"What's that noise Tommy Joe?"

"Fuck, the cat's out of the bag now for shure. Michael, give me a hand to carry the sack on deck."

Wyatt inhaled sharply, as Tommy Joe and Michael dragged a huge sack from the hold, over to the boom of the sails. A large body wriggled inside, and the top of the sack fell open to reveal the red headed and bearded face of McFadden, bound hand and foot, and gagged.

They removed the sack, and manhandled him to the boom, where they tied his hands to the sail, and his feet to a metal hawser. Bloodstains were splotched on Mc Fadden's white shirt, and Wyatt saw the fury in his eyes, bulging from their sockets. He grabbed Tommy Joe's arm, and pulled him to the other side of the boat.

"Tommy Joe, what the hell's going on? You can't keep someone tied up in a sack like that, no matter what he's done, he could have suffocated."

"Relax Inspector, can't you see there's holes in the sack for him to breathe through. We had to get him on board without anyone knowin'."

"But why?"

"Why? Because for one, when you gave me that bullet the last week, I checked it with the one poor Shep was shot with, and it was the same, exactly the same. McFadden, that fuckin' bastard over there he did it, he fuckin' did, he killed my dog. I knew it all along, I just needed the proof, an' you gave me that."He spat over the side, after he spoke.

"But this has to be proved in court. There are experts for that kind of thing, and anyway you can't abduct someone just for killing a dog. "

"Fuck the court, Inspector, did you fuckin' come down in the last shower or what? Nothin' will ever be hung on him, because everyone around here's scared shitless to go in the box against him, an' he knows that too. Anyway there's more to it than killin' a dog, a whole fuckin' lot more."

"What about the forensic and ballistic evidence?"

"Fuck the forensics, and balls to the ballistics. Believe me, he'll get off scot free, the bastard, but the people tryin' to nail him won't, I've seen it all happenin' before, so I fuckin'have. He has the fear of God in everyone."

"How did you catch him?"

"Michael and me, we were havin' a drink last night in the pub after work, when who comes in only his nibs there, an' him sittin' there drinkin' on his own up at the bar readin' the paper like lord fuckin' muck, surely waitin' for someone. Couldn't believe our luck, we couldn't. When the cunt went out later to the loo in the yard, we waylaid him comin' back. Whacked him on the head I did, with the hurleystick I got from the van. Broke it in two on his skull, I did, before I gave him a fuckin' rabbit punch on the back of the neck. Michael finished the job with a blow from a crowbar. That bastard is fuckin' strong, I'm tellin' you."

"But why didn't you tell Sergeant McSweeney?"

"Because it's not time to, but I will in due time, Inspector. You have a part to play in this too. We can get to the bottom too, about how yer man Duffy vanished. I hear you're good at the writin', is that a fact?"

"I suppose so, why?"

"I want you to write down the cunt's confession."

"How the hell are you going to get him to confess?"

"Leave it to me Inspector, I have me ways, not by to the book, mind you. But first there's something you ought to know about that effin rat." He spat again over the side of the boat.

"What's that?"

"That bollocks. He's been on my back for years, always lookin' for money for his fuckin' cause. I told him where to get off, with his murderin', thievin' ways. I never gave them a penny so I did, I wouldn't give that lot the steam off me piss. Then things started to happen at the farm, with animals poison'd, and machinery banjax'd. I wouldn't give in, a man has his pride. Then there was the boat gettin' blown up, an' poor Shep getting' shot, an' the fire at the house. But long before all these, a few years back, was when the big thing happen'd, yeah the fuckin' big thing." Tommy Joe paused, and rubbed his eyes. His face was grim, and his eyes had a faraway look, as he recalled the incident.

"Duffy, he booked the boat to go fishin' that day, an'

Michael, he went with him. They'd just reached the top of the Killary, an' were headin'on for Inishturk. They were passin' a small island out in the middle, an' Duffy was standin' there fishin' at the back of the boat, with Michael beside him, when two shots rang out.Duffy fell into the water, a bullet shot clean through his head. Michael was lucky he only got grazed in the shoulder. He cut the engine, an' dived in after Duffy, but when he got to the body, Duffy was stone dead in the water. Michael looked behind him an' saw the boat'd drift'd a good bit away. Michael, now he was never a great swimmer, but he somehow got back onto the boat, panick'd, exhaust'd, an' shocked to the marrow, he was.The poor lad, he's never been the same since, he went completely into himself he did, an' couldn't talk about it, or talk about anythin', ever. But I'm sure it was McFadden he saw that day, because he got awful agitat'd seein' him last night at the pub. I never saw Michael so worked up, 'cept when poor Shep died." Tommy Joe paused, wiped his eyes, and continued.

"That bastard over there, he did it, shure as I'm standin' here." He said, pointing at McFadden, and trembling with rage.

"How can you be sure?"

"The fecker, he had two good reasons. One, he wanted to get back at me, he'd threatened it often enough. Second, Duffy was courtin' his sister for a while, an' he thought Duffy was a spy, usin' his sister to get the lowdown on his crowd. Then he found out she was up the pole, the word was all over the place about that."

"But how can you be sure? Michael couldn't have told you all that. And what happened to Duffy's body? Why didn't you go to the guards?"

"Musha, one thing at a time will you, for fuck's sake Inspector. Michael was in such a state of agitati'n, when he came home that evenin', an' me waitin' for him on the pier, him bein' long overdue. I knew somethin' terrible must've happened, yeh the poor fellah, he couldn't talk, only nod and shake his head. I had to work out what happened, an' put two and two together. They never found Duffy's body either, must've drift'd out to sea, these things happen. I wait'd a couple of weeks to see if the body would turn up, but it didn't. Then...then I made me mind up, not to report the whole thing."

"But why not?"

"Look Inspector, I took it on myself to do it the way I did, I don't expect you 'r anyone to understand. Maybe I wasn't right in the head at the time, to do it that way, but I did. I didn't want poor Michael bein' put through all the Garda, media, an' legal hassle that was bound to happen, after what he'd been through already. An' him not bein' able to talk atall. Sure they'd have put huge pressure on the family too, that crowd, bad cess to them, the bastards. I said to myself, I'll wait, until the fuckers someday slip up, an' give me the chance to give them their comeuppance, and feck me if it wasn't yourself that finally gave me that chance an' I'm not going to waste it. Today, *I'm* the feckin' judge, jury, and execution'r."

"Hold on now, slow down a bit Tommy Joe, did Michael have any medical treatment for his condition?"

"No, but maybe he will later, when all this is over, I had to take that decision on my head too."

"But you can't just take the law into your own hands."

"No? Just fuckin' watch me do it. You have a pistol, can I borrow it a while, Inspector?"

"No." Wyatt said, alarmed. There was no way he could trust Tommy Joe with a loaded gun.

"Ok Inspector, so be it, if that's the way you want it. I have me own ways anyway, of gettin' people to spill the beans. An' another thing, there was these documents that bastard had on him at the pub last night, they showed plans an' stuff on the gold minin' premises, an' names and phone numbers of his friends. We have him now by the short and curlies for shure. An' I want you to write down every effin word of his confession." He handed Wyatt a pencil and notebook.

"Can I see the documents you got from McFadden?"

Tommy Joe fished a few crumpled sheets from his back pocket, and handed them over. Wyatt scanned the pages, which were scribbled and barely legible. He folded the pages and gave them back to Tommy Joe, who strode across the deck to McFadden.

"Are you ready to sing us a song, Big Bird?" He snarled, and yanked the gag off.

"Fuck you an' all yours. I'll make sure you fuckin' roast in hell for this. You're a fuckin' marked man, you'n that fuckin' dummy brother of yours. I shoulda finished him off before, when I had the fuckin' chance. Ye'll both regret this for the rest of yer fuckin' days." McFadden spat on the deck in front of Tommy Joe as he spoke.

Tommy Joe's eyes narrowed into slits, his forehead furrowed. He paused for a while, before walking slowly in a circle around McFadden.

"So we're not ready to sing yet, Big Bird are we? Well, we've got all day out here, so we have. Nice'n quiet here too, nobody will hear anything, even if there's a scream or two to frighten the birds. We're not going anywhere, are we? We'll soon see who's goin' to regret what, before this fuckin' day is out."

Tommy Joe is trying to use psychological tactics, Wyatt thought, and wondered if McFadden would crack. As he gazed across the deck, he felt trapped in some surreal nightmare. The boat bobbed in the mist covered swell, and the stillness was eerie. Tommy Joe had stripped, his muscles bulging beneath his tee shirt, his face set stony, and sweat was beaded on his brow.

A pair of ravens squatted on the side of the boat, their heads cocked in curiousity, as they waited to feed. A shriek from an invisible sea bird pierced the mist. Wyatt felt his stomach heaving in time with the boat, and shivered.

"Looks like its Plan B then, Big Bird.You may be sorry." Tommy Joe snapped, and shouted instructions to Michael, who pulled up anchor, and hoisted the mainsail. Soon they were sailing to various places in the fjord, marked with small, yellow buoys.

A while later the boat was back, anchored in the same spot, a heap of kelp-covered lobster pots strewn on the deck. Dark objects scuttled around inside the pots, and the air reeked of seaweed. Tommy Joe picked up a couple of pots, and brought them over to Wyatt.

"Have a gawk, Inspector, you'd never be knowin' what might come up from inside these pots betimes."Wyatt stared into the pots.

Inside one, two giant spider crabs fought each other over some bait. In the other pot, a lobster was locked in mortal combat with a huge brown crab. Wyatt felt the hair rising on the back of his neck.

"Try these on for size, Big Bird." Tommy Joe said as he slid back the gate of each pot and inserted one over each of McFadden's bound hands. Wyatt looked on in disbelief.

Minutes passed, before Tommy Joe took the pots off, and peered into them, shaking his head. He then emptied the remnants of the shells, crushed by McFadden's huge fists, onto the deck. Wyatt glanced at McFadden's face. Although defiant, he looked pale and shaken, the whites of his eyes showing.

"Blow me now, Big Bird, if you're not the tough bastard. Well those were just for starters. When you're ready to sing, just nod your head, ok? For the next course, two pots will be put on your feet. Can't say what'll be in them, that'll be the surprise, won't it? If that doesn't do the job, we'll move upwards for the main course, won't we?"He placed an unopened pot on McFadden's groin."Good pickings there I'd say. You might be singin' in a much higher voice, like them opera singers, after those boyos are finished with you, whaddya think?"Tommy Joe waited for his words to sink in, before continuing.

"And if that doesn't make you sing Big Bird, we'll have one final course for dessert, that'll fit fine over your face, problem is, if we go that far, you won't be able to sing for us atall, will you now?" As he spoke, he held a large lobster pot close to McFadden's face.

Wyatt glanced at McFadden's face, and saw stark terror etched on it.

When Tommy Joe asked the question again, McFadden's head nodded vigorously.

"Right Inspector, over here with the pencil and paper, Big Bird's gonna sing the sweetest little song he's ever sung."

Not long later Wyatt had written down McFadden's confession to every incident Tommy Joe recounted, including stealing the dynamite that blew up the boat, and firing the shot that killed Frank Duffy. His voice had no remorse, as he confirmed each accusation put to him by Tommy Joe.

McFadden signed his name under each written incident, as if everything was ok because of what was going on in the North. Lastly, Tommy Joe got him to sign the documents taken from him at the pub. Tommy Joe handed these to Wyatt, and told him to keep them in a safe place. Wyatt was amazed that McFadden had cracked so quickly under Tommy Joe's tactics, but he worried that afterwards he'd be like a wounded animal, bent on revenge.

Although elated that the mystery of Duffy's disappearance had been solved, Wyatt felt edgy about the process used to extract the truth. He beckoned Tommy Joe to the other side of the boat, out of McFadden's earshot.

"What do you intend to do now Tommy Joe?"

"I'll give a copy of the confession to the guards."

"Forget that, the evidence won't stand up in court, they were got under duress, he'll be released."

"I said I was handin' in the evidence, I didn't say I was handin' him in, did I?"

"What do you intend to do with him?"

"I intend to feck him overboard, let him swim with the fishes, like Frank Duffy. Drowned while makin'a getaway."

"You can't do that, that's murder."

"Try me Inspector, I'll fuckin' give the bastard a dose

of his own medicine."

"That's not the way the law and justice system works."

"Feck the law and justice, what justice did he give Duffy? We're doin' everyone a favour gettin' rid of that bastard."

"Tommy Joe, we need to talk about this, two wrongs don't make a right, it's just not cricket. You can't drown someone out of hand, just because it's convenient."

"Why not? The bastard deserves it. Fuck the cricket, an' what mercy or fair play did he ever show Duffy an' all his other victims over the years?"

"I know you're angry, but the law is the law, we must obey it, whether we like it or not. We're living in a democracy, not in the Dark Ages, it's not on, I won't have it." Tommy Joe was silent for a few minutes, and paced the deck, wringing his hands, before he replied.

"Ok Inspector, you win this time, I'll go along with what you say. But mark my words, you may regret it." Tommy Joe muttered, and walked to the other side of the boat, where McFadden lay.

"Your bacon's been saved this time, Big Bird. These sheets with your friends names on them, that's signed by you, are goin' to be kept in a safe place by the Inspector, an' he'll give them to the guards if you get up to no good again. I wouldn't be in your shoes for love nor money, if your friends find out you've spilled the beans on them. You're gettin' a fair deal, more than you deserve. Do I take it then that you will be keepin' on the straight an' narrow, from now on?" McFadden nodded his head. At that moment, the ravens honked and flew away in disgust, vanishing into the mist.

Later they handed their prisoner over to Sergeant McSweeney, saying Tommy Joe had caught him breaking into his house.

"Was that after he vanished mysteriously from the pub the other night, with his friends wonderin' what had happened to him, and the barman sayin' he upped and left after readin' the paper, and sayin' he thought he'd just gone to the loo? And then you left just a minute later, Tommy Joe? And had he not a lot of blows to the back of his head?"

"Sure Sergeant, we followed him, caught him breakin' into the house. We got him from behind."

"Ok, I'll believe you Tommy Joe, but thousands wouldn't. Breakin' and enterin' with intent, will you and Michael testify?"

"For shure we will, but that's nothin' to what we've got here." He handed the Sergeant the signed confession.

McSweeney scanned the papers, after removing his hat, and sat behind his desk, scratching his head. He whistled, saying it was dynamite, and confirmed many of his suspicions. McFadden would be charged, and remanded on bail. But he reckoned it could be argued by the legal beagles, that the confession was got under duress, and the charge wouldn't stick. How they had extracted the confession he couldn't imagine, as McFadden's image was of a hard man, tough as teak. Still, they would throw the kitchen sink at him, and hope something would stick. He asked if Tommy Joe and Michael would testify again in this matter. They agreed, and signed a statement for the Sergeant before they left.

When Tommy Joe later suggested a pint to steady their nerves, Wyatt didn't need a second invitation.

"There you are Inspector. Not a bad haul was it, for your first day's serious fishin'?" He plonked the pints on the table before him.

"You can say that again, but it wasn't exactly what I had in mind." Wyatt's head swayed back, as he swigged from the brimming glass. He remembered then that he had never used his new fishing equipment. Maybe another day, he thought.

"Look Inspector, I know maybe I got carried away today, but I couldn't help it, after him sayin' all them things about Michael, an' him after murderin' poor Shep, an' Duffy, an' all the other things he done to us. I'm glad you stopp'd me givin' the bastard his due desserts once an' for all. You understand we're on the same side? An' what happen'd on the boat stays on the boat. Can I count on you?" His eyes squinted, and his face was like granite, as he eyeballed Wyatt.

"Sure Tommy Joe, we're on the same side, you needn't worry on that score. What happened out there today stays out there."

Wyatt downed a few more pints, before he bade goodbye to Tommy Joe, and strode up the road to the hotel.

That night he tried again to write his report to Halpin, but was unable to focus on it, as the events of the day tumbled through his head. He realised his decision to follow the letter of the law could backfire. Tommy Joe's methods on the other hand were simple, effective, unorthodox, but they offended his sense of fair play. Anyway there was no going back, as the legal system was now in charge. He had to stay on red alert though, and watch his back.

He opened the bottle of whiskey he'd bought before leaving the pub, and poured a stiff shot. His hand trembled as he looked at his copy of the list of names of McFadden's accomplices. This document was vital to his safety from now, and it must be stored in a secure place, and he needed to work out the best way to use the information. Maybe he could take a short break from the area, and get his head together. The whiskey bottle was half empty when he fell into a fitful slumber. Visions of ravens, giant crabs, lobsters and lobster pots, and the hate on McFadden's face, flitted through his mind throughout the blackness of the night.

# Chapter 17

## *Haunted House*

Seamus Halpin was incredulous when Wyatt told him that Duffy's killer was behind bars. But he agreed with Sergeant McSweeney that the murder charge might not be legally enforceable, whatever about the breaking and entering offence. He asserted a good lawyer could overturn the charges, and prove the confession was obtained under duress. And he warned that Tommy Joe and Michael should watch out for retribution from McFadden. Wyatt omitted to inform Halpin that he had in his possession the signed sheet with McFadden's cronies' details.

"James, things have escalated, you're now involved in a murder case, up to your oxters. That man's dangerous, and so are his friends. Perhaps you should leave the area for a while, and finish your project report in Dublin?"

Wyatt wondered if Halpin was concerned for his safety, or just using it as an excuse to cut short his stay in the west. He paused before replying.

"Ok, I agree Seamus, but I have stuff to finish off here. It's best I stay a bit longer, there are issues I need to check out." In truth he knew what Halpin said made sense, it was now unsafe to stay, but he couldn't leave Leenane now, it would be like deserting a sinking ship.

"Ok James, it's your call. Be it on your own head, but I think you should get away for a while, and wait for the heat to die down. Take a break, leave Mayo for a while, you've earned it. You can do your report just as well somewhere else, out of harm's way." He must really be genuine about my safety this time. Wyatt thought. The thought of Sligo and his cancelled visit with Jenny then leapt to mind, their unfinished symphony.

"Good idea, Seamus, I might just do that, thank you. "

"You're welcome James, mind yourself." The phone

clicked dead.

Wyatt thought for a few seconds then rang Noel Kenny, his contact in the Mayo News. He briefed Kenny on the murder arrest, and told him to contact Sergeant McSweeney. Wyatt then asked him to come urgently to the hotel. When Kenny arrived, they adjourned into the lounge, and sat in a corner, facing the door.

"Thanks for the story Mr. Wyatt, we've got a scoop on it, and I can sell it to the big boys in Dublin."

"Good, let's say you now owe me one, Noel. The payback is that I need your help on a matter of importance."

"You've got it. Shoot." Kenny had his pencil and notebook in hand.

"No need for notes, the document I'm giving you now is a copy, and in it are details of McFadden's gang. It's for your eyes only, its top Secret, you understand? It must be kept in a safe place and only put it in the public domain if anything happens to Tommy Joe, Michael, or me. Understood and agreed?"

"Yes, you have my word, and hopefully that situation won't arise." Kenny stood up, shook hands, and left the hotel with the document under his arm, glancing about as he went.

Wyatt rang Castlebar hospital to learn Bridie's mother had been sent home. He rushed back to his room, and gathered his reports into a briefcase, putting the sheet with the data on McFadden's cronies in last. He put the briefcase into a rucksack, and hoisted it onto his back. After donning his new cycling helmet, he set off for Bridie's mother's house.

Showers wept on the landscape, the sun playing peek-a-boo in the clouds, and once, when it came out a rainbow arced over the Delphi valley. Wyatt wondered if it was a lucky omen, a pot of gold would come in handy. As he passed Aasleagh Falls he noticed people on the bridge, looking over the wall into the river below. They were chattering, and pointing downwards. He hadn't seen this kind of activity at the rapids since he arrived in Leenane, and his curiousity was aroused. He stopped, leaned his bike against the wall of the bridge, and peered over. Below, under the arch, were serried lines of salmon waiting to move upriver to the cataract.

His heart leapt, when he looked towards the falls. A salmon was breaching high in the air, defying gravity to climb the face of the waterfall. After failing many times, it clung onto something half way up, paused, and took another sideways leap, then with a final heave, it went over the top and out of sight up the river, back to where it was born, and all in the blink of an eye. He felt he had witnessed something special, a revelation of sorts, and wondered if his work had helped in any way in what he was seeing. He hoped so, and smiled to himself, thinking he would put the details in his next report to Halpin.

As Wyatt continued his journey to Bridie's mother's house, he passed a deserted cottage on the top of a hill. Ben Gorm towered in the background, and dark clouds hung overhead, another cloudburst about to spill onto the saturated land.

He pushed on up an overgrown track to the house, seeking shelter. The back door of the cottage was blown in, and inside rubbish was everywhere, along with the odour of farm animals. An old gents bicycle was parked in the kitchen, an upstairs model with the saddle tied to the crossbar by a piece of string. It seemed as if someone had left it there for safety before a journey, but never came back. The house had rodent infestation and dry rot, but most of the windowpanes and the roof were intact, except for a few missing slates.

Later, he continued his journey, as the sun shone on the dripping landscape. On arrival, Bridie told him her mother had undergone a hip operation, and would take up to three months to recover fully. She herself had taken three months compassionate leave to mind her. It would be full-time care for the next few weeks, she said, so there wouldn't be much chance of them getting together, unless he came to visit them.

Wyatt said he would love to call whenever her mother was well enough. Her mother was sleeping at that moment, and it would be a few days before she could have visitors. Wyatt was struck by Bridie's devotion to her mother, and how she tried to keep her in her at home when she could have made other, more convenient, plans. Guilt pangs shot through him, when he remembered how little time he had spent with his own mother, since *she* became confined to a nursing home.

Over a cup of tea he informed Bridie of McFadden's confession and arrest. At first she was shocked, but later said it didn't really surprise her. She wouldn't believe justice was done until he'd been convicted and sentenced in court, and she was afraid for his, and Tommy Joe's safety. He scoffed at this, saying he and Tommy Joe both had a healthy interest in living. She then suggested that he took a break from the area. They all want to get rid of me, he thought. He said he'd think about it, and before leaving asked Bridie about the deserted house in the valley.

"Oh, that'll be the O'Hara's cottage. Old Matty, he lived alone there after his wife died a long time back. He was a quiet, shy person, and didn't go out much. Then off with him one day to visit his son in the States, and he never came home. He'd be very old now, if he's alive at all. Around here they call it the haunted house, after someone thought they heard the banshee's croonin' there one night when the moon was full. It was probably just some poor creature pining for its mate, but no one ever goes next, nigh, or near the cottage since then." The idea of it being the perfect place to hide his files flashed through Wyatt's head.

Before leaving, he kissed Bridie lightly on the cheek, and said he would call every day to check on her mother's progress. He went to the room where he had stored his files, and stuffed them into his briefcase, hauling it back to his bike. He could barely fit it onto the back carrier. Soon he was back in the haunted house, and lifted some floorboards in a bedroom, stashing the briefcase there. Before replacing the floorboards, he checked that the file with the details of McFadden's gang was in the briefcase. He sighed with relief when it was, and replaced the last floorboard, thinking he had found the perfect hiding place.

Back at the hotel he picked up a letter at reception. It was typed and embossed with an English stamp and postmark, and smelt of a familiar perfume. A frisson of excitement shot through him, as he realised it was from Jenny. He rushed to his bedroom, and poured a whisky, his hands trembling as he sat back on the sofa to read it.

She said she was missing him, time out of mind, and couldn't wait to be with him again, and she hoped he felt the same way about her, deep in the heart's core. Her mother was recovering from depression, and though she loved her dearly, she knew she had to get away for a short break, or she herself would end up in a looney bin.

Her boss, the Bitch, was still giving her a hard time, with the magazine losing money, and she needed to get away from her too. Jenny had decided to take some holidays the next week in Sligo, and maybe kill two birds with one stone. Perhaps she could see him and also finish her article on Yeats, which she hoped to develop into a book. Anyway they had promised themselves to do it when they cancelled the last trip, hadn't they? There were so many lovely places and sights she wanted to revisit and show him, and they could hold hands and take life easy and walk by the sally gardens? She hoped he would not be old and foolish, and agree to come with her.

He re-read the letter and sipped his whisky. Her words touched him, and his heart told him to go, but in his mind he felt he was not playing fair with Bridie. Then he remembered Halpin's advice about laying low, and Bridie saying the same thing to him, and her being immersed in minding her mother. And then there was his previous promise to Jenny, their unfinished symphony. Would he regret going? Would he regret not going? He later wrote to Jenny saying he would love to meet her in Sligo, and could she give him the dates, and where she was booked.

\*\*\*

Redolent of the splendour of the Big House in its glory days, Lissadell was now a large, grey, decaying Georgian mansion, its gardens overgrown, and badly in need of restoration. Still, there was something about the place, Wyatt thought. He mentioned this to Jenny, who was poring over her book.

"Yes, you're right Jim many people coming here say that on their first visit. It's so rich in history. I think that's the attraction. Some of it is good, some bad. "

"Such as?"

"Well…let me think.The good, could be Yeats' words about the people of the house, the Gore-Booth sisters. The bad, maybe the illegal cutting down of the trees by the locals back in the fifties and sixties. There may even be other things further back."

"Just tell me the good."

*"The light of evening, Lissadell,*
*Great windows open to the south,*
*Two girls in silk kimonos, both*
*Beautiful, one a gazelle….."*

"Did Yeats fall for one of them?"Wyatt was curious after all he was involved with two women.

"Who knows? He was always attracted to women, and one was a revolutionary, the other a poet."

"Did the lady poet write anything famous?"

"Trying to catch me out, are you Jim? Well, actually there was a poem called "The Waves of Breffni".

"Really and how did that go?"

*"The great waves of the Atlantic sweep storming on their way,*
*Shining green and silver with the hidden herring shoal;*

*But the little waves of Breffni have drenched my heart in spray,*
*And the little waves of Breffni go stumbling through my soul."*

"Hey, I think I remember that poem from my schooldays." The words had caused a tingle to pass through his body. So much for people rubbishing leprechauns and fairies, he felt like someone had just walked on his grave.

"Quick Jim, let's take a few snaps, and get over to Knocknarea before the evening closes in."

They reached the car park at the foot of the mountain by mid afternoon, donned their walking boots, and headed up the winding path to the summit. Jenny told him that anyone on their first visit to Maeve's tomb would get a special wish if they carried a stone up the mountain and left it on her cairn. An old wive's tale, he thought. Although not superstitious or religious, he picked up a stone and put it in his pocket, thinking it no skin off his nose to carry a stone uphill.

Soon the Sligo countryside's patchwork mosaic of fields lay below them, as they ascended the barren, treeless terrain. Across Sligo Bay, Benbulben's sierra top loomed bare on the skyline. They were alone, and all was silent as the dead, save the music of birdsong. A mound of stones stood on the plateau at the top of the mountain.

The mountain top was littered with burial chambers, and he felt an aura of spirituality in the air. The ancient history of the country lay buried below their feet, with the holy quiet of the church, and the dead everywhere. Wyatt went over to the cairn of Queen Maeve, the High Queen of Ireland, knelt down, and placed his stone on it. After kneeling there a while and saying a silent prayer, he blessed himself, stood up and departed in silence. Disbelief stops here, he thought, surprised at the feeling he had inside.

"Made a special wish yet, Jim?" She broke the spell.

"Yes I have, but what has your poet friend got to say about all of this?"

"A lot, you should read some of it sometime."

"Maybe I will. We better make tracks back to the car. Otherwise we might have to spend the night on the mountain with all these dead spirits."

"You're right let's leave, it's a bit creepy here."

They rushed down the mountain in the half light of the approaching night.

\*\*\*

"Jim, what's that gun doing there?" She had come out of the bathroom, showered, showing more skin than clothes. He sucked in air.

"It's mine, and so is the bulletproof vest beside it. I was going to explain what happened since we last met, but just hadn't got around to it. It's a necessary travelling companion now, but I didn't want you to worry, or break the spell of this place."

He held her close, felt her trembling. He told her briefly about McFadden's chase on the mountain and his later arrest. She still had a worried look when he finished, and insisted on him bringing the gun with him when they left the hotel.

Later, under the haze of smoke in McGlynn's bar, over the noise of the fiddlers playing in the corner and the chatter of the scattered crowd, they recounted their day of magic. As they planned their next day's trip to Lough Gill and Benbulben, they sipped their drinks. Wyatt said he felt in awe of the place, though he had never believed in fairies, or the little people. Now he was not sure. You keep on drinking, Jenny said laughing, and then maybe you'll start believing in them.

And as they kept on talking, she told him a story she'd heard on her previous visit. Near Colooney, was one of the biggest collections of prehistoric burial chambers and standing stones in Europe, but over the years this had been whittled down to around fifty. The rest had either been destroyed or taken away, and a few years ago the local council had tried to turn what was left into a waste disposal site. Then there was such an outcry locally, the council had backed off. A rare victory for the environment and sensibility over greed and avarice, she said. He remembered grimly the disaster of the destruction of the Viking site at Wood Quay in Dublin, and the potential gold mining disaster in the Delphi valley.

"Let's drink to that." He said, raising his pint.

"Super. Let's drink to us too." Jenny smiled, and lifted her drink.

Time flew past the midnight hour, the air resounding to the noise of music, and banter about anything and everything, magical and mysterious, serious and delirious, until the owner asked those left if they had no homes to go to. Then the pub emptied, and the last of the revelers wended their weary way home. As they walked arm in arm down by the river to their hotel, they stopped to listen to the rushing water, and they held each other tight, kissed long and hard, and she whispered in his ear that she thought she had had found her Innisfree.

Later in their hotel room, in the double poster bed, they lay in each other's arms, feeling enwrapped in a cocoon away from the realities of life, and both wanted it to last forever. Nothing mattered to him, only her warm presence, ebbing and flowing, until he found himself sliding down a tunnel into a timeless place, magical and far away from his worries.

Next day on the way to Lough Gill, they passed a place where sally trees were grown for basket weaving in olden days. She held his hand as they passed by the place, telling him to take life easy, and he said he was. Then they came to a holy well under a hill, where legend had it miraculous cures happened in bygone years. A solitary old man knelt at the well, saying the rosary, and later they both drank from the waters, and said a silent prayer. Nearby stood a mass rock where outlawed priests said mass in Penal times. A small stone crucifix was carved into the top of the mass rock. Wyatt felt moved by a feeling of peace and mystery, just as he had been on Knocknarea.

When they reached Dooney Rock, on the edge of the lake, with the Isle of Innisfree visible further on, Jenny told him of a local fiddler immortalised by Yeats in a poem.

"What was so special about him?"

"He was like a pied piper he made people dance like a wave on the sea."

In his mind Jenny seemed immersed and entranced by the places they visited. Though he was sceptical before coming to Sligo, he now felt himself falling under some kind of spell.

Dromahair was their next stop, and they stoppeded for coffee and a sandwich in the local pub. The owner informed Wyatt of a session that night in *Shoot the Crows* in Sligo town. Jenny told him that there was a man from the area who dreamed of Faeryland, and finally discovered tenderness in his life before he died. Wyatt's cynicism about such things was waning, and he wondered if he might be changing into that kind of dreamy person.

The final place of seeing was Drumcliff, and casting their eyes on the grave where the poet's body rested, in the graveyard of the church where his grandfather had once been rector. Wyatt was taken by the simplicity of the place, overlooked as it was by Benbulben's bare head, where the poet had fished and sported the livelong summer days of his youth.

The music and drink flowed that night in Shoot the Crows. They drank to poetry and music, and to every thing and place they had seen that day. It was beyond anything he had expected. Jenny said it was better to experience it with someone you liked and loved, and hoped he agreed. Wyatt said he did, and later, under the canopy of the four poster bed, he told her beautiful she was, and that he loved her. She sighed, and said that was the nicest thing she'd ever heard, that she loved him too, and was going to prove it, and she did, in the nicest possible way.

They parted at Sligo airport the next day, both promising to write soon. Jenny dabbed a handkerchief to her eyes, as she vanished into the Departures Area. Wyatt waited until her plane was in the air, and waved to it, blowing a kiss upwards. He then took a taxi back to Leenane, and slept for most of the journey. He hadn't done any work on his project but felt refreshed and ready for anything.

In the hotel Wyatt opened his bedroom door, and noticed an envelope on the floor, with his name scrawled on it. He closed the door, tore it open, and scanned the words. It was from Sergeant McSweeney, dated that day, and marked delivered one o'clock. McSweeney said he had put it under Wyatt's door himself to ensure privacy, and was sorry to relate McFadden had been released on bail that day, and he wanted Wyatt to know that nothing could be done about it, as the bail money had been put up. Naturally, that's the way of the law in this land, Wyatt muttered, and read the letter again and again, a numb feeling inside, thinking you can run but you can't hide. He put his gun under the pillow, and opened the drawer beside his bed, where the half- full bottle of whiskey was stashed. Before going to bed he'd emptied it, but in spite of that, sleep only came stop start during the night.

# Chapter 18

## *I knew a Valley Fair*

Next day Wyatt decided to ring Halpin, and tell him of McFadden's release by the Garda. Within minutes he'd changed his mind, afraid it might look as if he was scared. Halpin might then pull the project and recall him immediately to Dublin. A knot of fear came in his gut, and he was dithering, but he was damned if he'd go running scared to Halpin. Instead he got stuck into his work pile, hoping it would settle his mind. But not long later, when the files and reports were sorted, he gave up, feeling his head wasn't right for it, feeling he needed to talk to someone. He rang Bridie, and asked how her mother was.

"She's doing well, thank you. It's nice to hear from you again, stranger. You said you would ring *every* day." She was miffed, the irony palpable. He had forgotten to call her as promised, and instantly regretted it.

"Yes I did. I…I…I'm sorry Bridie. I was away in Sligo, it… it slipped my mind. I…I…look I've got some worrying news. I can't talk about it on the phone. Can I come over?"

"Well… ok then….in that case. Maybe come in about an hour, if it's that serious. Mam should be up and settled in her chair by the fire then."

"Ok. I'll be there."

Damn, he should have rung Bridie, Wyatt fumed. It was so stupid it had never crossed his mind when he was with Jenny in Sligo. It seemed during that weekend his mind was away in some other world. All that was history now, but all it would have taken was a phone call. Damn.On his way to visit Bridie's mother he stopped in the village and bought two bunches of flowers, red roses and lilies.

Wyatt arrived on time, the exertion of cycling soothing

his nerves. Bridie seemed downcast when she opened the door.

"Surprise." Her eyes lit up, when he handed her the red roses.

"Jim Wyatt, you're a slieveen. You know the short cut to a woman's heart, but don't think you're getting off the hook. They're lovely so they are, hold on while I put them in water."

As she placed them in a vase on the table, and filled it with water, he relaxed. Her face was serene again, and her smile filled the room, lifting his spirits. It seemed when she was despondent, he was too, and when she was happy he felt better inside. What did this mean? He pondered. No point in going into all of that just now, after all, he didn't think about her when he was away with Jenny, did he? Some other day he would try to figure it out.

"I brought these for your mother. Don't be jealous."

"Jesus Jim, you can't give her those." She spoke with her hand over her face, smothering a smile.

"Why?"

"Because, you amadawn, those are lilies. Lilies are bad luck to someone when they're sick, they're only for funerals and other occasions. She'll think she's on the way out. Have you no sense atall?" She laughed.

"Oh, well... I see, better not then, what'll I do with them?"

"Don't you worry, I'll leave them in the church tomorrow. Now tell me all about this disturbing news?"

After he had related details of Mc Fadden's release, a frown furrowed her face.

"That's bad news alright Jim, but half expected, I suppose. I thought they might have kept him in a bit longer."

"So did I, he's only out on bail for the moment. It's still not over for him in court, and it won't be easy for him with the bail conditions."

"Don't you bet on it Jim, you've got to be careful, you'd never know what that fellah could get up to."

"I suppose not."

"I'll go out to the garden and pick some wildflowers while you have this cup of tea. Mam's still in the bathroom titivatin' herself for you."

"Really?"

"Yes she is, believe it or not."

Afterwards Bridie returned, and handed him a bunch of wildflowers.

"There, that should do the trick. I need to get to the shops and then over to see Tommy Joe. It's not easy being a full- time carer. Can I leave you with mam for an hour or so?"

"Of course, take your time." She waved to him as she lifted the latch on the door.

Wyatt went into the kitchen, where Bridie's mother sat in a wheelchair by a turf fire. Her thick grey hair was brushed back, her face sallow. Two crutches lay propped against the wall behind her. A picture of the Sacred Heart hung on one wall, beside one of the Pope. JFK's face smiled down from another wall.A Child of Prague statue stood in the middle of the mantelpiece over the fireplace. She looked up.

"You're a thousand times welcome Jim, sit you down there." She smiled wanly and pointed to a chair opposite her, and said it was the chair her husband used sit in.

"I brought these for you, Mrs O'Malley. I hope you're feeling better. " He said, and gave her the wildflowers.

"Musha, I'm grand. Ah, aren't they lovely? As wild as the wesht wind." She put the bunch to her face, and inhaled.

"Will you put them in water and leave them on the table over there where I can see them. They're better than any doctor's cure they are, they give my heart a lift." She handed him the flowers.

Wyatt left the flowers on the table and sat down opposite her. She had lost weight, and her face had gone gaunt. Wrinkles creased her forehead, but there was a sparkle in her brown eyes, and defiance in her drawn lips.

She said she'd be right as rain in a few months, and he believed her. Then she asked him to blow the fire aflame with the bellows, saying she could feel the cold in her bones, even though it was the height of summer. When the flames had licked the turf into a warm glow he put the bellows back in the grate beside the tongs. Bridie had left a tray set for tea on a table beside the fire. He plugged in the kettle, and waited for it to boil. In the corner of the room, he noticed an old cabinet gramophone, with doors at the front and a handle at the side, beside a pile of 78 records.

"Does it still work?" He nodded in the direction of the gramophone, which had a picture of a dog listening to music, on the lid.

"It does shurely Jim. A bit scratchy, but there's needles aplenty. I just love listenin' to the old records, it reminds me of the olden times, it's not for me all them new fangled gadgets. But I can't wind it anymore with the arthritis. Would you mind playin' a record for me?"

"Of course, there's no problem." He walked over to the gramophone, and lifted the lid. After changing the needle, he wound the handle, and picked up a record that was on the turntable.

"It's called "Eileen Aroon". Is that one ok with you?"

"Grand, it's my all time favourite."

He placed the needle at the starting point on the outer rim of the record, and watched the circles revolving like magic on the surface in endless circling rhythms. The sound was full of static and faded, but audible. Then he heard her joining in on some of the verses. She still has a voice, he thought, and knows all the words:

*"I knew a valley fair,*
*Eileen Aroon,*
*I knew a cottage there,*
*Eileen Aroon,*
*Far in that valley's shade,*
*I knew a gentle maid,*
*Flower of hazel glade,*

*Eileen Aroon.*
*Is it the laughing eye,*
*Eileen Aroon,*
*Is it the timid sigh,*
*Eileen Aroon,*
*Is it the tender tone,*
*Soft as the string'd harp's moan,*
*Oh, it is the truth alone,*
*Eileen Aroon.*
*Youth must with time decay,*
*Eileen Aroon,*
*Beauty must fade away,*
*Eileen Aroon,*
*Castles are sacked in war,*
*Chieftains are scattered far,*
*Truth is a fixed star,*
*Eileen Aroon.*

The words of the song affected him in a way that he'd never felt before. The sound of the needle screeching at the end of the record at the end, jerked him back to reality. Before any damage was done to the record, he lifted the arm and replaced it into its socket, and turned the gramophone off.

"Thank you Jim, that brought me back. It's so lovely, it... it's from the Irish." There were tears in her eyes, as she dabbed them with a hanky. He was moved.

The kettle boiled, and he filled the tea pot, leaving it simmering on the range. Over a cup of tea she asked how *his* mother was keeping. A dart of guilt shot through him, as it hit him it was weeks since he'd rung her nursing home. But he said she was keeping well. *Truth is a fixed star, Eileen Aroon.* The words flashed through his mind. No matter what danger he was in, he must see his mother in Dublin.

Soon Bridie returned, laden with shopping bags, saying Tommy Joe sent his regards and would be in touch. Wyatt rose to leave, excusing himself, saying he had to finish his report to Halpin, and would ring the next day. Bridie followed him to the door, and thanked him for calling, kissing him soft on the lips. Her arm came up behind his neck, and pulled him closer. Before she'd moved away, he'd felt the tenderness of her body, the warmth of her breath, and looked into the depth of her eyes. See you soon, don't forget to call, she said. I will, I will, he mumbled.

On his way back to the hotel, Wyatt stopped at the haunted house to check if his cache of documents was safe. It was. The place was littered with animal dung, and stank. He held his breath. At least the smell should be a deterrent to anyone coming here, he mused. As he left, it hit him someone could be spying on him, but a quick glance over the landscape revealed nothing. Proved nothing either, he thought, and decided not to come to the house again, unless he really had to.

Back in his bedroom he felt happy, and reflected on his improved relationship with Bridie. You value your friends here, he thought, and she was much more than a friend. Later that day, a message came from Clontarf nursing home in Dublin, saying his mother's condition had weakened, and he must come urgently. Don't panic, he thought, but he did. This can't be happening just now. But it was. He packed his bags.

Before leaving for the evening train to Dublin, he rang Bridie to tell her of his mother's condition. She said she would tell her own mother, and they would say a prayer. He thanked her, and put down the phone, saying he would be back in a few days.

On the train, his thoughts flashed in short spasms, back to boyhood memories of his mother. In his life he had rarely felt as close to her as she would have liked. He regretted this, and wondered if she would have preferred a daughter. In her youth she had been blonde and beautiful, and never short of admirers. *Youth must with time decay, Eileen Aroon*. She loved sports, tennis and horseriding, and his father's early death had left her a rich widow with many friends.She had plenty of time to enjoy life, with him away in boarding school in England. And she did, as he found out one day when he came across some old love letters stashed in the attic. *Beauty must fade away, Eileen Aroon.*

In later years gardening was her greatest joy. *Flower of hazel glade, Eileen Aroon.* Still, in the end, they only had each other. It was a pity they were not closer. She had seemed less than happy when he'd married an English lady, but had loved her grandchild. That was, until the accident. Damn the accident. But in the end hers was a lonely life. *Oh it is the truth alone, Eileen Aroon.* He knew it was partly his fault. I hope I don't ever end up alone in a nursing home, like her. He hoped someone would love him enough to put up with him at home.

The eucalyptus trees on the gravelled driveway bent in the breeze, as if sighing in sympathy with something. An eerie feeling crept through his body when he stood outside the nursing home. He felt as if a spirit passed through him. It seemed like a bad omen, and his suspicions were confirmed when the matron told him that his mother had passed away an hour earlier. Her last words were" Has Jim not come yet?" The words cut him to the quick.

In her room she was laid out in a white dress, her face serene, as if all her trials were over, and she'd happily taken her leave of the world. He touched her frigid hands to make sure, and said a few prayers, staying in the room all night. They had a lot of time to make up. Now it was he who was left all alone.

Next day came and went, visiting solicitors, making the final funeral arrangements. It was to be a cremation, her ashes spread around her beloved garden. When he rang Bridie with the bad news, she said how sorry she was, and would have attended the funeral, but for her mother's condition. But they would get a mass said in her memory. He thanked her, and put down the phone, wiping tears from his eyes. After the funeral mass, as he was about to leave with the hearse for the crematorium, someone tapped him on the shoulder.

"Please accept my sincere sympathies James. You know a mother is a mother, is a mother is a mother." It was Seamus Halpin. Dark suited, grey moustached, sombre faced.

"Thanks Seamus, it's very good of you to come here." They shook hands. A light rain fell.

"I know what it's like James, I've been there myself. Maybe you'd like to drop into the office for a chat, before you leave Dublin, no rush, whenever it suits you. I'm sure you have matters to clear up. Anyway, as I said you have my sympathy on this sad day. I'll take my leave now. Goodbye." Halpin replaced his dark hat on his grey head, and moved away towards the car park in the dismal drizzle, angel's tears.

Wyatt followed the hearse to the crematorium at Harold's Cross. The ceremony was simple, uninspiring and impersonal.Sadness gripped him as the coffin moved along the conveyor belt. When it reached the small doors, they opened as if by magic to let the body enter the nether world, and vanish from view. It was her wish, but he was a traditionalist. Such is the way of the world. To be scattered without trace in a garden. His preference was always a gravestone to lay flowers on, and where he could visit and think of the past. It was important, he thought, to keep a grave clean in respect of the memory of the person buried there. He wondered if anyone would put flowers on *his* grave.

The ensuing days went sorting her affairs out. Her solicitor advised him that after the house was sold, mortgage paid, nursing home bill settled, and his own probate fees, there *would* be a reasonable lump sum left. Not enough to retire on, he smiled, but Wyatt *was* the sole beneficiary. As he signed the legal documents, Wyatt said he was glad to hear the news, but had no intention of retiring.

Halpin was in affable mood when they met. He was still ensconced in the same office, with the same desk and coffee machine, and the same pipe in his hand, puffing a pall of vanilla flavoured smoke around the office. Wyatt cut to the chase, telling him of McFadden's release on bail. Halpin's muted reaction indicated he may have already known the news. Wyatt reckoned his brother must have told him.

"Sure you don't want to finish the report in Dublin, James? Sure you've no second thoughts on the matter?" Halpin's eyebrows arched, as he leant forward.

"No thanks Seamus, I'm making good progress on it down there. That few days break in Sligo helped, just as you suggested, and there are some final items to be checked. It's important to get it right, after all the blood, sweat, and tears, don't you agree?"

"Absolutely, my boy, but can you give me any idea when it might be finished?"

"It will be a few weeks, barring unforeseen circumstances." If only he knew it wasn't yet started, Wyatt mused.

"And there's just one other thing, James?"

"Yes?"

"It's about the matter of the gold mining in the Delphi Valley. I wouldn't get involved too much if I were you. It may distract you from finishing the report." Wyatt wondered if his brother had given Halpin an earful.

"But it's an environmental issue Seamus, and it will directly and indirectly impinge on marine life in the area."

"Yes, but at this moment, it's not directly on our radar. It's highly sensitive I grant you James, but it's also highly political. I mean up to the very highest level, right to the top. Get my drift? I think you'd be well advised to keep out of it, and stick to your original brief."

"Is that your advice or an order?" Wyatt guessed someone higher up had been onto Halpin.

"You can take it whatever you like." Wyatt decided to drop the matter.

"Ok Seamus message received and understood." Wyatt left minutes later to catch the evening train back to

Westport.

When he got back to the hotel, Wyatt rang Noel Kenny in the Mayo News. Kenny confirmed he'd heard about McFadden's release on bail, and had covered it in an article in the paper. But don't worry he'd said, the information on McFadden's gang was safely hidden. Wyatt should also be on high alert, he'd said, as McFadden would be desperate to retrieve the information. In fact, they shouldn't even be speaking to each other on the telephone. Wyatt agreed, and thanked him, putting down the receiver. A dry feeling came in his throat, the feeling he got when he needed a drink.

After a bath, he changed, dined in the hotel, and walked down to the village. Evening shadows slanted on the brooding mountains, a hush in the air, broken only by curlews croaking on the shoreline. The fjord was blood-red as the sun sank. Under his jacket he felt the jutting bulk of the Beretta. Who knows, he might meet McFadden in the pub? If McFadden was foolish enough to show his nose there, he'd be ready, he resolved. But he breathed a sigh of relief when he reached the sanctuary of the pub.

The first familiar face Wyatt saw inside was Sergeant McSweeney, seated at the bar. McSweeney nodded and came over straight away and sat beside him, a pint in each hand.

"There y'are Inspector, get that into you. Sorry to hear the bad news about your mother."

"Thanks Sergeant.That's just what I needed." Wyatt took a swig, and put the glass down.

"In case you think our friend, you know who, might show up, he won't. I've warned him that he's off limit here. So don't worry. He has to behave himself because of the bail conditions."

"Ok, but I'm not going into hiding just because of him."

"And rightly so, bhoy. Any problem and you just contact me, I won't be far away." McSweeney winked and moved back to the bar.

Wyatt saw Tommy Joe in a corner with his brother Michael and a few friends. Tommy Joe looked over, and their eyes locked. Within minutes, he too had come over, a pint in each hand. After sympathising with Wyatt on his mother's demise, he changed the subject.

"Dammit Inspector, we should have sent that McFadden bollocks to Davy Jones' locker, when we had the chance, it would've saved everybody a lot of time and money. Now the legal beagles have got him out, an' he's back persecutin' peace lovin' people."

"I'm beginning to see what you mean Tommy Joe, but it's not as simple as that, he's only out temporarily on bail."

"Yeh, but with an animal like that on the loose, a lot of damage could be done. The bastard should be behind bars, he's an effin' murderer."

"Eventually he'll be trapped and caught. But a man's innocent until proven guilty." Wyatt said, though inwardly not convinced, as the practicality of Tommy Joe's thinking sank in.

"Balls to all that Inspector, do unto others as they would do unto you, I say only do it first. That's my law, let's drink to that." He lifted his glass, clinking Wyatt's.

At the end of the night he rose to leave. Sergeant McSweeney came over, and said he would escort him back to the hotel. Wyatt politely refused, but the Sergeant insisted, and said it was his duty. Wyatt could get himself to the pub in one piece any night, he said, and *he* would ensure his safe return to the hotel. Wyatt had second thoughts, and accepted the offer, realising he was more vulnerable after a few drinks.

Next morning a letter arrived with a UK postmark. A tingle shot through him, thinking it was from Jenny, their covert tryst still embedded in his mind. He took his cup of coffee, and sauntered into the lounge to read it. After thumbing the letter open, he smelt her perfume on the pages. She hoped her shy, brave one of the heart was safe and well. She said the perfume was the one she had worn in Sligo, and did he remember it? And did he remember when they walked through the long dappled grass, she with apple blossom in her hair, into the orchard of love, where she had laid her dreams at his feet, for better or for worse. She hoped it was for the better, and when things were getting her down, she thought of Sligo. Did he? Her mother was unchanged, sadly, so was her boss, as bitchy as ever. Her book was taking shape in her head, and she would start writing it soon, but anything could tempt her from the craft of writing, and it did. Maybe she could wangle another trip over, when she had something to show her boss. She ended saying she loved him, and hoped their love would not grow out of fashion like an old song, and she hoped he would write soon, and she was counting the hours.

When he'd finished re-reading it, he lifted the coffee cup to his lips. It was cold. He grimaced, replacing it in the saucer, and gazed abstractedly at the letter. He realised he hadn't told Jenny of his mother's death in the hullaballoo of recent days, and resolved to do it now. Life could be complicated with two lovers, he pondered, both beautiful, and one a gazelle. Hey, he was thinking like Jenny now, one day he would have to choose, but not today. He went upstairs to his bedroom, and wrote a long reply to Jenny. The rest of the day went in preparing the groundwork for his report to Halpin.

The following day came fair and fresh, cumulus clouds flying in fantastic shapes across the sky. After posting the letter to Jenny, he rang Bridie. She was taking her mother to Castlebar hospital in the ambulance for a check up.

Wyatt went to his desk, and was immersed in his report until late afternoon, when he was interrupted by a phone call. It was Bridie, her voice agitated. She said she'd just arrived back from the hospital to find the house had been ransacked. No, she said, she hadn't rung the guards, he was her first contact, and could he please come straight away. After telling her he'd be there immediately, and not to panic, he dropped the phone, ran down the stairs, and out the hotel door to where he had left his bike, his heart thumping.

# Chapter 19

## *The Rising of the Moon*

Bridie had calmed down when he reached the house. The break-in had happened during a visit to her mother in Castlebar hospital, earlier that day, and the smashed glass panel in the front door above the lock indicated how they'd broken in. She had sussed the situation before her mother realised what had happened, and moved her into the kitchen, which was intact. She'd then checked the other rooms, afraid that someone might still be in the house. Drawers were scattered over the beds, and wardrobes emptied on the floor, but no valuables had been stolen. She'd thought that strange. After tidying the rooms, she'd returned to the kitchen, to find her mother pouring a cup of tea.

"If it wasn't money they were after, Jim, I wonder what it was? But to think someone was in your house makes you wonder what the country's comin' to. It makes your blood boil and it makes you scared. It's good to have a man in the house at times like this." She touched his arm, and he saw the frightened look in her eyes.

"I'm happy to help in any way Bridie, but I'm afraid I might have been the cause of the break in. If I was, I'm sorry." He put his arms around her waist, and pulled her close, their lips touching. He felt the softness of her body touching his, tender, yielding. She sighed in his arms, and he sighed too, then she pushed him away.

"Jim, get a hold of yourself, me mam's in the other room." Her face was flushed.

"Sorry, I got carried away."

"I'm glad you did, but please don't get me wrong, this isn't the time for cuddling and kissing. But what *were* they after?"

"Probably the files and documents I was storing here in

the spare room, don't you remember?"

"Yes I do of course, I'd forgotten."

"Let's go and check that room."

They found the room ransacked. Luckily, Bridie had not thought to check it before, and had no idea of its contents. Papers were strewn everywhere, and he gathered them up, put them on the bed, and began sorting them out. There were some documents missing, but none of huge importance, and he sighed with relief. When he had moved the files to the haunted house he had left some unimportant ones as a decoy in the room. Obviously, they were looking for was the page with Mc Fadden's gang's details, he reasoned. And they would continue searching for that, it wasn't over. They must be unaware of the haunted house's hidden contents, he reasoned, but it was no longer safe to go there. The thought sent panic waves through his body.

"Ok, that's it Bridie, there's stuff missing, but nothing that can't be replaced."

"That's good Jim let's have a cup of tea. We can tell the guards tomorrow, I just couldn't put up with all their questions now."

They were sitting in the kitchen, chatting with Bridie's mother, when a knock came on the door. It was Tommy Joe, and his brother Michael, with a bucket of spring water, and fresh fish from their boat. Wyatt felt reassured when he saw Tommy Joe's stocky figure framed in the doorway.

"Howy ye all doin'?" Tommy Joe raised his hand in greeting.

"You'll stay for tea?" Bridie's mother asked.

"Well...if it's not puttin'yeh to too much trouble?" Tommy Joe said, winking at Wyatt.

They left the water and fish in the pantry, and visited the washroom before sitting down. The stench of fish from their clothes was overpowering. Bridie gutted and pan-fried the fresh fish, and served them with fluffy mashed potato in butter.

"That was delicious. I suppose you two don't get fed

like this back home, Tommy Joe?" Wyatt said.

"That's for shure, Inspector. It's all right for some I 'spose, gettin' wined and dined in the best hotels." Tommy Joe spoke with a twinkle in his eye.

"Tommy Joe and Michael earn their keep here for shure, keepin' us in fresh water and fed with the freshest fish all the livelong year." Bridie's mother said.

"Our plan's not havin' to cook for ourselves, if we can help it. We're not in the ha'penny place compared to Bridie here, when it comes to cookin'. Yeh have to know yer strengths and yer weaknesses." Tommy Joe grinned as he spoke.

Later Wyatt got to speak to Tommy Joe alone in the living room, and told him the details of the break- in.

"The bad bastards, I saw the door smashed alright, bad cess to them. We should've finished that cunt McFadden off when we had the chance." Tommy Joe fretted, and paced the floor, punching his fist into the palm of his hand.

"What should we do now?"

Tommy Joe kept pacing the room for several minutes before replying.

"Nothin' Inspector, we do nothin' for now. We could spill the beans on McFadden an' give the details of his outfit to the press, jus' like we threatened him we'd do, or we could report it to the polis too but that won't get us anywhere. McFadden's desperate to get his shaggin' hands on them documents, an' he'll have a go again for them, but he might make a mistake next time, and then we'll settle his hash. I bet he's rattled, so he is."

"And if he doesn't make a mistake?" Wyatt felt inside that maybe he himself was getting rattled.

"Then we're all fucked, Inspector, it's a rock an' a hard place, but we'll tough it out. Shite, he's under fuckin' pressure too."

"I suppose."

"An' I'll tell you somethin' for nothin' Inspector."

"What's that?"

"Expect nothin' in this life, an' then you'll never be

disappoint'd."

"I'll think about that."

Michael entered the room, and soon he and Tommy Joe bade everyone goodnight, lifting the latch on the kitchen door to leave. Night had fallen outside, the sky clear, shot with stars, and as the door opened a shaft of moonlight slanted across the flagged kitchen floor like a tracer beam. Tommy Joe muttered about not needing a lamp that night to guide him home, as he walked with Michael into the ghostly- lit landscape.

Back in the kitchen Bridie was peering out the window.

"Oh look Jim, the moon is full tonight, its on the rise over the mountains."She cried.

Wyatt walked to the window, and peered through the panes above her head, resting his hands on her shoulders. He felt her softness, and his pulse throbbed, as he inhaled her odour, and he saw the moon rising above Ben Gorm into a star spangled sky. Soon the whole valley would be bathed in a lunar light, he thought, and soon night creatures would be on the prowl. The thought that someone might be out there spying on them hit him then, and sent a shiver through his body.

"Jim, I'm scared about staying here on my own, with mam. Maybe you'd stay here a few nights until things settle down a bit?" Her eyes had a scared-bird look.

"Of course Bridie, of course I will, but...but...what about your mother, what will she think?"

"Don't worry, I'll make up a story, I'll say I'm doing your family history, which is true anyway, and I need you here to get information. I'd like to show you my office, by the way."

"I'd like that too, let's do it."

She brought him to her study. It was compact and dimly lit. The large desk was littered with papers, and had a word processor in the centre, with two chairs in front of it. An angle poised lamp stood beside the desk.

"What's all this about?"

"My project, you goose, I'm researching the name

Wyatt and it's origins in this area. Do you not remember the name we found on the old gravestone, that day on Inisboffin?"

"Oh....yes, of course, indeed I do remember it very well...I had forgotten." How could he ever forget that day? And her body lying along the flat gravestone, as her towel slid to the ground. His mind wandered.

Bridie gathered up the papers, and started to put them in order.

"Sorry Jim I've been meanin' to sort these out before, the room's in a tip."

"Don't worry, I know the feeling, and how is the project going?"

"Slowly, but I think I'm gettin' there. I've got into some very interestin' areas, but it's too soon to say anythin' for sure. I need to check out a lot more things, *and* we're talkin' here of something that started in the eighteenth century, for God's sake. Anyway, I'm enjoyin' doin'it. By the way Jim, I need some information on your own family, if you don't mind, as far back as you can go. Birth dates, wedding dates, burial dates and burial places, and so on."

"Sure, why not? I'll do my best. I hope there won't be any skeletons leaping out of the closet."

"You never know your luck. A lot of things were brushed under the carpet in olden days."

"I'm sure, and it's still happening today."

Nearly an hour later, when Bridie was satisfied she had enough details about his family, she closed her files and strolled again to the window, gazing out.

"Jim, the moon's liftin' high on the mountains now. Let's make the most of it, and go for a walk to the lakeside. Mam's asleep in bed, and we won't be long, it should be safe enough."

"Sure, why not? Let's go."

Bridie covered her head with a shawl, while he donned his jacket, before they tiptoed from the house. Outside, she took a key from her pocket, and turned to lock the door, before they walked hand in hand down the path, lit in a ghostly glare.

The wind was dead, the night still as the grave, the moon radiant, high in a stellar sky. It shone all over the valley, on the barren hills and rocks, the treeless terrain, and silvery on the gurgling river where salmon and trout rested silent on its sandy bottom. It shone too on all the farm animals, frozen still creatures, statue-like in the fields, and beamed too on where the fox barked unseen in the distance. It lit up Bridie's face, in a glow that made her beatific and beautiful. His hand slid down her waist, exploring, while they walked, and he felt her intake of breath as he did this.

Soon a little lake appeared, shimmering. Bridie took off her shawl, and placed it on a grassy clump near where the lake waters lapped on the shore. They both lay on the shawl, and she asked him if he loved her, and he said yes he did. They kissed long and hard, then softly and deeply, as they both fell under the spell of the lunar landscape. Slowly they became entranced by the surreal beams, and lost all reason for anything, except loving each other.

Later she stood up, and straightened her dress, tossing back her hair. Then he arose, stretching his arms above his head, and put his jacket on. She came to his side, and looked up into his eyes.

"Jim you're wonderful, you know that, all my worries have been blown away. God, there's magic in the moonlight tonight for sure. And romance, and love, and it does funny things to your head too, the moon does, it surely does." She put her arms around his neck, on tiptoes, and kissed his lips again.

"You're not too bad yourself, you know Bridie, but maybe we should head back to the house in case your mother wakes." The thought someone might be spying on them had crept into his head again.

"Yes you're right Jim. I suppose all good things must come to an end, unfortunately. But there's somethin' I must tell you. Look, I don't know how to say it, and I hope you'll understand Jim, but first just tell me again that you love me."

"Of course I do, I do love you." He saw a frown crease her face, just like on the night of the Ceili when she told him of her fiancée's return from America. He encircled her with his arms and hugged her close.

"C'mon Bridie, let it out, tell me what's bothering you. After what's happened in the past few months, nothing will come as a surprise. Anyway I hope its good news for a change." As he spoke he fondled her hair, and laughed lightly.

"I...I suppose its good and bad news, it depends how you look on it."

"Look on what? Please tell me what's on your mind, Bridie."

"I....I'm goin'to have a baby Jim, there that's it, its out. That's what's on my mind."

"Wow, congratulations, that *is* good news." His voice was outwardly cool, but inside he was stunned.

"You've been to the doctor?"

"Not yet, you're the first one to know."

"Then how can you be sure?"

"I can absolutely assure you I am sure, it's not somethin' I'd be makin' up, is it?" She sounded irritated.

"No not really Bridie, I'm sorry it was just a reaction. It's a bit of a shock I suppose, and who is the father, may I ask?" A strange feeling came in his stomach as he spoke.

"Who do you think it is, you goose. *It's you.* I hope you're happy, I hope you think its good news. "

"Of course I do, that's great, I mean wonderful. I'm delighted. It's great news. I can't believe it."

He hugged her tight, kissed her lips, and as their stomachs pressed together he thought he could feel a swelling in hers, and he felt something was happening over which he had no control.

"Jim, I know this must be a big shock to you, but don't think it hasn't been the same for me. You're the first person I ever felt that way about, like going all the way with, I mean. Francie and me, we would never go all the way, until we got married. Sure, we did things but not that, and what with him bein' away in the States an' all. The families would've been scandalised if somethin' like this happened, you understand?"As she spoke he saw tears glisten in her eyes.

"Of course I understand Bridie, I love you, don't you know, to hell with the neighbours and begrudgers, and whatever they might say." But inside his mind was topsy turvy, and he hugged her again.

"What I'm tryin' to say Jim is, that there's no reason for us to get married or anythin' like that. You understand that, even though I *do* love you, I wouldn't want it to happen that way, out of pity, like."

"Yes I *do* understand, and I *do* love you, Bridie. Look, we've been through a lot together, and we know each other pretty well. Maybe we should just keep it as our little secret until things settle down a little."

"Of course Jim, that's grand with me, for the moment."There was a look of relief on her face as she spoke.

"By the way, does your mother or sister know?"

"My sister Nora's away in Dublin on a course, and doesn't know, neither does my mother I think, but maybe, well you never know. Mothers seem to have a way for sussin' things like that, but I don't really think she does."

"I suppose, anyway tomorrow you're coming with me to Westport to see the doctor, and get yourself checked out. Ok?" He smiled, as he spoke.

"Ok." She smiled back.

On the way back to the house they stopped to embrace, and as they did, Bridie looked towards the heavens and cried out.

"Look Jim see there, see the star falling."She pointed towards Ben Gorm.

"Yes, I see it." A sign of one's insignificance, he'd always thought.

"Usually it's a sign someone's died and is on their way

to heaven, but tonight I feel it's a sign my baby is on its way to earth."

"That's a nice thought."

He kissed her again, and put his arms around her, hugging her close, feeling her tummy in awe, as they walked back to the house along the moonlit path.

Some time later Wyatt put the light out and settled to sleep in his bed. Moonbeams still streamed through the window, lighting the room in a luminescent glow. Then a creaking sound rustled in the room, after the bedroom door had opened, and Bridie slid into the room, finger pressed over her lips. She tiptoed to the bed, and slipped her bathrobe off on the way, draping it over the chair beside the bed. She stood there a few moments, the moonlight bright on her body, and he was awestruck, thinking how beautiful she looked, hair black and long in the moonlight, dangling over her shoulders. Then she pulled back the sheets, and slipped in beside him.

"Sssssh, don't talk. Mam can hear the grass growin'. I think it must be moon madness or something tonight, has me here doin' what I'm doin'."She whispered in his ear.

No words were spoken after this, as he felt her skin touch his, beneath the sheets, and their lips spoke in silence to each other. In the stillness, his fingers traced the Grecian bend of her back, and he felt her stomach for a sign of life. All the time she sighed in approval, and she touched him too, and he thought that this must be what heaven is like. The night flew in a haze of love, until in his mind's eye he saw a star falling from the heavens, leaving a blazing, dazzling trail before bursting into a million pieces.

"God, I could easily stay the night, moonstruck I definitely am, I must get back to my room now, before I fall asleep." She whispered as she slipped from between the sheets, kissing his lips as she left. Moments later she had vanished from the room, while the moonbeams still shone their celestial light through the window, and her smell lingered in the bed beside him.

He rolled onto his back, and stared at the brightly lit ceiling. Thoughts cascaded through his mind like water over a cataract. No it wasn't a dream, he hadn't imagined it, Bridie *was* pregnant, and *he* was the father. As if he didn't have enough on his plate at the moment, *and* Jenny coming to visit the next week. How would he explain the situation to her? With great difficulty, he reckoned. He knew when he was with Bridie he was smitten with *her*, and Jenny never entered his mind, but the same happened with Bridie when he was with Jenny. How was he going to sort this out? Right now he didn't know. Right now all he knew was he loved Bridie. Everything was ok for the moment, as they'd agreed to keep it a secret, but that situation couldn't go on for ever.

Tomorrow, the visit to the doctor would have to be made, he reflected, and her mother might soon find out she was pregnant, but what's wrong with that? Christ, if she starts getting sick next week, the world and his wife will know it, and Father Flynn will be beating down the door to know about the wedding plans. The word wedding sent another wave of panic through his body, as he knew he wasn't ready for getting married again. Maybe down the road, but he'd have to think further on that. And what about his career when he'd finished the marine project for Halpin? His secure, well pensioned position with the state was based in Dublin, not Mayo, and that was assuming he survived in one piece.

He put out his hand, touching the gun on the table beside his bed, and felt better. There were other important issues, like staying alive, *and* he needed to stay off the bottle. What he wouldn't give for a whisky now, though. Then he remembered Bridie was carrying his baby, and that brought brought another worry into his head, another responsibility another mouth to feed. I must stop thinking all about me and my problems, he thought, get a grip and act sensibly, and not behave like before when I cracked up, hit the bottle, and blamed everyone else. No, this time I will behave responsibly, he vowed. And he continued looking up at the ceiling, and the moon continued sending silver slivers slanting through the window. It was a long night.

# Chapter 20

## *Bog Down in the Valley*

While Bridie was in the surgery Wyatt waited outside, pacing the corridor, hands behind his back. Sometimes he stared out the window, and wondered if all this was really happening. But when his gaze switched to the crowd queueing inside, he realised it was all too real. He fretted something was not right as Bridie had been with the doctor a long time, and they had borrowed Tommy Joe's van while he was away fishing. When Bridie finally came out, she told him as they were walking through the corridor, that the doctor had confirmed her pregnancy, and said she was six weeks gone. They went hand in hand in silence back to the van, and left at once, afraid someone might recognise them, and start putting two and two together. The inside of the van reeked of fish, but beggars can't be choosers, he thought. As the van gathered speed, he spoke.

"Was everything all right Bridie, you were in a long time with the doctor?"

"Yes Jim, everythin's fine. The doctor said I was to take plenty of rest, but he kept annoying me, and askin' pryin' questions. I told him it was none of his business so I did. I told him where to get off. I was a bit short with him I suppose, but he was kinda actin' like God, and I asked him who he thought he was, a doctor or a priest. Anyway he got the message, and backed off."

"Look, you're bound to be a bit stressed, and the stench in this van can't be doing you any good either. Phew, let's go for a coffee in Westport. We need to get some fresh air into our lungs."

Bridie insisted he stop at a shop on the way to get some air fresheners. She said it was a lost cause tryin' to make the van smell better, but she'd have a go at it anyway. Soon they were sitting in the gardens of a restaurant on the quays, seeing the sun's glitter on the wavetops in Clew Bay, sucking in the air.

"God Jim, I feel a bit better now, the view does help, and I really needed that coffee."

"Have another one, then."

"Maybe I will and by the way, after tonight you don't need to stay in the house with mam an' me. I don't think those people, whoever they are, will come back. Anyway, tongues'll wag if the word gets out about me being pregnant and you staying in the house a lot. Can't have them thinkin' things, can we?" She grasped his hand.

"I suppose you're right, I'll pack tomorrow and head back to the hotel, anyway I have things to catch up on back there."

"I'm sure you have, and you'll probably find a note there from Father Flynn. We got one today."

"About what?"

"They're havin' a final protest rally on Thursday against the minin' project an' it's goin' to be in the church on top of Croagh Patrick. It looks like Father Flynn's lookin' for divine intervention, an' he's wantin' everyone to be there. It's his last throw of the dice, he says, an' it's startin' at mid day at the car park in Murrisk. Will you be goin' Jim?"

"Yes absolutely, I've got to see it through, but I don't think you should go, not in your condition."

"I'd love nothing better than goin', even in my condition, but I can't leave mam in the house alone. You'll fill me in on what happens, won't you?"

"Of course I will, don't you worry, and I don't think the doctor would approve of you going either." He kissed her softly on the cheek.

"I suppose not, but I'd really love to be there."

After paying the bill, they strolled back to the van, and soon were chugging through Murrisk, past cloud capped Croagh Patrick, high and mighty on their left. As they slowed down, he glanced up at the mountain's pointed cone shape, mysterious and mist covered at the top.

"It looks foreboding, is it hard to climb, have you ever done it?"

"Many times, and it's a lot harder than you'd think."

"Thanks, I'll be careful then." He grinned.

After Murrisk, they turned left towards Lioscarney, into the valley behind Croagh Patrick. As they headed into the Delphi valley, they passed people bent over, panning for gold in a river. I hope its only fool's gold they're finding, Wyatt muttered.

Back in her house, Bridie's mother was watching the TV news in the living room. Another atrocity in Northern Ireland, another hotel bombed, with many innocent casualties. Wyatt felt frustrated, and wondered when it would all end. In the Presidential election Lenihan had lost more ground after his "mature recollection" that he'd phoned the President of Ireland, and Mary Robinson had leapt to pole position. Wyatt packed his bags and drove back to the hotel. After putting the bags in his room, he drove up to the harbour, left the van there for Tommy Joe, and walked back to the hotel.

When he returned, he picked up his mail at reception desk. Father Flynn's letter was in it, and also an urgent message to ring Sergeant McSweeney. He hurried up the stairs to make the call from his bedroom. McSweeney told him more explosives had been stolen from Glencorrig Mining's premises the previous evening.

"Don't know if they were for use up North or what, but big Pete, your friend unfortunately arrived back at the premises, unexpected like, in the middle of the robbery, and took them on, unarmed, the mad fool. He got kneecapped for his bravery, or lunacy, whatever you want to call it it, and the poor guy is now in Castlebar Hospital, recoverin'.I thought you'd like to know, Inspector, I've just been to see him, and I'm afraid he's not in great shape."

"Oh, I'm sorry to hear that. Its bad news, but thanks for letting me know, I'll go see him right away."

Wyatt reeled in panic his throat parched, and then told McSweeney about the break- in at Bridie's mother's house. The Sergeant noted the details, and said he would call there later, before asking Wyatt if he'd be at the mining meeting on Croagh Patrick.

"You bet I will Sergeant, you bet." Wyatt scowled, putting the receiver back on the cradle. He then took the pistol from his holster, checked it was loaded, replaced it in the holster, and ordered a taxi for Castlebar hospital.

Wyatt's visit was restricted to ten minutes as Pete was under sedation. The light was dim inside the room, and in the gloom he saw the shattered leg, encased in a huge plaster, hanging like a giant's leg from a hoist over the bed. Blood stains were splattered on the battered Stetson lying on a table beside the bed, and Pete's face was bandaged and covered in cuts and bruises. He's been pistol whipped as well, Wyatt thought grimly, as he sat on a chair near the bed. Pete's eyes flickered in recognition, and a wan smile came on his face.

"Howdy dude. Sorry, can't talk much."One of his front teeth was missing.

"They gave you a right going over, Pete."

"Shore did, coulda bin worse though, I guess."

"How?"

"Well, suppose I coulda bin pushin' up the daisies now. Never knew livin' could be so painful dude, still it should git better." He grimaced as he spoke, then picked up the kidney shaped enamel dish from the table beside his bed, spat blood into it, and put it back on the table.

"Were you armed?"

"Nope, they was though, dang it.Thought there was only two of them, I coulda handled that, but then this other guy, he took me from behind. It was that no good sonofabitch with the red hair, the one we had the punch up with in the pub after the hurlin' game. I knew his voice, once he opened his gob."

"McFadden, you mean."

"Yeah thet's the guy, thet's the mean no good

sonofabitch, made me lay face down an' shot me 'n the back of the knee. Doc says it was a .22 slug an' I was lucky it went through the fleshy part, not the bones. When he shot me he said I was lucky this time, it could have been in both legs, or between the eyes." Pete talked slowly and painfully.

"So you'll be able to walk again?"

"Yeah, that's what the doc says, but it'll be a while, a long while I guess. Listen dude, I want you to do me one big favour."Pete leaned over in the bed as he spoke, eyes bulging.

"Sure Pete, what is it?"

"You git that damn lily- livered sonofabitch for me, you git him for me dude."

"Sure Pete, nothing would give me greater pleasure." Nothing would be more difficult either, Wyatt rthought. A young, dark haired nurse then entered the room, and said visiting time had finished. Wyatt gave Pete the thumbs up sign and left the room, anger seething through his veins.

\*\*\*

Wyatt took the special bus for the mining meeting from Leenane village to Murrisk. The day began warm and sultry, the hot sun playing hide and seek in the clouds. Many had gathered in the car park under Croagh Patrick, mostly wearing walking gear and rucksacks, and all with climbing sticks. Among the milling crowd, he spotted Bridie far away, and she saw him too, waving back, and was by his side within minutes, smiling as she handed him a booklet. She said her sister had arrived home, and was minding her mother, andTommy Joe had brought her in his van.

While they waited he read the booklet, concerning local lore about Saint Patrick, and Ireland's holiest mountain. At the end of the Saint's forty days fasting and praying on the Reek, the mountain was awash with black birds, and Saint Patrick, not knowing if he was in Heaven or on earth, struck his bell at them. Legend has it no demon came to Ireland after that happening. Near the Reek was a place called Lugnademon, where Saint Patrick banished all the demons (in the form of snakes). St Patrick's Bell was now in a museum in Dublin. Wyatt's reading was interrupted by the stewards ushering the people in the direction of the gateway leading onto the mountain.

Soon Father Flynn blew a whistle to start the ascent, and the crowd surged upwards, quickly transforming into a long, winding snake of people, stretched along the rising, twisting trail. They trudged over rough, loose stones that slid and slipped beneath their feet. Bridie kept at Wyatt's side, stopping in sporadic sunshine to look back over Clew Bay, and saw it studded with its myriad drumlin islands, lying in the water like beached whales.

At the first station the procession stopped, and Father Flynn said a decade of the rosary, then they moved onwards and upwards in a raggle taggle line, the air becoming muggy. Wyatt started to feel hot and sticky inside.

Later, as they came from under the lee of the adjoining mountain, their faces were whipped by a bitter, gale force wind, driving in from the east. At the same time cloud cover dropped steeply, and a mist cloud enshrouded them. They climbed on up the saddle with visibility down to zero, and stumbled over the sharp, unstable stones, footsliding more than ever.

Progress dropped to a crawl, and Wyatt noticed some people were climbing in bare feet. Ouch, he grimaced, realising the Reek had aspects of Purgatory about it, and understood why some climbed it as a penance. He wondered what Bridie was thinking of, bringing herself and the baby through all this.

At long last the Chapel of St. Patrick and St. Patrick's bed emerged like a mirage. Everyone sought shelter inside the sanctuary of the Chapel, away from the wind and mist.

Bridie went to the wall at the back of the Chapel, and

eased off her rucksack, sliding down, as she propped her back against the wall. Her face was grey, and she seemed exhausted, breathing heavily. She's taken on more than she bargained for, I hope she doesn't regret this trip, Wyatt thought. She took out a water flask from her rucksack, and drank deeply from it.

"That was some climb." he said, offering her a sandwich.

"Yes. It was hell. I should've taken my own advice and stayed at home, like my mam said, but here I am, for better or for worse. It's even harder goin' down, you know." She spoke as she ate the sandwich, looking worried.

"The weather might lift." Wyatt said.

"It rarely does."

A folk group, two young boys and a girl, playing guitars, had started singing on the altar of the Chapel. Wyatt was struck by the words of the song, especially the chorus.

*They paved paradise,*
*And put up a parking lot,*
*With a pink hotel, a boutique,*
*And a swinging hot spot.*
*Don't it always seem to go,*
*That you don't know what you've got,*
*'Til its gone,*
*They paved paradise,*
*And put up a parking lot.*
*They took all the trees,*
*And put them in a tree museum.*
*Then they charged the people,*
*A dollar and a half just to see 'em.*
*Don't it always seem to go,*
*That you don't know what you've got ,*
*'Til its gone.*
*They paved paradise,*
*And put up a parking lot.*

A standing ovation followed, though most were standing anyway due to the overcrowding. Father Flynn donned his vestments and said mass. Afterwards, he disrobed, and spoke from the pulpit.

The mining company wanted to mine 700 thousand tons of gold-bearing ore from under Croagh Patrick, the priest said, using cyanide that would poison the waters in the region, and leave a crater behind, the size of Hiroshima or Nagasaki. Croagh Patrick embraced the religious history of Ireland, *their* history. Digging into the Reek was more than just digging into a mountain, it was digging into the religious heritage of the Irish people. There was a bog down there in the valley behind the Reek, and a bog must stay down in that valley.

*We* are the custodians of our religious heritage and we must preserve it for our children, and our children's children, he said. We owe it to them, *and* St Patrick. Judas sold his soul for a handful of gold, and we must not do the same. The priest said he felt sad lately that all his so-called loyal and trusted friends had deserted him for the easy life and the lure of money. But today he was comforted by the numbers supporting the rally, who had taken the trek up the Reek, and he felt now that with God on their side, they would triumph. Rapturous applause followed his words.

Wyatt noticed Sergeant McSweeney in the crowd, and waved, weaving his way through the crowd to him.

"It was a hell of a climb today, eh Inspector?"

"You could say that. I didn't see any of the usual faces from the mining company on the mountain today."

"Don't worry, they'll have their spies here, there's a Judas in every crowd."

"I suppose, do you think Father Flynn will pull it off?"

"It could go either way it's too close to call. We'll know soon enough, the Minister for Energy will decide next week. Safe journey down, Inspector, and you mind that pretty girleen on the way."

"I will, don't worry." They saluted and parted.

Wyatt then spotted Father Flynn on the altar steps, surrounded by an excited crowd. He pushed his way through, shook the priest's hand, and wished him good luck, and when he saw the look of gratitude in the priest's eyes, was glad he'd done it.

On the journey down, he gave Bridie his climbing stick so she had support on both sides. They then trekked back down treacherous, sliding stones on the saddle, through drizzling mist, and a whipping wind, before finally breaching the mist clouds, emerging into dazzling brightness below. It's like coming out of hell, Wyatt thought.

Back in the car park, Tommy Joe was waiting beside his van. They adjourned to Campbell's pub nearby. Wyatt studied the walls of the pub, covered with pictures of people climbing the Reek, and realised how big an event it was for so many. They toasted Father Flynn with hot whiskies beside the turf fire. Bridie had a coffee, and perked up after it. Tommy Joe offered Wyatt a lift back to the hotel but he declined, worried that Bridie should be taken home as quickly as possible.

When he reached the hotel, Wyatt picked up his post at reception. His heart raced when he saw an envelope with an English stamp, and realised it must be from Jenny. Back in his room, he poured a double whiskey, and read her letter, smelling the musk perfume.

Did he remember their trip to Sligo, her shy one, coy one of the heart? Romantic Ireland, was not yet dead and gone, it was deep in her heart as he was. Was it the same for him, and did he think about her always, night and day? *She* thought of him, time out of mind.

Her mother was now in a nursing home, and more's the pity, unlikely to leave it. But it was near to her family and relations, and so far her mother was not short of visitors. Her boss had serialised some chapters of her book on Yeats in the magazine, with sales increasing enough to allow Jenny a one month, all expenses paid trip back to

Ireland. Jenny couldn't believe her luck. It was as if all her birthdays had come together, she could arise and go to Innisfree, and stay in the hotel in Leenane, before moving on to other locations. She hoped he felt excited too, and looked forward to his reply.

He re-read the letter, aware of his predicament, falling for two different women, both beautiful, and one pregnant. There was only one solution now, but he wished there was someone he could talk to.

# Chapter 21

## *Give Me Your Hand*

Next day Wyatt woke jaded after a restless night, and unable to make inroads on his workload. It was time to contact Halpin in Dublin, but he was anxious, having done little work on the report. Maybe I should ring Halpin first before he rings me? Wyatt pondered. He knew his boss liked a coffee and smoke before starting work, so he rang him a half hour before his start time, intending to leave a message. To his surprise, Halpin was already in his office, and he was put straight through.

"Seamus, hello... sorry I couldn't get back to you yesterday. There was an emergency, a friend of mine was shot, and I had to rush to see him in Castlebar hospital. It was traumatic as you can imagine, and deeply worrying."

"Oh...well....I'm sorry to hear that. That's a nasty business James, anyone I know?"

"No, he's a Texan working on the mining project, and he helped me out of a jam once. I owed him one, I guess."

"Was he badly hurt?"

"Yes, pretty bad. He was kneecapped, and won't walk properly for a long while. Pistol- whipped too, and lucky to be alive, I suppose."

"Hmm... nasty stuff indeed James, nasty indeed. Its bad luck for him and it seems to be getting more like the Wild West down there. At least *you're* still in one piece. "

"You could say that, physically, but mentally I'm not sure. Anyway I'm sure it's the report you rang about, not my health."

"Well, now that you mention it James, how goes it?"

"Ok, getting there Seamus. Progress made, but still a lot to be done. I've some marine check-ups to finish, but I'm on the home stretch. A few more weeks could finish it, barring any more interruptions."If he only knew, Wyatt thought.

"You've had other interruptions?"

"Well…..yes, apart from my friend getting shot. Since the guards released McFadden, my room's been ransacked, and some files stolen, nothing I can't replace, but a mess was made everywhere. There's psychological warfare going on, and its hampering progress on the report."

"I'm sure it is, are you still sure you don't want to finish the report in Dublin?"

"Yes I'm sure thanks. I'll take my chances here."

"Ok, it's your call, but I can see you're having a lot of extraneous problems. Let's hope that's the last of them, and if you change your mind, let me know. I'll inform Finance, they're on my back as usual, we're way over budget, you know?"

"Yes, I *do* know, but between the two of us, all Finance do daily is to push a pen and if they make a mistake, they just take out a rubber and erase it. They live in the background, but down here you're on the front line, in fact you could say you're in the firing line."

"I *do* understand James, I know it must be frustrating for you there on your own, but it's the way of the world I'm afraid.Hmmm. Don't worry though, as you know we're both singing from the same hymn sheet, and everything *will* be noted on your file. Anyway, the door is always open if you should change your mind and decide to come up to Dublin to finish the report."

"Thanks Seamus, I'll keep it in mind, and keep you posted. By the way, I believe the decision on the mining project will be made this week by the Minister."As he spoke Wyatt wondered why Halpin was so keen to get him back to Dublin.

"Really, I didn't know that. Anyway, I look forward to your update by the end of the week, James, goodbye for now."

"Goodbye." Wyatt replaced the receiver, gritting his teeth. He was sure Halpin knew damn well about the mining decision.

Back in his room he wrote to Jenny, saying how delighted he was about her writing success, and told her of the pressure he was under to finish his project. It may be a good thing she's coming, he reflected, it will be a chance to explain everything to her.

After posting the letter, he rang McSweeney, and within the hour the Sergeant's lanky frame was seated before him, by the bay window in the empty hotel lounge. Wyatt ordered coffees, and while waiting they chatted about the mining rally on Croagh Patrick. When the coffees came, Wyatt took a sheet of paper from his pocket, and handed it to the Sergeant, who read it. A frown wrinkled the Sergeant's face as he read it again, then he eyeballed Wyatt.

"What the hell's this all about, Inspector? I know some of these guys personally, *and* some of their families."

"Hold your hat Barry, that's an original document, signed by McFadden, giving details of his comrades in arms. On the bottom he's signed that these people are part of his unit, and here's another paper he had on him, showing details of the mining company's premises…in his own handwriting." The Sergeant glanced at the document.

"Yes, I can see all that, its all very fine, but this is serious stuff, and dangerous too. Phew, how the hell did you get McFadden to give you this information?"

"He volunteered it to save his skin, when he was caught breaking into Tommy Joe's house. He was offered a deal, it's witnessed by Tommy Joe and me. You can check McFadden's signature with your records."

"Yes, I'm ok with his signature, but once his legal team can prove the signature was made under duress, the charges won't stick. McFadden will have to testify in person as well, and that just won't happen. Informers have a short life span in this neck of the woods. What then?"

"That's your call. These people are implicated in the murder of Frank Duffy, arson, blowing up a boat, break-ins to houses and twice into Glencorrig Mining's premises, and a kneecapping, need I go on. The ball's now in your court."

"Ok Inspector, I know that, but to get anything to stick in court, McFadden will have to be our star witness, against his own crowd. That's not credible, as he's not likely to sign his own death warrant. Even if he gets off scot free, he's brown bread for sure, there's no hiding place, no matter how hard or where he runs."

"Look Barry, McFadden's welfare isn't my concern, just tell me what you intend to do with this information?"

"Firstly, I'll have to discuss it with my superiors. If we arrest them, we'll have to release them again within days, if we don't get McFadden's sworn testimony."

"But at least they'll know you're onto them."

"Yes Inspector, I agree with you there, *that* would be something, but I need to talk to my superiors. This information is explosive, and thanks for bringing it to me."The Sergeant stood up, folded the document, and put it into the breast pocket of his uniform.

"You're welcome Barry, but don't forget that's the original copy, so please keep it safe."

"I will for sure bhoy. Good luck." They shook hands, and the Sergeant strode from the lounge. Wyatt remained for some minutes staring at the cold, untouched coffee on the table. He then glanced around the lounge, went to his room, and called Noel Kenny of the Mayo Times.

He told Kenny he had a scoop for him that could make the national headlines, and he'd have the newshounds in Dublin begging at his lap. Kenny was in Galway, but said he would leave straight away, and meet Wyatt at the hotel that afternoon.

Wyatt began tidying the mess in his room, trying to bring order to the chaos he felt engulfing him. Afterwards, as he started sorting the papers for his report to Halpin, it hit him that he hadn't called Bridie. When he rang her he apologised, but thought she sounded offhand, and she reminded him of his promise to ring her every day. She said she was feeling ok, but a bit nauseous in the mornings, and she didn't think her mother suspected anything about her pregnancy. She sighed then, saying she despaired of ever getting back to her job in the hotel.

"It's too early to worry about things like that, Bridie."

"I just feel so useless Jim, I need to be doin' something to stay sane. The only thing that keeps me goin' now is the work on your ancestry."

"You're looking after your mother too, aren't you? And now that you mention it, how is that genealogy thing progressing?"

"I'm almost there, and with a bit of luck I could be finished today. I'm so excited about it, and I hope you are too. Anyway we need to talk, Jim, about your ancestors, *and* another matter. Maybe you'd like to come for dinner tonight, mam would love to see you too."

"Sure Bridie, I'd like that, around six o'clock ok?"

"That's fine, Jim, see you then." He put down the phone, curious to know what she wanted to talk about. Then he went back to sorting his files, wishing he had someone else to do the job for him.

When Noel Kenny arrived in the afternoon, they adjourned to the hotel lounge, and sat in the usual corner by the window.

"Well, let's cut to the chase, what've you got for me thats so urgent Mr Wyatt? It better be good, I had to break the speed limit several times getting here."

"I think you'll find your journey's not wasted. Do you remember that document I gave you with the details of McFadden's buddies, that was only to be opened if something happened to Tommy Joe or me?"

"Yes, I certainly do remember it."

"Well, McFadden *has* stepped out of line again. There's been a theft of explosives and a criminal assault, so you *can* now publish all the details. You could say something like, say... .... based on information received, the Garda are about to arrest a number of people suspected of involvement in criminal activities in the county over a period of time, then give details of the recent crimes, etcetera."

"Ok got you, but what if the Garda *don't* arrest anyone?"

"You have the same information that they have. If they do nothing, you publish the names and details."

"The charges won't stick I'm afraid, McFadden won't testify against his own people. He's for the high jump anyway, when they find out he squealed on them. I'd hate to be in his shoes then. And what the hell about *me*, and *my* family for God's sake? If they knew I was the one who wrote the article, *we* would be in danger." His voice was strident.

"Yes…well…yes…you're right there Noel, I…I hadn't thought about that. Sorry, I should have, I certainly don't believe you should risk your life, or your family's, just for the freedom of the press. But there's a man lying kneecapped in Castlebar hospital because of these thugs, something has to be done to stop their lawlessness. Someone has got to put a stop to their gallop."

"Ok, I agree with that sentiment, but how, and without me or my family being put in the firing line."

"By making sure the Garda make the arrests first, that's *their* job. You might need to give them a prod, and I suggest you ring Sergeant McSweeney. Tell him you have a copy of the document, and your paper will anonymously publish an article divulging everything, if the Garda do nothing. Your article must only say the Garda have the information, and are studying it. On the other hand, if they *do* round the gang up, for whatever period, and the Sergeant tells you in advance, you'll have your scoop, and without putting your neck on the block. What do you think?"

After a few moments' thought, Kenny replied.

"It's worth a go, I know the Sergeant, and I can rely on him. I'll contact him, and let you know how it goes." He stood up then, shook hands, and left the hotel, glancing furtively about him.

When he'd finished working Wyatt freshened up,

changed, mounted his bike, and set off for Bridie's mother's house, stopping in the village to buy a bottle of white wine. As he travelled he felt edgy, and wondered if someone was spying on him. But he was also eager to know what news Bridie had in store for him, and hoped he might end up staying the night in her mother's house. That thought pleased him, as he might sleep better there, and be close to Bridie.

As he pedalled through the valley, he passed the haunted house, covered in evening shadow. So far the house had served him well as a haven for his files, he reckoned, but he knew he'd better call there soon, and check if things were ok.

He entered the white stone cottage by the open half door, and handed Bridie the bottle of wine. She looked pale and drawn, almost ghost-like.

"Thanks Jim, that'll go down well with the fish. Maybe you'll stay the night? We don't want you cycling home drunk and ending up in some ditch, do we?" She smiled as she took the wine, and kissed him on the cheek.

"Good idea, Bridie, I'd love to stay. We don't have the moonlight this week to light the roads either, more's the pity."

"Yes, it's the only street lightin' we can afford down here. Mam's in the kitchen, settin' the table, so go on in, she'll be waitin' for you. I've a nice fresh piece of hake I got today from Tommy Joe, and I'll have it ready soon."

Wyatt ambled into the kitchen. The rectangular oak table was covered by a damask tablecloth, with a lit candle in the middle, and a vase of wildflowers at the end. In the range the turf fire glowed, and a kettle simmered on the hob. A wooden dresser stood on a side wall, laden with willow pattern crockery. Bridie's mother sat beside the fire in her rocking chair, eyes closed, fingers flicking the rosary beads in her hands, face serene in the shadows. The radio was playing lowly, and when she heard him enter, her eyelids fluttered open.

"Ah, there you are, I was just sayin' the Angelus, it's

just gone six o'clock. Sit yourself down there by the fire, 'til Bridie comes in." She clicked the radio off.

"It's a fine custom, the Angelus, and how are you keeping Mrs O'Malley?"

"Pullin' the divil by the tail I suppose, but every day I'm gettin' a bit better, thank God. I heard you climbed the Reek for the minin' protest?"

"I did indeed, and I'm still recovering from the effort, I'm aching all over."

"I said five decades of the rosary for Father Flynn that night, so I did."

"Well done, hopefully it will all add up for him, and he'll win the day. God is a good ally."

"He is for sure, but the devil is a dangerous enemy too, and God knows theres many people down here in the pay of Satan. The good don't always prosper in this life."

"I suppose not, but you have to have a go, you've only the one life to examine."

Bridie came in then, carrying three dinners on a tray. She had her makeup on, and looked radiant, wearing a turquoise dress, her hair brushed back, shining, in a blue bow. Wyatt held his breath, as he eyed her belly, wondering if he detected a bulge.

He poured the wine for them both, as Bridie's mother was a teetotaller. Bridie said one glass was her limit for the night. Afterwards, sated by the pleasure of fresh fish well cooked, washed down by wine, in a relaxed and peaceful place, Wyatt came to realise how much he enjoyed and depended on their company, and wondered if they felt the same about him.

Later Bridie's mother said she felt tired, and went to her bedroom. When Bridie returned after putting her to bed, Wyatt finished off the last of the wine.

"I really enjoyed that meal Bridie but tell me, what's this news you have for me? I'm dying to know."

"I don't want you dyin' on me just yet, Jim Wyatt. Actually there are a couple of things on my mind, but firstly, how about a Gaelic coffee to polish off the meal?"

"That sounds great, the suspense is killing though." He drained the wine glass in one swallow, while Bridie boiled the kettle, and took a whiskey bottle from the cupboard.

After a short time, Bridie handed him his Gaelic coffee.

"There you are, see what you think of that." He raised the cream- topped glass to his mouth, and put it on the table, licking the cream from his lips.

"Great, a heavy hand with the whisky though. Are you ready to put me out of my misery now?" Smiling, he took another mouthful, while Bridie had an ordinary coffee. She now had a brown folder on the table in front of her.

"Ok, firstly I've finished the main part of my research into the Wyatt name that was on that gravestone on Inisboffin, *and* into your family history. You may be surprised, or even shocked, at what's come up in the process, and some of the conclusions I've made."

"Really, try me then." He grinned, raising the glass to his mouth again.

Bridie read from the notes she'd taken from the folder, saying she was quoting from reports she'd got during her investigation, and would try to keep it as simple as possible.

*"It all began with the building of Westport House in the eighteenth century. The original house was on the site of an ancient castle of the O'Malley clan. Westport House was built by a Colonel John Browne and his wife. He was a Jacobite, who was involved at the Siege of Limerick. His wife was a great grand-daughter of Grace O'Malley, Queen of Connacht in Elizabethan times, also known as the Pirate Queen. Unlike today, the house then had no lake or dam, and the tides rose and fell against the walls. The building works were started in 1730, and eventually completed in 1778, by James Wyatt, one of the greatest of all English architects. England is full of famous buildings designed by Wyatt, such as the Pantheon in Oxford Street, London. Wyatt also laid out the town of Westport. On the*

*south face of Westport House is the date 1778, and inside it are many ceilings, cornices, and fireplaces done in his best style. The dining room is also a fine example of his work."*

"Interesting Bridie, but where is all this leading?"

"It's leading Jim, to the fact that Mr Wyatt spent a good few years living in, and around Westport. He enjoyed life there to the full, and had designs not just on buildings, but on beautiful women too.

There was a woman who worked as a maid in the house, a beauty by all accounts, who had a son for him. She left after becoming pregnant, and went to live near Cleggan. Wyatt was generous in looking after her, and she used the name Wyatt when she arrived there. She wasn't the only woman to bear offspring for the bould James Wyatt during his stay in the west, but she's most likely the link to that gravestone on Inisboffin."

"Fascinating please continue, this is getting interesting." Wyatt whistled in surprise as he spoke.

"The roots of your own family, on your father's side, can be traced back to County Mayo. I can prove this with birth, death, and marriage certificates to beat the band, in spite of how hard it was to trace people in the Famine era, so here it is.

It's conceivable Jim, that your bloodline is linked back to this famous Mr Wyatt of Westport House fame. Maybe not to the family whose name we came across that day on Inisboffin, but to some similar situation arising from liaisons when he was in Westport. We're talkin' here Jim, about the law of probability, and nothing more, this is not an exact science, you know."

"So you're saying I could be related to a famous English architect of the same name?" He was astounded.

"Possibly but it's not definite. It's a good story though and it won't affect your financial status too much. You're still the same person I know, and these conclusions have no legal implications."She smiled as she spoke.

"I appreciate that Bridie, and I still feel the same person

too. Strange, it hasn't sunk in yet, but thanks for all your work in finding out about this."

"Don't mention it, I enjoyed it, in fact I've decided it's what I'd like to do in the future. I'd like to put an article about this in The Mayo Times, if it's ok with you. It would be good publicity for me and maybe for you too." A smile flickered around her lips as she spoke.

"Go ahead and publish it, it can't do me any harm." It was not his usual low profile approach, but what the hell, he thought. All he was thinking about was how beautiful she looked when she spoke, her face sunlight on water, and concentrated as she read from the files, her body breathing in and out, as he wondered about the little body breathing out and in, within her body.

He embraced her, smelling the perfume of her body, and thought he could already feel a bump in her belly. She wrapped her arms around his neck, pulling him down to her parted lips, and he felt the heat rising in their bodies. Then he pulled away.

"What is it, Jim?" Her eyes looked startled.

"Nothing, but you haven't told me the other news yet, I'd just like to know, then I can relax."

"Oh yes, it had slipped my mind for the minute."

"Good, put me out of my misery."

"Well Jim, it's just I've been thinking we need a heart-to- heart talk about our future, and the baby's. I can't keep it a secret any longer from my mother, and word gets around in a place like this. You understand? You love me, don't you?" Her eyes, blue and piercing, beneath black, arched eyebrows, arrowed into his.

"Of course, of course I love you, Bridie, more than anything, I do. Look, I *am* sorry I should have spoken to you sooner, but a lot of things have been happening lately." He wrapped his arms around her again.

"I know they have Jim, and look I'm sorry to spring it on you like this, but I had to, it was gnawing away inside me."

"There's nothing to be sorry about, we said we'd

discuss it at a later time, and that time is now."

"What'll we do then Jim?"

"We'll just tell your mother for now, Bridie, and ask her to keep it a family matter for the moment, and in a few weeks we'll make it public. I should be finished my work down here then, and I'll have a clearer picture of where I'm going. I just need some time to sort a few things out, before we plan for making a home for us and the baby. You have my hand, my heart, and my word. I'll always love you, you know that."

"Oh Jim, I do love you. I'm so glad we spoke about this, at least I can talk now to someone." She hugged him hard.

"Maybe we should continue this conversation in bed, Bridie?"Her eyes widened before she replied.

"Ok, let's do that." And they left the room, tip- toeing to the bedroom.

"I hope we don't wake your mother."

"Don't worry, her hearin's not great anymore, anyway she's got cop-on."

Bridie slipped out of her turquoise dress, and left it lying on the floor, then slid into the bed. She tossed back the sheets on his side, and asked was he not comin'in, and he didn't delay, and jumped in beside her, his clothes left in a heap beside hers on the floor. His lips sought hers, and the love she was giving, and his hands touched her body, tender, tingling, as her arms encircled him. And in his mind he could see them both sliding over the sheer edge of a cliff, deep down into a raging sunset, their love consumed by an orb of fire as it sank in a blood stained sky, and then disappeared beneath the rim of the sea.

# Chapter 22

## *Man of the House*

The news flash came on the radio next morning, while he was having breakfast in the kitchen with Bridie. The Minister for Energy had turned down Glencorrig Mining Company's application to mine gold in the valley at the back of Croagh Patrick. The reason given was the unique religious importance of the area. Wyatt was exuberant, and Bridie whooped, as they hugged and danced on the flagstones of the kitchen floor.

Then she ran upstairs to tell her mother. He rang Tommy Joe, who was cock a hoop, and told Wyatt there would be a celebration in Traynor's pub that night, the craic would be mighty, and wild horses wouldn't keep him away. We beat the bastards, he said. Wyatt said he would see him there. Before he left for the hotel he asked Bridie if she'd come to the pub.

"I'd love to, but only if mam comes along too. I think she will, in the form she's in now, but she'll not be able to stay for long. She's stormin' heaven now, thanking God for the good news. She says it's the best thing she's heard in years. Tommy Joe will bring us in the van, I'm sure.It's great news, I'm so happy."

"Good. I'll see you there then, and your mam, hopefully. Thanks again Bridie for all that genealogy stuff, *and* everything else."

Wyatt kissed her lightly on the lips, then crossed the room, lifted the latch of the door, and went out to the shed where he had left his bike. He looked up, when he got there. The clouds hung heavy with rain, and he donned his wet gear before pedalling down the boreen.

As he freewheeled down an incline on the road, the morning mist hid the mountains, and he pondered the revelations about his possible ancestry. It could be a two edged sword, raising his profile in the community. Vanity is the devil's disciple, his mother had always said. It'll probably be a seven day wonder too, but it *could* make him more vulnerable as a target. Maybe he should have kept it a secret. It wouldn't affect the pound in his pocket either. Ireland being the way it was, he would certainly get a slagging, probably starting that night in the pub. So be it.

Then, as he spun by the haunted house, gaunt and grim on the hill, the bones of an idea hit him.

Back in his hotel room, he'd just begun his report to Halpin when the phone rang. It was Noel Kenny from the Mayo newspaper, saying he'd met Sergeant McSweeney in Westport, and that McSweeney was vague about what action would be taken by the Garda against McFadden's cronies.

After a long and heavy discussion, McSweeney had agreed to speak to his bosses again, and said he would get back to him. The Sergeant *had* later rung Kenny, to confirm the gang *would* be rounded up in the coming days, as a gesture, but they would most likely be released later. Kenny said he had primed his media friends in Dublin of the developments. The trap was set, he said, and would soon be sprung. Kenny thanked Wyatt and hung up. Wyatt smiled to himself, believing things were going his way at last.

Just as he got stuck into Halpin's report, the phone rang again. Wyatt grimaced, and picked up the receiver. It was Sergeant McSweeney.

"I'm just getting back to you Inspector, after our meetin'. Decisive action, you'll be glad to hear, will be taken in the matter, in the coming days."

"That's good Barry, glad to hear it. Going to the pub tonight?"

"I am indeed bhoy, see you there."

Wyatt stood staring out the window, thinking. He was worried by the Sergeant's words, and what might happen when McFadden's henchmen were out on the loose again. They would be on the warpath for certain.

He worried too about Jenny's imminent visit, and how to deal with it. Maybe some of McFadden's friends might turn up at the pub that night. Deep down he knew things should get easier as time moved on, but at that moment he felt worn out, and unable to focus on the work in hand. He had to get outdoors, and clear his head about what he should do.

Then an idea flashed through his head. He remembered the fishing tackle he had bought a while back in Westport, and his aborted fishing trip with Tommy Joe. Yes, that was it, he decided, he'd go on a fishing trek on the river beyond Assleagh Falls, in the Delphi Valley. That cheered him up. He quickly put away Halpin's report.

\*\*\*

The sky was weeping as he started out from where the river ended its journey to the sea, where it splashed over stones heaped up by waves at its mouth. There was a high tide and the river was surging in spate. In the midst of the foaming surf and tawny waters, sea trout waited, ready to go upstream. Some were swimming at the top of the waves under a halo of spray from an off shore wind. Others swam lower in the water, held steady by their fins. They waited, and waited, patiently, ready to make their move. Then when the next high wave washed over the shingle bank, he saw a few fish slipping through.

Afterwards the other, hesitant ones vanished back into the dark waters. There they waited for the next surge from the sea to carry them over the shingle crest, before the tide turned. He stayed a while to watch more of their finny, silvery bodies slithering upstream, before moving upriver.

There was a meandering pathway beside the river, which he trod in his waders, past dripping heather and dead rhododendron bushes. He heard the sound of unseen sheep bleating in the distance, as he moved forward towards the seeping hills.

He dropped to his hands and knees to drink the clear spring water, and saw his face and the grey sky etched in the water below. He wondered if he would catch a salmon that day, a big one perhaps. In the past he had only caught trout. Trout were fine, but a salmon was the prize catch.

Then he remembered from his schooldays, the fable about how the salmon became the symbol of knowledge in Irish mythology. In the story, young Finn McCool had got the gift of knowledge accidentally, when he'd burnt his thumb after touching the Salmon of Knowledge, as it cooked on the fire. Thereafter, whenever Finn needed to know anything, he just stuck his thumb in his mouth. Wyatt wondered if he did catch one, would it give him the knowledge to sort out his problems. Better not build yourself up too much, he thought, shaking his head. It might never happen.

Not far gone, he came to a holding pool under a bank of willows, and sat down. After resting awhile beneath the dripping branches, he had lunch. Then he put the rod together, tied two flies, tested the knots, and flicked a first cast into the river. Nothing.

He wondered if poachers with their drift nets, had taken them all. There was another pool nearby. He moved further along the bank and tried it, but the results were the same. He knew it was against the rules to take salmon so far upstream, but today he didn't give a damn about the rule book.

Later, he moved further up the glen, and feared he would soon run out of river, as he saw the sheer side of the mountain looming large out of the mist, before him. He trudged over sodden, tussocky landscape, past ruined Famine cottages, with rows of overgrown lazy beds beside them.

After rounding a bend in the river, a fine deep pool appeared, inviting, beckoning. It lay in a clearing covered by a canopy of red berried rowan trees. He guessed it was a reservoir of water caused by a fissure crack in the rock formation and the surging spate of the river, which had happened ages of time ago.

The reel ratcheted wildly in his hands, as he loosed the line, making a cast into the dark pool. The fly sailed across the water from one side to the other, until he whipped it out, and cast it in again. This time the fly became locked, the line taut. Wyatt wondered, heart thumping, if he had a salmon on the line.

Then he realised he had no net. What a fool he was to forget it, he fumed. After playing the fish for a long time, he carefully steered it away from any snags that he could see in the river, and gave out plenty of line, not rushing things. No, he mustn't rush things. Take it nice and easy. Let the fish tire out.

His heart leapt when the fish breached, silver-flanked into the air, the reel whirring crazily in his hands. It *was* a salmon. It seemed to stare at him for a split second, straight into his eyes, as if asking for mercy. Then, as it plunged down into the depths again, he sensed the panic rising in the hooked fish, and felt the pull and turmoil through his fingers. Continuing tumult ensued, before gradually reducing as the fish tired, and the circles in the water grew smaller.

But it wasn't over yet. Many a fish had made a last minute escape, he knew, due to over-eagerness by the angler. Then he began to haul it over to a bank in the shallows. The fish, sensing the end was coming, made a last ditch effort to break free, but after the long fight its energy had ebbed, and he was able to move it back to where he wanted. He grabbed it by the tail, and landed it on the bank.

It was a fine specimen, a four pound grilse, wriggling on the grass. He took the fly from the salmon's neck, and looked around for his priest, or a rock, to execute the last rites. With a swift blow to the head, he'd finish off the dying fish, and have the makings of a fine meal.

But he hesitated to carry out the final act. Something

inside made him falter, prompting him to have compassion, and release the fish. The fish was struggling to breathe before his eyes. As he lifted the salmon in his hands, he could feel its fading pulse. He rushed into the shallows of the river in his waders, and with his feet wide apart, gently lowered the fish back into the dark waters, from where it had come. The wriggling motion in his fingers faded, and he saw the salmon swim slowly away in front of his eyes, before vanishing down into the deep.

He stood staring into the silent pool for a while, wondering why he had shown mercy to a fish, and why he had no regrets. In fact, he felt the better of it. Raindrops plopped into the pool. Time to move on, he reckoned. After packing his rod, he trudged back through tussocky bunches of rushes and iris leaves in a growing rain shower. He saw the river rise relentlessly in the rain, as he retraced his steps over soggy peat tracks.

When he arrived back at the spate stream, near where his journey had begun, it was teeming with fish. They were sea trout, warriors of the sea, waiting, trying to move further up the river. A van with markings of the Heritage Service was parked nearby. A man got out, dressed in green wellingtons and oilskin jacket.

"Nice day for ducks. I see you haven't had much luck with the fishin'?"

"No. It wasn't my day. Mind you, I caught one, but let it back. It was small. There's too many being killed these days anyway."

"There is indeed."

In the distance, down by the banks of the river, he saw men making a fish-trap with a mesh frame, and asked the man what he was going to do about it. Nothing, he said, it's not my area, it's the Bailiff's problem, and he continued scanning the landscape with his binoculars. Soon the poachers passed by, head down, carrying a salmon. The man was now writing information into a copybook. Such is the way of the world here, Wyatt mused.

He bade the man goodbye, and moved on past some stone ruins, over a rickety footbridge, towards a track that would lead him away from the river, back to his starting point. Just then he heard a splash, and turned to see a fine, silver salmon leaping from the river.

He felt better then, and wondered if it was the same salmon he'd released earlier. And if it was, he wondered if the salmon had winked its eye at him when it jumped, in thanks for its earlier release. And he wondered if he had gained any knowledge from his day on the river. Most likely not. He was no Finn McCool. All that was in his mind now, was the thought of a steaming, seaweed bath before heading off to the pub.

***

Inside Traynors the atmosphere was vibrant, buzzing with music and chatter. A smoke haze drifted over everything, and a log fire blazed in the corner, with the musty smell of wet clothes drying out wafting through the air. The place was packed more than he had ever seen it. It felt like they'd just won an All Ireland. When he spotted Bridie sitting in the corner near the fire, with her mother in a wheelchair with her, he made a beeline over.

"You made it. Good to see you Mrs O'Malley. Can I get you both a drink?"

"Thanks Jim. Just a coke for me and mam'll have a lemonade."

Up at the bar he bumped into Tommy Joe.

"Well, Inspector, I hear you're related to the fellah that built Westport House, yer man, what's his name? Well, could you credit that? Now don't you go actin' high and mighty, and make us have to call you m'Lord in future."

"News travels fast around here, Tommy Joe. Don't worry it's still the same old me. I'll see you later."

He took the drinks on a tray back to Bridie. Father Flynn was there, talking to Bridie's mother, and Wyatt shook his hand.

"Congratulations Father, you must be a happy man."

"Indeed I am, my prayers were answered, thank the Lord. Your support helped, and *was* appreciated, Mr Wyatt, as well as all those who attended the meetings. I thank you with all my heart, and may God bless you. That day up on the Reek, I felt that the good Lord was on our side. You know, they can have all their new fangled gizmos and gadgets, and gurus, but when all's said and done, you can't beat the power of prayer."

"I suppose. It certainly worked this time for you."

The priest turned then to talk to Bridie's mother. Wyatt handed Bridie her drink, and sat close to her at the fire, thinking how beautiful she looked, her cheeks aglow, and he told her so. She blushed, her face reddening in the fire's warmth, as he lifted his glass.

"Cheers, to us and to Father Flynn."

"I'll second that."

They clinked glasses and drank deeply. Then he looked around and spoke, lowering his voice.

"Bridie, I've been thinking about things since the other night, and I've got an idea."

"Oh, what is it?" Her eyes narrowed with interest.

"You know that old ruined house in the valley? O'Hara's I think you called it, the haunted house."

"Yes, of course I do."

"Well, I was wondering if you could find out if it's for sale. I've an inheritance since my mother died, and if the price was reasonable, I might like to buy it. It needs doing up, a hell of a lot of doing up. You said the owner left for the states a while ago. Who knows, he may have since died. His family might be glad to sell it."

"Would you be goin' to rent it out or what?"

"No, it would be just for the two of us."

"You mean, you'd come down to live here, and leave your big job in Dublin?"

"Maybe Bridie, I haven't thought that far ahead. Anyway what do you think?"

"I think it's worth a go, Jim. I'll get goin' on it

tomorrow mornin'. I know someone in Louisburgh that could find out. I'm over the moon about it." Her eyes shone.

"Just one more thing. Let's keep it and our other news between the three of us for a little longer, until things become a little clearer."

"My lips are sealed. And to make doubly sure, you'll have to seal them with a kiss, but not now." Her face beamed then, and he felt happy inside.

A short time later Ned Halpin stood up, tapped a glass, and asked for silence for Father Flynn to say a few words. The priest spoke briefly about the people's great victory in preserving the holy ground for the people against the mining company's wishes. When he finished, he thanked everyone for their prayers and support, then left the pub to a huge ovation. Bridie went soon afterwards with her mother, saying the priest would drop them home, and she would contact Wyatt the next day. He drifted back to the bar, where he met Sergeant McSweeney, who handed him a pint.

"There you are Inspector, or should I now be callin' you Lord of the Manor." His eyes twinkled.

"Oh that, so you've heard about that too. No, we'll stick with the old name Barry, if you don't mind. It's far from stately homes I was reared. Ned Halpin seems to have changed horses very quickly. He's turned poacher to gamekeeper in one go. One minute he's for the mining project, now it's as if he never was."

"The man's first and foremost a politician, and he's going up next year in the elections as an Independent. Like a lot of people, he just wants to be on the side that's winning. Once he was for the minin' for the jobs it might create, but now he's changed tack. Soon they'll have forgotten all that, and he's chasin' votes as always. Like most politicians, he wants to be popular with everyone. Sure isn't that how they get elected?"

"I suppose, but surely if something is right, you do it for that reason, and not just to be popular?"

"You're a bit wet behind the ears Inspector, considerin' your high falutin' lineage. They just do it down here if theres votes in it for them. Not always good for the country, mark you, but there it is."

"Do you think he'll get elected next year?"

"Every chance Inspector, he works hard, puts himself about, and he's popular with a lot of people."

"Barry, I'd appreciate if you could keep me posted on any developments in rounding up McFadden's gang. And if there's any news about McFadden himself."

"I will for sure bhoy. By the way, make sure you keep your gun handy at all times, especially for the next few days. Don't let your guard down. Excuse me now, I see someone at the bar who owes me a drink."

The Sergeant slipped away into the throng at the bar. The Sergeant's on the ball, Wyatt thought. He knew I had neither gun nor bullet proof vest on tonight. How stupid that was. I had forgotten. That was careless. Damn careless. Got to be more careful, he muttered to himself.

Soon he cornered Tommy Joe, who took two pints in his hands, and they walked to a quiet place at the door, where he told him of the Garda's pending action.

"That's good Inspector. You just keep your mouth shut, watch your back, and everything'll be fine."

"Don't worry Tommy Joe, I will."

Later in the night Ned Halpin crossed the room to Wyatt, and shook his hand.

"I believe you're related to the gentry, James. Congratulations. We'll have to find a way of celebrating that."

"Hold on now, it's not conclusive, it's just a possibility. Let's not rush into making assumptions."

"You're right there. Sure a few weeks ago we thought the minin' project was a sure fire thing to go ahead, and now look what happened. It sure doesn't pay to count your chickens before they're hatched."

"I suppose you're disappointed at the outcome?"

"You win some. Life goes on. I've an election next

year to think about. I'll probably be looking for your vote if you're still here."There was a wry grin on his face.

"I'm afraid that's not likely. Your brother is anxious to get me back to Dublin."

"Is he? Well you never know what's around the corner. Things have been happenin' down here since you came. We've agreed a program to upgrade our water facility plants, and procedures. It was long overdue too. We're submitting it for government approval at the end of the month."

"That's good Ned, I hope it'll be passed." They shook hands and parted.

It was late in the night before the usual sing song started. Wyatt went to make a quick getaway in case he was called to perform, but paused at the door when he heard Tommy Joe's voice, dedicating the song, which he said was his all time favourite, to his new boat, *The Connemara Queen*.

*"Oh! My boat can safely float in the teeth of wind and weather.*
*And outrace the fastest hooker between Galway and Kinsale.*
*When the black floor of the ocean and the white foam rush together.*
*High she rides, in her pride, like a seagull through the gale.*
*Oh, she's neat! Oh, she's sweet! She's a beauty ev'ry line!*
*The Queen of Connemara is that bounding barque of mine."*

The clapping at the end was ringing in his head as he left the pub. He glanced furtively around, and headed up the road in the darkness. As he walked he felt the place where his gun should have been. He had been careless. That could have been fatal, he thought, hurrying towards the hotel.

# Chapter 23

## *A Hive for the Honey Bee*

Bridie rang the next day, excited, saying she had news about the haunted house. The estate agent had contacted the family, and discovered old Matt O'Hara had died years ago in the states. The agent thought the family would be open to a reasonable offer.

"What's reasonable?"

"You'll have to speak to the agent yourself. You're the one with the money."

"Ok, let's do that today. Maybe Tommy Joe's van's available?"

"It is, he's away after the mackerel all week, and I've borrowed it already. I have to go see the doctor myself this mornin'."

"Oh. Is everything alright?"

"It's just a checkup, there's not a problem, everything's fine."

"I'll come along with you then."

"Thanks Jim but there's no need. I can drive, and my mam's coming too. She's due for a check-up too. There could be a lot of waitin' around in the hospital. You've all that work to do. I'll pick you up, if you like, in the afternoon at the hotel."

"Ok, that's great, see you then Bridie."

He put the phone down, glad to make inroads on his report before Seamus Halpin rang again. Before he started on it, he picked up his post in the lobby.

In it was a letter from Jenny, reeking of the musky perfume she wore in Sligo. The letter was short, and said her visit had been put off for another two weeks, her boss being up to her usual antics. Jenny thought she couldn't take much more the woman. She hoped they could make up for the delay when they met, as he was in her thoughts, time out of mind. She hoped he felt the same.

The news that she wasn't coming made him breathe easier. It gave him more time to get his head right. At least he didn't have to confront it now. Relieved, he wrote a short reply sending his love, and regretted the delay in her coming. By the time he had posted it, he was surprised to find half the morning had gone.

When Bridie arrived in the afternoon, he jumped into the driver's seat beside her.

"Everything go ok with the doc Bridie? Where's your mother?"

"I dropped her home first. She's in fine fettle thanks. She can get around the house now with the help of a stick. In a few weeks she won't even need that. The doc says she's done well."

"Good and what about yourself?"

"Fine……just fine, but the doc says I have to take things easy for a while."

"What's the matter? Nothing serious I hope?"His brow furrowed.

"No, my blood pressure's up a little, that's all. There's nothing to worry about, Jim. The doc says I just have to slow down for the next few months. It looks like my mam will be returnin' the compliment, and looking after me in the future."

"You've got to do what the doctor says, Bridie. Maybe you shouldn't be coming to Louisburgh?"

"No, I said I'm fine. I'll rest when I get home."Her face had a determined look.

"Promise, you're looking paler than the dawn."

"I promise. I better start puttin' my make-up on more often."

Bridie guided him to the estate agent's office, at the bottom of a hill near the centre of Louisburgh. She insisted on staying in the van, in spite of the stench. The agent's name was Jack McHale, and he advised Wyatt that there was twenty acres going with the house, which he agreed was a wreck. The asking price was less than Wyatt expected, but he feared the renovations could prove costly. McHale said nobody in the area was interested in buying the house, because it was reputed to be haunted.

"Surely people here don't believe all those old wive's tales?"

"You'd be surprised Mr Wyatt. The mind can play weird banshee tricks on a lonely, windy night in the country. Tell me, would you be goin' to live there yourself?" McHale asked, smiling, as Wyatt handed him a cheque for the deposit.

"No, it's an investment for my retirement."

"Good, I'll make arrangements for the vendor's solicitor to contact yours when you give me details of your legal advisers. Barring complications, everything could be finalised in a matter of weeks."

"That's good." They shook hands, and in a jiffy he was back sitting beside Bridie in the van.

"How did it go Jim?" She sounded anxious.

"I'm not sure. It looks like I've spent a heap of money on a broken down hovel in the back of beyond. But the haunted house image helped to keep the price down. That was good, but I bought it without giving too much thought to the deal. It's not like me…… no, not like me at all."

As he spoke he drove the van out onto the road, down the sloping main street, towards the bridge over the Bunowen River, where the road forked left for Leenane.

"You mean you *really* bought it?" She sounded incredulous.

"Yes. Did I do the right thing?"

"Well, that depends. What are you intendin' to do with it?"

"I told you before. It's for us, just the three of us."

"Oh Jim, that's great. I can't believe it. Are you sure?" Her eyes lit up.

"Yes."

"An' will *you* be livin' there too?"

"That's the general idea. But I can't say when. We need

to get a solicitor, an architect, and a builder. I'll need your help too, if you don't mind Bridie, you know the lie of the land down here. I don't want to put pressure on you in your condition, but I need to get on and finish this bloody project for Seamus Halpin before it drives me crazy. I'll organise all the money matters."

"Oh Jim, I'm so happy. Let's have a drink to celebrate."

"Well ok, let's do that. There was a pub back up the road called the *Bun Abhainn*, let's go back there."

They did a u- turn at the bridge, and drove back up the hill, parking outside the pub.

Inside they sat in a sunny nook by the window, and he sauntered to the bar.

"I feel over the moon. Here's to us." She said, and patted her stomach, lifting her glass.

"Here's to us."

And as they clinked glasses he looked at her, and thought her face a ray of sunshine on a winter's day.

"You'd swear you'd won the Lotto, Bridie. It's only a house, a wreck at that."

"No. It's more than that, Jim. It's going to be a home for us. I've always dreamed of having my own home, never thinkin' it would ever happen. Ever since I was at school, a long time ago, it's been in my mind, to really have my own dresser, an' crockery, an' all."

"Then maybe your dreams *will* come true, and maybe the wreck will live up to your expectations." He leaned across and lightly kissed her lips, smelling her fragrance.

"It…it will Jim, it will, I just know it will. I can't wait to tell mam. Don't you worry it'll only be the three of us that know about it. Sorry, four." She patted her stomach, and squeezed his hand as she spoke.

"Down the hatch, got to get you back home now, so you can rest. Doctor's orders."

"Yes, there's things to be done in sortin' the house, Jim."

"Tomorrow's another day. We've got all the time in the

world, and you must look after yourself."

As he put his empty glass on the table, he felt the bulk of the pistol beneath his armpit, but he was getting used to it now. It was his constant companion.

Wyatt dropped Bridie home, and drove back to the hotel, hoping to get in a few more hours on the report, before returning the van to Tommy Joe that night at the pub. When he arrived at the hotel, there was a message to ring Noel Kenny of the Mayo Times. It was urgent. The best laid plans...he fumed, rushing to return the call from his room.

"Thanks for calling back Mr Wyatt, I got some information today, I think you should know about."

"Good. What exactly is it?" Wyatt tried to sound cool, but inside felt the tension rise.

"The guards rounded up the people named on McFadden's document yesterday."

"Right, what then?"His heart thumped.

"They were charged with the break- in at Glencorrig mining company's premises, and with assaulting the man there. I can't recall his name." I can, its Pete, Panhandle Pete from Texas, Wyatt thought grimly.

"Yes, yes, and what then?"

"They were released today on bail. Their lawyers got them out, but the charge still stands. Apparently the case will rest on who'se prepared to put their life on the line, by going to court as a witness for the state. McFadden will hardly do that, will he? Anyway, he seems to be hidin' in the long grass, or maybe he's left the country. In that case it will depend if the man injured in the break- in at Glencorrig Mining Company can identify any of them, and more importantly, if he'll testify in court. I believe he's still in Castlebar hospital."

"Yes he is. I know him, I'll speak to him. Thanks for the information."

"You're welcome, and just one last thing Mr Wyatt."

"What's that?"

"Look out for yourself. These people are dangerous.

They won't think twice about putting a bullet in anyone."

"Thanks again, I'll watch my back. Goodbye." But as he replaced the receiver, he felt a tremor of fear tingle through his veins.

Nerves jangling, he abandoned work for the rest of the day. Visions of McFadden chasing him over massive, mist- covered Mweelrea, shot back into his mind. Damn, I need a drink, he muttered, punching the palm of his hand, and pacing the room like a caged animal.

That evening, he relaxed in a seaweed bath, changed, had dinner, and left the hotel for his long- promised drink. Outside the hotel in the gloaming, the sky bled from a searing sunset, with the air still as the grave, save some birds singing their last songs of the day. He looked about nervously, then entered Tommy Joe's van and headed for the village.

As he drove the van he felt the pistol's steel barrel prod his body. No fear of forgetting it this time, he thought, but still there was a lump in his stomach. Who were these people who had been released? Were they watching him now? Would any of them be in the pub tonight? Would Pete be brave enough to identify any of them in court? Where would it all end? Too many questions, but not many answers.

He needed to speak to Tommy Joe soon to sound out the problems. Tommy Joe seemed fearless, and seemed to have their measure. He glanced through the van window across the fjord towards Ben Gorm, and saw the mountain glint gold in the dying sun. All that glisters is not gold, he mused. When he parked the van he looked around slowly, and did so again before entering the pub door.

He sighed, relieved when he saw Tommy Joe and Michael seated at the bar, talking to some friends. They nodded to each other, before he headed to a table in the corner of the room. Tommy Joe soon followed him over, carrying two drinks.

"Howyeh Inspector, get that into you. I suppose you heard the news?"

"Yes, and I'm not sure what to make of it. It's a bit worrying."

"Divil the bit of worry it is. For the first time in their lives, some of them bastards is havin' the guards on their backs. Yes, an' they don't like it for sure. But bad cess to them anyway I say. The guards are only doin' what they're there to do."

"I wonder have they spoken to McFadden?"

"Who knows? They'll want to, for sure. But they still have this paper signed by him, givin' the lowdown on the lot of them. McSweeney has it, and he'll be here later. You ask him about that when he comes. Will you be havin' another drink then? You can't be seen in here with an empty glass in your hand." He grinned, and winked as he spoke.

"Sure Tommy Joe, fill them up again. Here are the keys to your van, and thanks for the use of it. I trust you had a good day's fishing?"

"Divil the bit of it we had, them feckin' seals made mincemeat of the nets. We spent half the day, meself and Michael, mendin' 'em. 'Twould scald the heart of a saint."

In a few minutes he was back, and put a full glass on the table.

"Get that into you, it'll do you some good. I see the Sergeant's just arrived. I'll leave you now to chat with him. And just one more thing Inspector."

"Yes?"

"That girleen Bridie, you take good care of her, she's special to me and Michael. We wouldn't ever like to ever see her get hurt." Tommy Joe winked, saluted, and ambled over to the bar.

"Don't worry, I will." Wyatt called after him.

Soon he was joined by Sergeant McSweeney, pint in hand.

"Things are hottin' up, I can tell you. I've never been this busy in my life. It all seems to have started when you arrived here, Inspector. Looks like you stirred up a hornet's nest. I think it's safe to talk here." McSweeney scanned the room before he sat down.

"Really, what gives?"

"Instead of havin' only McFadden to deal with, we've now got the problem of charging three of his gang with criminal trespassing, and they're out on bail, free to do what they like. We've got to get them behind bars. Pronto."

"But how? "

"Good question bhoy, easier said than done. I've been losin' sleep dwellin' on it."

"You're not the only one, Barry. What about the document McFadden signed, giving details of his gang?

"We're keeping that up our sleeve for the moment, Inspector. It's our ace in the hole and we'll play it when the time comes. They don't know yet that we have the lowdown on them, even if it doesn't stick in court. McFadden will be let off the hook, sayin' the information was got under duress. They'll be let out of jail then. Still, it's powerful stuff to have. It may put a stop to their gallop for a while." He paused for a slug from his glass, before continuing.

"The media have their hands on the info too. We have to put these three boyos in prison for a while. Cool their ardour. Some of the stuff going on up North would sicken a saint. Proxy bombing, that's their latest murderin' carry on. Gettin' innocent people to drive their vehicles, loaded with explosives, up to their targets, like human bombs. It's sickening and barbaric. We've got to bloody well do something about it."

"Can you pull it off Barry? I mean put them behind bars?"

"It depends. We need someone to stand up in court and testify. Someone brave enough to put their life on the line."

"What about the guy in Glencorrig Mining, the one who was injured in the break-in? Maybe he could identify some of them. I know him from the fracas after the hurling match. I could speak to him."

"Do you bedad? Well, that would be worth tryin'. The man's not from these parts either and he's still in the hospital I believe, but he's making progress, and could be out soon. We have him under security surveillance."

"I'll speak to him right away."

"Good, I'll be goin' now. Good luck."

The Sergeant placed his empty glass on the table, and left the pub. Wyatt followed a few minutes later. As he left the comforting light of the pub, for the wall of darkness outside, he waited awhile at the side of the road, checking if anyone had followed him. A few minutes later, he walked briskly back to the hotel, hand on pistol all the way. Though he felt the better of visiting the pub, he fretted in bed later. A nightcap of shots of whisky was followed by a night of fitful slumber.

When Halpin rang early in the morning, Wyatt felt tired and irritable.

"Is progress satisfactory on the report, James? Finance are on my back again, as you can appreciate."

"Yes, Seamus, I'm getting there."

"Can you be a little more specific James?"

"No, not really. Sorry, I'm doing my best, believe me."

"Ok James, no need to get tetchy. We're all in the same boat, aren't we?"

"Yes, of course. It's just the pressure of finishing off on these matters is getting to me. I'm not sleeping well either."

"That's to be expected down there. Sure you wouldn't like to finish it off in Dublin?"

"No. I need to be here to the end, to do it properly. I trust you'll explain that to the powers that be?"

"Ok James, so be it. I'll be in touch in a week."

Wyatt knew Halpin was annoyed, as he put down the phone. But so what? He fumed. It's ok for him, safe up there in his cushy office. Down here it's survival. God, he could do with a hair of the dog. Before starting back into the report, he decided to speak to Pete in Castlebar hospital.

When he saw the uniformed Garda outside the hospital room, he felt re-assured. Inside, Pete lay propped up in the bed, bandages gone, Stetson on the table beside the bed, looking perkier than before. The swelling on his mouth had receded, and the bruises were now splotched on his face in a yellowy blue colour.

"Howdy dude, good to see you." Pete's lips cracked in a grin as he spoke.

"You too Pete, how are you feeling?"

"Better dude, a heck of a lot better, thanks to them lovely physio gals here. They're givin' me a good goin' over. They've got me going great on the sticks, so they have. I'm gittin' out of here soon too. Back to the real world. Dang it, I can't wait to git outta here. "

"That's good, I'm sure you can't, you've had a hell of a time. Look, I want to ask you something about the break-in at Glencorrig Mines."

"Shoot dude."

"The guards have arrested three people in connection with it. They want to know if you would identify any of them, if they held an ID parade."

"I sure as heck would."

"And if you identified any of them, would you be prepared to swear it in court?"

"I sure would too."

"Are you certain? These men are dangerous. You would have police protection though."

"Sure I'm sure. We Parkers, we're afraid of nothin', heck we're Texans through and through."

"Good. I'll speak to the Garda. You're a brave man Pete. By the way, I trust you know the mining project isn't going ahead?"

"Sure do. Guess I won't be goin' nowhere for a while. It's a shame all that gold goin' to waste. An' the assayers sayin' too, that it was top drawer. But it'll be a while before we pull out."

"Ok, so long Pete." Wyatt waved as he went out the door, nodding to the Garda as he passed by.

Before starting back into the report in his room, he rang Bridie. She sounded exuberant.

"The architect will have plans by next week, and he's going to modernise it inside, but keep its character outside."

"That's good."

"It is. The solicitor is organised too. And I've a builder from Louisburgh appointed, he's a distant relation."

"That's great. I hope you're not overdoing it?"

"No. I feel on top of things now, and I'm goin' to take a rest now."

"That's good, please give my regards to your mother."

He put down the phone, and walked to his computer. The radio was playing low in the background. A news flash interrupted the music. Kuwait had been invaded by Iraqi forces under Saddam Hussein. World peace was threatened, the media said, oil prices and stock markets were in chaos. It all seems so far away and irrelevant to what's going on here, Wyatt muttered, as he proceeded to read his files.

The next morning he rang Sergeant McSweeney, and told him Pete was prepared to identify his assailants. The Sergeant was pleased, and said the ID parade would be arranged in the coming weeks.

A few days later another letter came from Jenny, doused in perfume. She would arrive in two days time, and wanted to tell him in advance of her changed circumstances. There was no one else she could divulge her innermost secrets to, except her dog Judd, who was coming with her. There had been another bust up with her boss, who had again tried to mess up her plans to come to Ireland. Jenny said she'd told her this time what to do with her job. Yes, she'd burnt her bridges this time, and there was no going back. She didn't care, the woman was an out and out bitch, and she'd had her fill of her. She would tell him the details when she arrived.

Her dream was to find a place of clay and wattles, with

bean rows growing all in a line, and build for herself there, a hive for the honey bee. Ireland was a country for old people and old loves, she said, and she would make her song a coat, covered with embroideries, out of old mythologies, from heel to throat. This time she was staying, she *would* follow her dream. Wyatt was alarmed, but realised there was nothing he could do about her decision.

***

The day Jenny arrived, Wyatt checked and found out she had booked into one of the chalets beside the hotel. He rang her, and invited her to dinner that night. She said she was tired after the journey, but would come anyway, as she needed to talk to him. In the restaurant she explained why she was now staying in a chalet. One reason was her dog Judd, a little mongrel, the other was her reduced circumstances. She had only her savings left, but needed the cash to finish her book on Yeats.

"I might be able to sell a few chapters to a magazine though, to raise a few bob before it's finished. Words alone are certain good, but they don't put bread on the table. Anyway it's super to be here. And also to see you." She sighed.

"You're brave to sacrifice everything for your art, Jenny."

As he sipped his wine, he thought she looked alluring in her black v- necked dress, with a string of pearls circling her neck, and the smell of her perfume in the air. Memories of their weekend in Sligo invaded his thoughts, though he knew everything had changed utterly since then.

"I know some people think I'm a crazy Jane, but I knew I just had to do it. It was like it was my destiny to leave and come here."

"I don't think you're crazy."

"Thanks Jim, you're super, I knew you wouldn't let me down."

"I won't, you can count on that." Inside, his thoughts churned.

"I have a few bob put by. I'll have to make it stretch until I finish the book, and add the halfpence to the pence."

"How long will the book take?"

"That depends. I think I'm half way there. Then I have to get somebody to publish it."

"And how hard will that be?"

"Good question, but who knows? At least I've had a few episodes published in England. I've had a few rejected too. That's pretty depressing. At least I learned one thing."

"What's that?"

"The stuff that I wrote after my previous visits here, were much better than the ones I wrote when I was in England. That also was part of my decision to come here. Of course, it wasn't the only one my love."She smiled and kissed him on the lips.Jenny excused herself just then to go to the bathroom, returning a few minutes later.

"Sorry Jim, out of season I'm afraid. How jolly inconvenient. And what have you been up to here since my last visit?" Her brown eyes burrowed into his.

There was so much to tell, he said, but he would tell her only a little that night. The rest could wait for another time, he thought, feeling relieved, as he told her about the mining protest rally on Croagh Patrick, and his salmon fishing experience.

"Oh Jim, that was terrific. And a happy ending too. I *do* love that. And the mining company got its comeuppance. Super. I might even use that story in my book. And I *do* love the idea of you as a fisherman, maybe going to a grey place on a hill, in grey Connemara clothes, at dawn to cast your flies, and with the down-turn of your wrist, dropping the flies into the stream. Was that how it was, my darling?" She grinned as she spoke.

"Yes Jenny, that's pretty close to what it was like. Maybe we should be going now?"

"Yes, we should be getting back, Judd might be making strange in his new surroundings."

When Jenny entered her chalet door, the dog jumped up on her in excitement. But when Wyatt came in after her, the dog yapped loudly and angrily, snarling at him, baring his teeth. It took Jenny a while and a walk around the garden to calm him down.

"Sorry Jim, Judd's just not used to strangers, but he'll be fine now he's got to know you."

"Maybe we should just say goodnight here and now, Jenny. You must be tired from the journey." The desire he'd felt earlier had ebbed, mainly due to the dog.

"I'm sorry Jim, Judd must be jealous. Anyway it's his first night here and he hasn't settled in yet."

"I need to get back to the hotel. I'm expecting an important call in the morning. I'll speak to you tomorrow evening." As he kissed her, he felt the warmth of her body, while the dog growled lowly at her feet.

As he ambled back to the hotel, he was glad he hadn't stayed, but knew he might have been tempted if the dog hadn't been there. Before things became even more complicated than they were already, he decided he must have a heart to heart with Jenny.

# Chapter 24

## *Green Fields of America*

Next morning he decided to visit Bridie, as he worried about her health. When he reached the cottage, she was resting in bed. Her mother let him in, and offered him a cup of tea, as she shuffled around the house, walking stick tip- tapping on the flagged floor. She had set the table with her best willow pattern delph. In the middle of the table was a plate of buttered scones beside the home-made jam.

"It's good to see you getting about the house again Mrs O'Malley."

"The sooner I can feck this stick into the wardrobe the better. Bridie, she made them scones last evenin', she's a dab hand at them."

"How is she?"

"As good as can be expected, but she's got to rest more. She'll be goin' back again this week for another check up. Do you want to see her now? I'll go and wake her, and tell her you've come to see her. She'll be glad to know you're here."

"Yes, thanks, I'd love to see her." He scoffed a scone, as she tapped her way out the kitchen door. Soon she returned.

"She said you're to wait five minutes more. She's in the bathroom, titivatin' herself."

Before strolling to the bedroom, he helped to clear the crockery. Bridie was propped up by a pillow in the bed, black hair brushed back, long and shiny, a smile lighting up her face.

"Thanks for comin' to see the invalid Jim. You'll get your reward someday."

"It's nothing, it's my pleasure." He kissed her lips.

"Everything's flyin' with the house."

"Good. And how are *you*?" She had a red flush on her

cheeks.

"The blood pressure's up and down, I have to watch it. I get tired more easily than before, but I take a few more hours in bed in the mornin' and evenin'. "

"That's good. You're going back for a check up this week I hear. Can I drive you to the hospital this time?"

"Thanks Jim, that'd be great. It's next Friday, and I'll get the van from Tommy Joe. I know he'll be out after the mackerel all week. The builder is rarin' to go on the house. He gave me a letter for you. It's probably his bill for the job, or maybe lookin' for an advance. The architect said the amount was ok to pay." She handed him the envelope, and after opening it, he glanced at the contents.

"That's great, I'll arrange the money this week. He can start now if he wants to."

"Ok, I'll tell him that. I can't wait for him to get goin'."

On an impulse, he told her about Jenny Marsh coming back to finish her book.

"Oh, that'll be that pretty English lady. I remember her now. She's nice, I like her. I'd like to meet her again when I'm feelin' better."

"Good, I'll tell her that. In the meantime, you take it easy. Ok?"

"I will, after I ring the builder."

"I'll be off then, and leave you to rest." He leaned down to kiss her.

"Oh Jim, before you go, there's somethin' I need to talk to you about." Her voice was low and serious.

"Nothing bad I hope?" He sat down again beside the bed, and held her hands.

"Not really, but I have to tell you I had a letter from America. It was from Francie."

"Oh. And what did *he* say?"

"He begged me to come over to him in the States. He sent me the money for the fare too, and more money, lots more. He'd heard I wasn't well, an' maybe he thought I was pinin' for him, or somethin'. Or else maybe he heard I was pregnant, an' thought I would be just dyin' to go out to him."

"And would you?"

"No, never, my home is here, where my heart is, and this is where I'm stayin'.With *you*, silly." She gripped his hands in hers.

"I'm glad of that. You had me worried for a minute. Did you write back to him?" He sighed with relief as he spoke.

"No, not yet, but I will write later today though, enclosin' his money. The nerve of him, thinkin' he could buy me off. How little he knows about me."

"Maybe he hasn't got over you yet. And I don't blame him, his loss is my gain. Anyway thanks for telling me about it, Bridie. I *do* love you. You take it easy, and I'll call again tomorrow."He bent over, and kissed her again.

"Thanks for callin' Jim, you know I love you too. I can't wait until the house is ready."She blew him a kiss as he left the room. Looking back, he smiled and waved, and blew a kiss back to her, before closing the door.

Rain drizzled soft on his oilskins, from a mist enveloping the valley, as he cycled back to the hotel. He could barely make out the shape of the haunted house as he passed by, but he saw the builder's van parked outside and smiled. He must be keen to do the work, he thought. Bridie will be happy to hear he's started.

As he pushed the pedals, he recalled Bridie's reaction to the news that Jenny had come back. He was surprised how calmly she took it, but was glad he'd told her, though a lot was left unsaid.

Back in the hotel, he dried out, and spent the afternoon working on Halpin's report. Afterwards he decided to clear the air with Jenny about his relationship with Bridie. He left the hotel, crossing the car park to Jenny's chalet, and rang the bell.

She opened the door, clad in tight fitting jeans and t-shirt, hair tied back, the dog yip yapping at her feet. Her eyes, brown, autumnal, gazed into his.

"Gosh Jim, you caught me on the hop, my hair's a mess

and I've rubbish clothes on. But I work better dressed like this, and I can take the dog for a walk without changing. Not that we could get out much today, with mist clouds tumbling down from the mountains. Still it was good weather for getting things down on paper. Nothing to distract me from my labour of words. But hey, look, the sun's breaking through at last. Smashing."She pointed up over his head.

"So it is. Maybe we could go for a walk now with the dog. There's a good place not far away. It's called the Green Road. It goes down by the Killary fjord, past some Famine ruins."

"That would be super Jim. Judd would love that. See, he's wagging his tail, as soon as you said the magic word "walk". He might even get to like you in time. Hold on a minute till I put on my walking boots."

Soon they were strolling along the old road on the south side of the fjord, sodden and slippery from mist and drizzle.

Across the inlet Mweelrea towered, ochre in the evening sun. Below, gulls lazed in the rolling water, serene after their day's toil. Ahead the path twisted as they threaded their way through ramshackle ruins, and lazy beds that people had laboured over, famine years ago. They passed the ruins of *Doire* where the whole village had vanished through death or emigration in the Famine.

"It's so sad Jim to see these ruins, and think how people lived in such a beautiful, but harsh place.I can almost feel their spirit reaching out to me. Can you?"

"Yes, it's sad the way it was. They broke their backs, and had nothing to show for it. Then the Famine came, and that was that. It was die or get out. Some people are born unlucky, and some get dealt a rotten hand. Where is God in all this? Maybe they get rewarded in the next life."

They tried to climb down to a lower pathway. Wyatt went first. As Jenny followed, she slipped on the dripping ferns, and landed in a muddy pool. He pulled her up by the hand.

"Oh Jim, it's the seat of my jeans, they're all muddy and wet." She was close in his arms, their bodies touching, and he smelt her perfume and felt her softness. He slid his hand behind her, and felt her wet bottom.

"Yes, they're wet all right. But there's no drying around here I guess."He looked down into her surprised eyes, feeling her body close and against his, and she not minding. And he felt himself being carried away. A few moments later, Jenny broke away from him.

"Jim, I don't think this is either the time or the place. Let's go back to my chalet. It's hard to be lovey dovey with a wet bum, and in wet panties. You can rustle up something to eat while I have a bath."

"Good idea. Let's do that."The blood pulsed in his veins.

On the way back Jenny stopped, and cocked her ear.

"Can you hear it Jim?"

"Hear what?"

"The curlew, silly. Listen."

"Yes, I can hear it now, so what?"

She turned towards the shoreline as she replied that it's crying brings tears to the eyes, and that there's enough evil in the crying of the wind. Then she turned back to him.

"Sorry Jim, I got carried away, silly me." She took his hand and they hurried along the pathway, with Judd following behind, tail wagging.

Wyatt looked into Jenny's fridge. It was nearly empty. He reckoned she was either on a tight budget or ate very little. He decided then to get some food from the hotel. Jenny was in the bath, so he left a note on the table.

When he came back later with two duck dishes and a bottle of red wine, she was seated at the table, sipping a glass of white wine. She wore a white dress with a low neckline, lips lined with pink lipstick. A pair of kicked- off shoes lay on the floor beside the sofa. On the table were a lit candle and a vase of wildflowers.

"Sorry Jim, I'm afraid the larder was bare. I must do some shopping."

"That's ok I'm not much of a cook anyway. It got me off the hook." He smiled, as he filled his glass.

"Your talents lie in other directions."

"If you say so, I hope you've recovered from your fall in the mud?"

"Actually I came out to see if you wished to wash my back, but you had gone to the hotel. I can be brazen and wanton as the dawn, you know. "A twinkle came in her eye as she spoke.

"Just my luck. Here's to us."

"Let's eat before it gets cold."

Later, food and wine gone, they sat on the sofa, with the dog whimpering outside.

"Judd's mad jealous of you."

"He better get used to it, it's a dog's life here you know."

The dog continued whining and scratching at the door. Finally, Jenny stood up and let Judd in. The dog lay on the floor beside the bed, sulking.

"Jim?"

"Yes?"

"I've just seen that gun on the chair. Are those bad guys still after you?"

"Not really, I just keep it as a precaution. You never know. I'll hang onto it until I've finished my project, its no load to carry."

"And what will you do then?"

"I'm not sure just yet. I've just bought a house up in the valley as an investment, with the money from my mother's estate."

"Oh really?"

Her eyes widened in surprise. He told her then of his relationship with Bridie, although feeling inside it wasn't quite the right time to do so. But it had welled up inside him, and he had to get it out. He told her how he had fallen for Bridie, when she had split up with her fiancée Francie, over not going with him to the States. Lastly he told her of

Bridie's pregnancy. Tears filled her eyes, and she reached for her handkerchief.

"Jim, I just can't believe it, how....how you've deceived me. How...how could you do it? You're a cad. You knew this all that time, and never said anything. How could you?"

She sobbed into her handkerchief, and the dog growled in sympathy.

"I'm sorry Jenny, I was smitten by you right from that time I met you on the beach in that beautiful place. Look... I....I didn't mean to hurt you."

"Well you certainly have. You've made a complete fool of me. You jolly well have. A complete fool."She sobbed.

"I do love you Jenny, strange though it might seem and I don't regret our love. It *is* possible to love two people, you know. Sure what about your friend Yeats? Wasn't he in love with two women in the poem? Both beautiful too." Wyatt knew as soon as he uttered the words, that it was a mistake. Too late.

"That's not the same, it's not the same at all. How could you?" Her eyes flashed, as she spat the words at him.

"I suppose its not. I don't blame you for being upset Jenny, but I had to tell you. I was waiting for the right time, but I don't think there was ever going to be a right time. I'm sorry if I upset you. But why should you be sorry for loving someone? I suppose I better be on my way then." She said nothing, still sobbing. He walked to the bedroom door, and turned.

"Jenny, I do hope you stay here, and we can at least be friends. And another thing, Bridie likes you a lot, and she would like to see you sometime. She knows nothing about us."

"Goodnight Jim Wyatt, there's nothing more to say. Its all over.You're a cheat, and a cad. You led me up the garden path, walked on my dreams. I don't ever want to see or speak to you again. Ever." She dabbed her eyes with a handkerchief.

"Goodnight". He said, and closed the door behind him. The dog barked after him. At least *he's* happy I'm gone, Wyatt thought. The truth sometimes hurts, and so does love. Why can't we always stay happy? I'm sorry Jenny is unhappy, deeply sorry. But I can't change the past.

Happiness sure is an elusive state of mind. Like a Holy Grail. Sometimes you think you have it, then it slips away, and comes back another day. Maybe she'll get over it. Time heals they say, and so does a good whiskey. Later in his room, he downed a few, before falling into an on and off sleep.

Next morning, his showdown with Jenny still weighed on his mind. He knew it had to be done, but felt upset, and wondered if he should go see her, but decided against it. Maybe she would get over it? No, probably not, he reflected. Or perhaps she would go back to England? He hoped not. But he had to do it, though he wanted them to part on friendly terms. His timing was bad.

He crossed the road, to the water's edge, and picked a bunch of wildflowers. As he picked them he heard the curlew's cry ratchet forlorn in the distance, and it stabbed his heart. Back in his room he wrote Jenny a short letter. In it he said he was sorry she was unhappy, but he couldn't live the lie any longer, and he hoped she would understand that in time, and they could at least remain friends. He put the letter in the wildflowers and left them at her door.

Later that morning Sergeant McSweeney rang. The ID parade for the break in at the Glencorrig Mines' premises, including the assault on a member of the staff, would be held in Westport Garda station the following Saturday week. Wyatt could attend discreetly, McSweeney said, and stay in a room nearby if he wished. There was a private entrance where nobody could be seen entering or leaving. Pete Parker was still under Garda protection, but it might be a support for him if Wyatt was in the building. Wyatt said he would think about it.

On Friday he picked Bridie and her mother up, and drove them to Castlebar hospital in Tommy Joe's van. They joined the queue in the waiting area. Finally Bridie's name was called. Wyatt waited, reading the paper, as Bridie's mother took a ball of white wool from her bag, and began knitting, needles clicking like a ticking clock in the silent room. Somethin' for the little one, she said.

Later, Wyatt had read the newspaper several times, and Bridie's mother was on her second ball of wool, but still there was still no sign of Bridie. He went to the hospital shop and bought a magazine. When he got back Bridie's mother was standing at the door, knitting needles put away, her face wrinkled in a frown.

"We'd best be goin' now." She said.

"Why?"

"The doctor, well he came just after you left. He said he was keepin' Bridie in for a while, sayin' he's not happy with her blood pressure. He said a good rest should do the trick, and you can visit her when she's settled in." Her face had a sad look.

He drove Bridie's mother home, and a few hours later was back in the dimly lit hospital room beside Bridie. Her face seemed red and blotchy in the half light.

"Sorry Jim, for all this trouble. I'm a right nuisance." Her smile seemed forced and wan.

"It's no trouble Bridie. You've been overdoing things. A good rest here and you'll be right as rain." He bent over and kissed her flushed cheeks.

"My sister Nora is comin' back from Dublin for a while to keep an eye on Mam."

"Don't you worry Bridie I'll keep an eye on her too. You'll be out of here before you know it."

"I will Jim, I know I will. But nine months is a long time." She sighed as she spoke.

"It is, but you'll be out of here soon, Bridie. A good rest is all you need." He took her hands in his.

Minutes later, she closed her eyes, and drifted asleep. He rose, and stood a few moments looking down at her, thinking how peaceful she looked. Like an angel. He sighed, kissed her forehead lightly and left.

At the hotel reception, there was a message from Jenny, and a brown envelope, which he stuffed in his pocket. Back in his room he read her letter first. She thanked him for the flowers, but said he needn't think that a bunch of flowers would change her feelings towards him. She was happy with her own company, and Judd's, and her work, and the fascination of doing something difficult kept her going.

He started to write a reply, then stopped, stood up, scrunched the paper into a ball, and threw it into the bin beside his desk. Better to leave more time to let the dust settle, he muttered.

Wyatt took the brown envelope out of his pocket. It was unstamped, had his name scrawled on it, and the hotel's address, and had many misspellings. He started, realizing it wasn't from anyone he knew. He tore the envelope open. The handwriting inside was almost illegible, and unsigned. After reading it several times, he shook his head in disbelief.

It said that Wyatt was to bring the paper this person had signed before on the boat, to Bun Dorca harbour the next day at one o'clock sharp, or someone close to Wyatt would be shot dead. It hit him like a bolt it was from McFadden, and was for real.

He froze and felt queasy, as his stomach knotted. He told himself to stay cool, and think straight, but felt panic surging inside. He sat down, and read the page again, then stood up and paced the room, pummelling his palms. Who's going to be shot? He wondered. Is it Pete in hospital, or Tommy Joe, or his brother, or even Bridie, or her mother? Who knows? What should I do? He needed to talk to someone. Tommy Joe, he's the man, he'll know what to do. Tommy Joe has the measure of McFadden, Wyatt thought, as he tried to reassure himself.

That night he drove to the pub in an anxious state. Inside, a man in a cap played an accordeon in the corner, a crowd milled at the bar, and the usual smoke pall hovered overhead. He relaxed somewhat when he saw Tommy Joe and his brother Michael seated at the bar. Tommy Joe spotted him and waved, calling out.

"What'll you be havin' Inspector? The usual? Ok, I'll be right over."

Wyatt found a table at the back in a quiet spot, with a view around the pub. Tommy Joe was beaming when he came over, a pint in either hand, the odour of fish rising from his clothes.

"Howyeh, get that into you. It'll do you good."

"You seem in fine fettle, Tommy Joe?"

"An' why wouldn't I be? Aren't me and Michael after havin' a famous week with the fishin'? Caught a boatload of fish we did. Yes, a mighty week it surely was. It doesn't happen to us that often, so we're celebratin'."

"That's good, and thanks anyway for the van. Here are your keys. I might need it again, though, as Bridie's been kept in hospital for observation. Just a precaution you know."

"Oh, is that so? Well, you hold onto the keys in that case. Can you bring me'n Michael to the hospital to see her tomorrow?"Tommy Joe's face had scrunched into a frown.

Wyatt agreed, and then told Tommy Joe about the ID parade the next week.

"Well now Inspector, on your own head let it be, but I wouldn't advise goin' into them Garda premises where they're doing the identifyin'."

"And why not?"

"Because McFadden's men'll be watchin' like hawks whoever comes and goes. You're a marked man already, don't you go courtin' trouble."

"I want to support Pete, it's a brave thing he's doing."

"It surely is, and some would say too that it's a mad thing he's doin'. Why don't you meet him later in the Clew Bay Hotel, that's where he's stayin'?"

"How do you know that?"

"I have me sources Inspector. He's got Garda cover

there too. It's a safe place to go."

"Thanks for the information Tommy Joe. I'll do that. Look, I need your advice on something very important." Wyatt lowered his voice, and glanced around.

"Hold on a minit, wait till I get a couple of pints."

Tommy Joe took the empty glasses back to the bar. When he returned, Wyatt told him about McFadden's letter. Tommy Joe frowned as he listened, and scratched his head.

"That fuckin' animal, he's come out of his lair at last. He fuckin' means business for sure."

"I'm sure he does. But what'll we do?

"First we'll have another drink. Let me think awhile about this a minit."

Minutes passed like hours before Tommy Joe spoke again.

"Ok Inspector, here's the plan. Me'n Michael, we'll be goin' fishin' near Bun Dorca harbour in the mornin', an' we'll bring our hunting rifles with us. We'll be handy if somethin' happens, so don't you worry. You just meet him just the way he says in the letter, and give him what he needs. I'll pick you up early in the mornin', and we'll go get the document. There's no choice. It's a rock and a hard place. Make sure you're armed when you meet the slieveen. Feck, I shoulda finished the cunt off that time we had him on the boat." Tommy Joe punched his palm as he spoke.

"I'll be armed and ready Tommy Joe, and thanks for your help and advice."Wyatt said, trying to sound calm, but inside his nerves jangled. It was surreal, it couldn't be happening, he thought. But it was.

Later, on his way to the bar to buy a drink for Tommy Joe, he bumped into Ned Halpin, the local Councillor.

"Ah, it's yourself James, and how's she cuttin'? Finished the report yet? I hope I get a good mention in it? Can I get you a drink?"

"No thanks Ned, I'm just buying one for Tommy Joe, I owe him one. Let me do the honours."

"Sure James. Thank you."

Minutes later, they were ensconced in the corner. The music was flying, with the accordeon player now joined by two fiddles, a banjo, and a tin whistle.

"This is a grand, private spot you've got here James. It's standin' room only in the rest of the house." Halpin lifted his glass.

"The early bird, that's me. Down the hatch."

"Look James, it's none of my business what you put in your report. What's done is done, I've done my bit and life moves on."

"Sure Ned, what's done is done as you say, but what I can't understand is why people can't do what's right for the environment, the people, and the country, when it comes to preventing pollution. The country's future is at stake after all. When something's right it's right. It won't go away either, it'll come back to haunt you, if you don't do the right thing. Without a doubt you'll pay for it later, and with a vengeance."

"You have a point there I suppose. I gather you're referring to the mining fiasco. I guess it's to do with priorities. There's only so much money to go around everywhere, and sometimes the priority lines get blurred."

"Is it not your job to ensure that doesn't happen in your area?"

"Yes, I suppose it is. But it's not always black and white, sometimes it's grey."

"Then you must get clarification. It's about doing the right thing, and not always about popularity, winning votes and getting elected. Speaking of which, I believe you're going up in the elections next spring?"

"Yes. I'm going forward as an Independent. Look James, or should I call you Inspector? Let's let bygones be bygones. I've heard in the grapevine that you lay claim to some ancestral connection with the venerable Mr Wyatt, one of the architects involved in the building of Westport House, and in the laying out of the town of Westport."

"That's what they say, but it's not definite. It's a good

story, though."

"Well, I have a good connection there, with the owner in fact, and we've come up with the idea of having a cricket game in Westport House to celebrate your ancestry, whether its proven or not. You get a team together and I'll organise the opposition. We have many people working in Castlebar hospital who play cricket. You get a few of your hurling friends to play, and we'll have a bit of fun. What do you say?"

"I never knew they played cricket down here?"

"You'd be surprised then to know that once upon a time it was *the* biggest game in Ireland.

"Really?"

"Yes really, James, back in 1870 it was the number one game in the country. Look, I have a booking for the game on Saturday two weeks in Westport House. The owner is away on holidays, but everything will be organised. So, how about it then? Are you on?"

"Well....yes, ok then, why not? It could be a bit of fun, as you say. Let's give it a go."

They shook hands and Halpin melted back into the crowd at the bar. It was unreal, Wyatt thought. The idea of playing cricket seemed so far fetched, when he thought of what he was facing into the next day. But he had to admit Halpin had a persuasive manner.

After scoffing his drink, Wyatt scanned the crowd. There was no sign of Sergeant McSweeney. As he looked at the faces in the pub, he wondered if any of them were cronies of McFadden.

With the wildness in the air and the music racing along, there would be many staying late in the pub. Into the dangerous hours. He decided then it was time to go, although reluctant to leave the heady atmosphere. He finished his drink, and slipped into the blackness outside, his hand gripping his gun, every step of the way back to the hotel.

In his room Wyatt paced the floor, and then sat on the bedside, pondering the imminent showdown with

McFadden, a whisky glass cupped in his hands. He felt stressed. He reckoned Tommy Joe had called it right, and there was no choice but to face the music. His stomach churned with a feeling he couldn't fathom, and there was a dry feeling in his mouth. It was fear, it had to be. This must be what a prisoner feels the night before his execution. Or maybe it's like the moment of truth when the matador faces the bull. Only who was the matador and who was the bull? At least he was prepared, and had Tommy Joe and Michael as back up.

Sleep would not come, though he emptied the remains of the whisky bottle. Ned Halpin's words about arranging a cricket match seemed trivial. Everything paled into unimportantance compared with what was to happen the next day. He had his suspicions too, that Ned Halpin was involved in the tampering with the lab samples, and the break-in to his room. He shivered, and his mind wandered back to McFadden's letter. He waited for sleep to come. And he waited.

# Chapter 25

## *As I Roved Out*

The next morning Tommy Joe arrived early at the hotel in his van. Wyatt was waiting, edgy after a restless night. He'd skipped breakfast, his stomach churning. They went straight to the haunted house to get the document Mc Fadden had signed. On the way all was quiet inside the reeking van. Wyatt fumed how anyone could put up with such a smell, day in day out. Both stared out the window grim faced, as the sun edged over the mountains. The forecast was for hazy sunshine, with little cloud or wind. Even the scenery outside failed to lift the air of gloom inside the van.

They reached O'Hara's cottage, and parked outside at the rusted gate. Tommy Joe stayed in the van, keeping guard while Wyatt rushed up the overgrown track to the house. He found the document, intact in the leather briefcase, under the boards, and breathed a sigh of relief. Mission accomplished. Soon they were heading back to the hotel, silence still reigning inside the van.

"I have it." Wyatt said his first words.

"I don't think we were followed." Tommy Joe finally broke the ice.

"I hope not."

Quietness came again. Wyatt continued staring out the window, grim faced, wondering if all this was really happening. Before alighting at the hotel door, he turned to Tommy Joe.

"Thanks for the lift."

"Ok Inspector, you're welcome. Just stick to the plan we agreed, ok? We'll be sittin' out there on the water waitin' until near the time. We'll keep our eyes peeled sharp for the bastard. We'll pull into Bun Dorca harbour if we see anythin' suspicious. You keep your eyes skint for that cunt, I wouldn't trust him atall."

"I will, see you later." Wyatt waved as the van rattled up the road towards the harbour, black fumes billowing from the exhaust.

Back in his bedroom Wyatt checked his watch. Two hours to go, just enough time for a coffee and toast in his room. Soon he sat sipping coffee at the window, gazing onto the rear of the hotel at the sunlit mountain. The Devil's bollocks, how appropriate, maybe I have a date with the man himself, he thought.

He tried to focus on how things might go when he met McFadden. Maybe the man would agree to cease his paramilitary activities when he got the document? No, not likely, wishful thinking, a leopard doesn't change his spots. Or maybe he'd agree to move to another location? No, that would only be moving the problem elsewhere, though it would make *his* life simpler. Maybe he might want the charges dropped too? Had he informed his cronies of what he had been forced to sign on the boat? Probably not.

After a while he gave up, deeming it a waste of time to try to second guess such a person. He looked once more at the mountain. The Devil's bollocks indeed. Que sera, sera, he muttered, replacing the empty coffee cup on the tray.

Wyatt jumped when the phone jangled on his desk. It was reception. Seamus Halpin was on the line for him. Jesus, he swore. He needed to speak to Halpin like a hole in the head.

"Tell him I'm away on business. Just tell him I'll contact him later in the day." If all goes well, he added to himself. The least amount of people involved the better. Wyatt wondered if the girl detected the edge in his voice.

He then stripped to his shoulder holster, removed the gun, and checked it, before replacing it in the holster. After unharnessing the holster, he donned a bulletproof vest. It weighed a ton. With the holster back on over the vest, he put his shirt back on. It concealed both gun and vest. His throat parched for a drink but he banished the thought.

After saying a prayer beside his bed, Wyatt rose, blessed himself, and checked his watch. Eleven fifteen, time to get going. Outside the hotel, he scanned all sides, as he walked to his bike. The vest was weighing him down, and he felt and moved like a robot.

He refilled the water carrier on the bike, and put his visibility jacket on, leaving the zip accessing his holster partly open. With the signed document folded and hidden inside it, he placed the helmet on his head, and pushed off, free-wheeling down towards the village, an ache tightening in his gut. At last he was moving.

Outside the village he stopped and scanned west to see if Tommy Joe's boat was out in the fjord, but there was no sign of it. Damn, he thought, I hope he doesn't let me down. I know he won't, Tommy Joe is a rock. But where the hell is he?

He checked his watch again. With little time to spare he re-mounted, and pedalled hard along the twisting road towards Aasleagh Falls. Soon he was coasting along the far side of the fjord, and looked over to the hotel, across the fjord's expanse of water. Black-faced horned sheep wandered, and grazed along at the side of the road, indifferent to the traffic. Perspiration dripped down his face, as the road rose before him, and the sun beat down from an indigo sky.

The weight of the bulletproof vest slowed his progress. Butterflies fluttered about the wild flowers in the hedgerows. He thought then of the butterflies he had in his stomach. Gannets shrieked and scythed into the waters below, and crows croaked overhead. Bun Dorca harbour must be close now, he guessed. Damn, he muttered, forget watching bloody nature, and just watch the way ahead.

The road swung inland, north from the fjord, and dipped towards a bridge. Beneath the bridge, the Bun Dorca River tumbled towards the sea, on a path gouged out through the rocks, over ages of time. Wyatt glided down and across the bridge, turning left at the far side, up an incline that would bring him to the harbour.

He rose from the saddle, swaying side to side, as he pumped the pedals to gain speed. A pothole loomed in front of him, and he swerved to avoid it. In that instant, he glimpsed a flash in the corner of his eye, near a boulder at the road at the top of the hill to his left. There was no sound as his head was smashed by something hard. He was jerked sideways by the impact, and man and bicycle parted company. As he sailed surreally through the air, towards the siding, his body was pummelled by another impact, this time between his shoulder blades. Wyatt's body plunged down the incline, and turned over and over, stopping at a boulder near the river's edge. The bike soon followed, coming to rest near him, and lay upside down, with its front spokes spinning in the sun.

Wyatt lay on his back beside a boulder, his head throbbing in the smashed helmet. Through slit eyelids he saw black turning bright, then black again, as he dipped in and out of consciousness. Moments passed, and when he blinked bright again, a giant figure came into his vision. He was silhouetted against the sun, and stood at the top of the slope, gazing down at him.

The figure was still for several seconds, just staring, like a frozen shadow. The shadow then moved down the slope in his direction, stopped half way, raised a rifle, and took aim. A shot rang out, staccato in the stillness. The giant figure teetered, and fell head first down the incline, coming to rest near Wyatt's body.

Minutes passed before Wyatt put the pistol back into its holster. The stench of cordite hung in the air. He had taken aim and pulled the trigger automatically, just like McSweeney had shown him. More minutes passed before he lifted his head, wondering if it was still attached to his body. It ached as if hit by a hammer.

He stood up after a while, easing himself onto one arm, and balanced on the boulder, surveying the carnage. The spokes of the bicycle wheel still spun, glittering and clicking in the sunshine. He grimaced as he inched over to the inert person beside him. Every part of his body ached.

He started as he stared into McFadden's dead face. There was a look of surprise on it, and a gaping bullethole where his right eye had been. A .22 rifle with telescopic sights, and a silencer on the end of the barrel, was clutched in his right hand. Blood oozed from the wound, forming a pool of crimson that trailed down to the river. Flies and insects were already buzzing around the body. Wyatt felt a wave of nausea hit him, and vomited into the siding. He struggled over to the wreckage of his bike, and unclipped the water flask, gulping the contents.

Then he stood, dazed, and leant against a boulder, realising he had just shot and killed someone. That made him a killer, but he didn't care. He felt elated, and his friends were safe now. It was survival, the law of the jungle. Do unto others as they would do unto you, only do it first, or something like that.

Wyatt took the battered helmet off his head, removed the paper he had hidden there, and put it in his pocket. He looked at the dent made in the helmet by the first bullet, which had clipped the helmet, and realised how lucky he had been. It could have been him lying dead on the ground. The bullet proof vest had saved his bacon too, with the other shots. Luck of the devil. The Devil's bollocks indeed, he muttered and smiled grimly to himself.

As he waited, Tommy Joe and Michael came rushing into view, and scrambled down the incline, breathless, rifles clutched in their hands.

"We came runnin' soon as we heard the shots. We came into the harbour, quick as we could, when we saw him parkin' his van on the pier, an' leavin' it with a rifle slung over his shoulder. He's deader'n a doornail Inspector, you sure plugged him proper. You saved me the pleasure, are you alright yourself?" Tommy Joe spoke, face red, eyes bulging, squinting in the sun, and breathing hard.

"A bit groggy thanks, but I'll be ok in a few minutes, I think. My head feels like a train hit it. And my bike is wrecked."

"Fuck the bike Inspector, that's the least of our worries now. I'll get you a new one for Christmas. I've news for you anyway."Tommy Joe said, as he leant over and peered at McFadden's body.

"What's that?

"It wasn't yourself that killed him."

"What? Then who did?"

"The bullet that did the damage was fired by Michael here. He was quicker'n me up from the harbour. Your shot only winged him."

"Jesus, what'll we do? Someone may arrive here any minute. My head's spinning, I feel faint. I can't even think straight, let's do something for God's sake. Quick."Wyatt felt a panic attack coming.

"Yer right, we've got to get movin', Inspector. We've put paid to that bastard at last, the bane of my life. He fuckin' had it comin' for a long fuckin' time." Tommy Joe and Michael grabbed the body, top and tail, and dragged it out of sight behind a boulder by the river. Then they hid the bike in the same place.

"Michael, see if you can find the keys in his pockets."Tommy Joe grunted.

Michael appeared a few moments later from behind the rock, and smiled, jangling a bunch of keys from his finger.

They left Wyatt with the body, and ran back to the pier. Soon they returned in the white van, and left it parked on the roadside. After taking a tarpaulin from the back of the van, they dragged it down the slope, and wrapped McFadden's body in it.

They stuffed the corpse in the rear of the van, and helped Wyatt up the slope, into the front seat of the van, putting McFadden's rifle in beside him. Lastly, the smashed bicycle was recovered and shoved into the back, beside the body.

Within minutes the van was parked on Bun Dorca pier, facing seawards.

"Good job Inspector, we were steeped to get away with no one happenin' along, after the noise of the shots."

"I suppose, it could've been a backfiring van. What'll we do now? Ring McSweeney?" Wyatt's head was still groggy.

"No, it'll only feck things up. There'll be legal hassle too. The bastard's buddies'll start wantin' revenge when they find out what happened. We'll only just have sorted this bastard out, when other bastards will take his place."

"What are you suggesting then?"

"I'm suggestin' this time we keep it simple. This time we do it right, I've the right idea for the bastard. You've got the paper he was lookin' for?"

"Yes."

"Right, then I'm suggestin' we put your bike in our boat, an' you too Inspector, an' then drive the bloody van off the end of the pier, with McFadden in the driver's seat. The water's deep as hell around here. Most likely the body, or what's left've it, will never be found. Just vanish'd, like the grand Lord Lucan himself. Done a runner. And hadn't they both a lot t' run away from too? If McFadden's ever found, no one'll know how he died, when the fishes have finished with him. Well, what do you say this time?"

"Well…it… it's just not right is it? There are rules and regulations to be followed. And people trained and skilled to deal with these matters." Wyatt thought deep down Tommy Joe's suggestion was simple and had merit. And he was relieved too that *his* bullet had not been the fatal one. But above all his head ached, and he just wanted out of this nightmare, and back to the sanctuary of the hotel, and most of all he yearned for a drink.

"Yer right, an' where did it get you the last time. McFadden released in days an' after us again."

Wyatt knew he wasn't thinking normally. He was wavering, and felt light-headed, everything seemed far away. The rule books were fine, but it seemed to him just then that Tommy Joe's words made sense. McFadden was dead anyway. The solution was simple.

"Ok, I...I agree...let... let's get on with it, let's do it your way this time. Let's just get it over with."

Michael checked the road, and gave the all clear. Wyatt and Tommy Joe pushed the van off the pier, windows half down, and watched it fill up and sink deep into the depths in a seething mass. Tommy Joe muttered good riddance when it finally sank from sight.

Wyatt had a sense of relief too. Now McFadden was out of his life for good, he thought. Amen to that, but Wyatt still felt uneasy. Michael ran over then, looking distressed. He had taken McFadden's rifle out of the van and was waving it in the air. Tommy Joe swore, grabbed the rifle from him, and flung it far out into the fjord after the van.

Back at Leenane harbour, Wyatt shook hands with Tommy Joe, and as he started walking back to the hotel with his broken bike, Tommy Joe offered him the use of his van the next day to get the bike fixed. Wyatt agreed and left the bike in the back of the van.

"One last thing has t' be done Inspector."

"What's that?"

"You give the docament with them names and things on it to the Sergeant tomorrow."

"Why?"

"He'll pick them up an' arrest them then, an' charge 'em. He's got McFadden's real signature now. But he won't be able t' find McFadden t' testify. The smart legal men will get 'em released. They'll go hell for leather after McFadden's ass, but they won't find him atall, what with him swimmin' down there with the fishes. All the more reason for McFadden to vanish, eh?"

"I...I get the picture, Tommy Joe. I'll...I'll do that tomorrow." Wyatt waved goodbye and trudged back to the hotel.

He rested for a few hours, and later lounged in the bath, trying to get his head around what had happened. He had shot, but not killed someone. Self defence, but he had no choice. Inwardly he was happy he was alive and McFadden was dead, but his head still whirled, unable to take it all in. He resolved nobody must be told of McFadden's fate. Except one person.

Within the hour he was in Castlebar hospital in the darkened room with big Pete. He had bullied his way in for five minutes, as it was past visiting time.

"Thet you dude." Pete's eyes flickered open.

"Yes Pete, just a flying visit. I've got some news I thought you'd like to hear."

"Yup, shore could do with cheerin'up. Shoot."

"Our friend McFadden won't be annoying you anymore. Or should I say, he won't be annoying anyone anymore. I just thought you'd like to know."

"That's shore as hell the best news I've had in a long, long time. Dang it, the sonofabitch had it comin'. Kickin' up the daisies is he? Died with his boots on? Buried 'n boot hill? Best news for a long time. Thanks dude, you shore as hell made my day."

"Good, but just before I go Pete there's one thing."

"Shore, shoot."

"No one is to know about what happened to him. And this conversation never took place. It's our little secret, just the two of us. Ok?"

"Shore thing, my lips are sealed. You just made me one helluva happy guy." He tried to smile through swollen, bruised lips. Wyatt left then, feeling better.

That evening Wyatt had his dinner brought to his room. Earlier, he had bought a bottle of whiskey at the bar. After eating, he went to his desk, whiskey bottle in hand and poured a stiff shot. His hands trembled as he drank it. He refilled the glass, took another mouthful, and let the liquid linger at the back of his mouth, before swallowing it. It felt good.

He lay back in the bed, and let thoughts of what had happened earlier that day swirl through his mind like a river. McFadden had tried to pull a fast one with the ambush, but it had backfired. Wyatt knew he had been lucky, and felt relieved. Now Mcfadden was dead, and *he* was alive. *That* was a good feeling. The more he thought about it, the better he felt. After all it could have been him swimming with the fishes instead of McFadden.

Here's to a long and happy life, he toasted himself. Still, you couldn't know what his cronies might get up to. No need to get complacent. He was glad Tommy Joe was on his side. He was a rock. Wyatt refilled his glass, and toasted tomorrow.

# Chapter 26

## *Sporting Paddy*

Wyatt rang Sergeant McSweeney, to say he would not attend the ID parade, but would meet Pete Parker later at his hotel. McSweeney agreed to pass the word on. Later that day, Wyatt drove Tommy Joe and his brother Michael to the hospital to visit Bridie. On the way he told them they were part of his team for a coming cricket match in Westport House.

"What sort of a nancy boy's game is that at all Inspector? Dressin' up with all them pads an' things. Hurlin', now that's a real man's sport."Tommy Joe said, eyes twinkling, face twisted in a grin.

"You're entitled to your opinion Tommy Joe. You'll find out soon enough if cricket's a man's sport or not. Can you round up a few more players?"

"Ok, count us in Inspector. I wouldn't miss it for love or money. I'll get a few of the hurlers to play. I might have to twist their arm a bit, mind you, but they won't often get a chance to play in a fancy place like Westport House."

As they left the hospital, Wyatt thought Bridie's health had improved, but Tommy Joe had a frown on his face when he got back to the van.

"That girleen, she'd better slow down a bit, an' take it handy. She's doin' too much, far too much altogether."He shook his head as he spoke.

"She'll be fine, another few days rest, and she'll be right as rain."

"I hope you're right Inspector. Maybe you can drop us off in Westport on the way back. We need to get some things for the boat."

Wyatt left them at the Octagon under the statue of Saint Patrick, parked the van, and walked down James' street, entering the dim light of the Clew Bay Hotel lobby. He waited there, reading a newspaper, and ordered lunch. It was late afternoon before Pete's large frame came through the door, stetson on head, leaning on a walking stick. He smiled when he saw Wyatt, and shuffled over, hand extended. They shook hands.

"Good to see you dude. Boy, am I glad to sit down?"

"It's good to see you too Pete. What'll you have? Tell me how did it go at the ID?" Wyatt was reassured when he saw the silhouette of the security Garda through the panes of the hotel door.

"First things first, a rye whiskey, double." Wyatt went to the bar and returned with a drink in each hand. He placed the whiskey in front of the huge Texan, who lifted it to his lips, gulped a slug, and put the glass back on the table.

"Boy, I sure needed that. Dang, it was tough goin' back there."

"Well, what happened then?"

"Well, first there was lots of shenanigans goin' on with this gang outside the cop shop. They wanted to know what I'd done with their missin' friend McFadden. I was gonna give them a piece of my mind, but the cops, they held me back, then pushed me inside."

"And what happened then?"

"I was hangin' around there then 'til they got them guys lined up proper. I was sure waitin' a long time. A helluva long time, it seemed like forever. My legs were giving me hell."

"Did you recognise any of them?"

"Sure did, two of them for definite, I'd swear it on a heap o' bibles. 'Course the one I remember the most, he wasn't there, was he? Our friend, the one and only Mr. McFadden. He's the one you sorted out dude, heh heh. You sure cooked *his* goose." Pete giggled at the thought, taking another swig of the whiskey.

"Ssh Pete, not so loud, that's our little secret. Remember?" Wyatt's stomach tightened as he spoke, and he pressed his finger to his lips, glancing around the room.

"Sure dude, sorry, I'll keep my big mouth shut 'n future. Anyways, they were all pals of McFadden. A nice little bunch of rattlers they were, all in all. Spat in my face, they did, when I pointed them out. Said I'd regret this day. As mean, an' ornery a crowd of snakes, as ever I laid eyes upon. I just said nothin'. I just looked them dead in the eye, an' said nothin'. Where I come from, we got ways of dealin' with snakes." Pete said, patting the gun bulging beneath his shirt.

"Sure Pete. But don't go getting trigger happy. This isn't the Wild West, the law will take its own course. What then?"

"Cops said they'd be charged, an' kept in jail until the trial. Maybe for a couple of months, more or less." His eyes were glued on the empty whiskey glass on the table.

"No bail then, that's good. Let me get you a refill." Wyatt headed back to the bar.

"There you are, I must say you're a brave man, Pete. What will you do until the trial happens?"

"I've got some work to do for a few weeks. Then I'll hightail it outta here for a while, until the heat cools off. Back to Texas I guess, yeah let's drink to that." He lifted his glass to his mouth.

"Pete, if you're around, how about coming to a cricket match we're playing in Westport House, two weeks from today."

"Cricket?" What the heck sort of game is that?"

"This could take a lot of explaining. You've heard the expression, it's not Cricket, haven't you?"

"Yeah, but I never knew what it meant though. What kinda rules are there?"

"Theres lots of rules, so listen and I'll try to keep it simple. There's two teams out there on the pitch, one in and one out. When a man who is in is out, he goes out and another man comes in, and when the whole team is in and out, the team that is out goes in. Get the idea?"

"Clear as mud, dude." Pete grinned.

"Good, you'll be able to impress folks back in the

States with your new-found knowledge. Cricket is also about fair play and honesty."

"Yeah, I sure as heck like the sound of that. We could do with a dose of that around here. Count me in, I shoulda got rid of this walkin' stick by then too. Yeah, let's drink to that." Wyatt refilled Pete's glass.

"Cheers. It must be a bit lonely living here in a hotel, and not being able to work?"

"Sure was at first. Now I play Texas poker with a few friends at night, and lately there's a pretty physio gal from the hospital, she comes to see how I'm doin'. And we're gettin' on famous. Sharon's her name, an' I think I'm fallin' for her, dude. Don't know for sure if she feels the same way about me though. Anyway, let's drink to her." He lifted his glass again in the air. Before Wyatt left, Pete thanked him for coming to support him.

"We're all in this together, Pete. See you at the cricket match." Wyatt said, and rose to leave the hotel, nodding to the guard outside the door, as he left.

Early the next week he got a call from Seamus Halpin. After chit chatting, they got to the nub of the call, and Wyatt promised the finished report would be delivered in two weeks. I need it then without fail, Halpin added. There's the rub, Wyatt thought as he held the phone in his hand. It struck him then, he *had* stretched his stay in Leenane to the limit, and time had now run out.

But he knew the stuff he was writing was explosive if it got into the public domain. For the first time in his working life, he felt he was doing something of real value. Whether it would make a difference, he was not sure. But he would do his damnedest to make sure it did. He sighed, and put the phone down.

Some days later, as he cycled into the village, he met Jenny, walking the road with her dog. He invited her for a coffee in the hotel. To his surprise, she agreed to meet him there in a half hour. When she arrived in the lounge she was dressed in a tight fitting tracksuit, her top unzipped, and a tight white tee shirt bulging beneath. His heart thumped. He pointed to the tray on the table beside him.

"The usual?" No milk, no sugar?"

"Yes please."She seemed distant as she sipped the steaming liquid. A silence ensued.

"I called to see Bridie in the hospital yesterday."Jenny said finally.

"Oh, that's good. And how did you two get on?"

"We got on super, really. We had some good laughs. It's jolly good medicine. She was really interested in my book. The time flew by."

"Good. I saw her the day before and she was in good spirits. And how is your book going by the way?"

"I hope to visit Bridie again sometime this week. About the book, well to be honest, it's hard going. I'd sent some chapters to a number of publishers in the UK, but this week I got three rejection slips in the post. It's downright depressing."She sighed.

"I'm sure it is. But don't give up it must happen to most people when they start off."

"You're right Jim, but it doesn't help much when it happens to you. Anyway, I have no intention of chucking in the towel. But it's upsetting."

"I'm sure it is. Have a refill?" She nodded.

"And there's another thing I have to worry about."

"What's that?"

"Money, lucre, or the lack of it. Adding the halfpence to the pence.Words alone are certain good, but you have to put food on the table. I was hoping to get some sort of advance on my book or maybe something for serialisation in a magazine. It hasn't happened so far, and my savings are running low."

"Oh. Will you be going back then to your old job in England?"

"No, never. I'd rather die than go back begging to that bitch. She would just love that. Rub my nose in it, she would. I'm staying here until I've finished the book, come rain or shine, even if it's mostly rain over here, I'm afraid."

"But what will you do if the money runs out?"

"It's not gone yet. I'll deal with that when I come to it. Meantime, I'll have to get some kind of work to replenish the coffers."

"That's easier said than done these days."

"True, but I'm starting a part time job in Traynors pub this weekend."

"Really? Good for you, and how did that happen?" Wyatt's eyebrows arched in surprise.

"I saw an ad in the window of the pub, it's as simple as that. I just applied, and bingo. He's jolly nice, the owner, and the money will be a help, even if it's not a lot. I'll have to keep adding the halfpence to the pence from hereon in. I can see it now as ever, in my mind's eye. The things you do for your art." She was smiling now.

"Fair play to you Jenny. You better watch out though, for those hot blooded males in the pub, when they have a few drinks on them. They won't be able to keep their hands, never mind their eyes, off you. Mind you, having a pretty maid behind the bar could help sales."

"They won't be getting their hands anywhere near me, and that includes you Jim Wyatt, as I'll be safely serving from *behind* the bar. Yes, I'm hoping business will improve, and if it does, I've been promised a rise. Put that in your pipe and puff on it."

"I will. Maybe you'd like to come walking with me again sometime with your dog?"

"No, thank you. I can't forget how you trod on my dreams, and after me giving you all the heart. Just now the writing is flowing, and I have to keep at it, while it lasts. Thanks for the coffee and chat, Jim. It was nice to have someone to pour your heart out to. Cheerio for now." She rose to leave.

"You're welcome Jenny, I enjoyed it too." As he glanced after her shapely figure leaving the hotel, he pondered what the males in the bar might think, especially after swilling a few pints. Damn it, he had to admit to a pang of jealousy. Still, good luck to her, he was glad she was staying, and that she had befriended Bridie in the hospital. Her perfume lingered in the air.

That night he rang Tommy Joe to book the van to visit Bridie the next day. As he put down the phone, he decided to visit to the haunted house. Yes, Bridie would like that, he thought. He would bring her up to date on the builder's progress.

Early next day, he picked up the van, and drove it straight through rain and low cloud to the house. The van of the builder, Des Keane, was parked outside. Inside, the cottage was transformed with new windows, and a conservatory at the back. After a tour of the house, he headed to the hospital.

Bridie brightened up when he told her about the house. Before that she had seemed despondent, but he put it down to her slow rate of recovery. Patience, she said, was a virtue she didn't have. Before he left she said she was giving up smoking forever.

"Why's that?"

"It's such a stupid habit. In hospital it brings it all home to you, when you see and hear what its doin' to some people in here. And I know it's bad for the baby too."

"I agree. I can't wait to bring you to see the house." He told her then about the cricket game. She said that even if she couldn't be there, her mother would love to go to it. Her eyes were now half closed with sleep. It was time to go.

"I'll tell your mother then, and arrange a lift for her. Goodbye Bridie, relax and take it easy. And get well soon."

He hugged and kissed her, and left the room, wishing she was better, and wishing she was leaving with him. And wishing she was coming with him to the cricket match. And wishing his stay in the west wasn't coming to an end.

\*\*\*

Wyatt surveyed the scene and was impressed. Ned Halpin

had done a good job with the arrangements in the grounds of Westport House. A marquee tent stood beside the green sward where the oval-shaped cricket pitch was marked out beside the lake. On the lake's waters, Wyatt saw people pedalling about in wooden swans. Westport House's exquisite Georgian shape loomed high and haughty in the distance, half hidden by woodland trees, and had a river flowing through exotic gardens at the front.

The weather was dry and fair, sun flickering in and out of fleecy clouds. A sprinkling of people lined the flag-marked boundary. Some were picnicking with their families, while others watched with curiosity the goings on of the flannelled fools, wearing forty shades of white trousers, as they scampered about the cricket pitch. The sheep droppings and lush green grass in the outfield should add to the colour of some players' whites before the end of the game, Wyatt mused.

Later in the dressing room, the first innings over, Wyatt put on his pads, thinking his team had a chance of winning. They had bowled and fielded well, and held the Westport team to a total of one hundred and forty runs in their innings. Ned Halpin had proved a surprise packet, scoring thirty runs, including a spiralling shot towards the boundary at the lake's edge, which Tommy Joe had chased like a man demented, miraculously catching the ball over his shoulder, only to topple over into the lake in the process.

The umpire raised his two hands in the air, signalling six runs. Tommy Joe was not amused, as he emerged sodden from the lake, and raised two fingers to the umpire, before he left the field of play to change into dry gear.

On another occasion, a batsman hit a ball high in the air towards a fielder. As they ran, both batsmen turned their heads to see if the catch would be held. In the process, they collided in mid-wicket, and one lay prostrate after the collision. It was the one who had hit the ball. When he revived, the umpire's finger was up, and he was told he was out, the catch being held. He stumbled back to the dressing room, shaking his head.

"What's this thing Inspector, it looks like a soap dish? And this other thing that looks like a bloody catapult. It doesn't look like what David used against Goliath." Tommy Joe said, holding the objects up for everyone in the dressing room to see, grinning ear to ear.

"One's called a box, Tommy Joe. The other's called a jock strap. It's not a bloody catapult. You put one into the other, and you wear it when batting, to protect your crown jewels." The rest of the team hooted with laughter.

"Balls to all that Inspector. No self-respectin' O'Malley would be seen wearin' any of them things. Haven't you a bat in your hand to hit the ball with?"

"It's your call, Tommy Joe. As you're batting at number ten, you're unlikely to find out if you need to wear a protector or not."

Wyatt then gave a team talk, and outlined the match strategy, before walking out to the wicket with Sergeant McSweeney to open the innings. McSweeney was soon out, cursing, for a golden duck. First ball.

The match see sawed back and forth, Wyatt batted through the innings, and useful scores came from the hurlers playing in their first cricket game. Three runs were needed to win, with five balls left, when the eight wicket fell. Tommy Joe strode to the wicket, bat twirling in his hands, without helmet, pads, or gloves. Wyatt guessed there was probably no protection inside his trousers either.

They parlayed in the middle of the wicket. There were four balls left in the over. The last batsman to come in the dressing room was Texas Pete, who could hardly walk, never mind hit the ball.

"Look Tommy Joe, there's little or no batting to come, so it's up to us to get the runs."

"Yeh, ok, sure thing Inspector. What'll I do?" Wyatt could see Tommy Joe was nervous, his lips twitching.

"Try and get a single, give me the strike, and I'll get the runs. Leave it to me. Ok?"

"Sure thing, Inspector."

"Watch this Indian quick bowler, he's fairly nippy."

"Sure thing, Inspector."

The first ball bowled to Tommy Joe leapt off a length, and struck him on the fingers, crushing them against the bat. He threw the bat on the ground, and swore damnation at the Indian bowler, who stood amused, hands on hips, grinning back at him. Tommy Joe was sucking his fingers, when Wyatt went down to speak to him.

"Your lower finger joint is out." Wyatt said, as he surveyed the damage caused by the ball.

"Not any more." Tommy Joe said, as he crunched the joint straight with his other hand.

"Ok. Remember what I said before, keep cool, and give me the strike. Leave it to me, I'll get the runs." Wyatt said, and went back to the non-striker's end.

"Sure thing, Inspector."

The bowler retraced his way to where his bowling mark lay flattened in the ground. He turned and trundled in again on a long, angular run up, and accelerated as he approached the bowling crease, arms whirling at the end like a windmill.

This time the ball was fast and full length on the stumps. Tommy Joe's bat flashed like a scimitar, and the ball soared high and long into the lake, scoring a direct hit on one of the wooden swans. The surprised occupants, unhurt and laughing, threw the leather ball back onto the field of play. The umpire's hands were up. Six, and match won. Ned Halpin shook Wyatt's hand as they left the field, and after a short speech handed him a special cup, to commemorate the occasion.

Back in the dressing room, Wyatt thanked everyone for their efforts, before turning to Tommy Joe.

"I'll overlook your total disregard of my instructions at the end. Tell me though, do you think now it's a man's game?" He said, as he eyed Tommy Joe's bloodied fingers.

"Well, it's not as much a cissy's game as I thought,

Inspector, I'll give you that. I have to tell you though, I did wear my box. I wasn't takin' any chances in that department. "He chortled, holding his hands over his crotch, while the dressing room rocked with laughter.

Later that evening in Leenane, the cup was filled in celebration and passed around many times in the packed pub.Wyatt was exuberant, thinking the craic as good as he could remember. It's a pity Bridie wasn't there, he thought. She was delighted when he rang her after the match. She said her mother had enjoyed it, and had never laughed as much at anything. Ned Halpin soon came over, arm outstretched.

"You carried your bat, fair play to you, Inspector, if I may call you that. A match winning innings it was, congratulations. The original Mr. Wyatt would be proud of you." He saluted with his raised glass.

"Thanks Ned, you're no slouch with the bat yourself."

"I played a bit in my youth, so I did. I hear you're finishing up soon here. Hope this was a good finale for you, and nothing nasty in your report about us locals."He said, grinning.

"Of course not." They clinked glasses as Tommy Joe, and Sergeant McSweeney joined them.

"Hard luck about the duck Barry, it was a good ball, swung late, and moved off the wicket."

"It would have got the bould Christy Ring himself out, an absolutely unplayable ball."

"What are you on about there Sergeant? Unplayable my arse, haven't you a feckin'bat in your hand to hit the ball with?" Tommy Joe was not sympathetic.

"And hadn't you a bat in your hand when the ball smashed your fingers? Just as well you put on the box too, or your marriage prospects could have been up the spout, Tommy Joe." McSweeney replied.

"Balls to that Segeant, as I said before, I have a healthy interest in women, even if I'm not married." Tommy Joe said.

"Healthy? That's a new way of puttin' it, Tommy Joe."

Ned Halpin said, smiling.

"And I'm going to prove it, Inspector. See that new girl behind the bar. I fancy her, I do. I've been up to the bar so many times already to order drinks, just to be near her, to speak to her."

Wyatt sneaked a sideways glance and saw Jenny busy pulling pints behind the bar. He hadn't seen her before with the crowd milling about. Just then she looked in his direction and winked. He nodded back.

"I'm sure every other single guy in the place, has the same idea as you Tommy Joe. You better get on your bike." Wyatt grinned as he spoke, and felt relieved at the attention Jenny was getting. When they were alone, Sergeant McSweeney checked nobody was listening, and spoke in a low voice.

"McFadden's friends were none too happy after the ID parade, when the big Texan identified them, though they got out on bail the following day."

"I suppose not."

"They were even less happy, when we picked them up yesterday and charged them with the crimes on the document signed by McFadden, the one you gave me. They said he was a cunt and a traitor…..an informer in the pay of the police. They were released on bail within hours, and they're gunning for McFadden's balls."

"I'd say they are."

"Funny thing, Inspector, what they don't know is that since Duffy disappeared a few years ago, we've had McFadden on our payroll, and got good information out of him on a lot of cross-border activities. We'd no idea he killed Duffy.They're after him now. I wouldn't like to be in his shoes. He'll end up like Judas. I'll be off now."Glancing about him, he vanished into the throng at the bar.

Wyatt's mind reeled at McSweeney's words. McFadden an informer.That's a relief, he thought, and downed another drink. His disappearance will appear more plausible.

Later he sidled over to the bar and ordered a round

from Jenny. He paid her when she filled the tray with drinks, and asked if he could leave her back later to the hotel. She agreed, and in the late hours they slipped separately out of the buzzing pub, into the darkness of the night, and met outside. They walked side by side, nattering until they reached her chalet door. The dog was barking inside.

"Thanks for leaving me home, my sporting Paddy. Some of those chaps in the pub were the worse for wear, and making offers in their cups. There was one in particular."

"Don't tell me.I can guess."

"Jim, I'm worn out after such a hectic night, I have to say goodnight now. You understand? Thanks for leaving me back." Her brown eyes glanced into his. Fleetingly.

"I understand, maybe a walk next week with the dog?"

"Maybe."She went inside and closed the door, and the dog stopped barking.

# Chapter 27

## *A Trip to the Cottage*

The wrap-up meeting with Seamus Halpin in Dublin seemed never-ending. Wyatt had expected a sense of euphoria, with the project now finished, but it had dragged into a third day, and he longed to be back in the west, beside Bridie. Thoughts of the previous two days' meetings swirled through his head, as he trudged up the three flights of stairs, past the broken lift.

On the first day, he'd produced his fifty page report on everything he'd uncovered in Leenane concerning water pollution, and his proposals for action. He felt hopeful and satisfied with the contents. But Seamus Halpin had lapsed into pensive mood, poring over the pages, muttering to himself, tapping pages with the stem of his pipe. Tampering with the pollution tests seemed to worry him a lot. Late that first afternoon, Halpin had adjourned the meeting until the next day, saying he required more time to peruse the document.

On the second day, Halpin had poured coffee, puffed his pipe, exhaling vanilla flavoured smoke towards the ceiling, and talked trivia about the economy. As Halpin was speaking, Wyatt's mind kept thinking about Bridie. He remembered glancing out the window, at the rain pelting the panes, and wishing to be back in the west. The weather seemed in keeping with the mood in the office. The monotony of the second day's meeting remained etched in his brain. Halpin became tetchy, worrying about the political fallout if the details got into the public domain. He also disclosed that some people in power in Dublin were unhappy with the decision to abandon the gold mining project.

Wyatt was irate at Halpin's lack of feeling for the environment on this issue, retorted sharply, and surprised himself that he had the nerve to do so. With his emotions back under control, Wyatt remembered that Halpin's brother most likely had briefed him of everything going on in Mayo in the three months, and may also have been involved in the tampering with the lab samples. He felt frustrated that so far his work seemed only to have led to Halpin getting the kudos of promotion and a bigger office. Halpin had ended the second day's meeting, requesting yet another day to study the implications of the report. Wyatt was glad to leave the office before his patience waned. It had been a difficult day, but at least it was over. All he wanted then was to get back to the west, and be near Bridie. He rang the hospital that night, and was told her condition was stable.

Wyatt knocked on the door, anxious at what the third day might bring. Halpin ushered him in, seating him before the desk, littered with pages from the report. The air reeked of stale tobacco. They were alone, and he wondered if Halpin was leaving himself room for some surprise off-the- record remarks.

"Here we are again James, day three. It should be the last. I've now given your work a thorough going over. It deserved it. Coffee?" As he spoke, Halpin appeared serious, pressing tobacco into the bowl of his pipe. He arose, struck a match, lit his pipe, and blew out the match. He poured two coffees and brought them back on a tray to the desk.

"Now to business, James. I don't need to emphasise the need for confidentiality in all matters relating to this project."

"You don't Seamus. Let's get to the nub of it, and discuss the issues outlined in the report, and what action is going to be taken to remedy them. You must be aware there are many things that need urgent action. The facts are all there."

"You'll have to be patient in these matters James, I'm afraid. The mills of government grind exceedingly small, *and* exceedingly slowly. *This* is no country for quick decisions. An inter-departmental sub-committee has been set up to investigate all matters arising from your report. I will be chairing it. No doubt clarification will be required on many things, and I will be in touch with you James, regarding them. In the meantime, you will be re-assigned to your old job. Thankfully in one piece too." In the ensuing silence, Halpin smiled smugly, and blew a perfect ring of smoke, which rose and hung like a halo over his head. Wyatt gritted his teeth. He emptied his cup in one gulp, before clinking it back into the saucer.

"May I ask if there's been any alteration to my conditions of employment, following this assignment?"

"No, none, you have been reassigned to your old job. Back to the grindstone I'm afraid. Your file will reflect the satisfactory way in which you discharged your duties. Also, you'll have to hand over the gun, which was indirectly funded by the Department. "Halpin leaned over the desk, feigning concern, and continued.

"The experience won't have done you any harm. And I'm sure you're glad to be back in the sanctuary of the city, after your escapades in the wilds of the west." As he spoke, a smug smile again spread over Halpin's face.

"I just can't wait to get back, I'm over the moon."Wyatt gritted his teeth, wondering if Halpin got the irony.

"Good, that's all settled then. You can have a few days off, to get your stuff back to Dublin. Any further questions?" Halpin rubbed his hands together, as if indicating the meeting had ended.

"Well yes, now that you asked, there….there *is* one question on my mind.Much as I appreciate your kind offer and words, Seamus, I have considered my position. I've decided to apply for leave of absence from my job for three years. I'm entitled to it I believe, because of my service."Wyatt saw the pipe sag in Halpin's mouth. It was several moments before he replied.

"I…I'll talk to HR about it, of course. May I ask what brought this on?"

"Nothing specific Seamus, I've just been examining my life, that's all. And I'd like to hold onto the gun too. It's a personal safety matter, as I will be living in the same area as before. I'm sure you'll square everything with HR, just like you did before, Seamus. Remember?"

"Of course…of course, I'm sure there won't be a problem. But you didn't answer my question. What are you going to live on?" Halpin's voice was curt, his face blank.

"I'll make do. I have a few ideas. Money isn't everything, is it? Anyway if things don't work out in three years, I'm sure you'll welcome me back with open arms?" Wyatt replied, relishing Halpin's discomfort.

"So I would appreciate Seamus, if you could speak to HR urgently. There's business I need to do in Dublin, but I'd like to finalise these matters today, as I'm sure you would. Perhaps if I called back in a few hours you could have all the papers ready for me to sign? Any monies due can be sent on later." He stared into Halpin's glazed eyes. Silence filled the room.

"If it's not possible, I'll stay another night in the hotel. But I'd like to get back to Westport today."

"I'll speak to HR, as I said. Call back at three o'clock, and I'll let you know the position."Halpin's lips were set in a grim line, as he spoke.

Wyatt left the building, tramping around the block, towards St. Stephen's Green, buying a sandwich and drink on the way. The clouds were lifting, and the sun dappled the park, spangling blobs of brightness through the trees onto the lunchtime people passing below. Steam rose from the footpaths. Rusted leaves coated the ground and crunched crisply beneath his feet. His spirits rose as he walked. He chose a seat near a pond, sat on it, and took out the folded newspaper, scanning the pages.

The world was in chaos after the invasion of Kuwait by Iraq, the previous month. Just like my own life, he thought. He folded and replaced the paper in his raincoat, ate his sandwich, and watched the ducks feeding beside the pond. In the distance he heard the marching sounds of a brass band.

He sat back and gazed at the children playing in the playground nearby, running and shouting, happy and excited with life, living just for that moment. Wyatt sighed. He envied them their innocence and happiness. It brought him back. He could never match their innocence again, but he *could* aspire to happiness. And he would. Love and happiness, happiness and love, like a hand in a glove. Yes I will, he vowed, the tension of the morning meeting now abated.

Wyatt rose later and sauntered around the park, taking in the colours and smells, and sense of history, his mind drifting back to the morning meeting. Halpin just didn't get it, why *he* wanted out. All Halpin seemed to worry about was his pension. It was probably how he coped with the monotony of his job, counting the days until he retired. Wyatt had examined his life, and was happy to be out of his permanent pensionable life for a few years. Happiness has many faces, he knew now, and so had love.

He stopped in front of a statue of the poet, James Clarence Mangan. *Do not despair for help is on the way, my dark Rosaleen,* he read. He wondered what Mangan would have thought of the state of the nation today, and hoped someday to study his poetry.

Wyatt ambled down Grafton Street, past worried shoppers gazing into windows. He turned right at Dame Street into Trinity College, through the arched entrance, straddling the statues of Burke and Goldsmith.

Memories of the years he had studied there washed through his brain, as he trod the cobbled quadrangle. There was a cricket match in progress in College Park. He stopped to watch it for a while, before exiting by Lincoln Place. He felt content. He'd needed that one last stroll around the city, before leaving again for the west. He wondered if it would be forever.

When he returned to the office, Halpin had his HR aide seated by his side.

"I hope you know what you're doing James. You could be taking a big risk." As he spoke, Halpin ticked off boxes on a page before him, before swivelling around to face Wyatt.

"Maybe, Seamus. Who knows? Time will tell. You'll send on all monies due?"

"Yes James, but first please sign these documents. Your pension will be frozen. I'll witness your signature. How will I contact you, if I need clarification on matters arising from the report?"

"You'll have to post a letter or telegram to this address. I'll let you know when I have a telephone number." Wyatt handed him a note with the address of the cottage on it.

"So you've got a place down there?"

"Yes. I'm off the payroll now. But any future work will be on an agreed fee basis. I trust that is ok with you? And what about the gun?" Halpin hesitated, and looked at his HR colleague before speaking.

"Yes James, both matters are agreed. I wish you good luck. And good health." They shook hands, and within minutes Wyatt had left the office, and was hailing a taxi for Heuston. He thought Halpin wasn't such a bad guy after all.

Wyatt rested on the train to Westport, lulled by the rhythm of the wheels clicking on the tracks. His mind buzzed when he awoke. Maybe Halpin thought it crazy for him to leave his sinecure city job, but there was no other decision. Or was he just trying to convince himself?

He knew finalising the report was the end of something, but also the start of something more important in his life. He had found love, and that was worth more than a thousand piffling pensions. There was unfinished business in the west, but Halpin wouldn't understand that.

Wyatt had kept copies of the documents. He was glad to have the pistol in his pocket, and patted it for reassurance. He knew he had to make a new start, to put bread on the table, but he wondered how. He would have to think more about that, and he closed his eyes once more, as the wheels continued clicking away.

***

Next morning Wyatt rang the builder, who told him the cottage was complete, and would appreciate a final payment.

"The extension is completely finished?" It was a week ahead of schedule.

"It is indeed. Would you like to see it?"

"Yes, I'll be there within the hour." He put down the phone, shoved his cheque book into his pocket, and peered out the window. It was cloudy but dry, a perfect day for a spin through the Delphi valley.

The builder's nameless black van stood inside the wooden gate, on the newly- gravelled driveway. They shook hands and did a tour of the cottage. Wyatt was impressed. Duck egg blue on the outside, it had retained its traditional shape. A split-level extension had been added at the rear, with double doors opening onto a south facing patio, taking in the lake and mountain views. Inside were new windows, plastered walls, and central heating, with solar panels on the southerly roof.

Bridie would be pleased. All she needed to do was pick the furniture. Apart from some minor snags, the house had been transformed. He wrote the cheque and handed it to the builder. He couldn't wait to get to the hospital to tell Bridie the news. He hoped it would help give her get home quicker. He pumped the pedals hard all the way back to the hotel.

When he reached his room, he booked a taxi for the hospital in Castlebar. Halpin could foot the bill, as part of his closing expenses. God knows he'd saved Halpin much expense over the months, by using the bike and Tommy Joe's van. He also knew it was not appreciated.

He paid the taxi driver, and asked him to call back in an hour. Inside, he was told Bridie had been moved to another room. While he waited at reception, puzzled why she had been moved, a young nurse approached him, and asked him to follow her, saying Bridie's doctor wished to see him. He followed, hoping there would be good news. Perhaps she *was* coming home.

The young doctor looked up from reading a file, motioning Wyatt to sit down. He had a narrow face, glasses, and thin lips. He said he was sorry but he had bad news to relate. Wyatt felt his body tighten.

"Is she all right?....Bridie I mean, and…and the baby."

"Yes, Miss O'Malley will be alright. She's obviously very upset, and under sedation. Last night, she miscarried, after a severe haemorrhage. Unfortunately. This outcome was a distinct possibility all along of course, but it came fast in the end, and before the baby had even reached three months. There is no reason why Miss O'Malley can't go on to have healthy children in the future. But there are no certainties in life, you know. You have my sincere sympathies." The doctor closed the file on his desk. He had related the results, all in a day's work for him, the meeting was now ended. He had spoken with clinical detachment. Wyatt seethed at the doctor's lack of feeling, as the shock from his words sank in.

"Can I see Bridie? I've just travelled from Leenane." The doctor hesitated, taken aback, before replying.

"Strictly speaking, the answer is no, she's under sedation. But I am worried depression might set in. It can happen in cases like this, particularly where it's the first pregnancy. So I will agree on this occasion, but absolutely five minutes only." Wyatt left the room in a daze.

Bridie lay asleep in the dimly lit room. He touched her hand. Her eyes flickered open.

"Jim, is it you? I'm so sorry." Tears glistened in her eyes.

"Don't be silly darling, the main thing is you're ok. The doc said you'll be fine."

"Oh Jim, I'm so glad you're here. It…it was terrible. The pain, and the blood, on the sheets and everywhere. I rang the alarm, but when they got here, it was too late….it was too late....she was gone.... my little girl was gone. I...I let her down. And you."She was sobbing hard. He felt a lump rising in his throat as he handed her a handkerchief.

"Don't blame yourself Bridie. These things happen. Only God knows why. The main thing is that you're well, and we love each other. The doc says you'll be fine for the future. You could even be out in a few days for good, after all the weeks you've spent here. The doc said if this hadn't happened you might have been in here for the full nine months, with the outcome still uncertain."Wyatt said, trying to sound positive.

"I'd have done it, I would, for the little one, and....and now she's gone, gone."Her grip tightened on Wyatt's hand, as she wept.

"Does anyone else know?"

"No. I...I told them here you would be the first to know."

"Good. Look, I'll tell your mother and family then."

"Would you Jim? That would be great. I love you. I always will."

"And I will always love you." He kissed her softly.

"And....and Jim, there's just one favour I want to ask of you."

"Of course.... of course, you name it, what is it?"

"There won't be any funeral for our daughter, because of her age, so I want you to plant a rose bush in her memory at the cottage. Her name would have been Rosaleen. She had dark hair too."She sobbed again.

"Of course, I'll have it growing in the garden, when you come home. The cottage is ready and waiting for you, as I am. I'll be living there too, as soon as you're well enough to pick the furniture."Wyatt remembered Mangan's words, and felt the tears welling, his façade of strength fading.

"Oh Jim...that's great,that's great."Her speech began slurring as the door opened, and the young nurse beckoned him out of the room.

The taxi was waiting for him outside. He looked at his

watch, and apologised, realising he was almost an hour late. The taxi driver said he hoped it wasn't bad news that had delayed him. Wyatt said it wasn't, but he knew the driver knew it was. They travelled in silence. It was a long journey.

Bridie's mother took the news bravely. She said it was the will of God, and she would tell Nora the bad news. She perked up when Wyatt told her that the cottage was ready to move into as soon as Bridie came home. The phone rang in the kitchen, and she grabbed it.

"'Twas the doctor from the hospital. He said Bridie had improved, and we could expect her home in the next few days. Thanks be to God."

"That's great news. She'll stay here for a while then?" Wyatt's heart beat faster. Bridie would to be home soon. The main thing now was that she stayed in good health. Together they would pull through. It would bind them even closer. She was the most important thing in his life. He needed her as much as she needed him.

"For sure.'Til she's right and ready to leave. You'll have a cup of tea and a scone?"

"Yes, that would be grand."

"There you are." she said, placing the tray on the table." And you'll be staying down here awhile? And what then?"

"Well firstly, there's some sorting out to be done on the cottage. Tomorrow I have to plant a rose bush in the garden, along with other things, and move my stuff from the hotel. I'll be borrowing Tommy Joe's van as usual."

"And what then?

"Oh, making a home of it for us both, with Bridie's help."

"And what then?"

"I have so many things to do then. Finding what to do first will be the problem. These scones are delicious."

He finished his tea in a gulp, and stood to leave, thanking her.

"I'll say a Rosary tonight for you both, and for the

baby. It'll be grand havin' you both livin' so near. It's a consolation for me." She said, dabbing her eyes.

He strode to the door, lifted the latch, and turned to ask where he could buy a rose bush the next day. She replied that there was a nursery outside Westport, on the Leenane road.

Wyatt thanked her, closed the door, and dashed outside, shielding his eyes. Clouds of ochre were mountains in the sky, as he mounted his bike. He pushed hard to get back to the hotel before darkness fell, heart hammering.

He longed for Bridie to be back with him, and vowed to be there, waiting for her when she did. He yearned for their new life together to begin, and thought the planting of the rosebush in memory of their dead daughter would mark the beginning of it. The thought that he was in a place of beauty, travelling a road where no one was unwanted, gave him solace. He remembered then the priest's words exhorting those without faith to travel the road to Leenane, and smiled, wondering if travelling by bike would be ok. He'd made the right decision, and had three years to prove it. And he *would* show Halpin.

He pumped the pedals, breathing hard, and no longer felt alone in his loneliness. There was no other place he wished to be.But he worried that McFadden's disappearance might come back to haunt him, that maybe McFadden's friends or family would come after him. He would somehow have to deal with this danger if it happened, and felt reassured by the pistol beneath his armpit.

He pushed ever harder on the pedals. Dusk fell as he passed Aasleagh waterfall, and he looked across the flat, blood red, waters of the fjord. Soon he reached the hotel, parked his bike outside, and inhaled deeply. When he gazed heavenwards, he saw pale stars winking and the crescent moon like a sickle over Mweelrea, with the evening star aglow below it.

## Acknowledgements

Many thanks to my wife *Deirdre*, for encouraging me into the world of words.

And to all the members of the Longtable Creative Writing Group, for their feedback and help in getting "The Leenane Inspector" over the line.

And Se Murphy, my computer "guru" for getting the book to production process stage.

And Gillian Mills for her encouragement and marketing help, and technical marine information, from the "Inshore Ireland" magazine.

In writing the book, I am indebted to the work of others, in particular:

"A Year's Turning" by Michael Viney.

"Connemara" by Tim Robinson.

"Footloose in the West of Ireland" by Mike Harding.

"At the Mouth of a River" by Sean Lysaght.

Most of all, I acknowledge the "magical" qualities of the landscape of Connemara, which inspired this book.

All proceeds from this book will be donated to Sightsavers Charity.